ALSO BY BRYAN GRULEY

Starvation Lake

A Touchstone Book
Published by Simon & Schuster
New York   *London*   *Toronto*   *Sydney*

The Hanging Tree

A STARVATION LAKE
MYSTERY

Bryan Gruley

Touchstone
A Division of Simon & Schuster, Inc.
1230 Avenue of the Americas
New York, NY 10020

First Touchstone trade paperback edition August 2010

TOUCHSTONE and colophon are trademarks of Simon & Schuster, Inc.

For information about special discounts for bulk purchases, please contact Simon & Schuster Special Sales at 1-866-506-1949 or business@simonandschuster.com.

The Simon & Schuster Speakers Bureau can bring authors to your live event. For more information or to book an event contact the Simon & Schuster Speakers Bureau at 1-866-248-3049 or visit our website at www.simonspeakers.com.

Designed by Renata Di Biase

Manufactured in the United States of America

10 9 8 7 6 5 4 3 2

ISBN 978-1-4165-6364-8
ISBN 978-1-4165-6401-0 (ebook)

for c and goo

and in memory of my mother

February 1999

I have learned that you can be too grateful for love.

She stood in front of the window across the kitchen, backlit from the glow of the streetlamp outside her apartment window.

"Darlene," I said.

But she just waited, watching as I set my hockey sticks against the wall, her arms folded across her breasts, her head tilted so that her mahogany hair fell across the left side of her face. She was barefoot in black panties and a scarlet bra.

"Why do you bring those things up here?" she said. "Nobody's going to steal them out of your truck, Gussy. This is not Detroit."

"I suppose not," I said. I pushed the door back open and stood the sticks on the landing outside. Snowflakes swirled around my head.

"Still storming?"

I closed the door. "Slowed down a little while ago."

"You're early. I'm glad."

I pulled my boots off, dripping melted snow on Darlene's throw rug. "Enright's was closed. We get out of the game and there's nowhere to drink."

"Did you win?"

"Tied, two all."

"You score?"

"Hit the post."

"Hmm," she said. "You do that a lot."

"Somebody cross-checked me in the back of the neck just as I got the puck."

"Did you get his number?"

"Didn't," I said. "Got an assist."

Darlene didn't seem impressed. She stepped away from the window and dropped her arms. Her pale body glowed through the shadows. She slowly drew herself into a boxer's crouch and put up her dukes. The hint of a smile crossed her face, her dark eyes glinting.

"Come on."

"What? This again?"

"Let's go. Wimp."

We had known each other since we were children growing up side by side in clapboard houses on the southwestern shore of Starvation Lake. I had never quite figured out how to know Darlene as an adult. But here we were, in Darlene's second-floor apartment above Sally's Dry Cleaning and Floral, spending more nights together than not in the year since she had formally separated from her useless husband, since he had left town without a divorce decree or a forwarding address. A married woman whose marriage was over.

I left my clothes in a pile near the door. She circled closer. I was more than aware that, as a deputy for the Pine County Sheriff's Department, Darlene had undergone expert training at how to take a man down and that her method might well involve my groin.

"Don't be a wuss now."

I made my move. I tried to secure her arms and keep her at a safe distance, but she slipped her right arm out and punched me in the shoulder.

"Ow."

"Wuss."

I still had a grip on her left forearm. Keeping an eye on her knees, I twisted sideways and tried to push her elbow above her head so I could use my weight to ease her back against the wall. But she wriggled loose and slapped me hard on the back of the head, loosing a giggle as she did. She had never spelled out the rules of these engagements, but I assumed I was not allowed to hit, maybe because I had no desire to hit.

I crouched and slid to my left and got a hand on her right hip, grabbing the hem of her panties, and shoved. That threw her off-balance and she stumbled back, laughing. I grasped her left arm under the elbow and pushed it as gently as I could up and back to move her toward the wall. But she screwed her body into me, whacking me in the chest with the heel of a hand and driving me back half a step, still laughing. I pulled her back in close to me, safer, and took her by the chin.

"What are you doing?"

Her eyes were lit with mischief and lust. I felt her fingertips brush the skin on my belly as they sought the inside of my thigh, and I shivered.

"What?"

"I don't fight, Darl."

"Oh," she said. She reached a hand up to caress my cheek. I felt the tension leach out of her body, and out of mine.

"You're such a girl," she said.

She slid her panties off and nudged me backward toward her bedroom.

I must have glanced at the phone on her nightstand when it rang a few minutes later, because Darlene grabbed the back of my neck and whispered hard in my ear, "Do not stop."

The phone rang this late only if something was wrong with one of our mothers or if the sheriff needed Darlene. And if the sheriff needed Darlene, then there was a chance that I, as executive editor of the twice-weekly *Pine County Pilot*, circulation 4,124, had a story to report.

The answering machine clicked on after four rings. I heard Darlene's recorded voice—"You know what to do"—over her stuttered gasps in my ear and I thought, Yes, I do, and rolled her over onto her back and felt her calves and her heels digging into my back, squeezing me into her.

The caller didn't leave a message. Which meant it was probably the sheriff. Our mothers left messages, but the sheriff, knowing I might be here, wouldn't take the chance that I would hear what he had to say, lest it appear in the *Pilot* before he decided it was time. I told myself to try to remember to call him the next day while Darlene clutched me to her breasts and pleaded, "Don't stop, Gussy. Don't stop."

For the moment, I forgot about the phone call.

I awoke as Darlene undid herself from my left arm and crossed the tiny room and dug her cell phone out of the brown-and-mustard sheriff's hat she'd left upside down on her dresser. The nightstand clock said 2:21. The cell phone's keypad shone on Darlene's face as she punched keys. I heard three beeps. Must be voice mail, I thought. She couldn't help herself.

She put the phone to an ear and turned away from me, facing the mirror over the dresser. I stared at the ceiling, replaying the goal I hadn't quite scored earlier that night. I'd parked myself at one goalpost, all alone. Zilchy had slipped out of the opposite corner, made a move on the defenseman, and zipped the puck right onto my stick. I'd had the whole damn net to shoot at. But I tightened up a little and the puck caught in the heel of my blade and I pulled the shot. Back when I played goalie, I would've loved hearing the clang of that puck off the post. Instead, I was just embarrassed. Still, we played, got a good sweat, there was beer in a bucket of ice in the dressing room.

And now I was in Darlene's bed.

I moved my head enough to see her reflection in the dresser mirror, but her hair obscured her face. I watched as she listened to the phone, then took it off of her ear, punched another key, put it back on her ear.

Now, as she listened, her head slowly bowed into her neck and she drew her right arm around her waist until I could see her fingertips against her left hip. I raised myself on an elbow.

"Everything OK?" I said.

She tossed the phone back into the hat, straightened herself, threw her head back, stared up at the ceiling. In the mirror I watched her shut her eyes and press her lips together.

"Darlene?"

"No."

"No, what?"

"No, everything's not OK."

I got to my feet and moved toward her but she spun around and pushed past me toward her closet.

"I have to go."

"Go where?"

She flung back the folding door on her closet and yanked out a deputy's uniform folded over a hanger, tossed it on the unmade bed.

"Let me just do this," she said. "Go back to bed."

"What happened?"

She shook her head and went out into the living room, snatched her bra and panties off the floor, wriggled them back on.

"Darlene?"

"It doesn't matter."

"You're getting dressed and going out at—"

"Just go back to sleep."

"Are you going to tell me—"

"Gus. I will call you later. OK?"

I watched her dress. She fixed her brass badge to her brown blouse, the tie clasp in the mitten shape of Michigan to her tie. When she moved to the dresser and reached around me for the hat, I put a hand on her shoulder. She looked up at me then. She looked like she couldn't decide whether to scream or cry.

"What's wrong?"

"I have to go," she said. She grabbed the keys and cell phone out of her hat, picked it up, and started out of the room. I let her go. At the doorway she turned and pointed her hat at me.

"Go back to bed, OK? I'll call you later."

"Where are you going?"

"Don't be following me."

I waited a beat. "All right," I said.

Darlene closed her eyes, took a breath. She pulled the thicket of her hair back on her head and stuffed her hat down around it.

"Please," she said.

They found her hanging in the shoe tree at the edge of town.

Gracie McBride had started the shoe tree some twenty years before, when she was sixteen years old and in love or at least lust with a boy from Sandy Cove, the next town over. His name was Ricky and all I remember about him is that he played football, not hockey, and that he went through one hell of a pregnancy scare with Gracie. No one told him that, even if Gracie did have a baby in her belly, there was no way to be sure it was his.

When she finally let him know her period had come two days after it actually arrived—Gracie liked to have fun with boys that way—Ricky was so relieved that he drank half a quart of Jack Daniel's and went out in his father's enormous Chrysler something and backed it over every mailbox on Sunset Trail between Horvath Road and Walleye Lake. It actually wasn't that many mailboxes, but enough for Ricky to spend a weekend in jail.

Gracie was so impressed that when he got out, she told him to bring his football cleats and drove him out to an old oak towering over Main Street about a mile east of Starvation. There in the summer midnight dark she took off her clothes and then Ricky's and after they'd writhed in the tall grass at the base of the tree, she tied one lace of one of his cleats to one lace of one of her high-top sneakers—she had dyed it a bright pink so you could see it from afar—and threw the pair over her shoulder and clambered up into the tree. Ricky told her this was a stupid thing to do, especially naked, but Gracie giggled and kept climbing until she could find no more branches that would hold her ninety pounds. Then she reached over her head and looped the pink sneaker and black cleat over a bough.

Gracie wasn't as good at climbing down, or at least she pretended not to be. Ricky put his pants on and tried to help her, but he was too heavy to climb as high as Gracie, and she insisted, giggling again, that she was too afraid to descend. He finally drove into town while Gracie sat on a high branch in the dark, wearing nothing, until a fire truck came and plucked her from the tree like a pussycat. When one of the Pine County sheriff's deputies asked her what the hell she was thinking climbing fifty or sixty or seventy feet into a tree naked in the dark, she said, "I don't know, officer. Didn't you ever do anything for love?"

Soon more shoes began to appear in the tree. At the high school, hanging shoes became a spring ritual for graduating seniors, which naturally prompted a brief, futile attempt by the police to stop it, seeing as the kids' hangings usually involved beer and sometimes ladders. But adults hung shoes in the tree, too, especially after a night at Enright's Pub. Out-of-state tourists saw the tree and pulled over and hung their own shoes and flip-flops, their equivalent of writing in the guest book at a rental cottage. Sometimes when a romance soured, one of the two lovers would bother to shinny into the tree and slice a pair of shoes away.

But mostly the shoes multiplied, and over the years the oak took on the look of a matronly ghost dressed in a ragged nightgown. And somewhere in her highest branches dangled a single snow-covered football cleat tied to a high-top sneaker faded to a dirty gray, the pink but a memory.

And way below the sneaker now hung Gracie herself.

The headlights on my pickup truck pushed through the dark, my tires creaking through the fresh eight inches of snow left by the blizzard that had howled through Starvation between supper and sometime after midnight. Wind whistled into the cab through a twisting hairline crack in the window next to me. Twice I had to slow down and steer around branches the wind had severed from trees.

I saw the dim pulse of blue and red police lights about half a mile ahead. The silhouettes of the bare trees etched skeletons on the linen sky. I pulled onto what shoulder there was and parked, reached into my glove box and pulled out a notebook, my cell phone, a ballpoint pen, and a pencil, in case the pen didn't work in the cold. I stuffed it all in my jacket and stepped out onto the road.

For the record, I did not follow Darlene. After I heard her clomp down her back stairs and roar away in her police cruiser, I dressed and hurried out across Main to the *Pilot*. The police scanner on the plywood shelf near my desk told me all I needed to know.

The tree stood in a clearing about twenty-five feet off the road, surrounded by a field buried in snow and ringed by woods. The cops hadn't taken the body down, probably had barely touched it yet except to ascertain that it was dead, as they worked to encircle the clearing with yellow do-not-cross tape.

I veered to the shadows along the right shoulder across the road so the cops were less likely to see me. It wasn't easy to see over the wall of snow piled high along the opposite shoulder, but it gave me a bit of cover. The sheriff generally didn't appreciate me showing up before he'd had a chance to determine what had happened and what he would tell me and my friends at Channel Eight.

I spied Darlene unspooling police tape at the far end of the clearing, a duty she might have chosen so she would not have to face the body of her oldest and best friend up close in death. The area around the base of the tree was illuminated by headlights and the flashing lights of an ambulance, a fire truck, and three police cruisers parked at haphazard angles along the road.

Two paramedics bundled in parkas and wool caps stood behind the open double doors of the ambulance talking with the sheriff. The sheriff, a man built like an elm tree in a knee-length brown parka and a fur-lined earflap cap, pointed at the body. One paramedic nodded. The other climbed into the back of the ambulance. The sheriff held up a hand, as if telling them to wait a minute, then started toward the tree. He had to lift his knees high to get through the accumulated snow. We'd had a lot this winter, more than we'd seen since the 1980s. When the sheriff reached the hanging corpse, he stopped and played a flashlight slowly up the limp body. The light flashed white on her face.

"Jesus," I said to myself.

The wind gusted near the tree and Gracie swayed back a few inches, then swayed forward again. Not much of her face was visible through the jagged scraps of ice and snow that clung to her forehead and cheeks. Patches of white covered much of the rest of her. She was wearing something dark beneath all the snow and ice. Maybe a black leather jacket, a pair of black jeans.

Her left foot appeared to be shoeless. She could have lost a boot as she kicked away whatever she had stood on. I couldn't tell if the foot wore a sock. And whatever Gracie had climbed up on must have fallen into the snow. She hadn't climbed nearly as high as she had all those years ago. Just enough to secure herself to one of the sturdy boughs eight or nine feet off the ground. She wasn't ninety pounds anymore either.

Stray snowflakes blowing around had dampened the first page in my notebook. I flipped back to a dry page, took off my right glove, grabbed the pencil, started jotting some notes. I had reported on one suicide before, before I'd left Detroit and returned to my hometown, Starvation Lake, back when I was still covering the auto industry for the daily *Detroit Times*. A laid-off middle manager for Superior Motors, a big auto manufacturer, leapt from the Ambassador Bridge spanning the Detroit River between Detroit and Windsor. Hitting the water didn't kill him but the current sucked him under, and his body, in dark suit, white shirt, and red print tie, fetched up on Fighting Island downriver. My four paragraphs got buried at the bottom of A14 or 15.

I figured Gracie would get similar treatment in the *Pine County Pilot*. Newspapers didn't care much for suicides, unless they involved rock stars. The editors would argue that you could never truly prove anyone had committed suicide without knowing exactly what they were thinking right up to the last milliseconds before they died. Even if there was a note, you couldn't be positive that the dead one hadn't felt a desperate urge to call it off, to save himself as he plummeted toward the sidewalk, or whether the carbon monoxide so flummoxed her that her fingers weren't able to roll the car window down. Maybe it was, in the very end, just an accident.

This was no accident, though. Gracie had many choices that had led her to this final one. I can't honestly say that, as I stood watching her body rock in the wind, I felt much sympathy for Gracie. But I felt for Darlene.

Brilliant light flashed across my notebook. I stopped writing and looked up. The sizable upper half of Pine County sheriff Dingus Aho loomed over the snowbank in front of me, his flashlight extended.

"This is a crime scene, young man," he said. "Better get going."

I shielded my eyes against the glare and took a step closer.

"Dingus," I said.

He waved the flashlight beam toward my pickup.

"I'll ask you once to get in your truck and go home," he said. "If I have anything to say, you'll hear it later."

"Sorry, can't hear you," I said, moving close enough that I could see the ice striping his handlebar mustache. "That's Gracie McBride, isn't it?"

"I have nothing to say at the moment."

Despite his bulk, it was sometimes hard to take Dingus seriously because he still spoke in the singsong lilt of a Finn who'd migrated down to Starvation from the Upper Peninsula.

"This would be the first suicide in the shoe tree, wouldn't it?" I said.

"Nice try. Now move along."

I scribbled something illegible in my notebook, just to let Dingus know I wasn't giving up. Not that it mattered much. Early on a Monday morning, Channel Eight would have an entire day to cover the story before Tuesday's *Pilot* came out. And I doubted we'd run much anyway. A woman who'd been racing toward the gates of hell for most of her life had arrived a bit quicker than we'd all expected. Not much news there, actually.

"Dingus, could you at least confirm—"

"Gus!" he said, turning the beam on his face. "Look at me."

I stopped writing. The light gleamed on the badge pinned to the front of his earflap cap. He jerked a gloved thumb over his shoulder.

"You don't really want her to see you here, do you?"

I looked past him and saw Darlene and another deputy moving toward the ambulance. Dingus was right, I really didn't want Darlene to see me, but I didn't know how that could be avoided.

"I'm just doing my job," I said. "She'll have to understand."

"She'll *have to*, huh? I think you know her better than that."

"I guess."

"Look—off the record?"

"Sure. It's Gracie, right?"

He shrugged. "It's getting dangerous to drive a Zamboni around here."

Gracie had driven the ice-resurfacing machine at the hockey rink where my buddies and I played late at night. Starvation's last suicide, about a year before, had also driven the Zam at the rink.

"You going to do an autopsy?"

"Up to the coroner. But it's pretty standard procedure."

"Uh-huh." I nodded toward the tree. "What happened to her other shoe?"

A vehicle approached. Both of us turned our heads. Twin yellow beams shined between the headlights. Dingus squinted in disapproval as the Channel Eight van rolled closer.

"Damn it all," he said. He shouted at his deputies. "Let's move it, people. Get her down and into that ambulance chop-chop. I don't want her mother seeing this on TV."

I stepped back to the opposite bank and watched as the deputies and paramedics lowered Gracie from the shoe tree. I expected Darlene to stand aside but she shouldered her way in and took hold of Gracie around the waist.

"Careful," she shouted. "Be gentle with her."

The ambulance doors slammed shut as the Channel Eight van's passenger door swung open. Out jumped a slim woman in a quilted black parka. She shot me a frown before bounding up the snowbank, waving a microphone over her head. "Sheriff! Sheriff Aho!"

I looked past her and saw Darlene at the back of the ambulance. She held one gloved hand flat against the door. She dropped it only after the ambulance pulled away, churning snow in its wake.

I wished I could wrap my arms around her. Later, I thought.

I stuffed my hands in my pockets and started back to my truck. As the ambulance siren faded in the distance, I heard the muffled ringing of my cell phone in my pocket. It could only be one person.

"Darlene," I said. "I'm really sorry."

"Did you think I wouldn't see you?"

She was upset. I decided I'd let her be.

"Sorry. Gotta do my job."

"You always say that."

Cold stung my knuckles. I switched the phone to my other hand.

"We don't do much with suicides anyway," I said.

"Good."

"Yeah, no need to embarrass her mom."

"That's not what I meant."

She said it with such force that I stopped and spun around toward the shoe tree. "What do you mean?"

"Gracie did not—oh, goddammit, Dingus. Hold on."

I waited, watching the police lights flicker in the branches of the shoe tree. Darlene came back on.

"I've got to go," she said. "We'll talk later. I love you."

Clouds the color of bone hid the morning sun when I stepped onto Main Street just before seven o'clock.

Exhaust snaked up from three pickup trucks and an SUV idling in the angled parking spaces that ran down both sides of Main to where the street veered southwest at the eastern shore of the lake. The trucks had been left running to stay warm while their owners ate breakfast at Audrey's Diner. I imagined four grizzled old men in plaid flannel shirts buttoned over thermals sopping up egg yolk with white toast and talking about the chance for more snow, about the Detroit Red Wings' goaltending problems, about that new hockey rink going up in town, and maybe, if they had heard by now, about Gracie McBride.

A brittle gust of wind off the lake raked my face as I crossed Main at Estelle Street. Up and down Main stood two-story clapboard-and-brick buildings erected decades before, when the town of Starvation Lake—known back then, at the turn of the century, as Sleepy Corner—was civilization to the lumbermen who'd come north to demolish forests of pine from Lake Huron across to Lake Michigan. They had drunk and fought and sometimes killed and then, when the forests had all been leveled to stumps and pine needles, they had gone, leaving the settlement and other places like it to figure out how to survive.

Starvation had lasted by luring just enough tourists from Detroit and Chicago and Cleveland to come north to party and swim and boat and snowmobile. For a time, Starvation was Michigan's secret resort darling, one of the few inland towns that could tempt tourists away from Traverse City and Charlevoix and Petoskey on the big lake. But Sandy Cove and other little lakeside villages caught on and started grabbing for the same vacationers. There had been a time, too, when hockey teams from all over Michigan and even from outstate came to Starvation to play against our kid hockey team, the River Rats. I had been the goaltender on the greatest of those teams and, to some of the townsfolk—actually, a lot of them—the most disappointing.

If you counted, as I had, you would see that about one of every three buildings on Main had a sign in the window that said FOR LEASE OR SALE BY OWNER. Vandals had destroyed one side of the marquee on the shuttered Avalon Cinema. The Dairy Queen had closed its doors the day after Labor Day and the owner couldn't say whether he'd reopen come summer.

Still, there was the diner, the florist, Fortune Drug, Kepsel's Ace Hardware, the old marina, a bait shop, Parmelee Gilbert's law office, a dentist, Repicky Realty now where Boynton Realty had once been, Enright's Pub, and Big Larry's Party Store, closed Mondays and Tuesdays during winter.

And there was the lake, named for a drought that had almost dried it up until one of FDR's make-work projects built a dam to divert the Hungry River. As I saw it walking up Main toward the *Pilot*, the lake was a vast field of white, crisscrossed with snowmobile tracks and dotted with the dark trapezoids of ice-fishing shanties. Wisps of low clouds shrouded the tops of trees crowding the bluffs on the far shore. The lake stretched north and west from the town in a seven-mile crescent, spring fed, clear as tap water, as deep as 250 feet in some places. In summer it would come alive with the roar of boat motors and the squeals of children.

I stopped at the locked front door of the Pine County State Bank. The doorknobs of every shop along Main had been rubber-banded with glossy green-and-yellow brochures. I undid the one on the bank door.

"Media North Invites You to the 21st Century!" the cover said. Media North was the company that in the past year had bought up the *Pilot*, Channel Eight, and just about every other media outlet from Grayling north to the Mackinac Bridge, including billboard firms and video rental stores. The brochure described the all-in-one packages the company was bringing up north even before the city dwellers in Detroit and Lansing and Ann Arbor would have them: cell phones, beepers, satellite TV, the Internet. I had a Media North cell phone, but this was the first I'd heard that we were in the Internet business. I wondered if it meant we might get new computers for the newsroom.

Probably not, I decided.

I glanced across the street at Audrey's Diner, thought of going in for a bite, decided against it. I loved Audrey's coffee and her gooey cinnamon buns—loved Audrey, too, had known her since I was a boy—but I'd been avoiding her place of late. I'd written some stories for the *Pilot* that had angered more than a few of the locals, and Audrey's was their favorite soapbox. Letters to the editor wouldn't suffice; better to tear the local editor a new one while he tried to eat his pancakes and bacon. Nor did I care to hear their gossip about how and why Gracie met her end.

I stopped on the sidewalk beneath the shake shingles hung over the front window of the *Pilot* offices. A new logo in slanted, foot-high letters— MEDIA FORCE NORTH—had just in recent days been painted across the latticed glass in spaghetti sauce red. I had taken the sign that had previously hung there for years—PEERLESS PILOT PERSONALS WILL PUT YOU ON THE PATH TO PLEASURE AND PROFIT—and given it to my mother as a souvenir. She hung it on the wall over the beer fridge in her garage.

Behind the darkened front counter a sliver of light bled from the door to the newsroom. Either I'd left it on or, more likely, Philo Beech was already at his desk. I hoped the former and stepped inside.

"Good morning," Philo said. He looked up from his computer and gave me a prim smile before returning his eyes to whatever he was doing.

"Morning," I said, throwing my coat on the back of my chair. I might've said, "You're in early," but after two months of working with Philo Beech, I knew that seven o'clock was not early, not for him.

"Wow," he said, swiveling in his chair to face me. My new boss, seven years younger than me at twenty-eight, was wearing a sleeveless argyle sweater—the blue-and-black one he alternated daily with a red and gray— over a starched blue dress shirt with a button-down collar. "Philo" rhymed with "silo", which was how he was built, a slender cylinder one head and a half taller than me, topped with horn-rimmed glasses beneath short dark hair moussed to stand at attention. He had to stack three telephone books beneath his computer screen so he wouldn't have to crook his neck down to see. "I don't know how you guys do it."

"Do what?"

"The gray," he said. "The constant gray. I mean, I can take the cold and the snow. You know what they say: 'There's no bad weather, just bad clothing.' But the gray, the clouds, the constant overcast. Jeez-oh-pete, we haven't seen the sun in what? A month?"

"Actually, Thursday morning," I said. "I was up early."

"Ha!" he said, raising his arms over his head. "I missed that—I wonder why?" He looked around our windowless little newsroom. "Boy oh boy, how do you guys keep from offing yourselves?"

Any other morning I might have chuckled lamely and said something like, "That's what Enright's is for," because that would be true. But on this particular morning, with my still-fresh memory of Gracie hanging in the shoe tree, I could think of nothing to say to Philo's stupid little joke. I just ran a hand through my thinning brown widow's peak and, as politely as I could, gave him a look that said his foot was in his mouth.

"What?" he said.

"Well," I said. I looked over my shoulder at the police scanner. "Did you turn that off?"

Philo looked at the scanner and shrugged. "It seemed like a waste of electricity to have it on this early in the morning. I mean, we publish twice a week, it's not like . . ." He threw his hands up in the air. "OK, I give. Why?"

I told him about Gracie McBride. It took longer to make him understand what the shoe tree was—apparently he hadn't noticed it yet in his brief time in Starvation—than what had happened there. When I finished, he crossed his long legs, folded his arms across his chest, and sighed.

"That is extremely sad," he said. "Did you know her?"

"Not very well."

I didn't say more because I wanted to see how interested he really was. I didn't tell him that Gracie had been my girlfriend's best friend, that she'd been dating my own best friend, that she was my dead father's dead cousin's daughter, my second cousin, and an adopted daughter of sorts to my mother.

"My condolences," he said. "Will you be writing it up?"

"Sure," I said. I smelled Windex on the air; he'd been cleaning again. He had a screwy theory that a clean newsroom was a more efficient newsroom. "We don't usually do much with suicides."

"People don't like to read about them, do they? I certainly don't. It's always, you know . . . I suppose this woman had problems with drinking and drugs and whatnot, the usual?"

"Usual" wasn't a word anyone who knew Gracie would have used to describe her. But Philo's question reminded me of what Darlene was saying when she'd cut herself off a few hours before, her husky voice insistent in my ear: *That's not what I meant.* It had kept me from sleep when I'd gone back to her apartment, alone. Was Darlene going to tell me that Gracie had not taken her own life? That someone else had hung her in that tree?

Gracie had left Starvation for Detroit as a very young woman. She was gone for nearly eighteen years. Nobody heard much from or about her while she was downstate. Then Gracie quietly returned to town, and moved into her mother's trailer in the woods near Walleye Lake. That ended one morning with Gracie's mother firing a 12-gauge into the air and yelling, "You owe me, you little bitch, you owe me more than that," as Gracie escaped into the summer trees, laughing in threadbare pajamas. Darlene later told me Gracie and her mom had argued over a game of euchre they'd lost at the Hide-A-Way Bar the night before.

Gracie took a room with a kitchenette at the Hill-Top Motel. She talked her way into a job at the hockey rink concession stand, making cocoa and popcorn for $3.50 an hour. I hadn't known her to be a hockey fan—she'd certainly never attended any of my games—but she learned to sharpen skates and drive and maintain the Zamboni. She ditched the motel room for the cot in the Zam shed at the back of the rink.

I saw her when I went to play in the Midnight Hour Men's League. She'd be on the Zamboni, circling the ice perched on the stool she needed to see over the steering wheel. Gracie put down a good sheet of ice, smooth and hard enough that it didn't get too chipped up for at least half a game. Some nights after hockey I'd see her late at Enright's, where the proprietor, my old friend Soupy Campbell, served her double gin and Squirts and slowly sweet-talked her into his bed. Or maybe Gracie sweet-talked him.

There was an appearance of normalcy. Gracie and Darlene got together once a week for greasy ham-and-pineapple pizza at Riccardo's across the river from downtown. If they talked about Gracie's downstate years, Darlene did not let on, or at least not very much. I chose to believe that Darlene wasn't deliberately keeping things from me but protecting her friend's privacy, knowing that Gracie and I, though we were second cousins, though we had spent a good deal of time around each other as kids, had never really gotten along.

I assumed that Darlene knew many things about Gracie that I did not know, that I really didn't think I cared to know. But now that she had been found dead, I was curious, of course, mostly because of what Darlene had left unsaid on the phone.

"I don't know much," I told Philo, "but Gracie could drink most guys under the table. Drugs? Not sure. Maybe. She did a bunch of stuff when she was a kid, but that was a long time ago."

"Obviously some issues there," he said. "A few grafs then. 'Apparent' suicide, unless the police confirm the real thing."

"Right. They won't. Not here."

Philo clapped his palms on his knees and stood.

"Now," he said. "We have a bit of decent news on the financial end of things. An opportunity to consider."

I leaned back in my chair. Philo had been named managing editor of the *Pilot* on the fifteenth of December. I was already executive editor. It was explained that he outranked me. I tried not to care. I told myself that I already had so many bosses at Media North headquarters in Traverse City that one more couldn't make much of a difference. Especially not Philo, who had written exactly two bylined stories since arriving, one on a routine school board meeting, the other on the arraignment of a man for stealing a dog, both of which required corrections (he misspelled the names of both the school board president and the dog, Zuzu). Before that, he had worked at a couple of nothing papers near his home back east.

His blunders did nothing to change the impression he gave that he felt he owned the place. It took me an afternoon of phone calls to Traverse City to determine that Philo was actually the nephew of Jim Kerasopoulos, the chief executive of Media North.

He began to pace between the leaky watercooler and the copier-and-fax machine that had been low on toner for two weeks. His penny loafers clacked on the linoleum, almost but not quite drowning out the buzz of the fluorescent lights overhead.

"Let's hear it," I said.

"Hutch's Hockey Heaven wants to lock in a quarter-page ad twice a week for a month, ramping up to a half page when the new rink opens," Philo said. "That alone"—he stopped and closed his eyes as he counted on his fingers—"is close to twenty percent of current budget and would help push us up, quarter to quarter, a couple of percentage points."

"Nothing to sneeze at," I said, although, in truth, I knew almost nothing about ads or circulation or anything but putting stories in the paper, such as they were in a town like Starvation. I knew ads brought in money, and money gave me space in the paper. The rest I left to the business guys.

"No, sir," he said. "Better up than down, which is where it's been going for the last two years."

"Maybe we could get some toner," I said. "I had to call the Kiwanis the other day because I couldn't read the flyer they faxed about their mostacciolli dinner."

Philo hesitated for a second before resuming his pacing.

"Even better," he said, "the rink itself has proposed a month's buy of full pages in the weeks before it opens followed by a special section—they're talking eight pages, full color—about the rink, the local hockey team, et cetera. That's a little gold mine in and of itself. Then they'll renew the weekly ads on a month-to-month basis depending on local interest, which I'm sure will be no problem to sustain. The town is dying for this."

Starvation was indeed eager for the new rink. The old one, once called the John D. Blackburn Memorial Ice Arena after an old River Rats coach but now called simply Starvation Lake Arena, was a little more than thirty years old, almost as old as me. It had always been a patchwork job. It had opened as an outdoor rink, complete with hockey boards and goal nets and refrigeration pipes running invisibly beneath the ice to keep it hard through the occasional warm winter day.

I could still remember the thrill of stepping out onto the ice for the first time as a five- or six-year-old and how I yanked my mittened hand from my father's and then promptly fell down, wondering if I was smelling the secret chemical that froze the ice in the snow that scraped my cheeks. That night, Dad, Mom, and I stood along the boards with hundreds of people from Starvation and Kalkaska and Sandy Cove and Mancelona and cheered for the River Rats midget squad against some Detroit team. I didn't care that the Rats lost by five or six or that I had to get up on my tippytoes to see over the boards. I had a foam cup of hot chocolate from a thermos Mom had brought and I rolled the miniature marshmallows around in my mouth until they melted away.

By the time Dad died of cancer—I was seven years old—the rink had a ceiling and walls built on two of the four sides. A few years later, the town scraped up the money to close the north and south ends, which meant goaltenders no longer had to blink against snow and sleet being sucked through one end and out the other.

Bad memories lingered, though. The River Rats had lost their one chance at a state championship in that rink. I was the goaltender who'd given up the overtime goal that lost the title game. Eighteen years had passed, and I thought I had finally gotten over it. The town had not.

Now a wealthy man had come from downstate to build a brand-new rink with no bittersweet history. He had brought millions of dollars and a fourteen-year-old son who some said was the best young hockey player Starvation had ever seen. The boy happened to be a goaltender.

"That sounds terrific, Philo," I said. "What's the catch?"

Philo stopped pacing and looked at me. He was standing in front of a desk in the back that had nearly disappeared beneath old copies of the *Detroit Free Press* and *Chicago Tribune*. The pile wasn't going to grow because Media North—actually, Philo—had canceled those subscriptions.

"It is a great opportunity for us," he said.

"Yep. Are the ad guys in Traverse working it?"

"Of course. But we can't rely on them to carry the entire load."

"Well," I said, "you don't want me selling ads, do you?"

Philo walked over and sat against my desk, pushed his glasses up his nose, folded his arms. Now I heard the fluorescent lamps. I hated that buzzing. It made me feel lonely, even with this long hockey stick of a man sitting next to me on my desk.

"Look," Philo said, "I only minored in journalism at Penn, but I got my master's in it at Columbia. I have a deep and abiding appreciation for the historical separation of church and state in news organizations."

"I'm Michigan, no grad school, but agreed."

"Emphasis on 'historical.' As you know, the present-day realities of newspaper economics do not fit very well with many of the historical templates that our forefathers, with the very best of intentions, constructed for us."

I was beginning to wish I'd just gone to Audrey's. "And your point is?"

"All right. I really don't have to tell you this, but look: if we have no business—and we certainly don't have much at the moment—then we have no newspaper, which means we have no place to do your journalism. No money, no stories."

My journalism? I thought. I'd left my naïveté about newspapers being a calling at the *Detroit Times*. I'd worked there for more than ten years, writing mostly about the big automotive companies. I came damn close to winning a Pulitzer Prize reporting about a certain model of pickup truck that burned a lot of people to death. But I went to some extremes in my reporting methods that got me fired instead. In the end, it did not matter that my stories were true.

So here I was, back in my nothing hometown.

"Right," I said. I planted the soles of my boots against the edge of my computer stand. "But if you don't do good stories, you have no business either."

"That's very true," Philo said. "But I think you would agree that 'good'"—he held up his hands and waggled his fingers to signify quote marks—"is a subjective matter. We can count the dollars coming in, and we can count the dollars going out, right down to the penny. But good stories and bad stories all look the same on a balance sheet, if you know what I mean."

"Oh, I know what you mean. If the stories I've done about the new rink showed up on your balance sheet, they'd be entered on the 'bad'"—I waggled my own quote marks—"side of the ledger, huh?"

"I didn't say that."

I had written a few stories for the *Pilot* suggesting that the rich guy building the new rink might not have all the money he needed to build it, that it wasn't clear where he was going to get it, that he might have to cut a few corners to get the rink up in time for the state hockey playoffs in March, as everyone in town had hoped. It was as though the entire town believed that a new sheet of ice set beneath a shiny new roof with a nice new concession stand and four new locker rooms with showers that actually spewed hot water would make the River Rats winners, as though it had nothing to do with whether they were fast and tough and determined enough to beat the powerhouse Compuware and Mic-Mac and Honey-Baked Ham teams from downstate.

For Philo, it was actually a simpler matter. He had been dispatched to the *Pilot* by his CEO uncle to fix the finances. He would not be judged on whether we hung plaques on the paneled walls for our sterling reporting and writing and photographs but on whether we paid the bills and had some left over to transfer into Media North's bank accounts. The rich guy building the rink was offering us a blank check that—assuming it cleared—promised to solve Philo's problem, at least for now. The guy just wanted us—that is, me—to go a little easier on him.

I can't say as I blamed him. Hell, a new rink sounded great. I didn't like ice-cold showers any more than the next guy. And I really couldn't blame Philo. He was a smart young man with a bright future who was trying to prove he could walk the tightrope between elusive truth and hard reality. I had tried it once myself and fallen flat on my ass.

"Hell," I said, "the Internet's going to save us anyway, right?"

"Go ahead and laugh," Philo said. "The world is speeding up, my friend. The earth's spinning faster on its axis. People are going to want their news now"—he snapped his fingers—"instantaneously, pronto, *immédiatement*. The Web will get it to them when they want it, where they want it, how they want it."

I stared past him at the clock on the wall: 7:28. Mom wouldn't be up for a while. I wanted to get over there before she turned on the news.

"How about a coffee with cream? Can the Internet get me that? Or do I have to walk all the way over to Audrey's?"

"Forget the Internet," Philo said. "Look, Gus. I know—I know all of this ad stuff sounds, well, shitty probably, especially to a guy who's done such exemplary work—"

"Work that got me fired."

"—not just in Detroit but here in Starvation, those stories you did last year about the old hockey coach here—"

"No, no, no, Philo, you haven't been spending enough time listening to the codgers at Audrey's. That was all the work of another reporter who's since gone on to greener pastures. Man, I couldn't write my way out of a—"

"Goddammit!" He slammed a hand down on the top of my desk, rattling the pens and pencils in my Detroit Tigers beer mug. "Stop fucking with me."

I took my feet down.

"Whoa," I said. "Settle down, man."

Philo took off his glasses and pointed them at me. "I know what you're capable of," he said. "I've read your stories, including what you did at the *Times*. I know you can hang this guy like that silly stupid loser hanged herself last night. All I'm asking is that you give him a fair shot."

"How have I not given him a fair shot?" I said. "He doesn't return my calls."

"Have you spoken with his lawyer?"

"I thought you read my stories. The lawyer's quoted: 'No comment.'"

Philo rubbed his eyes. He slid his glasses back on.

"'No comment' just isn't good enough," he said.

"You want me to put a gun to his head?" I said.

"Come on, Gus. I think we both agree that this rink—that *any* new building around here that employs actual people—would be beneficial. But Mr. Haskell has now halted construction because of your stories."

Laird Haskell was the rich guy building the rink. I knew why he was dodging me. He and I had a past Philo didn't know about.

"Bullshit," I said. "He stopped building because he didn't have the money, because he was taking cash from Peter to pay Paul and his subcontractors walked."

Philo sighed. He looked up at the ceiling. The poor kid was doing his best. I doubted Columbia had prepared him for this, especially the amoebic water stain he must have seen blackening the ceiling panel over his head.

"Haskell," he said, "would like to meet with you."

"News to me. When?"

I got up out of my chair and pulled out my cell phone. No wonder I hadn't gotten a call from Darlene. I had left the phone off. I kind of liked the thing but I was still getting used to it.

"Today," Philo said. "I'm waiting to hear the precise time."

"He called you?"

"Not exactly. But I'll get back to you."

"Happy to meet with him. Why didn't you just say so in the first place?"

Philo walked back to his desk and, standing, punched a few computer keys. He didn't say so in the first place because he'd wanted me to hear about that ad opportunity first.

"Time still not certain," he said. "But it'll be at his house. Someone else will be with him. His lawyer, I assume."

"Great."

"You know the house?"

"I've seen it once or twice."

You could step outside the *Pilot* and see it from Main Street, the biggest house on the lake, peering out from the northeastern shore.

"Thank you," Philo said. He looked up from the keyboard. "Would you mind bringing me a coffee? No cream, four sugars?" He reached into his pocket.

"I got it," I said. "Back in a few."

As I started out of the room, Philo called after me, "Hey, Gus."

I stopped and turned to face him.

"Yeah?"

"Hockey's really a big deal here, isn't it?"

"You're catching on."

"Where I grew up, we play lacrosse."

"Tough game. You never saw hockey?"

"Well, not in Annapolis, but they had it in D.C., I guess, but it wasn't . . . I don't know . . . it wasn't like it seems to be here."

"No, not like here. Here, it's everything."

Outside on the sidewalk, I turned my cell phone on. There was indeed a message. Waiting for it, I felt the dry morning cold rush down the open neck of my coat and thought of Darlene asleep the night before, the warmth of her bare shoulder blades against my chest.

"Hey," I heard her say. She wasn't quite whispering, but she was trying to keep her voice down. "I'm guessing you'll be at Audrey's. Don't believe everything you hear, OK? I'll try you later. Love you."

"Me, too," I said, dialing her back. I watched Audrey's as I listened to three rings and a click followed by her voice.

"You've almost reached Pine County sheriff's deputy Darlene Esper. Please leave a message, keeping in mind this is not Books on Tape."

I'd heard the message plenty of times but still it made me smile. The phone beeped. "Darl," I said. "Got your message. Don't worry. I hope you're doing all right. I'm thinking about you."

* * *

The little bells on the door at Audrey's Diner jangled when I walked in, and every head in the place turned. The smells of bacon grease and maple syrup washed over me.

"Morning," I said, as friendly as I could without making eye contact with anyone. I went straight to the counter across from where Audrey DeYonghe was bent over the griddle in a crisp white apron over a smock embroidered with yellow and orange flowers, her hair tied back in a walnut bun wrapped in a hairnet. She glanced over a shoulder at me, smiled, turned back to the pancakes she was flipping. "Good morning, Gussy," she said. "What'll you be needing today?"

"A vacation is what he needs," came the voice from the back of the restaurant. Elvis Bontrager, squeezed behind his usual table, spoke through a mouthful of half-chewed egg and sausage. "A nice long vacation," he said, "so we can get our damned rink built."

Elvis was my personal Greek chorus. Whatever I wrote in the *Pilot*, from a few grafs on the upcoming Rotary Club lunch to a half page on the school board spending a thousand dollars on a "fact-finding" trip to Chicago, I could count on Elvis to let me know, in front of everyone at Audrey's, what he didn't care for. That turned out to be pretty much every word I wrote—or failed to write, if he thought there was something I should have written. It wasn't because Elvis didn't like the *Pilot*; he just didn't like me. Hadn't liked me since I let that goal in that cost the Rats the state title. Liked me even less when, instead of marrying his niece, one Darlene Bontrager—now Esper—I took off to make my name as a big-time reporter in Detroit. And I had heard he wasn't too pleased that I was now fooling around with Darlene, even though, at least on paper, she was still married.

"How are you today, Elvis?" I said. There was no sense in arguing; his ears might as well have been filled with cement. I pointed at a spot just below his shirt pocket, where a chunk of cheese-covered sausage had fetched up on the roof of his potbelly. "You're missing the best part."

Elvis kept his eyes on me while his wife, blushing, reached across the table and plucked the scrap off of his shirt.

"You got the scoop yet on the McBride girl, boy?" he said. "I'm thinking not."

"Why do you have to talk about this here?" Elvis's wife said.

My eyes swept the room. The music of forks and knives on china kept playing. Everyone kept their eyes on their raisin French toast and American fries. But nobody was talking because they were all listening. They must have been so grateful that Elvis was willing to be a loudmouth. It was hard to get the really tough questions answered talking behind people's backs.

"Gracie?" I said. "What happened?"

"You know what happened, son," he said.

"Gussy," Audrey said. "What would you like?"

"Thanks, Mrs. DeYonghe. Two large coffees, one cream only, one no cream, four sugars."

"Nothing to eat?"

Audrey glanced sideways at Elvis to keep him shut up. He was shoveling potatoes into his face, his red suspenders straining against his girth. I would have loved to sit down and savor one of her Swiss-and-mushroom omelets, but I hadn't time nor did I want the hassle.

"Uh, sure, how about some rye bread, grilled?"

"Coming right up. With blackberry jam? I made fresh."

"That would be great."

She leaned over the counter and touched one of my hands. The aroma of lemon wafted off of her face. "I'm so sorry about Gracie," she said.

"Thanks."

"How's Darlene? And your mother?"

"It's a shame is what it is," Elvis said.

I ignored him. "Darlene's working, so that'll distract her for now. I'm going to go over to Mom's in a few minutes."

"Good. How is she otherwise?"

"You mean . . . right. Her memory's not so good some days. Maybe it's just old age. She'll be sixty-six soon."

"Let's hope," Audrey said.

"It's a damn shame," Elvis said again.

"Yes, it is, Elvis," Audrey said. She took out two slices of rye, picked up a knife, and started spreading butter on each slice. "She was a young woman with her whole life in front of her. And a grieving mother. And others who cared about her. Leave it be."

"That ain't what I'm talking about," Elvis said. "Ain't no shame in Gracie McBride killing herself. It's about as surprising as a blizzard at Christmas. Was just a matter of when."

"Elvis," his wife said.

Audrey laid my rye slices on the griddle. Elvis waved his fork over his head, upon which a blue polyester baseball cap announced "Cupid Rhymes with Stupid."

"The shame is that in a town like this, we'll now have to have a long and—I might add—very expensive investigation into why she did it and how she did it and all the other hoo-hah that goes along with it."

"Our tax dollars at work."

I looked to my right. The complaint had come from Floyd Kepsel. Elvis was emboldening his audience. I had to get out of there.

"Precisely, sir," Elvis said. "We have somebody trying to give us a brand-new hockey rink—*give* it to us, no strings—and we cannot get that done. But now we will go about spending untold hours and days and money wringing our hands over this, this young woman's stupid . . ."

I'd seen Elvis worked up plenty of times, but not quite like this. I understood that he was disappointed—distraught, upset, totally pissed off—about the rink. There weren't many River Rats fans more devoted than Elvis, especially now that he had a sixteen-year-old grandson—big kid, pretty good feet, lousy hands, hard slap shot—skating right wing for the team. But I hadn't told the new rink's contractors and subcontractors to pack their hammers and go home; they did it on their own when the money stopped coming.

Nor had I hung Gracie in the shoe tree.

"What do you want me to do, Elvis?"

"Forbear, son."

"It'll be three grafs in tomorrow's paper. Relax."

"I will not relax. Let the girl go to the grave she obviously desired, and let us build the rink we desire."

"What does one have to do with the other?"

Elvis came halfway out of his chair, then sat back down. "You don't know, do you? You don't know the connection?"

I shrugged and immediately wished I hadn't.

"You didn't catch the TV news this morning?"

I had that sinking feeling a reporter gets when he's about to find out he got scooped. I glanced behind the counter. Audrey had slathered my rye slices with jam and was hurrying to wrap them in wax paper.

"I was busy."

"Hah!" He looked triumphantly around the diner. "So you don't know about the suicide note."

It was no surprise to have a suicide note at a suicide. But I knew nothing about Gracie leaving one. I reminded myself of what Darlene had said about not believing everything I heard. Audrey handed me the foam cups of coffee and the brown bag folded around my rye slices. I gave the room my best knowing smile.

"Stay tuned," I said.

Elvis and some of the others were still chuckling as the door jangled shut behind me. Actually, they were starting to piss me off. A young woman was dead, and even if she wasn't my favorite person in the world, she deserved better than to be shunted aside for the sake of a hockey rink.

I put the brown bag under one arm, balanced the coffees in one hand, pulled out my cell phone, and dialed Darlene, hoping everyone in the diner wasn't watching. When her voice mail came on again, I said, "Damn it," and stuffed the phone in my pocket.

three

Steam was curling out of a pan on the stove in my mother's kitchen
when I pulled my truck onto the shoulder across the road from her
little yellow house on the lake.

The house perched atop a short bluff that tumbled down to a crumbling concrete sea wall and a floating dock that was now propped on a pair of metal sawhorses above the shoreline. Mom had sold our boat years ago, when I'd first gone to Detroit to work for the *Times*. Now her house, along with Darlene's mom's house next door, was among the few remaining from when the first autoworkers and retired Detroit cops and firefighters came north to build their weekend retreats and retirement places.

Most of those cabins, with their screened-in porches and corn brooms standing by the back doors for sweeping sand out of kitchens, had been sold off and ripped down to make way for the fat-faced two- and three-story homes built by the guys who actually ran the auto companies, and doctors and lawyers from Chicago who rarely showed their faces at Enright's or Audrey's. Guys like the one supposedly building us that new rink.

The old things about the lake that Mom and I liked—the cinder-block garages lined up along the beach road, the smell of ammonia in the garbage to keep out raccoons, the sounds of dinner plates being cleared from a picnic table in the August dusk—were slowly disappearing. Mom liked how the old houses were tucked humbly back into the shoreline woods, just visible enough from the water that you knew whose dive raft was bobbing out front. The new places, she complained, seemed to be vying with the lake itself for attention. "People can build whatever they like," she would say, "but they should remember that the lake is not just a fancy coat of paint."

We took solace in the lake itself. On summer evenings, we'd sit on our oak swing atop the bluff and watch the setting sun make eddies of pink and tangerine undulate on the water. It was enough.

I had come back to live with Mom after staying for a while in a tiny apartment directly above the *Pilot* newsroom. Shortly after Media North took over the paper, I received in the mail a one-page letter addressed "Dear Tenant." It said my lease, which was about to expire, would not be renewed because my drafty, leaky, cramped apartment that smelled faintly of mildew apparently was part of "Media North's ongoing efforts to maximize shareholder value." Mom was happy to have me back, and I was glad to be there, not just for my old room or her pot roast and Swiss steak suppers. I was worried about her. She seemed to have aged more than a year in the past twelve months.

The kitchen lights were on but I didn't see Mom. As I approached the back door, I heard music playing inside. It seemed a little early for that.

"Hello?" I said, opening the door.

It took me only a few seconds to recognize the song. Mom usually played it just once a year, on the anniversary of my father's death:

If ever I would leave you
It wouldn't be in summer . . .

An open bag of turnips sat on the kitchen counter next to a glass baking pan containing a pork tenderloin smothered in rosemary. I looked into the pot steaming away on the stove. There was nothing but a little water in it, as if some had already boiled away. Why was Mom cooking so early anyway?

I turned the stove off and looked through the kitchen into the living room. My mother rocked gently in her favorite easy chair to Robert Goulet's crooning. She had dragged the chair from its usual position near the fireplace to the picture window where she could gaze out onto the frozen expanse of the lake. Bunched about her shoulders was the blue-and-gold River Rats afghan she'd knitted for me when I was in high school and then had claimed for her own.

"Hi, honey," she said.

She'd seen me in the reflection in the window.

I leaned over and kissed her on the cheek. She reached up with a one-armed hug, her pajama flannel soft on my neck. She had been crying.

"Hi," I said. "Are you cooking?"

She gave me a blank look, as if she didn't understand the question. She didn't remember. I waited. She turned her gaze back to the lake.

"Turnips," she said.

"Turnips?"

"I was going to make turnips. Last week, I bumped into Gracie at the drugstore and I promised I'd make them for her the way she likes them, mashed with lots of butter and salt and parmesan."

Liked them, I thought. I put my hands on her shoulders, tried to find her eyes in the window reflection.

"I'm sorry," I said.

"It was the last time I saw her."

Gracie had stayed with us on and off after her father—my own father's cousin, Eddie—had had his chopper blasted from the sky over a jungle in Vietnam. She was one year older than me. As a kid, she lived with her mother mostly in between her mother's boyfriends. My mother would come home from bingo saying she'd heard that Gracie's mom had been seen wriggling her butt on the lap of some new out-of-town guy at Enright's. "Better get Gracie's room ready," she'd say, and I'd dread having to share my tiny bathroom with all of Gracie's perfumes and hairsprays and boxes of tampons. I never understood why, but she always seemed to get her brightest red lipstick smeared on the mirror. And I hated mashed turnips, especially when Mom made those instead of potatoes.

Mom and I quietly watched the lake. Robert Goulet sang. She loved his voice, a voice so big, she said, it could fill up the sky. As if to prove her point, she would wait until my father was out on the lake in our little runabout with the ten-horse Mercury outboard, then she would put Goulet on the stereo and blast it over the outdoor speakers so my father could hear it all the way out at Pelly's Point. "Nobody sings like that anymore," she would say. "Not even Frank sings like that anymore."

My father teased her that she loved Robert Goulet because he looked like Dad. "You mean," my mother would tease back, "you look like him." And then he would bow in his paint-spattered coveralls, the drywall contractor with the dimpled chin and eyes as blue as the lake, and she would curtsy in her polyester slacks and Ban-Lon shirt, the housewife with the waves of hair and the smile that could light up the sky, and they would whirl around the living room while I watched from the kitchen, sheepish but happy.

My father died not in the summer but the late fall. My mother dated now and then but never came close to remarrying. She never spent a night outside our house unless it was with relatives downstate, and no man, at least none I saw, ever stayed in our place past supper. She was not happy when I left home for Detroit, and though she was proud of my success there, or at least told me she was, she was quietly relieved when my failures sent me back to Starvation. "You're all the man I need in my house," she would tell me, explaining that she was too busy for a man, too busy with her two-day-a-week job at Sally's Dry Cleaning, too busy with her bowling and ceramics and euchre and church and Meals on Wheels.

But I think she clung to the memory of her Rudy, my father, because he'd already hurt her in the worst possible way, and she would never take a chance on being hurt that way again. Instead she put all of her heart into me and into her friends, the closest of them all women. While I could see that they made my mother happy, I knew there was a part of her that she had locked away forever in the deepest shadows of her heart, and it made me sad.

Today was not the anniversary of my father's death. But I understood why Mom was playing Robert Goulet anyway. When I was in high school, I had come home from hockey one evening, hungry and tired, hoping Mom would have dinner on the table. But when I'd walked into the kitchen, the stove had been quiet, the table clear, and Robert Goulet was playing on the stereo. Although I had forgotten, that day was in fact the anniversary of my father's death—and the same day of the month, by chance, the twenty-second, of Gracie's father's death—and Mom and Gracie, who was staying with us at the time, were in each other's arms, dancing in the darkened living room between the sofa and the armchairs, a girl and a woman grieving the men they had lost.

I remembered this as I stood with Mom now, feeling her shoulders rock back and forth beneath my hands. The song ended. I walked over and turned the stereo off.

"Can you play it again, dear?"

I took Mom's chair in both hands and swiveled it around to face me. I sat on an end table. She bunched the afghan around her.

"It's all so sad," she said.

"Yes. It's very sad."

"How is Darlene doing?"

"Devastated, I'm sure, but she's been out working the case all night, so I suppose she's distracted, for now at least."

"Good. Will you give her my love?"

"Of course."

Mom looked up at the ceiling and sighed. "Those two," she said. "They were nothing but trouble."

Gracie was nothing but trouble. I pictured her on the night before she left town for college, having barely made it out of high school, a wisp in blue jeans, swaying to and fro on the roof of the Volkswagen bug she had painted orange to match her hair. Her nipples jutted against the T-shirt she'd torn short above her belly button. She waved around a bottle of Boone's Farm as she sang off-key to "Joy to the World" blasting from the VW's eight-track player.

Darlene danced and clapped and sipped from a Schlitz tallboy on the ground beneath Gracie. She shook her head shyly and laughed when Gracie motioned for her to climb up there too. Soon two boys and then a third climbed up there and little Gracie lowered herself to her knees and disappeared within the tangle of gyrating hips.

"Well," I said, "Darlene knew when to stop."

My mother nodded.

"How are you two doing?"

"OK."

Mom held her look for a moment. She didn't really believe me. I supposed how we were doing depended on how you defined "OK." Darlene quietly worried that I would run back to Detroit; I wondered why she hadn't finalized her divorce.

I'd asked her more than once when she was going to switch back to her maiden name. "I like how Esper sounds like whisper," she told me. "Darlene Bontrager sounds like a fat person."

"Were you with her last night?" Mom said.

"Yeah, until she got the call."

"You let her go alone?"

"She was on duty, Mom. She couldn't have me along."

"But you went out there anyway, of course."

"I have a job to do, too."

Mom rocked back in her chair, pulled her hands out from under the afghan, and laced them together across her lap, bracing herself.

"Yes," she said. "You do."

"What's that supposed to mean?"

"She's family, son. You have to get to the bottom of it."

"Mother, forgive me, but get to the bottom of what? She hung herself. I'm sorry about that. But that's the way it is."

"Why did she hang herself? Why would she do that?"

Though I could not answer them, the questions themselves didn't baffle me as much as why my mother was asking them. Did she really think there was something more to know other than that Gracie's entire life seemed to point to an end like this one?

"I know you loved Gracie. But it's not like this is shocking."

"It may not be shocking, but it is a shock, at least to me." She looked up at me. I saw fresh tears in her eyes, more angry than sad. "Gracie did not deserve this, Gus. She did not deserve this. She was starting to come around. She was starting to settle down."

I thought, How could she not deserve what she chose? But I did not say anything. I dropped to a knee and put a hand on one of my mother's. "Mom, she was sleeping with Soupy. She was drinking with Soupy. That isn't quite settling down."

"Soupy has a good heart."

"Yes. And a hollow leg and the maturity of a ninth grader."

Soupy Campbell was my oldest friend. We had played hockey together since we were kids. He was one of the boys who had climbed atop Gracie's orange VW on that drunken high school night. I could still see him swaying his hips as he chugged from a quart bottle of beer.

Something about that memory bothered me.

"What is it you always say about your work?" Mom said. "'You don't know . . .'" Her voice trailed off. She was struggling to remember. She had been doing a lot of that lately.

I started to say, "You don't know what the story—" but she cut me off: "Don't." She stared at my hand on her knee. "'You don't know what the story is . . . until it's in the paper.'"

"Yes."

She lifted her head. "You're making assumptions here." She hesitated. "I hate to say this, but I think you may be letting your emotions cloud your judgment."

"What emotions?" I said.

"Please, Gus."

My cell phone rang in my pocket. "Excuse me," I said, pulling it out.

"Those things will be the death of civilization. Why couldn't they, just leave them down in Detroit with the rest of the rat race?"

"Get with it, Mom," I said as the phone rang again. "Media North is bringing us into the twenty-first century."

"This one's plenty hard enough. Put that down."

I figured it was Darlene, and I wanted to talk with her, though not in front of Mom. I stopped the ring. "Sorry. Where were we?"

Mom hesitated, then said, "It's not your fault that you were an only child, honey."

"What's that supposed to mean?"

"An only child gets used to having things his way. Then you suddenly had Gracie in your world."

"She liked having things her way too."

"And you didn't appreciate it. You didn't like Gracie."

"That's not true."

It really wasn't. I didn't dislike Gracie any more than she disliked me. Our house just wasn't big enough for both of us. Or maybe Mom wasn't.

Over the years we had found a way to coexist, largely by avoiding each other, even after Gracie returned to Starvation the year before. When I saw her at the wheel of the Zamboni, I usually called out, "Hey, Gracie," and she'd nod, if not smile. I sent her a drink or two when I saw her sitting on her stool at the back of Enright's, her Kools and Bic lighter at the ready. Sometimes she acknowledged it, sometimes she didn't.

But now, as my mother prodded me, I was thinking of Gracie's old VW. She'd gotten rid of it a long time ago, of course, and I was trying to remember what she had been driving recently, besides a Zamboni.

I stood again.

"Gus?" Mom said.

"Do you remember what kind of car Gracie had?"

Mother looked at me blankly.

"Mom," I said. "Did you go to the doctor?"

"The what? Oh. Yes. I mean—yes. Yes, I did. Yesterday."

"Yesterday was Sunday, Mom."

I walked into the kitchen and stared outside at the garage. Mom's car, a tomato red 1995 Buick LeSabre, was parked inside. Gracie had driven an old lady's car too. It had been in a photograph on an inside page of the *Pilot*. After a long Two-fer-Tuesday evening at Enright's, Soupy had nearly driven it off the Estelle Street Bridge into the Hungry River.

I walked back into the living room.

"What's with all the rosemary on the pork roast?" I said. "It looks like a pine branch."

Mom furrowed her brow. "It's good for you," she said. "I saw it on that channel, the one that, you know. With all the recipes. They said it's good for your digestion and circulation. Gets the blood flowing to your brain."

Ah, I thought, a home remedy for creeping senility.

"Hey," I said. "What kind of car did Aunt Helene drive when she used to come up from Bay City?"

"That was years ago."

Long enough ago that Mom might remember.

"A Ford, wasn't it?" she said, brightening. "A hideous green thing."

"Yeah. An LTD. That's what Gracie drove. Not quite as big, but just as green and ugly. With a big rust spot—a hole actually—in the back of the trunk lid."

"Why does this matter?"

I stood there remembering the night before. My mind's eye traveled up and down the snowbanks on either side of the road. I saw police cruisers, the ambulance, the fire truck. I did not see an ugly green Ford LTD with a rust hole in the trunk lid.

"I would have noticed that," I said, thinking aloud.

"What?" Mom said.

"Gracie's car, it wasn't there."

"Where?"

"At the shoe tree."

"No?"

"No. How the hell did she get out there? She couldn't have walked in that storm, although I suppose—" My cell phone rang. "Hang on." I didn't want to miss Darlene twice. I answered. "Yeah?"

"Beech here."

Philo. I wished I hadn't picked up. "What's up?"

"It's on with Haskell. Eleven fifteen."

"Sorry?"

He paused. "Laird Haskell. Your appointment."

"Oh, right, sorry. OK. I'll be there. You coming?"

"Unfortunately, no, I have a meeting in Traverse City. Buzz me when you're done, OK?"

"I'll try."

"Gus."

"Yeah?"

"Just . . . just keep in mind now is really not the time to stand on principle."

I was too stunned to answer right away. Philo said, "Talk later," and hung up the phone.

"What's wrong?" Mom said. "You look surprised."

Surprised wasn't quite the word.

"Nothing," I said. "Where was I? Gracie's car. That's right. It wasn't there. I guess—"

"No, Gus."

"—she could have walked."

"No."

No.

As a reporter for the *Detroit Times*, I had written plenty of stories about people killed in or by cars and trucks. Regardless of whether I saw the blood spilled across asphalt or just heard about it from a police sergeant over the phone, I felt for the dead. I felt they'd been wronged, whether it was by a faulty steering suspension or a drunk driver or even their own innocent mistake. I felt for them even though they were strangers. Or perhaps, more accurately, *because* they were strangers. Because I knew nothing of their flaws. How they always grabbed the last piece of French toast for themselves. How they sucked up to their bosses and lied to their wives. How they used silence to punish their children.

But I knew all of Gracie's flaws. Or imagined that I did.

I thought of her sitting on Mom's lap in that very chair, the two of them sharing a box of Jujubes and chattering about the girls at school— "phony-baloneys," Gracie called them—who wore too much makeup and the kind of blouses that would make the boys notice their boobs, both Mom and Gracie hopelessly blind to Gracie sitting there with her eyelids

painted indigo and her T-shirt tied in a fat knot tight beneath her bud-
ding bosom.

It wasn't that I thought Gracie somehow deserved her fate; it was more
that I believed it was where she alone had aimed herself, a destination she
had mapped out, consciously or not, years before. I had nothing to do with
it then, so why should I have anything to do with it now?

But there were questions I could not answer: How did she get into the
tree? What did she stand on before she dropped to her death? How did she
get out there? All by herself. In a storm that had torn branches from trees.

I thought of Elvis and the others at Audrey's snickering over their
breakfast plates. Boneheads, every one of them.

"All right, Mom," I said.

My phone started ringing again. I ignored it.

"All right what?"

"I'll be looking into this. There must be an explanation."

Mom allowed herself a faint smile. She shrugged the afghan off her
shoulders and stood. "You better get going then," she said. "I'm going to put
those turnips on."

four

L ook," Gracie said. "Is it dead?"

She had spotted the white-tail lying beneath the boughs of a Scotch pine in the woods near Jitters Creek. July sun dappled the deer's back but the trees were thick enough away from the creek bed that most of the animal lay in shadow. It held its head up straight, its eight-point antlers reaching into the branches above its head. Its eyes were closed. I'd never seen a deer with its eyes closed.

"No," Darlene said. "It's sleeping."

Gracie took a step toward the deer. I grabbed a fistful of the back of her T-shirt. "Don't," I said. "It might be hurt. Dad said never mess with a hurt animal."

"It's just a deer," Gracie said, yanking herself away. "What's it going to do?"

"It can put a hoof right through you."

"It'll never catch me."

"Yes, it will," Darlene said. "Deer are fast."

"They run like deer," I said.

Gracie sneered. At eleven, she was a year older than Darlene and me, and she thought she was a lot smarter.

"Ha-ha-ha, booger face. I'll just go jump in the creek. I'll bet he can't swim." She started toward the deer again. This time Darlene grabbed her by the arm. "Wait." Darlene bent and picked a dead tree branch off the ground. "Let's test him first." She took two tentative steps toward the deer and tossed the branch at its back. The deer didn't budge.

"See, he's dead," Gracie said.

"Let me try again." Darlene found a bigger branch lying on a bed of pinecones. She threw it end over end and it glanced off the deer's neck.

The deer opened its eyes. All three of us jumped back.

"Oooooh," Gracie cried. We scrambled behind a tree and watched. I felt my heart pumping hard. The deer's head swiveled slowly in our direction. The rest of him did not move. His eyelids drooped.

"He's hurt," I said.

"Poor thing," Gracie said. Again she started to move toward the animal and again I grabbed her. This time she didn't try to pull away.

"Gracie. That deer will kick your butt."

"But we have to do something."

"We should call the ranger," Darlene said.

"What ranger? There's no ranger."

I let go of Gracie.

"Your mom's is closest," I said. "We can mark the spot and go tell her."

Our bikes waited back on the two-track road that wound down through the woods. We had planned to do some bike-diving into the creek, flying down the hill over the bank into the water. But Gracie had insisted on seeing if we could find a new path through the trees. "We can slalom," she had said.

Now she looked at me, then at the deer, at Darlene, at the deer again.

"No," she said. "Let's leave the deer alone."

"Leave it alone?" Darlene said. "A minute ago you wanted to go right up and pet it. We can't leave it alone. It'll die."

Gracie shrugged. "Everything dies. I don't want to tell my mom."

"She's not going to know we were bike-diving," I said. "We're not even wet yet."

"She doesn't give a crap anyway," Darlene said.

"No," Gracie said.

"We can't just leave it here to die. Somebody might be able to help it."

"Not my mom, or her—just leave it."

"Ler what?" Darlene said.

"This is stupid," I said. "We should tell someone. You're going to be bragging about it anyway."

"Just wait, Gus," Darlene said.

I waited. The girls stood there watching the deer. Its eyes were closed again. Finally, I said, "I'm going to count my steps back to the road so the police can find it." I turned and started walking back toward the bikes.

"It won't be the police," Gracie said. "Gus." She shouted it as I took big running steps up the hill.

After I told Mrs. McBride that the deer was twenty-eight steps down Jitters Trail, twenty-three steps to the right, and fifty-three steps down through the trees, she picked up her phone. When Gracie heard her say, "Bucky boy," into the phone, she punched me in the ribs.

"Ow," I said. "What are you doing?"

"Butthole. I told you."

I looked at Darlene. She looked away.

Four hours later, the deer was hanging antlers up from a joist in Gracie's mother's carport, dripping blood onto an oil-stained piece of cardboard. The fur around its neck was matted, and some had been worn away so that patches of pink skin showed through. One of the deer's hind legs jutted out from its body at an unnatural angle that made me think of the day the winter before when my friend Jeff Champagne lost a skate edge and slid into the boards and broke a leg.

I didn't know what the smell was in the carport, but I knew I didn't like it.

A man named Ringles stood looking the gutted animal over. Blood smeared the "Matilda" tattoo on his left arm. He turned to Shirley Mc-Bride, who was leaning against a garbage can sipping a longneck bottle of Drewry's.

"See where he got me?" Buck Ringles said. He fingered a tear in the rolled-up sleeve of his flannel shirt. "Fucker jumped up like he was coming for me. Goddamn leg's broken in two places, but the fucker would not give up."

"Buck."

"Oh. Sorry." He grinned at Gracie, Darlene, and me. "Bastard would not give up."

"You going to try to get a license?" Shirley said.

Ringles rubbed the gray stubble on one of his sunken cheeks. He was two heads taller than Shirley, skinny but for the belly that sagged over his belt. He and a cousin made their livings cleaning out septic tanks. Shirley had dated them both, off and on. For the moment, she was with Buck.

"Don't know," he said. "You know, you can get a license if you hit one with your car. My ex-brother-in-law did it when that doe run into him up on M-32." Buck touched the deer's skewed leg. "This one looks like he got hit himself."

"Maybe your car hit it," Shirley said.

Ringles grinned. "Maybe." Then his eyes brightened. "You think the DMV'll let me have a license for strangling a deer in self-defense?"

They both laughed.

We had overheard him earlier telling Mrs. McBride how the deer had died. Buck Ringles had taken his hunting knife into the woods—"just in case," he said—but was afraid that he might inadvertently cut himself in a struggle. He crept up on the deer from behind. When the deer suddenly turned and raised itself up on its front legs—"lurched," as Ringles put it—Ringles clambered atop its back, removed his belt, and quickly looped it around the deer's neck, pulling one end through the buckle and yanking with all of his strength.

When the deer lost consciousness, Ringles jumped off and found a tree branch. He brought it down on the deer's head again and again until he heard something crack and the head lolled over, limp. My stomach went queasy as we eavesdropped from Gracie's bedroom, hearing Buck's voice rise as he described himself swinging the branch.

Now, as we stood marveling at the garroted deer in Mrs. McBride's carport, Ringles reached beneath his potbelly and whipped off his belt. "Look here," he said. We saw specks of blood and short gray hairs stuck to the belt buckle. Ringles stepped back and whacked the deer on its rump. "That'll last to winter," he told Mrs. McBride. "Stew, steaks, chops, a whole damn smorgasbord. All free. And a nice little rack for over the fireplace to boot."

"You owe me," Shirley said. She was smiling.

Buck Ringles winked at her. "Don't worry, baby. You'll get everything you're owed and more."

"Oh, I will, will I?"

Gracie turned and stormed out.

"Where you going?" Buck Ringles called after her.

"She don't know," Shirley said. "She's always pissed off about something. It'll pass. How about another beer?"

Darlene and I found Gracie in her bedroom, sitting on the edge of her bed, clutching a pillow to her chest.

"It's boring here," I said. "Let's go back to Jitters."

Gracie gave me a look filled with anger. She turned to Darlene. "Tell him to go away."

"What did I do?"

Darlene sat down next to Gracie. "He didn't mean for that to happen."

"But it happened," Gracie said. "Tell him to leave."

"So the deer's dead," I said. "Everything dies, remember?"

"Get out of here."

I turned to Darlene.

"What?" she said. "It's not my house."

"What if it was?"

"Tell him."

Darlene looked at Gracie, then at me. "You better go."

"What? No. No, I'm not going. This is dumb. Come on, let's go down—"

"Get out," Gracie said. "Do you hear me? I hate you."

I heard her say it again, louder, as the kitchen door banged shut behind me.

five

I waited until I got into my truck to call Darlene.

"Esper," she said.

"Good morning."

"Jesus."

"Yeah."

"My God, Gus, I am so—" She stopped herself. I imagined her holding the cell phone close to her face, ducking away from the sheriff and the other deputies. "I am so sick of being a girl."

"What?"

"Being treated like a girl."

"What happened?"

"Dingus sent me back to the department."

"You're at your desk?"

"I'm handling the frigging press. We're off the record, by the way."

I decided not to make a joke. The "press" would be me and the woman who went on the air for Channel Eight. I started my truck, pulled it into Mom's driveway, threw it in reverse, and backed it onto Beach Drive.

"I'm sorry," I said. "Are they thinking—"

"Don't you dare take their side."

"I'm not. I just thought—"

"I know what you thought. You thought, This is my oldest friend, maybe I shouldn't be working on this."

"No." I really hadn't. Yet.

"Well, that's what Dingus said. 'Maybe you should take a little time, Darlene.' He can kiss my buns."

Dingus, I thought, might also have worried that she would tell me things she shouldn't. He didn't always mind me knowing things, but he liked to be the one who decided what I knew or didn't and when.

"Maybe he'll reconsider."

"I'll make him."

I let the conversation pause as I veered onto Main Street and passed the old marina, Repicky's, Enright's, Sally's, Audrey's, and crossed Estelle where the businesses gave way to two-story houses on either side of the road, their sprawling front porches buried in snow.

"How are you really?"

"I'm pissed."

"I know, but, I mean, you know, with Gracie and all."

"Are you going to write a story?"

"I have to write something."

"Like what?"

"Are you handling the press now?"

She softened her voice. "Like what, Gussy?"

The houses fell behind me and fields of white opened beyond both road shoulders. An occasional fence post knotted with barbed wire poked through the drifts. A new cell tower jutted into the sky high above the tree line.

"I don't know. If I had to write it this minute, I don't know how I could write anything but apparent suicide. But I have yet to hear from Dingus—"

"Screw Dingus."

"—and you cut me off last night and then you left me that weird voice mail this morning. Luckily, I don't have to write this minute, but I will a little later today, so any help you can give me . . ."

"Hang on," Darlene said. I imagined her looking around her office to make sure no one could overhear.

I pulled the truck to the side of the road, not far from where I had parked it the night before. Down the road, the lights of police cruisers flickered near the shoe tree.

As far as I knew, a pair of my old hockey skates still hung from one of the higher branches. When I was still a very young man, Darlene had brought along a paper grocery sack on one of our dates and insisted I take her to the tree. It was the summer before I left Starvation Lake. Parked near the tree in my truck we made love; I remember searching for her eyes in the dark.

Darlene pulled her jeans on and took the paper bag from the flatbed and beckoned to me. From the sack she produced a pair of her softball spikes, still flecked with dried mud, and a pair of my skates she'd gotten from my mother. "Now," she said. I climbed as high as I could and hung them next to each other on the only branch I could find without shoes already hanging from it. Perched on a branch, clinging to the tree trunk, I looked down and felt glad to hear her laugh and see the sweat on her forehead glistening in the moonlight.

It was not enough to keep me in Starvation, though. As I said, I was a very young man. Three weeks later, I left town for what I thought would be forever. Darlene refused to visit me in Detroit; we would either be together at home, in Starvation, she told me, or we would not.

Years passed. We didn't talk. It was awkward when we bumped into each other on my infrequent visits north. Darlene began to see a former minor-league hockey player named Jason Esper.

Just before they married, I heard through the grapevine that Darlene had climbed into the shoe tree after a night of drinking and torn her spikes from the branch. Hearing that, I imagined her hair swinging to and fro across her back as she clambered angrily from one branch to another.

More years passed before my troubles at the *Times* sent me back to Starvation, where I happily found Darlene in a marriage empty enough that she would reconsider me. Now, with her voice in my ear, I hoped that what had happened to her friend in that tree wouldn't make it harder on the two of us.

"So there was no car," I said.

"No," Darlene said.

I stared through my windshield at the distant crooked bough of the shoe tree where Gracie had been hanging the night before. One of the cops turned and pointed at my truck.

"And no ladder, nothing to stand on."

"Nope."

I wasn't accustomed to Darlene talking about cases. We had a loose rule that we didn't talk to each other about what we were working on. It was more Darlene's rule than mine; it wasn't like I was sworn not to divulge the contents of next week's school lunch menu. But Darlene was staunch. She'd talk about the doughnut sprinkles that got stuck in Dingus's handlebar mustache, about the other deputies' cheating on overtime, about how they had contests to see who could write the most speeding tickets on a holiday weekend. She almost never talked about specific cases.

"Any footprints out there?"

"Covered or blown over."

That reminded me. "One of her feet was bare, wasn't it?"

She waited, begrudging me this detail. "Yes."

"Have you—"

"No. We haven't found the other boot, unless it's up in the tree. Dingus is trying to get a cherry picker out there, but the snow's an issue."

"Well, how the hell did she get up there?"

"I don't know. Maybe she had help."

I thought of the stool Gracie had sat on driving the Zamboni. Soupy was always joking that she really needed a booster seat on top of that so she didn't drive the thing through the boards.

Then I thought, Oh, holy Christ, Soupy. He and Gracie had been seeing each other, less discreetly than they no doubt had imagined. Soupy had closed Enright's early the night before. I hadn't thought too much of it then, given the snowstorm, though it wasn't like Soupy to close his bar even one minute before he could sell—or drink—one last beer. Now I had to wonder whether Soupy had driven Gracie out to the shoe tree. Nobody could be that stupid.

Except maybe Soupy. My stomach tightened. He wasn't capable of hurting anyone intentionally. But he was damned good at hurting himself.

I decided against asking Darlene about Soupy. Instead I said, "So what about your voice mail?"

"Did you go to Audrey's?"

"Yeah. Elvis was holding court."

"I figured. What did he say?"

"He said the cops—you guys have a suicide note. Said it was on TV this morning, why the hell hadn't I seen it, blah blah."

"Which is why I left that message."

"So there is no suicide note?"

"No . . . well, there's a . . . it's complicated. She had a piece of paper on her. Some people might call it a suicide note, people who knew about

Gracie's"—I thought I heard a catch in Darlene's voice—"you know, her flair for drama."

"A piece of paper? Like what?"

"It wasn't a suicide note."

"So, what then?"

"She was trying to tell us something."

That she was suicidal? No. No car. No ladder. A shoe missing. "What exactly did she write?"

"She didn't. The people at that new hockey rink did." There was a pause. I thought Darlene might have been collecting herself. "A rejection letter. One page."

"She applied for a job at the new rink?"

"Yes. The same job she has—had at the old rink."

"Was the letter dated?"

"Not sure. They haven't let me actually look at it. But I assume it's recent."

It seemed a little strange that the owner of the new rink, or his minions, would be making decisions about jobs when the rink was barely a skeleton of structural steel. Might Gracie have gotten the job if construction hadn't stopped? Now I understood what Elvis had meant by the "connection" between my rink stories and Gracie's death: my stories, by halting construction, had killed Gracie. Elvis had quite an imagination.

"And they told her no?"

"Yes. They told her to go to hell."

"Forgive me, Darl, but why would anybody think that's a suicide note?"

"Most people wouldn't. But we're talking about you-know-who."

She meant Pine County sheriff's deputy Frank D'Alessio, who probably had leaked the detail to Channel Eight. "Where did you find it?" I said.

"In a snowdrift a few feet from where she was hanging."

"So she could have just dropped it."

"Or it could have fallen out of her pocket as she was being dragged up into the tree."

I tried to imagine it. A man? Two men? It wouldn't be a woman. Not with Gracie. No, it would be a man, or men. But why? I had no idea. All I could think at that moment was that the answer was likely to be found somewhere other than Starvation Lake. Somewhere downstate.

"When do you expect to hear from Doc Joe?" I said.

"You mean Doc Slow?" Doc Joe was Joe Schriver, Pine County medical examiner. He was not known for expediting cases. "We'll probably figure this out before he rubber-stamps it."

"You've positively identified—Jesus!"

A rapping on the window to my left startled me. I turned and saw D'Alessio standing in the road outside, a long flashlight in one hand.

"What?" Darlene said.

I lowered my voice and put a finger up to let D'Alessio know I'd be just a moment. "I have a visitor," I told Darlene. "You-know-who."

"Gus," Darlene said, "somebody wants us to think this was a suicide. Somebody who really didn't like Gracie."

D'Alessio rapped the butt end of his flashlight on my window again, harder. "Open up, fuckhead."

I took another look at the shoe tree. "You're right," I told Darlene.

"Gracie was no angel but—"

"I know. She didn't deserve this. Don't worry. I'm on it."

C old whipped across my face as I rolled my window down. D'Alessio had hidden his eyes behind unnecessary sunglasses.

"Frankie," I said. "What's up?"

"Can't be parking here." He jerked a thumb in the direction of town. "Got to move it along."

D'Alessio had come to Starvation from Detroit as a boy. His father had been a Detroit cop who got sick of the shot-up streets and falling-down houses, so he came up north and bought a grocery store in town. Frankie had a wife and a couple of kids. He skated in the Midnight Hour Men's League. Not a lot of skill, but a knack for whacking the top of your skate with the heel of his stick when you weren't looking, something I hadn't had to endure when I was playing goalie.

He also carried a barely disguised hard-on for Channel Eight's on-air reporter, Tawny Jane Reese.

"What do you think?" I said. "I hear you've got a suicide note."

"Crazy little bitch," he said, meaning, I assumed, Gracie. "No comment."

"It's not a suicide."

"All communications with the press should be directed to the sheriff or the on-duty press liaison."

I chuckled. "Tell me, Frankie. How do I get you to leak me stuff like this so-called suicide note? I hope Tawny at least gave you a hand job."

I didn't really think she'd ever given in to D'Alessio's come-ons, but I was sure she regularly used them to her advantage.

"You want a tip?" D'Alessio said. He grinned and leaned his head down so he could look at me over the tops of his glasses.

"I'm not giving you a hand job."

"Meat's back."

I tried to look nonchalant. "Who?"

"Fuck you," D'Alessio said. He leaned his head back but kept the grin in place. "You know—the guy whose wife you been banging."

He meant Jason Esper, Darlene's estranged husband. I had heard rumors that he might come back to Starvation after leaving Darlene and town many months before.

Those of us who played hockey called him Meat for how the knuckles on his right hand looked after dozens of fights in the lowest of the low minor leagues. Like pounded meat. Darlene had told me that Jason went through periods when it was too painful for him to put his hand in his pocket. He also happened to be about as big and muscled as a steer.

"Aha," I said. "Well, welcome back, Meat. Why's he back? Did someone beat his video golf record at Dingman's?"

"I hear he's fixed himself up pretty good," D'Alessio said. "But you can see for yourself tomorrow."

Tuesday night, Soupy and I and our team, the Chowder Heads, had a first-round playoff game in the Midnight Hour Men's League.

"No shit, huh?" I said. "Meat's playing?"

"Yes, sir. Last time you saw him on the ice, he was skating for the Pipefitters, wasn't he?"

The Pipefitters was the team from south of Detroit that beat us in overtime in the 1981 state final.

"Yeah," I said. "But he was young, didn't get a lot of ice time."

"He'll get plenty tomorrow, unfortunately for you."

"Can't wait."

"Deputy!"

The shout came from the shoe tree. We both looked to see Dingus waving his arms over his head. He didn't seem happy. D'Alessio, flustered, gave him a thumbs-up, then looked back at me.

"Move it along," he said. "I'll see you at the rink or"—he smirked again—"maybe in the hospital."

I swung my truck around and headed back in the direction of town. As I turned north on Ladensack Road, I tried Soupy's cell phone. As usual, he didn't answer. Probably still in bed, I thought. I didn't bother to leave a message he wouldn't bother to retrieve.

* * *

The Starvation Lake Arena, in all of its cinder-block glory, squatted in a parking lot ringed by snow-laden pines and birches.

I slowed to let a snowplow pull onto the road in front of me. I was glad to see the lot empty but for a single Dodge pickup. Snow was piled high against the marquee on wheels near the roadside, but I could still make out the advertisement for that night's game. "River Rats v Mar ue te, 7 o'clock, SRO", it said, the "q" and a "t" missing from "Marquette". I smiled and shook my head. It had been a long time since the Rats had commanded standing-room-only crowds. Back then, I was the goalie, Soupy was the all-state defenseman, and the Rats were one of the best squads in Michigan.

I drove around to the back of the building and parked. A rusted oilcan overflowed with beer cartons covered in snow. The door to the back of the rink was locked so I walked around to the front, hoping I was alone.

The sweet smell of refrigerant filled my nose as I pushed open one of the double doors between the arena lobby and the rink itself. The only sound was the hum of a generator beyond the walls somewhere. I walked to my left and stopped on the rubber-mat floor behind the net I had tended as a kid for the River Rats and, many years later, in the Midnight Hour Men's League.

I'd liked the vantage all those years I was a goalie: the rink spreading out in front of me, the bleachers rising to the shadows beneath the ceiling on my left, the benches and penalty boxes stretching down the dasher boards to my right, the opposing net facing me two hundred feet away, the banners dangling from the rafters overhead. When a crowd had gathered, I could feel the glass behind me groaning against their weight, hear them cursing me or praising me, no matter what I did. Some were on my side, some weren't. Sometimes you couldn't tell the difference.

Finally, I had had enough of throwing myself in front of flying pucks, enough of people firing pucks at my head. A year before, I had ditched the mask and leg pillows and chest protector, grabbed a stick with a hook on the blade, and started playing on a wing. It felt good to be on the bench bitching about the goalie instead of being the one on the other end of the bitching, good not to be alone between those iron pipes.

I scanned the rink, looking for whoever had parked the Dodge outside. Sometimes old folks came and walked circles around the perimeter for exercise. None were there on this morning. The preschool figure skating class wasn't due for another hour. I knew these useless facts because I read them each week on the press releases someone sent to the *Pilot*. I peered up at the banners. The last, in faded Rats blue and gold, had been hung in 1987, when the team won the regional final before losing in the state quarters. The best—or the worst—was the banner from 1981, when my own Rats team lost in the state final, in that very rink, because of the goal I allowed into the net I was now standing behind.

A noise came from the concession stand. I turned and saw a cardboard box marked Koffee-Kleen Filters appear on the counter. Whoever drove that Dodge was working back there—probably a kid a year out of high school who'd work in rinks and on construction sites between unemployment checks his whole life without ever leaving Starvation Lake. I ducked my head and skittered around the corner of the rink boards to my right, hoping no one had seen me.

Staying low, I scrambled along behind the benches and penalty boxes toward the back of the arena. The floor peeled up in places. Chilly drafts blew over me through thin cracks in the walls. An electrical outlet box hung haphazardly off the back of the announcer's box, spewing bare wires. Puddles had formed where water had dripped through the sieve of a roof. Even though the Rats were finally winning again, skating stride for stride with the downstate teams for the first time in years, the town was letting the rink go to pot.

The town council, chaired by none other than Elvis Bontrager, had planned the year before to pay for refurbishments. Then Laird Haskell showed up at a council meeting one night with a box of glossy blue-and-gold folders embossed with the slogan "River Rats: Return to Glory." He had a goaltender son who would keep other teams off the scoreboard and a bank account that would build the finest hockey facility in Michigan, complete with a weight room, two Zambonis, a bar called the Stanley Club—and a new scoreboard with a video screen that would show replays of his son's brilliant saves. "We'll build this," he told the council, "and the championships will come."

The council, without asking a single hard question about when or where he was going to get the money, gladly set aside the plans to fix the old rink and started shoveling our tax dollars toward helping Haskell. What reason was there to doubt him? He was a wealthy man—just look at his enormous house on the lake. Why would he propose a new rink if he couldn't pay for it? Why throw money at the old rink when a free one was there for the taking?

At the back of the arena, I looked back over the top of the boards toward the concession stand and saw Johnny Ford doing something at the frozen yogurt machine. So that was his Dodge in the lot. He wasn't out of high school yet. Either he didn't have morning class or he was skipping.

He hadn't seen me, I decided.

I crept past the two extra goalie nets leaned against the back wall and into the high-ceilinged bay where the Zamboni stood dripping water on a concrete floor. Johnny must have run it just before I'd arrived. I walked around the Zam once slowly, smelling gasoline, looking for anything that might give me an inkling as to how Gracie had wound up in the shoe tree.

Three tall plastic buckets embossed with Miller Lite logos sat along the back wall, one filled with rags, another with clotted snow. Next to the buckets stood a broom-sized squeegee and a pair of shovels. Along a side wall stood half a dozen carbon-dioxide tanks beneath a fuse box.

I glanced once more out the Zamboni bay to make sure Johnny wasn't coming, then ducked under the yellow police tape strung across the doorway into the shed that Gracie had called home for the past few months.

I smelled something like incense mixed with the unmistakable odor of marijuana. The town had so lost interest in the rink that nobody even cared if the Zamboni driver smoked dope. Maybe that's why Gracie had been turned down for a job at the new rink.

The floor in Gracie's home was concrete. A scuffed wooden workbench ran alongside the wall to my left. A pegboard above the bench was empty, maybe because Gracie was too short to reach it. The bench was strewn with tools, cans of oil and paint and WD-40, greasy rags, some purple-and-orange marking pens, and an old Detroit Red Wings cap frayed around the bill. Gracie had worn the cap whenever she ran the Zam, her fading reddish hair streaked with silver straggling out the back.

I stopped for a second and thought, She must've taught herself to use the tools to keep the Zam in working order. I had never given it a thought before she died, when my pals and I were playing and she was driving the Zam. Before she returned to town, I had never known she was handy around machinery, that she didn't mind getting dirt under her sparkly pink-and-purple fingernails. Nor did I have the slightest idea what she had done for a living during her years downstate. Never cared either.

When Gracie last lived in Starvation, she'd slung ice cream cones at the Dairy Queen. Business was especially good on her Friday nights because she always wore the tiniest, tightest top she could find, and boys would come all the way from Torch Lake to flirt. The luckiest one would get a cone that came with a wink and a question: "Extra sprinkles tonight?" More than a few times, the lucky one was Soupy. And Soupy being Soupy, I was never short on the details of what happened in the backseat of his Chevy Nova or the woods around Gracie's mom's trailer. "The Gymnast," he took to calling her, or sometimes "Nadia."

Beyond the bench stood an old wooden filing cabinet, a small refrigerator, and Gracie's cot. As quietly as I could, I pulled out each drawer of the cabinet to see what I could find. Three of the drawers were empty and one contained a smattering of file folders filled with papers, some of the folders marked with dates from the early 1990s. Dampness had stuck the edges of the paper together. Maybe the cops had already taken all the revealing stuff, if there was any. Could there be a diary? A journal? I couldn't imagine Gracie having the patience to sit and write in one.

Atop the fridge stood four empty bottles of Gordon's gin, their caps removed; two unopened bottles; and one bottle still about half full. I opened the fridge. The inside of the door was lined with sixteen-ounce plastic bottles of Squirt, the grapefruit soda pop Gracie splashed into her gin. I counted the bottles: ten unopened, one not quite empty. Five bottles of Blue Ribbon waited in the back of the fridge. For Soupy. The fridge's top shelf held a loaf of wheat bread that hadn't yet been opened, a package of cheddar cheese, and a bunch of low-fat strawberry yogurts. I picked up one of the yogurts and looked for the expiration date. March 11. More than four weeks away.

Gracie had just bought all of this stuff, I thought. Why would she go grocery shopping if she knew she was going to kill herself? She wouldn't.

I closed the fridge.

Her cot was unmade. There was a pillow, a sheet that looked like it hadn't been washed in weeks, and an afghan identical to the one my mother had made for me. Mom had given it to Gracie when she'd left for downstate. I imagined her asleep, breathing refrigerant and paint fumes.

Beneath the cot I spied a green-and-gold Wayne State University duffle bag. I reached under and pulled the bag out. It was unzipped. I poked around inside. There were a couple of Squirt bottle caps and, in a zippered pocket inside the bag, a blue plastic hairbrush with black bristles.

"I'll be goddamned."

My mother had bought me the blue brush at Fortune Drug when I turned nine. I kept it proudly on the top of my dresser. Gracie, during one of her extended stays with us, took it and hid it. I threatened to beat her up but she laughed in my face. She said my mother would kill me if I touched her.

She was right about that. So I waited for her to go out to the lake one day and snuck into her room and went through her things until I found the brush in the back of her underwear drawer. I was grossed out, as Gracie surely had intended, but I wanted my brush. She stole it back while I was asleep that night. "You're a little bitch," I told her the next day, and my mother heard me and made me stay in my room for the duration of a sunny Saturday afternoon.

Then Gracie told Darlene about the brush and the next thing I knew, Darlene had stolen it from Gracie and Gracie was calling her a slut. My mother finally figured out what was going on, but instead of using her motherly prerogative to order the brush returned to its rightful owner, she filched the brush herself while she was over at Darlene's having coffee with Mrs. B. She let Gracie and me know she had it over dinner at the picnic table that night, and Gracie laughed so hard that she choked on a mouthful of hot dog.

By the next morning, Gracie had pilfered the brush from Mom, and by night, I'd grabbed it and hidden it in the freezer box of the fridge in the garage where Dad used to keep his Carling Black Labels. Mom found it there and hid it in the bird feeder on the beach. Gracie took it from there and didn't have it a day before Darlene stole it and stuck it beneath her mattress.

I didn't even think about using it on my hair anymore. Once Mom joined the game, the brush became something entirely other than a brush. It was now *the* brush. And it wasn't so much the having of it that mattered, but the keeping of it, the not losing it to someone else, at least for me. Maybe it was because I was a hockey player; one-goal games and sudden-death overtime were much more about fear than triumph. Once I had the brush in my possession, I tried not to give it a thought—then I would wake up in the middle of the night to see my bedroom door being swung shut by one of the thieves in my life, Gracie or Darlene or my own mother.

I came to hate losing it. It was my brush, after all. And it didn't matter who had it, or where it was; if I didn't have the brush in my possession, I blamed Gracie, because she had started the stupid game. And whenever the rest of us seemed to have lost interest, Gracie would find the brush and secretly return it to me, then wait a few days before stealing it back, just to show me that she could make me feel that sting. I was an idiot, of course, but I fell for it again and again. Occasionally I would try to reconcile Gracie's nasty streak with her lot in life, having lost her father and been forced to live with her crazy mother. Of course I'd also lost my father, and though my mother wasn't crazy in the same way Shirley McBride was, it was clear whose side Mom was on when it came to the brush. And I let that gnaw at me too.

The last time I had had the brush in my hands, I was a senior in high school and Gracie was in her first semester at Wayne State. Her mother had gone out of town with her latest boyfriend and locked Gracie out of her trailer, so Gracie spent Christmas with us. On Christmas morning, I found a gift from Gracie beneath our tree. I couldn't remember ever getting a Christmas present from Gracie. She watched, smiling, while I undid the shiny red-and-green paper and silver bow. Inside was the brush. Gracie wanted me to laugh.

I tossed the brush at her. "Keep it," I said.

"Gussy," Mom said.

"Don't be a baby," Gracie said.

"Or give it to her," I said, pointing at Mom. "Or Darlene. Or whoever you like. I don't want to see it again."

"Gus," Mom said. "Gracie is trying to be nice."

"No. She's messing with me. She'll probably steal it back tonight."

"You're an asshole," Gracie said.

"Grace Maureen McBride!"

That was one quiet Christmas dinner.

The taunting began a few years later. I had just begun working at the *Detroit Times*. As a rookie reporter, I didn't get a lot of mail. One day an envelope showed up, postmarked Detroit. The address was handwritten. I wondered if a reader had seen one of my stories and written a nice note.

But there was no note. Just a color photograph of the brush balanced in the right hand of the *Spirit of Detroit*, a bronze statue outside the city-county building downtown.

"Fuck you, Gracie," I said. I tore the photo into shreds and threw it away.

Over the years, the photos kept coming, one every six months or so. The brush on the edge of the boards at Joe Louis Arena. The brush dangling from the hand of a hot dog vendor at Tiger Stadium. The brush on a blackjack table in a Windsor casino. The brush on a railing along the Detroit River at dawn. I trashed them all. Finally I started recognizing the envelopes and tossed them without even opening them. The photos stopped coming sometime in the early 1990s, and I forgot about the brush.

Until I found it in Gracie's duffle bag.

I didn't use brushes much anymore on what was left of my hair. But I stuffed it in my pocket and kicked the bag under the bed.

A calendar hung on a nail on the wall over Gracie's pillow. I had never noticed it before but then why would I have? My infrequent visits to this room were usually to chase a beer or two for Soupy while he showered after a game. Now I leaned in and saw, to my mild surprise, that the calendar came from Pandit's Shell & Service in River Rouge. I tried to picture it. River Rouge was one of the little blue-collar pockets south of Detroit where steel was once made and cars built. Why the hell would Gracie have a calendar from River Rouge?

The calendar was correctly turned to the page for February. Way to go, Gracie, I thought. Each day was struck through with an X etched in black ballpoint pen. Some X's were the squiggles a drunk would make, but they were all there—except on the last day of Gracie's life. Maybe that made sense, or maybe it did not. I tried to imagine what she might have been thinking. I couldn't.

When Gracie scratched the X across the day *before* she died, did she know for a certainty that it would be her last full day on earth? If she knew she was going to die, why wouldn't she have struck through the actual last day as well? On the one hand, I was surprised that Gracie had maintained this daily discipline at all; on the other, I figured she of all people would relish the flourish of being able to X out her end for everyone to see. She could have been smiling no matter what the outcome was going to be.

I unhooked the calendar from the nail and flipped the page back to January. There wasn't a single X mark there.

"Goddammit, Gracie."

I put the calendar back on the wall.

I leaned back against the workbench and wondered whether the cops had spent any time here. The county had whacked Sheriff Aho's budget twice in the past year; he couldn't afford overtime. Darlene had been complaining that her regular hours had been cut. Maybe a deputy had just hung the police tape and left the room for later. Or maybe they'd done a quick dusting for fingerprints, though I couldn't see what good it would have done. They would have found me and Soupy and Johnny Ford and a dozen men's league players who had wandered back to bum a beer.

I had been back in the Zam shed myself two nights earlier, the night before the night Gracie died.

"Gracie," I'd said when I walked in.

She was standing at the bench, her hands streaked black with grease, fiddling with something metal that must have come from the innards of the Zamboni. Within her reach stood a tall blue plastic cup embossed with a gold River Rats logo, a toothy rodent carrying a hockey stick like a pitchfork.

Gracie didn't seem to notice me at first, though I was standing six feet away. I watched her for a moment. She was just tall enough to get her elbows up on the bench without having to stand on something.

"Gracie," I said.

"This . . . this fucking piece of shit," she said, slamming the part down on the bench. She grabbed a rag and swiped it across her face, leaving a black smudge on a cheek. She looked up and down the bench, apparently not finding what she was looking for, then finally turned to me and waved an arm toward the fridge. "Are you blind? Get your own beer."

"Didn't come for a beer," I said. "But I'll take one, thanks."

I slid past her. She was wearing black-and-green snowmobile pants hitched by suspenders over a red flannel shirt unbuttoned to her bosom. I reached into the fridge and grabbed a Blue Ribbon. I twisted the cap off and pinged it into the metal wastebasket beneath the bench.

I reached into my coat pocket and produced a pair of gray wool mittens, a red "G" knitted into the back of each. Mom had made those, too. In high school I had had a pair with blue "G"s on the backs. I would wear them as I was leaving the house, then trade them out for black leather gloves, because I was terrified of what I'd hear if I walked into the hockey dressing room with those mittens on.

"Got your mittens," I said.

Gracie had the Zamboni part in her hands again, staring at it with her head cocked to one side. "You know," she said, "you play like a pussy out there."

I almost coughed up the beer I'd just swallowed.

"What?"

"You heard me. You think I don't watch?"

My team, Soupy's Chowder Heads, had beaten the Dead Wings of Murray & Murray Funeral Home that night, 5–2. I thought I'd had a pretty good game.

"Did you see my two assists? Including on the game winner?"

She swiveled her head around to look at me. "Only pussies talk about assists," she said. "So you give the puck to Soupy, he scores. BFD. You still play like a pussy."

"What the hell do you know about hockey?"

In my entire thirty-five years, I could not recall Gracie ever saying a word to me about hockey except to complain about the reek of my equipment drying in the basement of Mom's house. She never seemed to care. She never came to a Rats game, at least not that I could remember, unless it was to drink and smoke dope with the burnouts and the football players who clustered behind the rink before we played, hoping the cops would ignore them. I figured she'd taken the job at the rink because it came with a cot and a fridge and a concession stand she could lift food from, not because she gave a rip about hockey.

"I know enough," she said, turning her eyes back to the Zam part. Without looking she took up the River Rats cup, swished it around a little, and took a drink. "Enough to know you ought to have your ass back in the goal."

"How the—you never even saw me play net."

She set the cup back down. "It's obvious you shouldn't be playing wing.

I mean, you've got good enough wheels and you're smart enough to know your hands ain't so hot so you've got to get the puck to other people. But you don't like mixing it up in the corners and in front of the net, so you might as well just put your mask back on and get back in the goal where it's safe."

"Are you kidding me? Did you ever take a slap shot to the neck?"

"What are you being so pissy for? I didn't say you were a pussy. I just said you play wing like a pussy. There's a difference. You're a goalie. Be a goalie, for fuck's sake. Just be who you are. At least you have the chance."

"Thanks for the advice." I slapped her mittens down on the workbench. "Here."

"Ah," she said, her dull eyes brightening a little. She picked up her drink with one hand, the mittens with the other. She drank again while staring at the mittens as if trying to recall where she'd last seen them.

She had left them at Riccardo's Pizza a few nights before after she and Darlene had had their weekly pizza and Greek salad. They had said their good-byes and Darlene had gone to the ladies' room. She noticed the mittens sitting on their table on her way out. Gracie was already in her green LTD, about to pull out of the parking lot. Darlene ran outside waving the mittens over her head. But Gracie gunned her engine and Darlene stood in the lot watching the lights of the LTD recede over the Estelle Street Bridge. Later that night, Darlene gave me the mittens and asked me to drop them off at the rink. She wouldn't see her friend again until Gracie was hanging dead in the shoe tree.

Now Gracie tossed her head back for the last drops in her cup. She set the cup down and pushed away from the bench, mittens in hand.

"Hmm," she said, to no one I could see. "Don't want to lose these again."

She lurched toward me as if I weren't there. I stepped aside, watching. She grabbed the cot by a leg and dragged it away from the wall, the metal legs scraping on the concrete. She slid around behind the cot and eased herself down to her knees.

On the wall next to her was a heating vent. She set the mittens on the cot and reached into her snowmobile pants, producing a set of keys. She used a key to unwind the two screws holding the vent grille in place. The grille clattered to the floor. Gracie leaned down to peer into the vent.

"Gracie," I said. "What are you doing?"

She didn't seem to hear. Totally shit-faced, I thought. All that talk about the way I played wing was just gin-and-Squirt babble.

Gracie reached into the vent with her left hand up to her elbow. The hand came out holding a baggie filled with marijuana. Her stash. I wondered whether the heat flowing around the baggie could turn her room into a giant bong.

She stuck the bag back into the vent. She took the mittens in hand and reached back inside. This time her hand came out empty. "Gracie," I said, but she did not acknowledge me. It took her a couple of tries, but she fitted the grille back onto the vent and redid the screws. She stood, moved out from behind the cot, shoved the cot back into place, and rubbed her grease-stained hands together. Then she looked up and noticed me as if I'd just walked in.

"How the hell did you get in here?"

Now I crouched behind the cot. The screws on the vent grille came out easily enough. I was careful to lay the grille quietly on the floor.

I leaned my head down and looked inside. It was too dark to see much. I stuck my left arm in, expecting to feel a lumpy cylinder of plastic. But my hand found only the vent's flat metal walls. I lay down on my side so I could shove my arm in farther. My knuckles banged against the back wall of the vent. I swept my hand all the way to the left and then back to the right.

I found it in the back right corner. Something small and soft. I squeezed it in my palm and pulled it out.

In my hand rested a tiny white shoe. A baby shoe. For the left foot. With a blue satin ribbon intertwined in the white cotton laces. I took it by the ribbon and let it dangle in front of my face.

Was it Gracie's own shoe? Why would she have saved it? Why would she have stuffed it in this vent? Where was the other shoe? If this shoe was hers, then why a blue ribbon, why not pink?

Down near the tongue of the shoe, a rust-colored key was tied to the ribbon.

I undid the key from the ribbon and slipped it on to my key chain. I put the shoe in my pocket with the brush. I replaced the grille, backed out from behind the cot, and was about to swing the bed back into place when I heard footsteps behind me. I turned around.

"Excuse me," Johnny Ford said.

I'd seen him around the rink a few times but never up close. He always seemed to be scuttling around in the rafters like a squirrel, messing with the arena lamps, crisscrossing the bleachers with a trash bag.

"Johnny," I said. "Good morning."

He looked at the floor, nervous. His black jeans sagged atop his unlaced lumber boots. I noticed a mustard stain on the "N" of his Hungry River Rats sweatshirt. The shirt bagged around him, his left forearm hidden in the pouch.

Until his accident, Johnny Ford had been a promising young River Rat center who handled the puck like his stick was part of his body. Working a summer job at Grandview Golf Club, he was mowing at the edge of a pond at number 10 when the mower caught up in some damp weeds and stalled. Johnny reached in to dislodge them, and twenty-two pounds of snapping turtle bit off the first three fingers on his left hand and vanished with them into the green murk. There was a screwup at the hospital; the hand became infected and had to be amputated. He never played hockey again.

"Uh," he said, "I don't think you're supposed to be back here. I mean, you're not." He tossed his head toward the police tape. "You know, the cops."

"Yep, saw it," I said. "Sorry. I didn't touch anything. Just wanted to look around, see if there were any, like, pictures or anything I could use for the paper. I would've asked the sheriff for permission, of course. She was my second cousin, you know. Gracie, that is."

Johnny looked around the room. "You find any?"

"No, not really. Nothing I can use. Guess I'll check with her mother."

He just stood there, saying nothing.

"You going to run the Zamboni now?"

It was a dumb question I hoped would distract him. "Already did."

"Did Gracie ever let you?"

"Once." He turned back to me. "You better go."

"OK." I put my hands in my pockets, made sure I still had the brush and the shoe. Not that I had any idea what use they would be.

"Sad thing, isn't it?"

Johnny shrugged. I wondered, for just a second, if Gracie might have seduced him, just for kicks. Probably not, I decided.

"You didn't see a cell phone around, did you?" he said.

"A cell phone? You have a cell phone?"

"Used to. She borrowed it."

"She borrowed your cell phone?"

"For twenty dollars."

"Oh. Well, no. Didn't see it. Sorry."

He looked around the room again. "I got to get back."

I took a step closer to him. "Hey, Johnny, do me a favor, will you?" His face told me he wasn't sure. "You know the expression 'What goes on the road stays on the road'?"

"Nope."

"Ha. Well, it's a hockey thing. I was hoping maybe you'd kind of think of me coming here like that. One skater to another. I don't want to get the cops pissed off. Especially when one of them's my girlfriend, you know?"

"I'm not a skater anymore."

"Just between us then?"

"Twenty bucks?" he said.

I gave him a ten and two fives. I was less worried about the sheriff finding out I was snooping beyond his police tape than I was about everyone else in town hearing it.

On the way back to town I dialed Darlene's cell. It went immediately to voice mail. "Remind me," I said. "Which shoe was Gracie missing?"

My password opened Philo's computer.

The techies hadn't gotten around to disabling the override the *Pilot*'s previous owners had bestowed upon me as the boss of exactly three people. I supposed that they would get around to it, and then Philo probably would have the ability to pry into my e-mails. But for the moment, Media North's organizational inertia was working in my favor. While my truck idled in the parking lot behind the newsroom, I scrolled through Philo's e-mails. I wanted to confirm a hunch.

The subject line on a 9:14 a.m. e-mail read, "RE: hskl meetng." I opened the e-mail. *Now is not the time to stand on principle,* I thought, remembering what Philo had said to me on the phone. I read the e-mail.

> phi—
>> haskell & 1 other 11:15 his place
>> great opp here. No time 4 soap box.
> jmk

"Figures," I said to myself.
I closed up the computer and headed back out to my truck.

Only through the naked trees of winter could you see Laird Haskell's home from the road. And, on this gray morning, Haskell himself, coatless on his porch.

After more than twenty-five years suing auto companies for building unsafe cars and trucks that killed and maimed and burned people, Haskell was a bona fide millionaire. He had lived in Bloomfield Hills near Detroit among many of the executives who appeared as defendants on his lawsuits. He had bought his house on Starvation as a weekend getaway in the mid-

1970s after seeing the lake when he'd come to watch his nephew's Port Huron team play against the Rats.

Many years later, it turned out that his own son was quite a player. Minding the net for HoneyBaked Ham's peewee team in Detroit, Taylor Haskell had let in, on average, fewer than two goals per game and registered an astonishing twenty-three shutouts in the fifty-six games he had played. But Laird Haskell was not satisfied, not with the coaching of his son, or with the players around his son, or with the fact that, every few games, HoneyBaked's other goaltender would get a chance to play. He moved his boy to Little Caesars, then to Emmert Chevrolet. But nothing was good enough for Laird Haskell, who, like so many deluded hockey dads and moms, believed his son was destined for the NHL.

Haskell sold his Bloomfield Hills home and moved his son and wife to the palatial house on Starvation. They hadn't been in town a month before Haskell appeared before the town council to say he had bought a thirty-acre parcel of land on which he planned to build the River Rats a new home, the Felicia Haskell IcePlex, with his own $7.5 million, all cash. He just needed a property tax break and a little help getting utilities hooked up.

I hadn't seen him up close in years. Once in a while I'd glimpse him on the lake, shirtless at the wheel of his cruiser, or directing his help at his boathouse, which was about the size of Mom's cottage. In Starvation he kept a low profile for a man who had made his name as one of the most effective plaintiff's lawyers in the country, the scourge of Detroit's automakers. He dispatched his attorney to most of the public meetings about the rink. Of course he showed up for every River Rats game to watch his son tend goal. But even there, he kept to himself; he had paid to have a small private box built in a high corner of the bleachers, where he served cocktails to men and women who came from places other than Starvation and vanished afterward, presumably to hotels or bed-and-breakfasts in the real resort towns, Charlevoix or Petoskey or Traverse City. Normally this would have been the source of much carping and gossip around the breakfast tables at Audrey's, but no one dared to speak ill of Laird Haskell once he'd offered to build that rink with his own money.

He waved to me as I eased my truck down a steep winding path plowed to the bare concrete. Fake gas lamps glowed along both sides of the path.

Haskell ambled off the porch and stood waiting at the end of the drive. The house loomed up before me, three stories of cream siding, picture windows framed in maple, cantilevered decks someone had bothered to shovel. Plumes of smoke wafted up from a brick chimney. Even the firewood stacked neatly against the house had been swept clean of the night's snow.

As I parked, Haskell approached, smiling. I wished he wouldn't. The veneer of familiarity made me uncomfortable, even if we had in fact known each other for a good many years. He was grayer and thinner on top than I remembered, a small man, no bigger than me, who moved with the sureness of someone who had calmly accused chief executives to their faces of murdering the people who had died in their cars and trucks. His paunch nudged a little more firmly at his starched denim shirt, but Haskell was well kept for a man in his sixties. His smile, in particular, looked just as sculpted and willful as I'd seen it when he was beguiling juries and making himself wealthy.

I hopped out of my truck, automatically patting my back pocket for my notebook. Haskell stepped up and took my right hand into both of his.

"Long time, Gus," he said. "I guess it really is true: you can run but you can't hide."

"You talking about me or you?"

He laughed and put an arm around my shoulders. "Let me show you my shack," he said, as if I'd never written a single story calling the money behind his project into question, as if he'd never had his lawyer order me to stop calling the Haskell home at the dinner hour, as if we were old friends who'd bumped into each other at the country club.

The case was *Willing v. Superior Motors*. It was 1991 and I was covering the auto industry for the *Detroit Times*.

Laird Haskell represented the estate of James P. Willing, a forty-one-year-old father of five who was killed when he ran his four-door sedan into the back of a panel truck on an interstate in southern Ohio. The lawsuit alleged that Willing's antilock brakes had failed due to negligence on the part of the car's manufacturer, Superior Motors.

At Haskell's invitation, I appeared one morning at the thirty-fifth-floor offices of his firm in one of the glass-and-steel towers of the Renaissance Center on the Detroit River. A secretary led me to a conference room.

Four square white boxes marked WILLING were stacked against one wall. Six yellow legal pads and three blue felt-tipped pens waited at the seat where the secretary, a woman named Joyce, deposited me. Bottles of orange juice and Coke huddled on a silver tray. "Take all the time you need," Joyce said. "Feel free to help yourself to a beverage. Sandwiches will be brought in later."

"If I wanted to copy some pages, is there a—"

"I'm sorry. Mr. Haskell has directed that nothing be removed from the room, including copies. You may take notes, of course."

"OK."

"And," she said, pausing at the door, "you were never here."

I grinned. "Of course not."

I spent the next five and a half hours going through the documents in the boxes. There were depositions, internal Superior Motors memos, various court pleadings. All told, the documents showed how the engineers at Superior had detected problems in the development of the company's new antilock brake system. They had advocated design changes that, according to certain memos, would have cost Superior a few pennies per vehicle. A "safety economist" for the company had prepared a cost analysis estimating that the potential cost of litigation over the design of the brakes would be less than what it would cost to implement the changes. The analysis calculated the cost of a single human life at $432,124.68. The design changes were never made.

I ignored the stamps on the front of many of the documents saying they had been sealed by court order. That was Haskell's problem, I figured. I had wanted to write about the Willing case for months, but the state judge overseeing the case had, at Superior's request and over Haskell's objections, blocked public access to all documents obtained in discovery between the company and the Willing family. So there wasn't much to write about.

Until Haskell's secretary phoned me one day and asked if I'd like to spend a few hours in a conference room with some boxes of paper. I readily agreed that anything I saw or read would be off the record until Haskell gave me the go-ahead to write my story. It was better than nothing, and I couldn't imagine that Haskell wouldn't want me to tell the world how Superior had behaved prior to the untimely death of a father of five.

I had eaten a turkey sandwich, gone through nearly three of the boxes, and filled three legal pads with notes when Joyce came into the conference room around two thirty that afternoon and said I would have to leave because the conference room was needed. I was so excited about the prize-winning story I was already writing in my head that I never wondered why a firm with offices taking most of an entire floor in the Ren Cen didn't have other conference rooms available.

"OK if I come back in the morning?" I said.

Joyce smiled politely. "Mr. Haskell will be in touch."

I went back to the *Times* and told my editor to prepare a big display space in Sunday's paper. We could start the story on A1 and open a page, maybe two, inside. I didn't bother telling him that I couldn't publish a word of it until Haskell gave me permission. I wasn't worried in the least that he wouldn't give it to me.

I began to worry a little when neither Joyce nor Haskell returned my calls the next day, or the day after that. Late that night, I got Haskell's answering machine. "We plan to run this Sunday," I said. "You're going to love it." Technically we weren't supposed to tell sources when stories were running, especially stories that affected companies owned by public share-holders. But how could I get Haskell to release me to write without him knowing when? I didn't think it could hurt.

On the Friday before the Sunday that my story was supposed to run, I received a phone call from a flack for Superior, an unctuous gnome of a man named Snell. I'd been trying to reach Haskell all morning, to no avail.

"I don't get to say this very often," Snell said. "But it's a great day for American jurisprudence."

"What are you talking about?"

"I understand you're working on a story."

I could almost hear his smirk.

"I'm always working on stories, Dave. What's up?"

"I don't think you're going to get to write that story."

"Which story?"

He tittered. Then an echo came over his voice as he switched to a speakerphone. "I've got Howie Reichs with me."

Howie Reichs was Superior's top safety executive.

"Hello, Howard," I said, knowing he hated being called Howard. "To what do I owe the honor?"

"Augustus," he said, imagining no doubt that I didn't like being called Augustus. I actually didn't mind. "I hate to disappoint you, but you'll have to find another company to crucify this Sunday."

How did he know it was Sunday? Only Haskell knew that.

"We're going to be making an announcement shortly, and I wanted you to be the first to hear."

I let my head drop into a hand. I knew what he was going to say.

Thirty minutes later, the company issued a two-paragraph statement: Superior had settled the Willing matter. The terms were not disclosed. The statement quoted Laird Haskell as saying the settlement "served the best interests of the Willing family while addressing the complex safety dilemmas posed by this admittedly complicated matter."

My story never ran. The world did not find out about the design defects in the antilock brakes. But over the course of the next year, Haskell represented seven additional clients who sued Superior over the brakes. Each time, the cases were settled quickly and the terms were not disclosed. A story in the *American Lawyer*, quoting anonymous sources—Haskell, I guessed—estimated that the firm of Haskell, Sherman & Toddy had collected more than $20 million in contingency fees on the brakes cases. People kept dying, Haskell kept collecting, and my scribblings on those legal pads went unseen.

I called Haskell every day for months. Each day, Joyce would kindly tell me she'd give him my message; she may well have, but I never heard from him. I kept track of his firm's cases, though. One morning I cornered him in a men's room at the federal courthouse on Lafayette. He had just started to pee when I walked in and stood next to him at the adjacent urinal.

He turned and smiled at me, not the least bit surprised. "Hello, Gus," he said. "We're a little old for a sword fight, don't you think?"

"I know what you did."

"Really?" He peered into the urinal. "Then what are you doing here?"

I had come prepared. "You hear of the Miller family in Austin?"

"Austin, Texas?" He turned and faced me, shook himself off, zipped up. "No. Should I?"

"They don't exist anymore," I said. "They rolled their minivan when the brakes failed. Husband, wife, three little kids. All dead."

Haskell stepped to a sink. He squeezed pink soap onto his hands, washed them in cold water, splashed water on his face. He snapped a paper towel from the dispenser and dried his hands, then patted his cheeks and forehead dry, watching himself in the mirror as he did.

"Did you hear me?" I said.

"I heard you." He reached into his suit jacket and produced a slim leather case from which he plucked a business card. He handed it to me. "If someone is in need of legal advice in this matter, they really should call me."

He started to leave. I stepped in front of him.

"Are you serious? You almost got me fired."

Our eyes met. I was younger and stronger and angry enough to beat his face in with the soap dispenser. But his eyes told me I was no more important to him than the guy who'd be swabbing the toilets that night.

"So that's what's important here? Your job security?" he said. "Maybe you should go back to your newspaper and write a story. Meantime, I have to be back in court. Excuse me."

"I haven't checked my voice mail yet today," Haskell said. "Have you?"

We were sitting at a round mahogany table in his office on the third floor of his home. Haskell had his hand on a multi-line phone in the middle of the table.

"Uh, no," I said. "Why, did you call me?"

"Ha," he said. "I meant, 'Have you checked *my* voice mail?'"

It was a joke. I had lost my job at the *Detroit Times* two years before because I had learned some things about accessing a certain auto company's voice-mail system that I would have been better off not learning. Haskell had had nothing to do with my demise but undoubtedly had heard about the details on the attorney grapevine in Detroit.

"Ah," I said. "Got it."

"Sorry. I didn't know if that was still raw. Apparently so."

Behind him one half of a credenza was crowded with pictures of Haskell with his wife and son, in ski attire atop a mountain, on a sailboat, in front of the White House. There was a picture of Haskell in a tuxedo and his wife in a ball gown with President Clinton and the first lady. The other half held pictures of the son in goaltender gear, holding the wide blade of his goalie stick aloft, hugging a teammate, posing in a blurry shot with a man in a Detroit Red Wings uniform.

Above the credenza, framed reproductions of front pages of the *Detroit Times*, the *Detroit Free Press*, and the *American Lawyer* lined the paneled wall. Headlines on each shouted the size of verdicts Haskell had won against auto companies: $28.1 million, $94.4 million, $42.8 million. I couldn't help but think of the one case that was not on his trophy wall, the one I'd covered for the *Times* that had set me at odds with Haskell and gotten me in trouble with my bosses. Nor could I help wondering again how he could be coming up short with the money to build that new rink. What exactly was the problem?

"It's fine," I said. "I like it here."

"You landed on your feet, man. And of course who wouldn't like it here, huh?" He swept an arm toward the big bay window facing the lake. I looked. Mom's house was a fuzzy yellow speck in the tree line on the opposite shore.

"I hear you've been staying with your mother," Haskell said. "That's a good son, in my book."

"The rent's free. The food's good."

"Oh, my, you must have heard." He leaned into the table and shaped his face into one reflecting concern. "That girl."

Gracie, I assumed.

"Yes. Not a girl, really."

"Did you know her?"

"A little."

"It's terrible. Her poor mother."

"Yeah. She worked at the rink, you know."

"Did she?" he said.

"Drove the Zamboni. Sharpened skates."

"Ah." Haskell gazed out the window again, crossed his legs, ran his fingers along a crease in his corduroy slacks. "Suicide is so . . . so selfish, don't you think?"

"It's not a suicide," I said.

"Really? Is that what the police are saying?"

"They aren't saying yet."

Haskell shook his head. "I had a client once—did I ever tell you this story?—this client had a son, an only child, four years old, who'd been gravely injured when he was thrown from a minivan. He actually died while we were at trial due to complications related to being a quadriplegic, which should have worked to—well, that's beside the point."

"Right."

"The defense put my client, the mother, on the stand. About as brazen a move as I've seen in all my years of lawyering. They asked her a lot of questions about how the boy was situated, where she'd bought the car seat, how well she secured him, et cetera. They even asked about her husband supposedly leaving her. All of it patently irrelevant, trying to blame her for their own client's egregious negligence. They got her crying, of course. I assured her they were out of order and I'd get her testimony thrown out by the judge. But . . ."

He let his voice trail off for dramatic effect.

"And she killed herself?" I said.

"Unbelievable."

"She'd lost her son and her husband. And she must have felt guilty."

"No," he said, leveling his eyes on me as if I were a member of the jury. "She was just afraid to get on with her life."

"What happened with the case?"

"The family had been through enough. We settled."

"I guess you missed out on a pretty big payday there, huh?"

"A payday had nothing to do with it."

I felt more comfortable now. I pulled out my notebook, set it on the table, and opened it to the first page. I took out a pen and wrote HASKELL and the date across the top of the page. I made sure to write it big enough that he could see it.

"Ah, well," he said. "Time for the business part of the meeting. We should probably discuss some ground rules."

"What? You asked me here, Mr. Haskell."

"Call me Laird, please. Look, my understanding—"

"I'm the only one here, Laird."

"I'm sorry, I'm not being clear. My attorney had a discussion with a helpful intermediary for your organization, and my understanding was that we were going to visit for a while and we could work out what you might want to write, if anything, in your little paper."

"You talked to Kerasopoulos," I said.

"I'm not at liberty to say."

The e-mail I had read in Philo's computer had come from Jim Ker-asopoulos, my boss, Philo's boss, Philo's uncle, the president and chief executive of Media North Corporation, and Haskell's intermediary. Ker-asopoulos was a businessman who saw nothing wrong with sticking his nose into news coverage. I actually didn't mind his gaining me access to Haskell. But he was not going to set the terms for how I made use of it.

"Well, Laird, I'm here, and I'm happy to listen to whatever you have to say, so long as it's on the record. I also have a few questions I'd like to get answered for my little paper."

Haskell grinned and slapped his palms on the table. "Because the public has a right to know. Is that it?"

"Something like that."

"Is this your way of getting a little payback?"

"Payback for what? I'm just doing my job."

"It's my money, son. Don't forget that. My money's building that rink."

"Not entirely. There's sewer and water and roads and police and fire paid for by tax dollars. You're also getting a nice little property tax break. And while your rink stands out there with the wind blowing through the steel, the town's letting the old rink rot."

"Fair enough," Haskell said, raising his hands as if in surrender. "But I have something for you today and, frankly, I think it's a pretty big story for this town. We can give it to you exclusively, if you can help us out a bit."

"Help you out how?"

"Nothing special, nothing extraordinary. Just a little balance. The next time you're going to quote a subcontractor bitch—excuse me, complain about allegedly not getting paid, I wish you'd check with me about what the sub's actually accomplished to warrant being paid."

"Are you kidding? I have called you repeatedly and—"

"Yes, yes, I understand. I have been remiss at responding to your inqui-ries because I've been, well, I've had other priorities. I apologize. I realize now that I have let the stories in your paper make it even more difficult for me to complete this project. But I will complete it."

"When?"

"You'll see. Soon. Very soon."

I wrote that down in my notebook.

"Wait," Haskell said. "We are not on the record."

"Did I ever say we were off? When exactly is 'very soon'? By next season?"

Haskell folded his hands on his chest and fixed his gaze on the table.

"Do you want to hear what I have to tell you?" He lifted his gaze to me. "Or should we just give it to Channel Eight?"

I thought of Elvis embarrassing me that morning at Audrey's Diner. I was not about to get one-upped by Channel Eight twice in one day.

"What do you got?"

"Off the record?"

I set my pen on the table. "For now."

"Two items," Haskell said. "Something we're going to announce shortly. And something else I can't really tell you about yet. Just a heads-up."

Christ, I thought. That's how it went when you agreed to go off the record.

"What's the second thing?"

"You have a paper tomorrow, is that correct?"

"That's right."

"And then your next paper is Saturday?"

"Yep."

He gave this a moment's thought. "If I tell you, then you cannot use it in the paper in any way, shape, or form, is that correct?"

"If you—"

"Never mind. Look, let me be candid, all I can say at the moment is that we might be seeking a bit of help from the town."

"Financial help?"

He considered for a moment, his way of letting me know, yes, it was financial help. Then he said, "I'm afraid that's all I can say."

"Come on."

"I'm sorry. Things are in a delicate stage. I'm being as helpful as I can."

On the contrary, he was giving me just enough information that it could, in theory, handcuff me if I happened to hear something more specific from someone else. That's why he'd asked about my not being able to use it in any way, shape, or form. Although I hadn't answered that question, Haskell might remember things differently, if it served his purpose. But what could I do? If I hadn't gone off the record, I'd have nothing. I knew Haskell was as slippery as a bass on a bad hook, but I had no choice, or

I thought I had no choice, but to deal with him any way that I could. At least he was speaking to me.

"That's pretty disappointing, Laird," I said. "So I better be able to put whatever your announcement is in tomorrow's paper."

Haskell brightened. "You will." He picked up the phone, punched two numbers, and said into the phone, "Felicia. Yes. Could you send him up? No need for you to—no. No. Yes, I understand. Thank you, dear." He returned the phone to its cradle, stood up, and walked over to the door, pushing the button on the doorknob that locked it. "I guarantee you will love this."

He waited at the door, smiling. I heard footsteps in the corridor outside the door, then the sound of someone trying to open the door.

"Whoa, one minute," Haskell said. He undid the lock and held the doorknob. "It is my distinct pleasure," he said, "to introduce to you the new coach of the Hungry River Rats."

He swung the door open and there, filling up most of the doorway in a blue-and-gold River Rats sweat suit, was Jason Esper.

"How are we doing today, Coach Esper?" Haskell said as he pumped the hand of Darlene's husband. Jason was looking at me, just as surprised to see me as I was to see him. I decided I'd better stand up.

"Meat," I said, using his nickname. I extended my hand. "Congrats."

He tilted his head slightly and allowed himself a small, amused smile. Haskell nudged him in my direction. Jason took my hand. I felt the calluses on his knuckles, the scars of a hundred minor-league hockey fights. He held tight when I tried to release. "You can call me Coach," he said. He let my hand go.

"Midget squad?" I said.

"Yep." He turned to Haskell and handed him a manila envelope.

"Thank you," Haskell said. "Let's sit down for a minute, shall we?"

I'd always thought of Jason as big, but he looked bigger than ever as he eased himself into a chair. He had indeed cleaned himself up since the last time I'd seen him. That afternoon eight or nine months before, he was hunched on a stool at the Kal-Ho Tavern in Kalkaska, a can of Busch Light and a empty shot glass in front of him, his lighter lying atop a pack of Marlboros. I'd stopped for a patty melt on my way back from a meeting at corporate in Traverse City. If Jason noticed me, he gave no indication. He sipped and smoked with his half-open eyes on a soap opera on the television hanging over the back bar. A jagged line of clotted blood crossed the bridge of his nose.

Now, sitting across the table next to Haskell, Jason looked as lean and strong as I'd seen him since he was the mullet-headed winger, number 28, skating for the Pipefitters all those years ago. Scars from sticks, pucks, and his nightly scraps cut thin slashes beneath his eyes and along his chin. But his blue eyes were bright, his blond curls clung tightly to his head, he wore a neatly trimmed blond goatee touched with gray. A different man, at least in appearance.

I looked at Haskell and said, "What about Poppy?" Dick Popovich had been the midget coach for five years. He'd never gotten the Rats out of the regionals. With Haskell's boy, Taylor, in goal, people figured he had a chance.

"He's retiring," Haskell said.

"Of course. And we're so desperate for a winner that we hire a guy from our archnemesis to get us there."

"I hired him," Haskell said.

"I might have Poppy give me a hand with the goalies," Jason said.

"Goalies need all the help they can get," I said.

Jason gave me a mirthless wink. "You ought to know, eh, Carpie?"

Jason had been sitting on the opposing team's bench when I allowed the goal that cost the River Rats the state title eighteen years before. He'd moved to nearby Mancelona with his parents as a teenager. He was quick and agile for a tall kid. And mean as a snake. Our coach begged him to defect from the Pipefitters to the Rats, but his parents had other plans—college hockey and then the NHL. He lived with a teammate's family near Detroit during the Pipefitters' season and spent summers up north. Our paths didn't cross much.

While I was taking journalism classes at the University of Michigan, Jason skipped college for Canadian juniors. He played one game in the NHL and later wound up skating for two hundred dollars a game in minor-league towns like Raleigh and Baltimore, where people went to hockey games to drink beer and howl for players to spill one another's blood. I had heard he was briefly a celebrity in Hampton Roads, Virginia.

Local youngsters wrapped their knuckles with white tape to emulate their brawling hero.

He was briefly a celebrity in Starvation, too, after he retired from the minors and moved to town to sell insurance in the early 1990s. By then I had been working in Detroit for years and planned to stay until, as I dreamed, the *New York Times* or *Washington Post* hired me away. I never quite understood how Jason managed to woo Darlene. In a matter of weeks, my mother had told me, their romance went from a few weekends in Jason's cabin in the woods to a wedding in the Pine County Courthouse. After hearing that, I wasn't able to bring myself to go back to Starvation for months.

Darlene didn't like to talk about her years with Jason. Everyone in town knew that he was much better at video golf in bars than he was at selling insurance, which was why he and Darlene could manage only to rent the little apartment over Sally's that she lived in now. I teased her once that she had married Jason because he had skated for the team that had made me the town goat, that she had wanted to make me jealous. She went silent for two long nights, which made me think that what I had said in jest might actually have been a fact.

Which meant I never had to bring it up again. It was all in the past anyway, I told myself. But here Jason was, sitting across from me, my girl-friend's *husband*. I wondered what Haskell knew about it, whether Jason had told him or he had heard it around town. Hell, I wondered what Jason knew.

"So, first practice is what?" I said. "Boxing lessons? How to get the other guy's jersey over his head?"

Jason folded his arms on the table and leaned forward.

"This is a whole new package, my friend," he said. "I'm here to prepare young men to be winners in life, on the ice and off."

"Precisely," Haskell said, placing a hand on Jason's arm. "Past is past, now is now, and the future for the Hungry River Rats is brighter than ever, with a new rink, a new coach, and some fine new players."

"That's right," Jason said. He glanced at Haskell, who removed his hand from Jason's arm. Then Jason turned back to me. "I'll tell you the same thing I've been telling his son: Winners win. Players play."

"And goons goon. Isn't that what they say in the East Coast League?"

"I don't expect you to understand."

He seemed pretty cocky for a guy who'd lost his wife to me. I turned to Haskell. "How much are you paying him?"

Coaches normally received their annual pittance from the local hockey organization funded by parents and fans and silent auctions and sponsors like Enright's and Fortune Drug. But I assumed that, if Haskell was handling the announcement, he would be writing Jason's checks.

Haskell slid the manila envelope to me.

"Everything's in there," he said, and I knew my question wouldn't be answered. "Press release, bio, photo, and other materials you may find helpful. It's all yours. Nobody else has seen it."

"How much is he getting to be coach? I don't think Poppy makes more than like fifteen hundred."

Jason started to answer but Haskell quieted him with a gently raised hand. "Candidly," he said, "I don't see how it's relevant."

"Look, if you're paying him out of your pocket, or your unbuilt new rink's pocket, then I guess it's none of my business. But you said you might be seeking a 'bit of help' from the town, so I think—"

"Whoa," Haskell said. "Hold on there, mister. That was off the record."

"I understand, but I still heard what I heard, and my question—"

"No." He wagged a finger back and forth in front of his face. "You don't even know that, sir. I never said it. That's what off the record means."

Jason sat back and knitted his hands atop his head, enjoying the show.

"I know what off the record means," I said.

Haskell looked at his watch. "My gosh," he said. He picked up the phone again, punched two numbers. "Fel," he said, "are you taking Taylor?" He turned away and lowered his voice, but I could still hear him. "Not—no. No. He needs to do his balance class. He has not been—dear? Dear? He hasn't been getting from post to post like he—I'm sorry, but—please, Felicia, that's simply not fair. He is not going to be playing in the New York Philharmonic so let's just put that whole fantasy to rest." He listened for a few seconds. I glanced at Jason, who'd let a barely disguised smile creep onto his face. "I understand that's how you feel," Haskell said.

He hung up the phone and pushed his chair back. "I'm afraid that's all the time we have. Thank you for your time, Gus."

"I had a few more questions."

"I'm sorry," Haskell said. "I didn't realize how much time we'd already spent. But feel free to call me if you have follow-ups."

"This afternoon?"

Haskell gave me one of his jury frowns. "Today is really not going to be good. Try me tomorrow."

"I have a paper to put out."

"Great," he said. He pointed at the envelope. "You have a great front page story right there. Which reminds me. I have a question for you."

"I thought you were out of time."

Jason was smiling more broadly now.

"Have you been made aware," Haskell said, "of our plans for advertising in your paper when the rink opens?"

"I don't have a thing to do with advertising, Mr. Haskell."

"Really?"

"Really. Love seeing it, though."

The door opened and a buxom rail of a woman in jeans and a cashmere sweater the color of oatmeal appeared. I recognized her initially from the pictures on Haskell's credenza; then I remembered seeing her at the rink, once with her son, another time with her son and husband. Her silver hair, drawn back into a billowy ponytail, belied the youth in her emerald eyes. Her left wrist was wrapped in an Ace bandage. Bracelets in silver and gold speckled with highlights matching her eyes covered her other wrist.

"Did you hurt yourself, dear?" Haskell said.

Her eyes darted from Haskell to Jason to me, where they lingered for an uncomfortable second before returning to her husband.

"Slipped on the back porch. Our plow crew missed a spot."

"Let me see that."

Haskell reached for her injured hand but his wife pulled it away.

"It's fine," she said. "I really would rather Taylor not miss another piano lesson."

"Dear, I thought—"

"I went ahead and called his trainer and he said he'd move the balance session back an hour. So Tay can do both. I'll have him back here for his pregame meal in plenty of time."

Haskell gave her a look long enough to make me wish I was somewhere else. Felicia folded her arms. As she did, she took a tiny step backward.

"I see," Haskell said. "We can talk about this later."

"If you like."

"Have you met Gus?"

I stood and extended my hand. "Gus Carpenter, Mrs. Haskell."

"Of course," she said. A smile flickered on her face. Her handshake dug a fat diamond into my palm. "Nice to finally meet you."

For a second I wondered if she was being sarcastic. I figured she was the one who'd insisted that I stop calling the house for her husband.

"Yes, ma'am. Sorry for all the phone calls."

"No trouble at all." She looked at Jason. "It's nice to see you, too, Jason."

"Felicia."

"I have to be going," she said to Haskell. "But I can show Mr. Carpenter out."

"Thank you, dear," Haskell said. He reached for my hand. I shook without thinking. "Call if you need anything."

"Not at the dinner hour, please," Felicia Haskell said. "Come."

I slid past Jason. Neither of us made a move to shake hands.

"See you," I said.

"You going to be at the game tomorrow night?"

"I'll be there."

"Keep your head up."

eight

You had to be hungry to eat at Riccardo's Pizza, and not because the portions were especially large. The pizza tasted as if grease had been ladled on instead of sauce. The stromboli should have been served with a chisel and hammer. The mozzarella sticks lay in your belly like lead sinkers. But it was cheap. And I was curious.

I stood at the counter, breathing garlic as Aerosmith blared from a boom box in the back, the sole lunch customer at seventeen minutes after noon. Riccardo's did most of its business late at night when the drunks came pouring out of Enright's.

"Anybody home?" I called out.

There were three tight booths and a wall cooler filled with bottles of pop and chocolate milk. Next to the cooler was a small hole in the wall plaster that hadn't been fixed since the last time I'd been in, with Darlene, weeks before. I remembered hearing it was made by a napkin dispenser flung across the room.

The pizzeria sat on a steep rise above the river. I stepped to the window and peered down on downtown Starvation Lake. My gaze fell upon the door to Darlene's apartment, set atop a set of outer stairs leading down to a railed sidewalk that ran along the river. I recalled the night before, how she'd grappled with me before we slipped into our lovemaking.

"I thought you don't eat here no more."

Stefan Bellissimo stood behind the counter in a white apron streaked with spaghetti sauce, hands on his hips, a butcher knife in one hand. Beneath the apron he wore a threadbare River Rats T-shirt. A hairnet mashed his black ringlets to his forehead. A ballpoint pen protruded from behind his ear. Flour powdered his thick eyebrows and mustache.

"Belly," I said. "How are you, buddy?"

"Don't give me that shit. You know what you did."

The men's hockey team I played on, the Chowder Heads, had for years ordered postgame pizzas from Belly's joint. But I had finally persuaded our captain, Soupy, to switch to Gordy's in Fife Lake. The pizza was better and Gordy usually threw in fried mushrooms.

"Hey," I said, "I still bring Darlene in."

"Darlene brings Darlene in. I'm one of your paper's biggest customers. You can't even bring your boys by?"

"What? One ad a week?"

"Look at that," he said, pointing at his booths, where he used old *Pilots* as tablecloths.

"Ah. Well, I'm here. What's good?"

"Don't be pulling on my dick. The pizza's good."

I squinted over his head at the backlit menu on the wall. Belly had owned the place for something like ten years, in which time it had been called Zito's, Sicoly's, Fat Tony's, Provenzana's, Enzo's, Mizzi's and, for a time while he dated an Irish woman from Sandy Cove, Hickey's. He kept changing the names, he said, for marketing reasons. The pizza stayed the same.

Today's "Rats Special" was a grilled cheese sandwich with pepperoni. Too risky, I thought. Maybe a cold sub. Just $2.95 with chips. Pretty hard to screw up.

"What did Darlene have the other night?" I said.

"What she always has. Small Greek salad, ham-and-pineapple pie."

"What about Gracie?"

"What?" Belly said. "You want food or not?"

I wanted to know what Gracie and Darlene had talked about there. The minute I had left Haskell, I'd forgotten about his little announcement and returned to the questions about Gracie swirling in the back of my mind: Why the fresh groceries if she'd planned to off herself? How did she manage to hang herself on a high branch without a ladder? What about the calendar with the dates crossed out in February but not January? Was she counting down the days till her death, and if so, why hadn't she crossed off the final day? What about the single baby shoe left in her hiding place? And the key attached to the ribbon? Her ever-present Wings cap was hanging in the Zam shed; had she made a conscious decision to leave it behind? Or had she been forced to leave? And if so, why? Why would her worthless little life matter that much to anyone?

"Yeah, yeah," I told Belly. "Italian sub, extra peppers."

He waved the butcher knife around. "I'm not hearing a lot of enthusiasm."

"You want me to sing?"

He put the heels of his hands against the countertop and leaned forward. Beads of sweat along the tops of his eyebrows glistened in the overhead light. "Let me ask you a question: You got a problem with us?"

"No problem," I said. "I just happen to like Gordy's—"

"Not that. That pissed me off but I mean like the whole thing. You got a problem with the whole town. It's like we're some bunch of fucking hooples who can't do anything right, and you're going to set us straight."

"Hooples? What are you talking about?"

"You know what I'm fucking talking about. You know how much the game means to this place."

Belly, who did not play hockey but attended every Rats game and supplied half-price pizzas for team functions, always referred to hockey as "the game," in the same sort of bizarre sacred intonation that baseball freaks used about their tedious sport. I loved hockey, loved watching it, loved playing it most of the time. But love to me didn't require reverence. It was just a game.

"What's your point, Bel?"

He plucked the pen from behind his ear, a greenish order pad from an apron pocket. "My point is, why do you got to jam this guy up in the paper?"

"What guy?"

"The guy who's building the rink. You seen his kid play yet? Patrick Roy rolled into Kenny Dryden."

"The old rink's not good enough for him?"

Belly slapped the order pad down on the counter. "Ain't the point," he said. "The point is, a new rink equals a new attitude—we can win. We ain't had that around here. You of all people ought to know that. We're like the goddamn Lions. No matter what we do, we lose because we think we're going to lose. Something's got to change to turn that around. This rink, the guy's kid is our chance. Why do you have to fuck it up?"

I really hadn't tried to fuck it up.

As a player, I was delighted to hear I'd be skating on a fresh sheet of ice and dressing in a room where my feet didn't stick to the rubber-mat floors. As a reporter, I grew skeptical after two subcontractors left me late-night voice messages saying they had not been paid and Haskell wasn't returning their calls.

I started stopping by the Pine County Courthouse every few days to see if any lawsuits had been filed against Haskell. Soon there were three. I wrote a fifteen-inch story and scheduled it for the front page, above the fold, where we had run earlier stories about the rink's progress. I made repeated calls to Haskell and his attorney. They ignored me.

I was surprised to see the next morning that the story did not appear on the *Pilot* front page. Only later did I learn that Philo Beech, who'd been in meetings at headquarters in Traverse City, had read the story there and, without consulting me, decided to shorten it and move it to the bottom of page A6. When I asked him why, he explained that anybody could file a lawsuit and, without a response from Haskell, the story really wasn't fair and balanced.

Philo was sitting with his boots up on his desk behind a two-day-old *Wall Street Journal*. I listened from my swivel chair across the room, speechless. What proof did we have, Philo said, that the subcontractors had actually completed the work they claimed to have completed? These disputes could just be run-of-the-mill contractual spats best left to the involved parties. At least the story hadn't been killed outright, he said; I should be happy it had run at all. So blithe were his criticisms that I got the impression that he was relaying something he'd heard from someone else. He finally put the paper down and, for the first time in his little soliloquy, actually looked at me: Had I finished that feature on the outhouses-on-skis race that Sandy Cove was planning for the weekend?

I swallowed my pique, kept my mouth shut, and stayed on Haskell, sneaking calls and e-mails and half-day trips in between chamber of commerce press releases, school board meetings, and girls' volleyball games. I combed through every local, county, and state file and database where I might find a reference to him, his Detroit firm, or any related business entity. There wasn't much. I filed requests for documents under the Freedom of Information Act with four different state agencies. I wrote and e-mailed Haskell and his lawyer; I called Haskell at home at night; his lawyer threatened to sue us; Philo ordered me to stop calling.

I started driving past the construction site each morning before work. A cubical shell of rust-colored girders and columns had risen amid the mounds of mud and scrap and snow. Dump trucks and backhoes and bulldozers were parked around the site. I never saw them moving. I saw smatterings of workers on some mornings, none at all on others. I bought a disposable camera and, on four consecutive Fridays, drove to the site and from my truck window took four black-and-white photographs, one from each corner of the structure. I had them developed, shuffled them like playing cards, and left the stack one night on Philo's desk chair.

The next morning, I was working at my computer when I spied him in the reflection of my screen, flipping through the pictures and looking puzzled.

"Gus," he said, "are these yours?"

I swiveled around. "Yep. I thought we could run a sort of sequence of photos showing the progress they've made on the new rink."

"Interesting idea," Philo said. He riffled through them again. "Did you mark the order you took them in?"

"I didn't. But you can figure it out, can't you?"

Philo regarded my grin through his horn-rims. "A little game, huh?"

He spread the sixteen photos out on his desk. He quickly discerned the four different angles and arranged the pictures accordingly. Then he stood back and folded his arms. After a few moments, he said, "I don't see it."

"You don't see what?"

"The progression. Which one goes before—" He stopped himself. "You're pulling my leg, aren't you?"

"Not at all. That's how it is."

"That's how what is?"

"That's how the rink is. Four weeks. Zero progress. Lots of trucks and piles of stuff. But nothing actually being built."

"Well," Philo said, "if you put these in the right order—"

"Be my guest."

He pushed his glasses onto his forehead, snatched up a picture in each hand, and brought them close to his face. He looked at one, then the other, then back at the other. He picked up a third picture, then a fourth. I saw the back of his jaw flex as he ground his teeth. He flipped his glasses back down.

"These could have been taken on the same day."

"You're right, they could have," I said. "But they weren't."

"OK, I get it. May I keep these?"

I never saw the pictures again. I watched the court docket for Haskell's replies to the lawsuits and, when those inevitably appeared, I used them as excuses to write stories. Philo seemed relieved that Haskell was getting his public say. I doubt Haskell was pleased, though. Although the stories invariably ran short and at the bottoms of inside pages, I was able to shoehorn in tidbits from my far-flung fishing—liens placed on various Haskell properties around Michigan, litigation over the sale of his Bloomfield Hills house, a delinquent property tax bill on the same. Maybe it all added up to not much; after all, Haskell was a lawyer, and lawyers litigate. Or maybe it meant he'd eventually leave Starvation Lake holding a multimillion-dollar bag.

The town council didn't seem to think much of it. Nor did the zoning board, nor the road commission. They all did whatever Haskell's lawyer asked, every step of the way. I wondered why I was even bothering to report things that nobody heard or wanted to hear anyway.

Then late one Friday in January, just early enough for us to make deadline but too late to do much additional reporting, Haskell's lawyer faxed over a three-paragraph press release stating that construction on the rink had been "temporarily suspended." No shit, I thought. The second paragraph said, "The local media's campaign to derail this well-intentioned project has emboldened certain of our creditors and made it difficult at this time to come to an understanding about the most expeditious path forward. However, we are confident . . ."

That story ran on the front page, above the fold. Twenty-three messages awaited me on my office phone that morning.

"Why can't you just leave us alone?" said the first.

"Stick to screwing up hockey games instead of rinks," said the second.

The rest were the same. Different words, same rebukes.

"I don't know," I told Belly. "Ice is ice, attitude's attitude. The Rats are playing pretty well in the old barn."

"What's the matter with you?" he said. He set the knife down, tore his hairnet off and threw it aside, his curls tumbling down onto his forehead.

"You cursed this place with your fuckup twenty years ago or whenever the hell it was. Now you don't want to help a team that could put the curse to rest?"

This wasn't going well. I wanted to ask about what Darlene and Gracie had discussed. "Christ, Belly, I'm just making a living. Are you going to make my sub? Or—or should I have something else? What did you say Gracie had?"

"The chick who offed herself? Jesus, what the hell do you care?"

"Maybe I'm superstitious."

"Fucking hockey players." He picked up the butcher knife and pointed it at me. "Well, I don't know what the hell she had, pal. She was in here twice this week with two different babes and I can't keep it all straight in my fat head." He smiled. "Come to think of it, might've been an Italian sub. So maybe you're taking a big chance, eh?"

I turned away and looked through the window to town. A sheriff's cruiser pulled into a space in front of Kepel's Ace Hardware. The door opened and Darlene got out. I looked back at Belly. He was pulling his hairnet back on.

"She was in twice?" I said.

"Yeah," he said, tucking his hair under the elastic with the same fingers that would be putting provolone on my sandwich. "OK, enough preaching. You ain't hearing me anyway. I'm going to make your sub."

I glanced outside again. Darlene crossed Main and turned into the alley that led to the river walk and the stairs to her apartment.

"Hey, Bel, never mind," I said. But he'd already gone back into the kitchen and turned the music up loud, an old Rod Stewart tune. I pulled a five-dollar bill out of my jeans pocket and set it on the counter. "Bel," I said, trying to make myself heard over Rod. "I gotta go."

"What?" he yelled.

"I gotta go. Hey, tell me—who was the other babe?"

"What?"

"The other babe with Gracie?"

"Onions raw or grilled?"

I looked out the window again. Darlene was ascending her stairway two steps at a time. "Goddammit," I said, and rushed out the door as Belly yelled again, "Raw or grilled?"

* * *

She was already coming back down the steps when I arrived at the landing. She stopped when she saw me. She had a shoe box under one arm.

"Hey," I said, trying to catch my breath.

"Hey."

She saw my look at the shoe box.

"They're just letters," she said.

"Are you taking them in?"

She looked down at her boots, trying not to cry.

"Darl," I said. She turned and went back up the stairs.

She finally stopped sobbing.

I stroked her hair as her tears dried on my chest. Her bedroom was silent but for the rumble of an occasional pickup passing on Main Street.

When we'd entered her apartment, Darlene had dropped the shoe box on her kitchen table and shoved me up against the refrigerator. She brought her lips to mine and kissed me hard, unbuttoning my shirt, her deputy's badge digging into my rib cage. Then she grabbed me by the waist of my jeans and dragged me into her bedroom, though I did not have to be dragged.

We had made love twice before either of us said a word, Darlene crying in between and afterward in whimpers and shuddering sobs. "Ah, Jesus," she finally said. She turned to face me, propped her elbows on my belly. The imprint of her sheriff's hatband was still on her hair. She didn't like the hat, thought it framed her face in a way that made it look fat, but she kept it on when she was on duty so nobody would take her any less seriously than any male cop.

"I'm sorry," I said.

She settled her face into the heels of her hands and rubbed her eyes, then let her chin fall to my chest. "If she had just killed herself, maybe I wouldn't be crying. Maybe I'd just be angry."

"Gracie was Gracie," I said. "Hard to account for anything she did, without getting into her head."

"She didn't like people messing around in there."

"Did I ever tell you about the prom?"

"What prom?"

"Senior year. The prom. I wanted to take you."

"You were probably too chicken to ask."

"Not exactly," I said. I shifted in the bed so that Darlene straddled my left leg. I liked the feel of her skin warm around my thigh. "You were sort of on and off with that football player."

"Pete Klein. God, he was gorgeous. But really, I was just trying to make you jealous."

"You succeeded. But still, as you say, I wasn't really sure whether to ask you. So I went to Gracie."

"No."

"Oh, yeah. I figured, she's your best friend, she'll know your deal, she's a romantic, she'll level with me. Big mistake."

"What did she say?"

"She said—and I quote—'What makes you think you're good enough?'" Darlene giggled.

"What's so funny?" I said.

"You said you wanted her to level with you. What did you expect?"

"I thought you'd be on my side."

"I am. Now. But . . . it doesn't matter."

"What?"

I waited.

"Gracie told me."

"Gracie told you what?"

"That you might ask me."

"Yeah, right. So stay away from your phone, eh?"

"No," Darlene said. "She said I should go with you."

"She did not."

"Yes, she did. Anyway, you didn't ask me."

I sighed. Darlene let her head fall to my chest and we lay quietly for a few moments. Then I said, "I did a little snooping at the rink."

Darlene lifted her head. "Gus. That's a crime scene. I hope you didn't touch anything."

I didn't reply.

"Oh, God. You're going to get me fired."

"I thought you wanted me on this, Darlene. The town would love to smack a suicide label on it and get back to building their rink."

"Did you or did you not—wait. Your voice mail. Why did you want to know which shoe Gracie was missing?"

"The left one, yes?"

"Why?"

I rolled out from under her and dug the baby shoe out of my coat pocket. The hairbrush was there too but I reflexively left it hidden away, as I would have when we were stealing the brush from one another years ago. I laid the baby shoe on the sheet next to Darlene and sat on the bed. The cheek under Darlene's left eye twitched once. I saw tears welling again.

"You want me to put it back?"

She bit her lower lip, put a hand on my forearm, squeezed. "That's what she was saying."

"Gracie? When? What are you talking about?"

"The other night. At Riccardo's. She kept talking about how her life was a failure because . . . because . . ."

"Because why?"

She shook her head. "She wanted a kid."

"No."

"Yes."

"Can you imagine what a disaster—"

"Shut up. She was serious. She said her time was running out."

Maybe Gracie should have considered that when she was partying away her body, her mind, her heart, the men who took to her. But then I did not really know what her life had been like all those years in Detroit. Even though we had lived in the same town for a long time, we rarely took any trouble to seek each other out, apparently content to live in our separate worlds, mine a submersion in newsprint and sources and late-night calls from phone booths, hers I had no idea what. At my mother's insistence, I tried to call Gracie once in a while, but I couldn't keep up with her ever-changing phone numbers and finally gave up. I wish I could say that I felt bad about it. There were no calls from Gracie, after all.

I saw her once, or thought I did. I was at Joe Louis Arena watching the Red Wings in a playoff game against the Chicago Blackhawks. A woman I was dating from the *Detroit Free Press* was supposed to join me but had to work late so I bought myself a standing-room only ticket and went alone. I stood with a twenty-four-ounce cup of Stroh's with my back to the wall along the aisle between the lower and upper bowls of seats, watching Roe-nick and Larmer and Chelios trample the Wings' hopes for a Stanley Cup. At a stop in play I looked to my right to check the scoreboard for the shots on goal and there she was.

At first I didn't recognize her. Gracie had always been cute. The boys liked the way her sharp cheekbones set off her languid blue eyes, the narrow gap between her front teeth, the barely discernible overbite that imbued her smile with a hint of secret mischief. Her body, taut as a guitar string, and her willingness to share it had helped keep her in boyfriends.

But this Gracie following a tall man with black hair slick with mousse and a cashmere topcoat down to the rink-side seats was more elegant and beautiful than I had ever seen. Her auburn hair tumbled over a charcoal turtleneck. She carried a fur coat over one arm. She seemed straighter, taller, less mousy. Maybe it was the turtleneck. Or the fur.

The man, who also wore a turtleneck, stopped and turned with a suave smile and an offer of his hand. She took it and edged into her seat, laying the fur across her lap and fluffing her hair as she settled in. She looked more like a Grace than a Gracie. I tried to keep an eye on her, but the fans behind her kept jumping to their feet and blocking the view. At the end of the second period I went to the men's room and when I returned to my place against the wall, she was gone.

"Why didn't she just have a kid?" I asked Darlene.

She just looked at me.

"OK, dumb question. Hard to bring up a kid in a Zam shed."

"Which was really her point," Darlene said. "She kept saying, 'I fucked up my life, I fucked up my life, and I can't fix it.'" She nodded at the baby shoe. "I think I know what that is."

I picked it up and turned it over. "You do?"

"You really want your prints all over that?"

"What do you think it is?"

She set her chin atop her fists and fixed her eyes on the pillow in front of her. "She had an abortion."

"When she was downstate?"

"If she'd had one here, we'd all know about it by now, wouldn't we?"

"I suppose. She didn't tell you?"

"Not in so many words. But every now and then, she would talk about kids, and, you know, she'd get all misty and after a while she just stopped making sense."

"Would she have had it recently? Or a long time ago?"

I was thinking of Soupy. But I wasn't about to bring him up. I wanted to ask him about it before the police did, if they hadn't already.

"I don't know," she said. "I don't know if she actually had an abortion. I just have this feeling. Whenever she got into one of her little crying jags, she'd always be saying something like, 'Don't ever give up what you got, because you can never, never get it back.'"

"Wait," I said. "Why would she have a shoe if she had an abortion?"

"Come on, it's Gracie. She might've gone to Kmart and bought one."

"Just one? Where's the other one?"

"Gussy . . . I don't know."

"You know, Darl, maybe she actually had a baby and adopted it out."

"Do you think she'd go through that? Nine months? No drinking?"

I didn't have to think much. "No," I said.

I watched Darlene staring into the pillow. I felt for her. She and Gracie went back as far as Soupy and I did. As little girls, they'd combed each other's hair, painted on each other's makeup, worn each other's clothes. When Gracie was on one of her extended stays at our house, she'd often go next door to sleep at Darlene's. I could still picture them sitting knees to knees in their one-piece bathing suits on the dive raft in front of the house, the last of the day's sun bathing their tan shoulders, them waving their arms, leaning back to giggle, chattering about whatever they chattered about.

I thought I knew what Darlene was thinking: if only Gracie had never left Starvation, maybe she would have been all right.

But how could Gracie not have gone? It was late in her senior year of high school. In my junior English class, room 211, we were discussing *One Flew Over the Cuckoo's Nest* when we heard a shrieking in the hallway that every one of us immediately recognized as Gracie McBride. "Oh God, oh God, oh God, it's so cool, so so cool!" Our teacher dropped his book and rushed out to see what the commotion was about, and five or six of us got out of our seats and followed. We saw Gracie spinning her way down the hall, the orange plaid pleats of her skirt whirling out from her hips.

"I'm going to college," she sang. "I'm going to college."

An anonymous donor had offered to pay Gracie's full tuition, room, and board, so long as she attended Wayne State University in downtown Detroit. The donor, whom everyone in town assumed was a Wayne grad, had made the gift in honor of Gracie's father, who had been awarded the Purple Heart posthumously after Vietnam. Gracie's mother raised a brief stink about being entitled to some of the gift, seeing as she was the one who had lost her husband. No lawyer would touch it.

That fall, Gracie left for Wayne. It was September 1980. Almost eighteen years would pass before Gracie walked Main Street again. Not once in those years did she even visit, and most folks in town forgot about her. Except Darlene, who called her now and then and visited downstate once or twice. And my mother, who spoke with her each month on the twenty-second, the anniversary of Gracie's father's and my father's deaths.

"What the hell did she do in Detroit?" I said. "How did she survive?"

"I don't really know," Darlene said, and I could tell it hurt her. "She was always vague when I asked her, or she made jokes: she was dancing in a strip club, she was selling coke. For a while she worked as a secretary somewhere. A real estate company, I think." She nodded toward the shoe box on the table. "That's why I dug that out."

"She never graduated from Wayne."

"No."

I slid across the bed and placed my palm lightly on Darlene's shoulder. She reached up and touched my fingertips with hers.

"Speaking of out-of-towners," I said. "When were you going to tell me Jason was back?"

"Who cares?"

"Have you seen him?"

"Nope. Don't care to either."

"I saw him. He looks good. A lot better than he did."

"I really don't want to talk about him right now."

She twisted around to see the clock on her stove. "Crap," she said. "Lunch is way over. Dingus is going to be p.o.'d."

I waited on the bed while she put her uniform back on, fitted the hat on her hair. She grabbed the shoe box and came to the bed, standing over me. She leaned over and kissed me on the neck.

"You were sweet today," she said.

She was almost out the door when I called after her. "Hey. How about I make you spaghetti tonight and then we can go to the Rats game?"

"OK," she said, and she was gone.

A soggy dishrag lay on the bar at Enright's. Somewhere a faucet was running. The air tasted of mustard and pickled eggs.

At the far end of the long, whiskey-colored bar sat two regulars, both men, one stool between them, always one stool between them. They nursed their longnecks and lit cigarette after cigarette, never saying a word, just staring into the rank air in front of their unshaven faces, their eyes drifting up to the soundless television behind the bar.

Taking my own seat a few stools away, I considered for a second whether they might be contemplating where their lives had taken that wrong turn, how they had wound up spending every afternoon in a dive on an anonymous Main Street, shoving their last balled-up dollar bills across the bar. But they were more likely wondering how they were going to get out of splitting that pile of logs their old ladies had been bitching about since New Year's.

"Trap—you want Thousand Island?"

Soupy leaned out of the kitchen at the other end of the bar and shouted at me, using the nickname he'd given me when I first started playing goaltender. I wasn't playing goalie now, but the nickname remained.

"On the side," I said.

"Blue Ribbon?"

I looked at the clock behind the bar. It bore the slogan "No Wine Before Nine." All the numbers on the clock's face were nines.

"Why not?" I said.

Soupy threw the dishrag in a sink behind the bar and set the beer in front of me with a plastic basket containing a cheeseburger and onion rings bleeding grease into a red-and-white checkered napkin.

I wanted Thousand Island dressing on the burger but I was so hungry that I picked it up and took a bite first. My teeth crunched through the charred crust and into the juicy red middle. The bite was too big and the melted Monterey Jack stuck to the roof of my mouth. Soupy wasn't good at much besides hockey, but he sure knew how to make a burger.

"Boffing'll get you hungry, huh?" he said.

I popped an onion ring into my mouth. It was the frozen kind but good anyway, crisp and hot.

"What are you talking about?"

"Fuck you," he said. "I was going to the bank and saw you chasing the little lady up her stairs there, lover boy."

"I was not chasing."

"Nothing like a little afternoon action to break up a dreary day."

"Mr. Carpenter declined to comment."

Soupy leaned his elbows on the bar. Ketchup and grease streaked the white apron he wore over his Northern Michigan University T-shirt. His blond hair was tied back in a ponytail that hung between his shoulder blades. He knew I'd come to ask about Gracie, and I knew he'd probably do what he could to avoid talking about her. Soupy liked to jaw about hockey and beer and fishing and how to get women into bed. Everything else was small talk.

"How's the bluegill wrapper?" he said.

I plucked the top bun off the burger and added the dressing, replaced the bun, took another chomp, just as big. Even better. I bit into half an onion ring, cooled it all down with a pull on the beer.

"Bleeding red ink," I said. I made a show of looking around the bar. Pictures of Soupy as a kid in his River Rats blue-and-gold hung up and down the knotty pine walls in between the big brass hooks where snowmobile riders hung their helmets. There were no pictures of me, but Soupy had installed the goaltender's mask I no longer wore on the back bar between bottles of Mohawk root beer schnapps and Southern Comfort. The back-lighting gave the mask the look of a skull. A few bottles down stood two of Gordon's gin, one full, the other half full, both marked on the label with a big black "G."

For Gracie. Everyone else got Beefeater.

"When are you going to rename this dump 'Soupy's'?"

The summer before, Soupy had sold the town marina his family had owned for fifty-some years and used the cash to buy Enright's. At the time he was actually trying to quit drinking, so he joined the legions of other drying-out northern Michigan drunks who reckoned the best way to be sure they were genuinely sober was to test themselves every single day by getting other people drunk. He quit the quitting thing pretty quickly. He kept the bar.

"You know what it costs for a lousy goddamn sign?" Soupy said. "Anyway, it'd be like putting up a billboard for the IRS: 'Over here, dudes.'"

"Good point."

My cell phone started ringing from my shirt pocket. I considered answering, but the jukebox was wailing "Moondance."

"You going to get that?" Soupy said.

"Can't hear in here."

He leaned closer. "That lard-ass in the coveralls plays that damn song about seventy-two times a day."

"At least it's not 'Dream Weaver.'"

"These guys think this is their goddamn living room. That one had his daughter's fucking baby shower here the other day."

"Must be good extra cash, though."

"No. Lost my ass giving toasts away. And they left without paying the bill. Assbag down there"—Soupy jabbed his elbow in that direction without looking—"says put it on his tab."

"That's not good," I said. "Kind of makes you wonder how a guy can afford to shut his bar down early with all his hockey pals coming in."

Soupy ignored me. "So we tied, eh? Heard you hit the post."

"Yeah. Where the hell were you?"

"Can't be missing empty nets, Trap."

"Where were you, Soup?"

Soupy never missed hockey. When the Chowder Heads were skating, he left Enright's in the hands of his other bartender, Dave Lubienski. But Soupy had been a no-show the night before. Then we found the bar closed hours before last call.

"Loob's wife had a chicks' night out, and he had to stay with the kid. I tried to get Tatch to fill in but as usual he had his head up his ass." He picked up the dishrag and began wiping down the sink behind the bar. "Ready for the game tomorrow? The Linke boys were in last night talking shit."

The Linkes played for the Mighty Minnows of Jordan Bait and Tackle, our first-round opponents. Soupy was trying to change the subject. I decided to play along, for now.

"Should be fun," I said. "Did you get the hats?"

"Oh, Trap, fucking-ay, hang on."

Soupy hurried back into the kitchen. Every year, he bought the Chowder Heads hats for the playoffs. He thought they brought us good luck. His team hadn't actually won the playoffs in three years, but Soupy did not relinquish his superstitions easily.

He emerged wearing a red wool cap with a fluffy white ball on the top and black tassels dangling to his shoulders. A pair of soup spoons crossed to look like hockey sticks were embroidered into the front of the hat.

"Awesome or what?" Soupy said. The regulars glanced up, unimpressed. "I ain't even going to wear a helmet, man."

"Sweet," I said. "Is that mine?"

"Fucking-ay."

He tore the cap off of his head and threw it at me. I pulled it on my head and looked in the mirror behind the bar, mugging. Soupy laughed and reached over the bar for a hand slap.

When I had played goalie for the Rats and for Soupy's men's league team, the Chowder Heads, Soupy had always been my best defenseman, the smartest at staying between the puck and me, the most adept at stealing the puck and hurrying it to the other end of the ice. If an opposing player gave me the slightest bump, or whacked one too many times at my pads, I could count on Soupy giving him a stick shaft to the back of the neck, maybe a glove to the face.

After his hockey career evaporated in a steam of booze and drugs in the minors, Soupy had stopped expecting much from life. It didn't take much to make him happy anymore. A case of beer, a bag of barbecue chips, a Red Wings game on the tube, a new cap for a playoff game. Gracie's return had been a bonus. She was at once the new woman in town, since she'd been gone so long, and a familiar one, who knew Soupy well enough to have no expectations, except for a few drinks, a little reefer, a night in his bed.

For a while I had been glad for him. But eventually came the creeping suspicion that my apparent satisfaction with Soupy's lot was a symptom of my own complacency, a sign that I too was now willing to settle for a day-today existence in Starvation, with none of the visions I once carried around about changing the world with the things I could find out and write down.

"I like it," I said, stuffing the cap in a coat pocket.

"Yeah, buddy. Calls for a shot."

He snatched two glasses and a bottle of Jack Daniel's off the back bar and poured us two fat shots. I really didn't need it, but it gave me an opportunity to change the subject again.

I raised my glass. "To Gracie," I said.

Soupy hesitated before clinking my glass. He drank the Jack down in a gulp, winced, poured himself another, swallowed that. I drank half of mine, set the glass down. "You all right?" I said.

"Fine."

I knew he'd enjoyed sleeping with her, because he talked about it almost constantly. I wasn't sure whether he'd gotten his heart as involved as his pecker, because he didn't talk about that.

"Sorry, man. I know you liked her."

"Yeah. Cool chick."

"Are we going to talk about it?"

He picked up the dishrag again, held his arms up in an exaggerated shrug. "What's to talk about? Obviously she wasn't happy. So"—he looked into the sink—"she did what she did."

"No, Soup."

"Chickenshit, if you ask me."

"No." I lowered my voice. "She didn't kill herself."

"How the hell do you know?"

"Cops been to see you?"

He sneaked a look at the regulars. They weren't looking, but the jukebox was off again, so they could hear. For months, Soupy had imagined, or pretended to imagine, that only a few locals knew that he and Gracie were sleeping together, even though she came into Enright's every night around nine, sat at the same end-of-the-bar stool beneath a picture of young Soupy celebrating after a goal, drank her eight or nine gin and Squirts, stayed until the bar was empty, and left through the back door with Soupy.

"What the hell would the cops want with me?"

"You tell me. Soupy Campbell closed his bar early last night. That's front-page news right there."

"There was a big fucking storm last night, you know."

"There's a big fucking storm every two weeks and you never close early. And you weren't at the rink. You think Dingus isn't going to notice?"

"Dingus?" He was getting louder now. One of the regulars had turned his head to watch. Soupy looked at him. "What's your problem, Lenny? You interested in settling up?"

Lenny returned to his cocoon. Soupy glared at me.

"What the fuck, Trap? You selling me out to your girlfriend?"

"Oh, Jesus, give me a break. You could get yourself in trouble here, buddy. Where were you?"

"Good question," came a voice from the front of the bar.

We turned to see Sheriff Dingus Aho standing in the open front doorway, his cruiser's lights flickering on the street behind him.

"Damn," I said. "This is not good."

"Christ, Dingus," Soupy said. "Did you have to use the lights? I got a business to run here."

Dingus spared Soupy the handcuffs. By the time they pulled away, Soupy in the backseat staring straight ahead, a small audience had gathered on the sidewalk, and Soupy's bar had closed early for the second time in less than twenty-four hours.

"What's all the hubbub out there?"

Phyllis Bontrager asked me the question as I came through the front door of the *Pilot*. Her eyes, replicas of her daughter Darlene's, widened behind the huge lenses she'd worn for as long as I'd known her. As kids, we had called her Tweety Bird.

"You didn't see?" I said. "The cops took Soupy in."

Mrs. B pursed her lips and popped her glasses up onto her head. She was standing behind the front counter wearing a red cardigan with the shapes of reindeer heads knitted into it. A game show flickered silently on a black-and-white TV at the other end of the counter.

"Are you all right?" she said.

I must have looked worried, though I was telling myself the sheriff was probably just going to grill Soupy before letting him go. He could have done it more quietly, but Dingus had his own way of doing things.

"Yeah, I'm OK," I said. "Worried about Soupy."

"You're a good friend, but Alden Campbell wouldn't hurt a flea," she said. Alden was Soupy's real name, but Mrs. B and my mother were the only ones who called him by it. "How is your mother?"

"Not so good."

"Yes. This is difficult for her. I went over this morning as soon as I saw her up."

"Thanks. I must have just missed you. Have you seen Darlene?"

She shook her head no. "She woke me up in the middle of the night. I was glad she did, of course, but she wasn't making any sense. All I could hear was that Gracie was"—she stopped, searched for a word—"gone. Then I just sat up all night."

"I'm sorry," I said. "What do you think?"

She picked a pile of advertising invoices out of her in-basket, started stacking certain ones on the counter to her left, others to her right. "Alden didn't really think he could close the bar early and nobody would notice, did he?"

"Who knows what goes on in that head?"

"Do you think he knows anything?"

"No. I mean, he probably knows *something* about what happened to Gracie, hopefully not enough to get himself in trouble." Damn Soupy, I thought. He was a month older than me, but seemed like a little brother half the time. "Mail?"

"On your desk." She flipped her glasses down again. "School menus. The phone bill. A notice from the Boy Scouts on their March fund-raiser. The county extension newsletter; this month's focus is winter mildew. Revised town council agenda. Two letters to the editor: one from Jill Smith about the restrooms at the senior center; one from Danny Braun about your stories on the new rink—I can read that one if you'd rather not." She tipped her head so that she was looking at me over the rims of her glasses. "And something from Detroit."

She loved me like a son. And mistrusted me like the punk next door who had once broken her daughter's heart.

"Probably a parking ticket I never paid," I said.

Philo appeared behind Mrs. B in the doorway to the newsroom. "Good afternoon, Gus," he said. He usually used that line on me when I showed up at 10:00 a.m. Now the wall clock over his head said 1:20. I had plenty of time to finish what I had to do for Tuesday's paper, but that wasn't what counted with Philo. He had a punch-clock in his head that his uncle had installed.

"Sorry, Philo. I was out gathering information."

The look on his face told me he was not impressed.

"One other thing," Mrs. B said. "Shirley McBride stopped in."

Gracie's mother. "Here? How was she?"

Philo pointed one finger at the newsroom then disappeared back there.

"Oh, you know. It's all about Shirley. She said she was on her way down to see Parmelee." Parmelee Gilbert was the only lawyer left on Main Street. "Something about a life insurance policy."

"Gracie's life insurance? Don't tell me."

"Her uncle supposedly sold her a policy not too long ago."

Gracie's uncle was Floyd Kepsel, Shirley's brother and the owner of Kepsel's Ace Hardware. He sold life insurance on the side and was a town councilman.

"How much?"

"I don't know. Shirley, as you know, isn't always crystal clear."

"But if it's more than a hundred bucks . . ."

"Exactly. She was doing her entitlement thing. You know."

"Yeah." I'd seen it on display at assessment appeal meetings. Shirley was the exceedingly squeaky wheel who rarely got the grease, or at least never enough to satisfy her. "Is she stopping back here?"

"Gus!" I heard Philo call out.

Mrs. B jerked a thumb toward the back. "Go."

Philo was on the phone so I tossed my coat on a table strewn with yellowing *Pilots* and started on what I had to get done before deadline: Rewrite the school menu, Boy Scouts, and extension service items into briefs. Write the Jason Esper story. Get the sheriff to talk to me about Gracie, then write that story, doing everything I could to avoid the word "suicide." Now Gracie supposedly had a life insurance policy. Who would take the trouble to buy a life insurance policy if they were deciding when and how they would die?

I left the rest of the mail for later, although I glanced at the Detroit piece to see if Mrs. B had peeked inside. It didn't appear that she had.

The message light on my phone was on. I dialed. There was one message: "The animals are restless," came a raspy voice.

I deleted the message, fished my cell phone out of my coat pocket, and dialed a number I didn't want on the *Pilot* phone bill, which Philo now spent half an hour going over each month. He was either looking for pennies to cut out of the budget or trying to figure out who my sources were. Probably both. Our cell phone bills went straight to corporate.

The raspy voice came on my cell phone: "You didn't hear this from me."

"Good afternoon."

"Whoa, whoa, whoa—don't be saying my name."

"I won't. What do you know?"

It was Clayton Perlmutter, town councilman and self-appointed curmudgeon. I didn't trust him as far as I could throw my hockey bag. But he spent most of his days on the two phones in his house deep in the woods, trading this bit of gossip for that one until a lot of little bits added up to something that mattered. I had to keep him closer than folks I actually trusted, because he actually knew things they didn't. In my eighteen years as a reporter, I had come to the reluctant realization that it was better dealing with liars and thieves than with people who didn't know anything. Or people who were just plain stupid. Perlmutter was not stupid.

"Your old pal Laird," Clayton Perlmutter said, "has visited with a few select members of your town council—not including yours truly, naturally, because he knows where I'd tell him to go—with a great big hat in his hand."

"Really? I thought you were the one with the hat."

I heard the low bark of a dog in the background. Perlmutter muffled the phone and yelled, "Shep. Can't you see I'm on the phone?" He came back on. "No, son, no hat for me. That's past history, you know that."

"Of course."

He fancied himself an entrepreneur. A year before, he'd gotten into some trouble with the state of Michigan for using research grants to support a sasquatch museum he'd never actually opened. Now he was proposing to build an Up North Hockey Hall of Fame on a couple of acres abutting the land where the new rink would be. He didn't have a nickel to build the thing, but that wasn't the point. Perlmutter merely wanted to scare Laird Haskell into buying his little plot at a handsome premium.

Until Haskell did, Perlmutter would be juggling his phones and spreading rumors and trying to make trouble on the council.

"So, anyway, old Mr. Haskell, it turns out, ain't as rich as he looks."

"I think we've written that."

"Ha," Perlmutter said. "Nobody wants to believe it."

Philo walked over and sat on my desk. He crossed his loafers and folded his hands on his knees. I smiled, pointed at the phone, held up a finger, and pressed the phone harder to my ear.

"Anyway," Perlmutter continued, "the big rich lawyer now wants the town to give him a little loan. You know, just a short-term thing, no strings attached, thirty days same as cash, like we're some kind of special bank for millionaires."

"Really? How much?"

"Oh, not much at all. And of course it ain't because he's having any financial problems. It's just a little cash-flow glitch is all."

"How big of a glitch?"

"He just needs a little six-figure bridge loan."

"Can you be more specific?"

Shep barked again in the background. "Oh, give or take, about one hundred thousand smackeroonies."

No shit, I thought. So that was what Haskell meant by "a bit of help"—a pretty hefty bit for a town that had to have bake sales to raise the money to buy a new backstop for the softball field. I doubted the town council had a hundred grand cooling in a bank vault somewhere. I sat up a little straighter in my chair, happy for the interesting turn of events, even happier that I knew and Haskell didn't know that I knew. Philo was watching, so I tried not to look too happy. Plus I'd still have to get it confirmed elsewhere.

"Impressive."

"Maybe next he's going to sell us the Brooklyn Bridge, huh? You know, it might be nice to have all of this in the paper before it suddenly shows up at Wednesday's council meeting. Otherwise, it's a done deal, and I got a feeling we ain't never going to see that hundred K again."

"Well, thank you, sir," I said. "Not sure we'd be interested, though."

Perlmutter paused a moment, then let loose with a guffaw. "Oh, someone listening in, huh?" he said. "You are a regular Geraldo Rivera, sir. A regular Geraldo Rivera. Over and out."

I ended the call and looked up at Philo.

"What's up?" I said.

"Who was that?"

I riffled through my mail for the town council agenda and tore open the envelope. "Some whack job," I said. In the middle of the agenda, below old business, an item had been added: "Executive Session re: capital construction." That would be where the council went into a private caucus and wrote Haskell a big check.

"Are you sure?" Philo said.

He had watched me carefully. But before I told him anything, I wanted to do a little more reporting on Perlmutter's tip. Bosses couldn't always be trusted with good stories. The more time they had to think about them, the more time they had to mess them up or kill them outright.

I tossed the council agenda on my desk. "Would you like a story about how the White House is scheming to poison our lake so it can be turned into a cooling pond for alien spaceships?"

"Hmm," Philo said. "I think not."

"OK. Going for another correction tomorrow, Philo?"

"Pardon me?"

I gestured at my computer screen. "I was looking at the obit you wrote for old Mrs. Guthaus. Where the hell is Toussaint, Arizona?"

He looked at me, dumfounded. "Two what?"

"Tou-SANT." I said it with what I fancied to be a French flourish.

"Oh," he said. "Tucson. I would have caught it."

"Let's hope. You know, you've kind of got to imagine your corrections ahead of time. That's the best way to avoid them. If you can imagine a correction—"Tucson is a city in southern Arizona. A story in Tuesday's Pilot misspelled the city's name"—then you have to double-check it."

I prided myself on this. Once I got out of bed in the middle of the night and called the printing plant to make sure that a caption referring to a shotgun said shotgun and not rifle, a common mistake among pointy-headed journalists who'd never held a real gun in their hands.

"So you've said," Philo said. He uncrossed his loafers. "How did your meeting with Mr. Haskell go?"

"Fine."

"Did you get a story?"

I thought for a second. "At least one."

"Right." I figured he already knew about the new Rats coach, courtesy of his Uncle Jim. "And how was the body language?"

"Fine. Everyone's fine."

Philo cleared his throat. "My meeting in Traverse was unnerving, to say the least."

"I'm sorry to hear that."

"Yes. Long story short: revenues are way behind budget, and the budget was conservative to begin with." Philo looked nervously around the room. "I don't know where else to cut."

I recalled him on his first day at the *Pilot*. A week before Christmas, he bustled around the newsroom like a kid about to open his presents: just twenty-eight years old and the managing editor of a real newspaper. A tiny newspaper, an obscure newspaper, a newspaper that didn't report much news that anybody outside of Starvation Lake cared about, but a newspaper nonetheless.

He had told me then how he had decided to eschew the route taken by his grad-school peers, which was to turn summer internships at the big dailies into full-time jobs that would someday have them covering the White House or Wall Street or wars in foreign hells. "I want nothing to do with the Washington media mob and the whole backstabbing New York scene," he'd said. "I want to learn this from the ground up, get the ink in my veins, if you know what I mean." Part of me found his purity and naïveté endearing. Another part wondered if Philo had failed to land any internships and had fallen back on his uncle.

Either way, I couldn't help but feel for him now as his eyes darted around our wretched little newsroom, looking for ways to clip a few pennies off our monthly outlay. There in the corner was the desk of our old photographer, who had worked on and off at the *Pilot* longer than Philo had been alive; Philo had had to call him up and fire him on New Year's Day. There on Philo's desk was the mug jammed with ballpoint pens Philo had sneaked one by one out of the Pine County State Bank. There on a shelf were the last three legal pads in a package that had to last until the end of the month.

"Philo," I said. "You went to journalism school."

"I did."

"Why?"

He laced his fingers together in front of his argyle sweater. "Because I like the way newspapers can knit communities together."

He must have read that somewhere, I thought.

"And you understand how newspapers do that, right? They do it by telling people things they don't want to hear."

"Please," Philo said.

"Well, why aren't you doing journalism then, however you want it?"

"I'm the managing editor of this newspaper."

"You're the Bob Cratchit of this newspaper."

"You must mean Scrooge."

"Nope. Scrooge was the boss. You aren't the boss by a long shot."

I saw him look at the thermostat on the wall near the back door.

"Go ahead," I said.

He couldn't help himself. He slipped off the desk and walked to the thermostat and actually turned the heat down. I laughed.

"It's not funny," Philo said. He came back to where I was sitting and stood over me. "We could let you go. Would that be funny?"

It didn't hit me as hard as he might have hoped, because I didn't think he was serious. After all, who would actually put stories in the paper if I was gone? Philo spent most of his time writing e-mails and going to meetings about all the other businesses Media North was now in, cell phones and television and the Internet and billboards and video rentals.

"Hilarious," I said. "Tell you what, why don't you just fire yourself? Get the hell out of here and see the world, get drunk, get laid, do the things you really want to do. What's that you always say? 'Earth's turning faster on its axis.' What are you waiting around here for?"

"What makes you so high and mighty? What are you, thirty-seven, and you're still messing around in Starvation Lake?"

"Thirty-five. And, hey, it pays the bills. I don't have a trust fund, pal."

"Pardon me?"

"Come on."

"What do you know about me? You know nothing about me."

"No offense," I said, "but you're miserable and you know it." I felt Mrs. B move into the newsroom doorway. "You came here thinking you were going to run this little empire and knit these nice little towns together and take over for Uncle Jimbo. But it's not working out, is it? You fire me and you won't have time to worry about the Internet anymore. You'll have to go to things like drain commission meetings. Ever go to a drain commission meeting? It's actually even worse than it sounds."

"Well, let me tell you something, *pal*," he said. "I just might do that. But you know what that means? Huh? It means we're all goners."

"Right, right, we're all goners. But the Internet, that's going to save us."

"That's right. Print's kaput, my friend."

"I'm not your friend."

He pointed at me. "Our biggest cost? Those big damn presses that print the paper. And the trucks that have to haul it around. When we're rid of those, we'll have—"

"Squat," I said.

"We'll be in the money. You'll see. I'm going to make them see."

Although Media North had an Internet business, it did not yet have the *Pilot* itself on the Internet. Philo had stood before Kerasopoulos and the other directors of Media North and patiently delivered his Internet-is-our-future speech. They had listened politely, as if they were indulging a boy asking the company to sponsor his Little League team, then moved to the next order of business. They wouldn't even let us have our own experimental website. Kerasopoulos said we couldn't be handing our stories over for nothing; that would be the death of us. He would also have a harder time controlling the news if the *Pilot* had an instant pipeline.

"All they can see is their 401(k)s and their pensions and their long-term bonuses. They're not about to piss all of that away on your—"

"Excuse me."

It was Mrs. B. Philo turned. "Yes, Phyllis?"

"I'm sorry, I thought you two might like to know. Channel Eight just had a bulletin. The River Rats have a new coach."

I jumped out of my chair. "You're kidding."

It hadn't taken Haskell but two hours to burn me.

"No," she said. "It's Jason Esper."

"And what do you think about that, Mrs. B.?"

"What do you think I think?"

She wasn't her daughter's estranged husband's biggest fan.

"Who cares?" Philo said.

"There's something else," she said. She drew her reindeer sweater around herself. "They said the police are going to charge Alden in Gracie's death."

"Impossible. Charge him with what?"

"Alden who?" Philo said.

"They didn't say," Mrs. B said. "They just said he'd be charged."

"There's a difference between being charged and being taken in for questioning."

"I'm just telling you what was on TV."

I felt Philo staring at me. My heart was in my belly, partly for Soupy, partly because I'd just been scooped. Twice. In about thirty seconds. On the two biggest stories to hit Starvation in a year.

I could blame Haskell for the first one; he'd obviously turned around after our meeting and leaked it to Channel Eight. Or maybe Jason himself had, I thought, maybe while I was in bed with his wife. On the other, I had no one but myself to blame. Then again, even if I knew the cops were going to charge Soupy, what the hell was I going to do with it? The *Pilot* wouldn't be out till the next morning.

Excuses, I thought. It felt lousy.

I turned to Philo. "Alden is Soupy, the guy who owns Enright's. The thing about him could be bullshit. Channel Eight gets stuff wrong all the time. I'll chase it."

"OK," Philo said. "The coach is a bigger story anyway, don't you think?"

No, I thought, the murder of a Starvation Lake citizen is way bigger. But I said, "Maybe. Just think, Philo, if we had our own Internet page, we might have beaten Channel Eight to both these stories." I grabbed my coat. "I'll be back."

"Where are you going?" Philo looked up at the wall clock over the copier. "You don't have a lot of time."

"You want to help?"

"I wish I could," he said. "I have to do this budget."

"No problem," I said, and gave Mrs. B a light squeeze on the shoulder as I headed out to Main Street.

Afternoon already had begun to succumb to night. I turned toward the lake. Low hanging cloud banks pinched the tree line against the far end of Main. I walked down the block and sat on a bench beneath the marquee of the old Avalon Cinema, remembering the smell of popcorn on the air when my mother had brought me there as a boy to see *Willy Wonka & the Chocolate Factory*. Now all I could smell was winter.

I had to make a few calls I didn't want Philo to overhear. I dialed the numbers for three town council members who, if I caught them at the right time, might not mind talking. Most had shut me out since I'd started writing about Haskell and the new rink. A potato chip bag skittered past my boots as each of the calls landed on voice mail. I left bare-bones messages saying I needed clarification on a council matter; no need for them to know that I was prowling for another Haskell story.

I needed to confirm what Perlmutter had told me. Haskell had told me just enough off the record to tie my hands. Clever, I thought. Or stupid on my part. Now I had to write my story as if I'd never heard him say what he'd said about seeking help from the town. But I had to get the story. Everyone in town deserved to hear what the council was about to do before it was done and Haskell cashed his check, even if they didn't want to hear it, which was probably the case. And I had to get back out ahead of Channel Eight.

Most important, I wanted to know what was going on with Soupy. I tried Darlene's phone. She didn't answer. "Hey, stranger, just checking in," I told her voice mail. I shoved the phone back in my pocket and felt the old hair brush I'd found in Gracie's Wayne State duffel. I pulled it out and scrutinized the stray hairs stuck in the bristles, auburn and gray.

I remembered what Mrs. B had said about a life insurance policy. So far

as I knew, suicides often nullified life insurance policies; the beneficiary—
I assumed it was Gracie's mother, Shirley, based on what Mrs. B had
said—was unlikely to get a penny. Even if it was obvious that Gracie was
murdered, even if the police investigated her death as a homicide, someone
would have to prove it or the insurance company could take forever to pay,
if it paid at all.

And Soupy? Did he drive Gracie out to the shoe tree and boost her up
to the hanging bough, then just leave her there to die? No way, I thought.
Although he and Gracie were far from in love, they were having a hell of a
good time. Or at least Soupy was.

"Dude," he had whispered to me late one night as we dressed for a game.
"I got no legs."

"Why?" I said, digging for a roll of tape in my hockey bag.

"Gracie. I got to the rink early to get my skates sharpened and she
hauled my ass back to the Zam shed."

"No."

"Yeah. Ever fuck on a Zamboni?"

I tried to imagine precisely how they had done it, decided I didn't want
to know. "Good old Nadia," I said.

"More like Evel Knievel."

I had to shut this conversation down. Without looking up from the
sock I was winding with tape, I said, "So, you going to marry her?"

"Marry her? Trap, she won't even let me take her to a movie. The
woman fucks like there's no tomorrow."

And now there was no tomorrow.

I didn't believe the cops were going to charge Soupy with a thing. More
likely, I thought, the sheriff was trying to squeeze him for information.

So my next stop had to be Dingus—if Dingus would even talk. He
didn't do phones. I would have to go see him, hope whoever was at the
front desk—maybe Darlene—would tell him I was there. I looked at my
watch. I had enough time if he didn't make me wait too long, if he agreed
to see me at all.

I was about to get up from the bench when I felt a tap on my shoulder.

"You are truly deep in thought, young man."

I turned to see Parmelee Gilbert, attorney-at-law, in a charcoal topcoat
and a wool scarf the color of a carrot.

"Impressive," he said. "Would that all of us in Starvation think so hard about what we're doing."

"Hey, Parm," I said. "I wish I knew what I was doing. How are you?"

"Staying busy." He peeled the leather glove off of his right hand and extended it. "I am very sorry for your loss."

I knew he meant it. "Thanks. Mom's taking it pretty hard."

"These sorts of things are never easy," he said, and he meant that too. He slipped his glove back on. "Please extend my sincerest condolences."

"I will, thanks. Did you see Gracie's mom?"

The question took him by surprise. He folded his arms behind his back and leaned slightly forward, a polite smile on his face. Parmelee Gilbert was nothing if not polite. As Laird Haskell's lawyer, he never failed to return my calls and politely decline to comment or to make his client available for questions.

"Shirley McBride?" he said. "I did speak with her, yes."

"Ah, sorry," I said. "Attorney-client privilege?"

He stood straight again, and peered past me down the street. "Would you care for a cup of tea?"

Twin mugs of tea steeped on coasters on Parmelee Gilbert's desk. He sat in a leather chair behind the desk and lifted each of his legs to strip the slickened rubbers off his wingtips. The shoes gleamed with what I assumed was that morning's polish. "I apologize," Gilbert said, while setting the rubbers on a rug, "that I haven't had you in before."

From the straight-backed chair facing his desk, I could have laughed without being rude. Gilbert himself might have laughed with me. He had so thoroughly stonewalled me on my Haskell stories that I had almost given up on calling him. Of course I couldn't actually give up; I had to keep trying, at least so I could tell the faithful readers of the *Pilot* that I had. Each time I called, he would thank me for calling with my "pertinent questions," ask me to give his best to my mother, and promise to get back to me "with the clearest possible response I can offer."

And then, invariably, he would call me at 5:40 p.m., twenty minutes before my deadline, to say, "We're sorry, but Mr. Haskell prefers not to discuss these matters in the press" or "With our apologies, Mr. Haskell is focused exclusively on the positive aspects of this extremely vital project for

Pine County and Starvation Lake." He was a lawyer representing a lawyer. Sometimes I would wonder: Did Gilbert think at all like Haskell? Did he envy Haskell's success? Or envy Haskell himself?

Gilbert always thanked me yet again for giving his client—never him, always his client—the opportunity to comment. He always declined, no matter how or how many times I asked, to say anything further. To my occasional attempts to get him to guide me one way or the other on an off-the-record basis, he would merely say, "With all due respect to you and your colleagues, in my experience there is no such thing as off the record."

I knew reporters at my old paper, the *Times*, and our rival, the *Free Press*, who would have been pleased, even relieved, to have Gilbert's nonresponse; it's so much easier and quicker five minutes before deadline to insert "*so-and-so declined to comment*" than to have to shoehorn in a last-minute point-by-point rebuttal of every fact and nuance in your story without making it a he-said, she-said jumble that threatened readers with whiplash. "*No comment*" made a reporter's job simpler. Unfortunately, simpler had never had much appeal for me. If I had preferred simpler, I never would have left Starvation, never would have gambled away my job in Detroit, never would have left the blessed sinecure of my crease and goalposts and mesh to play wing.

I had to grudgingly respect Parmelee Gilbert for refusing to go off the record. He was correct, of course, that there was no such thing. There was fact and there was fiction and it didn't matter whether you said it was "according to a person familiar with the matter" if the person supposedly familiar was lying or ignorant or stupid. I had known plenty of lawyers and flacks who viewed off the record as an opportunity to dissemble and obfuscate. Gilbert hadn't been terribly helpful, but at least he'd been honest in his unhelpfulness. So I didn't laugh when he apologized for not having me in before.

"You're doing your job," I said. "I just figure you could bill a lot more hours by actually answering my questions."

He smiled. "Milk? Sugar?"

"A little of both, please."

While he finished preparing the tea, I looked around. For a lawyer who had hung his cedar shake shingle on Main Street for more than thirty years, Gilbert's career mementoes were scant. Framed degrees from Michigan Tech, a bachelor's in American history, and the University of Detroit law school decorated the otherwise empty wall to my left. A hot plate rested on the windowsill behind him. On his desk was a telephone, two pens and two sharpened pencils lined up alongside one another, and a blotter calendar neatly jotted with appointments and reminders. On my right, a waist-high bookshelf was lined with law tomes and a few slim editions of a book, *Ghost Towns of Michigan.*

Atop the shelf stood a photograph of a smiling girl in braces and pigtails entwined with white ribbons. She was wearing a cheerleader's blue sweater embroidered with an interlocking "P" and "C" for Pine County High. Her name, I knew, was Carol Jo Gilbert. Had she lived, she would have been in her mid-forties.

When the girl was fourteen, her mother, Gilbert's wife, had taken her downstate on an annual Christmas shopping trip. They went from store to store in the big Northland Center mall north of Detroit, stopping as always at Sanders for lunch. The mother left Carol Jo to finish a chocolate soda while going to a pay phone to let her husband know they were having fun.

Carol Jo wasn't seen again until the ice melted on a pond near Harbor Beach where her killer had dumped her. I remembered hearing about it as a boy, the hushed, anxious whispers, the shaking heads and furrowed brows, while eating breakfast at Audrey's with my mother. Carol Jo's killer was never found.

Two months after Carol Jo was buried, her mother, who had not been seen outside the Gilbert home since the funeral, showed up at Sunday Mass in the middle of the priest's homily. Mom and I, sitting in the front row, heard the murmur rising in the pews behind us and turned to see Mrs. Gilbert, in a wrinkled flannel shirt with the tails out, walking purposefully up the center aisle. She stopped in front of the communion rail. From the lectern astride the altar, Father Emmett gave her a sideways glance but continued with his sermon.

Her first scream stopped him. *You have nothing for me,* she yelled. She raised an arm and pointed at the tabernacle. *You have nothing but death.* Father Emmett stepped away from the lectern toward Mrs. Gilbert—*Mary Jo,* he said—but she kept up her wail as if he weren't there, as if none of us were there. *You are nothing. You are nothing but death.*

Darlene's father and two other men came out from their pews and tried to take Mary Jo Gilbert by the shoulders and settle her down but she pushed them away and continued her keening. Father Emmett hopped over the communion rail and approached her with his hand out, palm down, as if to bless her, but she slapped his hand away. I turned and watched the men drag her down the aisle until my mother twisted me around and told me to mind my own business.

Late that night, Parmelee Gilbert called the police to say his wife had gone to the grocery store hours before and had not come home. Early the next morning, two officers appeared on Gilbert's front doorstep on Ambling Street. They told him his wife had been found in the woods a mile north of the lake. She had used a garden hose to feed the tailpipe exhaust back into her car. After burying Mary Jo, Parmelee Gilbert sold the home where the three of them had lived and bought another house two blocks away.

I had to believe that was why he had invited me in.

Now he walked from his house to his office each morning, Monday through Saturday, and returned home each night around six, carrying a brown leather satchel under one arm. His caseload was mostly mundane and domestic—probate, real estate closings, property tax appeals. He politely declined to handle divorces or disputes between neighbors, surrendering that business to lawyers in other towns. He was a fixture at town council and county commission meetings but rarely if ever showed up for more social events like hockey games or euchre tournaments or even the annual Kiwanis Christmas brunch. Such aloofness was normally frowned upon in Starvation Lake, but Parmelee Gilbert was forgiven, more because of Carol Jo than his wife.

He picked up his tea and gestured for me to do the same. "You inquired about Mrs. McBride," he said.

I sipped. He'd gotten the sugar just right. "Yeah."

"Please. I want to make it clear that she is not my client."

"Got it. But I heard—"

"You heard that she is curious about the existence of a life insurance policy connected with the unfortunate demise of her daughter."

"That's right."

He propped a wingtip against the edge of his desk and pulled his left sock taut on a pale calf. "I am not in position to confirm that there was or wasn't a life insurance policy involved in this matter," he said. He repeated the sock pull on his right leg. "But I can confirm that I have agreed, as of this morning, to represent the Haverford Life Insurance Company of Traverse City."

"This morning?"

He sat up straight, picked up his mug, and looked at me over the top of it. "That is what I said."

"But you can't confirm that Gracie had a life insurance policy?"

"That would, as you say, violate the attorney-client privilege."

"We are on the record, yes?"

"Unless I say otherwise."

So he was confirming that Gracie had a life insurance policy without leaving his fingerprints, all while staying comfortably on the record. Why else would Gilbert have been hired that very morning?

I imagined Shirley McBride storming into his office, demanding her cut of the insurance proceeds, threatening to go to the paper, which of course she already had. Now Gilbert was trying to keep things calm and accurate and within his control.

"Sorry," I said. "This probably isn't comfortable for you."

"It's my job."

"So Shirley is the beneficiary?"

Gilbert gave me a tiny smile, then took it back.

"I didn't say there was a life insurance policy. However, just for your information, if there was in fact a policy, I would not be at liberty to tell you who any beneficiaries might be, as that would indeed violate attorney-client privilege as well as the potential beneficiaries' privacy."

"Understood."

I wished I had looked more carefully through the file folders and papers in the cabinet in Gracie's Zam shed. The policy might have been in there. What a dope I am, I thought.

"In addition," Gilbert said, "strictly for your background information, life insurance policies are frequently voided in cases where the insured has inflicted death on him- or herself. In effect, there would be no beneficiaries in such a case."

"Right. And you think Gracie was a suicide."

"Gus, for the record, I have not said that the deceased is in any way related to my being retained by the Haverford Company. I trust that what-ever you write, if you write anything, will reflect that."

"Understood. But why would someone who planned to kill themself bother with a life insurance policy?"

He sat back in his chair and folded his hands in his lap.

"Off the record?" he said.

"Off the record?"

"Yes," Gilbert said, as if he went off the record as routinely as he tied his tie every morning. He looked down at his folded hands. "As you can imag-ine, I feel terrible for Mrs. McBride and everyone who knew the girl. The loss is no less, whatever the cause." He stopped. I waited. He looked up, his eyes flitting to the photo of his daughter before returning to me. "But who can divine the workings of a single human heart? Who really knows what a person thinks and believes when he or she decides to do whatever they do?"

I thought of Gracie sitting on the edge of her cot in the Zam shed, alone, weary, bedraggled, alcoholic. Why would anyone have wanted to kill her? Who could possibly have had a motive?

"Yes," I said. "But you have a client with money on the line."

"I am not speaking for any client."

"Sorry. Will I see you at town council Wednesday?"

"Back on the record. Always possible. My clients frequently have busi-ness before the council."

"I'm sure I'll be there."

"Well then." He stood. "I have an appointment to get to."

"How can I help you?"

Pine County sheriff Dingus Aho leaned back against the front edge of his gray metal desk, thick arms folded across his thick midsection, one hand twirling a curl of his mustache. The room smelled of Tiparillos and, strangely, perfume. Dingus had kept me waiting outside his office for half an hour. He didn't usually make me wait. I had only an hour or so to file my stories and write up the other junk waiting back at the newsroom. I cut to the chase.

"No way it's suicide."

"You knew her," Dingus said. "What do you think?"

Since I had returned to Starvation a year and a half before, Dingus and

I had come to an unspoken trust that we would not deliberately waste each other's time. Even in the typical cop-and-reporter cat and mouse, there was purpose. He had his, I had mine, and he had learned that I might actually know things that he did not. In the hallway outside his office hung a framed copy of a *Pilot* front page. The banner headline read, "Police Uncover Porn Ring." We had helped each other on that story. Dingus could have had a byline.

Darlene merely tolerated my relationship with Dingus. I knew it rankled her that the sheriff could seem more forthcoming with me than with his own deputies. I told her that a big part of his job was managing information, and sometimes he had to pay more attention to someone digging for it than to people who were beholden to him for their jobs. "Bullshit," she replied. "It's because you're a boy."

"Hell, Dingus," I said. "I didn't know Gracie. She didn't live here for years."

"You guys were in Detroit together."

"No. We were just there at the same time. We might as well have been living on different planets."

He stopped twirling his mustache and squinted one eye. "And you had no idea whatsoever what she was doing down there?"

"Nope."

"You know, of course, I can't talk about an ongoing investigation."

I'd heard that line before. He wouldn't have had me into his office if he didn't want me to know something. Or wanted something from me.

"What's with the leaks to Channel Eight?" I said. "You want to get on TV? Or are you just trying to help D'Alessio get laid?"

Dingus ignored that and moved around behind his desk. His swivel chair groaned as he sat. He moved a half-filled doughnut box aside, reached into a drawer, and came out with a glossy black pamphlet. "I like this," he said, waggling it in front of his face. "Some vagrant gave it to me in Florida when I was down there for a conference."

I saw the title on the pamphlet cover: *Hiding from God.* Dingus read aloud: "'When we open the newspaper, we see for the most part bad news. We see more of the dark side of humanity than the good and decent side.'" He looked over the top of the pamphlet at me. "Here's the best line: 'The newspaper is simply a snapshot of the darkness that is within each one of us.'"

"I was definitely thinking that the other day as I was typing up the St. Jude Society's lost-and-found list."

Dingus set the pamphlet on his blotter and pointed at my face. "Don't give me that smart-ass bull. Your sister's dead and all you care about is your stupid little scoops?"

His singsong voice sometimes made it hard to take him seriously. Not at the moment. His mood tasted like all the sharp metal in the room, the angle-iron chairs, the star points on his badge, the shelf brackets, his pistol.

"She wasn't my sister," I said.

"For all intents and purposes, she damned well was. Nobody took better care of her than your mother. I had the distinct privilege of being reminded of that about an hour ago when Gracie's other mother was sitting in that chair you're in now."

"Shirley?" That explained the perfume.

Dingus snatched a yellow Post-it note off his blotter and slapped it down on the desk in front of me. I leaned in. The perfume filled my nostrils. Shirley usually used enough to deodorize a ballroom. I peered at her scribble, which listed to the right:

MUST TALK. URGINT NEWS. PLEAS CALL 231 555 3671.

"This is for me?" I said. "She's threatening you?"

"Hell's bells, it would take me all night to tell you how many times she's told me she'd be going to the *Pilot* with this little birch or that. She's the least of my worries."

I ignored the vibrating cell phone in my pocket.

"What did she want?"

He jumped up from his chair and paced to the back of the room, where a pair of particle-board shelves held cans of pepper spray, an assortment of black-and-chrome-colored handcuffs, and a photograph of Dingus's ex-wife and current girlfriend, Barbara. "She wants me to find a murderer," he said. His voice turned sarcastic. "She wants her daughter *avenged*. She wants *closure*."

I imagined Shirley pounding her fat pink fist on Dingus's desk, the bracelets she bought out of the clearance bin at Glen's rattling, her bleached blond perm bouncing. She'd be wearing Kmart designer jeans pushing the zipper flap open and one of those $17.50 THROW AWAY THAT CORK! sweatshirts from the Just One More Saloon. Around town it was said that Shirley had sold her dead husband's Purple Heart medal for $33.50 on an Internet auction site. It wasn't hard to believe.

"She wants the life insurance proceeds," I said. "And she's going to raise a stink about it. But there is a murderer, isn't there, Dingus?"

"I'll be goddamned," he said, turning away from me.

A light on Dingus's phone started to blink. He didn't notice. He was pacing from the shelf to his desk and back. The light went off and Dingus stopped in the middle of the room and held his arms out wide. His face flushed red.

"Why?" he said. "Why the hell did she have to come back here?" He pointed at his phone. "That thing's been ringing all day. Every damn member of the county commission and the town council's calling to tell me, 'Leave it alone, Dingus' and 'Just let it lie, Dingus.'"

"Nobody wants a murder around here," I said. "They have more important things to worry about."

"Shirley's just trailer trash to them, not worth the overtime," Dingus said. "That doesn't surprise me one bit. But they're calling Doc Joe, too." The county coroner. "They're not supposed to do that. Doc, he gets the faintest whiff they might cut his budget, he'll sign whatever they want."

"Are they threatening to whack you too?"

"Funny you should ask."

Dingus stepped to his desk, grabbed a file folder, and plucked out a sheet of paper that had come over a fax machine. He handed it to me. "You can't have this," he said. "But you can read it."

The fax had been sent at 11:18 that morning. It was signed by town council chairman Elvis Bontrager. The town, which had long ago eliminated its own police force for lack of funds, now relied on the sheriff's department and contributed to its budget. Elvis's letter said an allocation of money for the purchase of two new police cruisers might have to be "temporarily delayed" because of "reconciliation issues" that had recently cropped up.

Damn, I thought. Laird Haskell, who probably didn't know and certainly wouldn't have cared, was picking Dingus's pocket. Instead of paying for better public safety, the council was about to give $100,000 to a supposed millionaire so he could build a hockey rink. Great for the story I was about to write. Not so great for Starvation. Unless, of course, the River Rats won a state championship. Then everything would be fine, and it wouldn't matter to a soul if the local cops had to resort to bicycles to do their jobs.

"That sucks," I said, handing the letter back. "They can just do that?"

"They can just do that," Dingus said. "And that's not all. They're talking with the county commission about more cuts. Just between us."

I thought about Darlene. For all of her carping about Dingus and the other "boys" at the department, she loved being a police officer. She would hate to lose her job so the town could have a shiny new hockey arena.

"Why do they give a rip?"

Dingus might have been the only person in town—except, perhaps, my mother—who didn't care about hockey. He'd never played it, didn't watch it, and probably thought it just caused him a lot of grief, what with all the postgame bar fights and drunks steering their way out of the rink parking lot.

"Who knows?" he said. "Maybe they think a big murder investigation'll spook their bankers and that rich fellow will walk and they won't get their precious rink. I don't know what the hell these people think."

"What are you going to do?"

He sat down heavily in his chair. His phone started blinking again. "I plan to proceed with—"

There was a knock at Dingus's door. It opened and Deputy Frank D'Alessio ducked his head in. He gave me a *What the fuck are you doing here?* look before telling Dingus, "Sheriff, you have a call."

"I can see that," Dingus said. "Who is it?"

D'Alessio glanced at me and said, "Uh, a council member."

"Which council member, Deputy?"

"Chairman Bontrager."

"Not now."

"He said it's important."

"Tell him to go cut a hole in the lake and jump in."

D'Alessio grinned. "I'll tell him you'll call back when you can."

Dingus watched the door close.

"So," I said, "you're not really going to charge Soupy, are you? You just leaked that to buy yourself some time with the politicians."

Dingus shrugged his acknowledgment. At least he hadn't used me like he had Channel Eight. "I could still charge him with obstruction, though."

"He's not talking?"

"No, he's—excuse me."

A different light on his phone was blinking. Dingus picked up the phone and turned in his chair until he faced away from me. But I could still hear him, as he undoubtedly knew. "What's up, Doc?" he said.

A full minute passed. "OK. Let me know. Thanks." He turned around and hung up the phone. "Goddammit—why did she have to come back here?" He said it less to me than to himself. "You know, whatever happened to that girl—and we are off the record here, son—whatever happened to that girl has nothing whatsoever to do with the people of this town. Nothing at all."

"Why don't you send someone down to Detroit?"

"No," he said. "They're not going to have that."

"They?"

He waved at his phone. "The whole lot of them." He shook his head. "I told her not to come back here. I told her never come back."

"What are you talking about?"

He pushed back up from his desk and walked to a file cabinet in the back corner of the office. He stretched a key ring on a retractable tether from his gun belt to the top drawer and unlocked it. He took out a brown accordion file, put it under one arm, locked the drawer, walked to the door, and opened it.

"This way," he said.

I followed him out of his office. We walked down the corridor past the entrance, me glancing into offices to see if I might catch a glimpse of Darlene. I did not. At the end of the hallway we reached the locked door that opened into the Pine County Jail. Dingus peered through the little window crosshatched with steel. The door buzzed and Dingus pulled it open. He turned to me then and casually handed me the accordion folder.

"Hang on to this," he said. "Do not lose it. Wait here."

I took the folder and stood waiting, hoping no one would walk up and ask me what I was doing with a folder stamped CONFIDENTIAL on both sides. I stuffed it under an arm and glanced up at the surveillance camera screwed into the wall above the door, peering down on me like a crow on a telephone wire.

The door buzzed again. It opened and Soupy stepped through, Dingus right behind him. Past his shoulder I saw Darlene walking away and had to stop myself from calling after her.

"I'm releasing Mr. Campbell to you," Dingus said. He turned to Soupy. "I'm not through with you. If you even think about taking any out-of-town trips, we'll have you back in here before you hit the interstate. Got it?"

"Got it," Soupy said.

"You tell them anything?" I said.

Soupy and I had just pulled out of the department lot, my headlamps carving the blackness into cones of white.

"I'm going broke, man," he said. "Just get me back to my bar."

He wasn't going to talk. Not now. There'd be time to push him later.

There were all sorts of questions I hadn't gotten the chance to ask Dingus: What about that rejection letter Gracie had supposedly gotten? Why was she wearing only one shoe when she died? How did she get up into the shoe tree? Where was the ladder? Where was the car? Dingus might not have answered any of them. He usually gave me only what he wanted me to know, so that I might, in doing my own job, help him.

So I was dying to see what was in that accordion folder I'd stuck beneath my seat.

I glanced at Soupy. The way he was staring out his passenger window, I had to wonder if he was actually distraught over Gracie's death, if he realized, facing the cops, that Gracie actually had mattered for more than whatever she did for him in bed, or on a Zamboni.

We rode in silence for a mile. Then, without turning to me, Soupy said, "Got something to tell you."

"What's that?"

"I'm not yanking your chain."

"About what?"

He shifted in his seat until he was looking out the windshield. "They put me in that room where the prisoners see their lawyers," he said. I'd been in the room once for an interview myself. There was a table bolted to the floor, a few hard-backed chairs, a single window covered with a metal cage. "I'm looking out at the back lot, and who rolls up but Meat."

"Jason?"

"Yep."

My heart was suddenly racing. "And?"

"He wasn't there to pick up his safe-snowmobiling certificate, Trap."

He told me he saw Darlene come out to meet Jason. She wasn't wearing a coat. I imagined her holding her arms tight around her bosom, her breath billowing around her head. Of course Soupy couldn't hear anything. Then someone came to take him to another room.

"Well," I said, "they probably have divorce details to work out."

"Maybe. Didn't notice any lawyers out there."

I kept my eyes on the unfurling white road, my lights flashing on the lower halves of tree trunks whisking by in the dusk.

"Thought you'd want to know," Soupy said.

"Yeah. Thanks." The lamps along Main Street were coming into view ahead. "They didn't, at least when—?"

"No. No touchy feely. But . . . I don't know."

"You don't know what?"

"Looked to me like he wants her back or something."

I cackled. It came out sounding like someone else. "That ain't going to happen."

I dropped Soupy at Enright's and went around the block to the *Pilot* back lot, where I sat in the dark checking the messages on my cell phone.

The three council members I had called said they would have no comment on whatever story I was working on. A fourth whom I had not called also left a message saying she wasn't interested in commenting. I had to figure they knew what I was going to ask.

The fifth message came from Darlene. She said she had to work late, don't bother making spaghetti dinner, she'd catch up with me at the Rats game, or later. She loved me. She had to go.

Relax, I told myself. She still had issues to work through. She wasn't going anywhere. Everything would be all right. I'd try her again later. We'd lock her door against the night and hide beneath her blankets.

I switched on an inside light and pulled the accordion folder out from under my seat. A label pasted to the top of the folder was inscribed in felt-tip pen: "McBRIDE, Grace Maureen, 08/26/95."

I reached inside and pulled out a stapled bundle of pages, maybe fifteen in all. It was an official Pine County Sheriff's Department report. I flipped immediately to the last page and, sure enough, there was the signature of then-deputy Dingus Aho. "Fucking-ay," I said.

I looked at my watch: 5:21. I had thirty-nine minutes to write two stories and a few briefs. No sweat, I thought. But, as much as I wanted to see whatever Dingus wanted me to see, I did not have time then to sit and read that police report. There was no chance of it going in that night's paper, and if I didn't get my work done on deadline, I'd have a call from Jim Kerasopoulous waiting for me at eight o'clock the next morning. I had no desire to talk to Kerasopoulous, not about my dedication to my job, not about the future of the *Pilot*, not about the weather.

I slipped the folder back under the seat and started across the lot toward the newsroom. By now Philo was probably panicking. I started to write the Gracie story in my head. I wasn't about to write the standard "apparent suicide" story, but, given what I had heard at the sheriff's department, I had to be careful about using the word "murder." *Foul play*, I typed on my imaginary keyboard, *may have played a role in the macabre death of a Starvation Lake woman . . .*

I stopped in my tracks.

Starvation Lake woman?

I turned and trotted back to my truck, unlocked the door. The inside light came on. I reached under the seat and slipped the police report out of the accordion folder. I wanted to see just one thing. It was typed on the very first page, just below Gracie's name and house address: "Melvindale, Michigan."

Melvindale sat just south of Detroit on the northwest border of River Rouge. River Rouge was the old steel town where the X'd-out calendar hanging over Gracie's bed had come from.

I knew Melvindale. I'd played hockey there when I lived downstate and drank in a bar called Nasty Melvin's. I hid the folder and locked my truck. Walking back to the newsroom, I had a feeling I might be visiting Nasty Melvin's again.

eleven

I knew there was a problem when I heard Philo say, "Oh, God. They've stopped the presses." He was staring into his computer screen, hands frozen over his keyboard, his face a crimped mask of worry.

"Why?" I said.

Only once had I heard anyone actually say the words "Stop the presses" without sarcasm. It wasn't because the pope had died or a passenger jet had plunged into the Detroit River. It was because some layout guy pasting up pages got miffed at his boss for not letting him take the night off to go to a Tigers game.

At the *Detroit Times*, we were running a wire story inside the paper one night about a man who'd been convicted of sodomy. We ran a mug shot and, beneath it, short captions that identified him as so-and-so from Wichita, "convicted sodomist." But instead of the sodomist's photo, the ticked-off layout guy inserted a picture of a well-known Detroit industrialist named Cochran. There were a few nervous laughs until the executive editor caught wind of it. He didn't actually say, "Stop the presses," he said, "Jesus H. Christ, we're all going to get fired." His secretary then picked up her phone and called the printing plant and gave the command. The layout guy got suspended for a week, but the suspension was set aside after his union appealed.

Philo looked across the room at me. "They're stopping it for your stories."

Uh-oh, I thought. I'd had stories spiked before, but never two on the same day. "Which?"

"Both. Shit, shit, triple shit. I knew I should have looked at those."

"I thought you did."

"No. No time. You didn't give me any time." He picked up his keyboard as if he might slam it down. He reconsidered, let it drop lightly back onto its tray. "Goddammit, Gus."

"Sorry, Philo." Although I wasn't, really. "I wrote the stories and I'll stand by them. Not your fault."

"You might not have much to stand by. They're totally redoing the hockey coach story and"—he squinted at his screen—"the dead lady story too, cutting that to a brief."

"A brief? Who's 'they'?"

"Who do you think?"

The call from Kerasopoulos came ten minutes later. Philo kept his voice down but I overheard him say "at least half an hour"—which I took to mean how late I'd been—and repeat "Yes, of course" and "Sorry" four or five times. Finally he hit his hold button and turned to me. His expression vacillated between angry and shattered.

"It's the boss," he said.

I hit the blinking button and picked up my phone.

"What's up, Jim?"

"Please tell me who your source is." Issuing from the speakerphone in his Traverse City office, Kerasopoulos's voice sounded even more like a foghorn than usual.

"I'm sorry, what was that?"

"Your source. Who's your source?"

"Would you mind getting off the speakerphone?"

"I would." So he wasn't alone. Fat ass, I thought. I thought it not solely because Kerasopoulos indeed had a fat ass, but because he was a fat ass through and through with his fat-assed way of thinking that whatever he did or thought or said was absolutely correct. I knew it was stupid to think this, but I couldn't help myself.

"Apologies, Jim, but I'm reluctant to discuss sourcing when I don't know who else is listening in." I was bound to disclose my sources— or at least most of them—to a superior, but I didn't have to be careless about it, especially in an echo chamber like Starvation.

"Excuse me?" he said.

I imagined him leaning his double-wide torso out over his conference table, cheap paintings of white-tailed deer and mallards on the paneled wall behind his salt-and-pepper head.

"Which story are you talking about, Jim?"

I heard a click—the hold button—followed by silence. I figured he was inquiring about the story on Jason Esper being named coach of the River Rats. About midway through the story, low enough where Kerasopoulos might not notice it, I'd slipped in a couple of paragraphs about the town council planning to convene in private to consider the Haskell loan. I felt pretty good about it. The taxpayers of Starvation needed to hear it, even if they didn't want to.

There was another click and Kerasopoulos came back on.

"The room is clear, sir," he said, though he remained on speakerphone. "I would advise you not to test my patience any further. Now, please tell me who told you the rink developer wants a loan from the Starvation Lake council."

That was easy, and even if Haskell was eavesdropping, I didn't mind outing him. "The developer himself, Laird Haskell," I said.

"And on what basis were you speaking with him?"

Kerasopoulos, who had set up the meeting, knew damn well what basis. "At the time, we were off the record," I said, "but—"

"So you just violated that agreement willy-nilly? This is not Detroit, Gus."

Oh, man, I thought, this was like having the puck on my stick in front of an empty net. My ready reply had popped into my head while I was talking with Dingus. "Sorry, Jim, but Haskell promised me the scoop on the hockey coach. Then he went and leaked it to Channel Eight, so the off-the-record deal's off."

"That's your answer?"

"He broke the agreement, I didn't."

"Well, Mr. Big City Reporter, you are an idiot."

"Excuse me?"

"You are an idiot. Mr. Haskell did not leak that story—I did."

The "I did" echoed through the speakerphone and reverberated in my ears. If what he said was true, I had truly fucked up.

"I'm sorry, how did you—"

"As chief executive of a company that oversees what I consider to be a sacred public trust, I try to keep myself abreast of everything happening in our communities," he said. "When I heard about the new coach, I thought it was important enough news that we shouldn't make our viewers and readers wait to hear it. You seem more concerned about pursuing your various vendettas against citizens who are trying to accomplish something good for the community."

Citizens trying to buy a pile of ads in your paper with the community's money, I thought. "They're not vendettas," I said.

"As for the other story, I'm not about to have the *Pine County Pilot* indulge your lurid conspiracy theories and phantom sourcing. 'Sources familiar with the case'? What the hell does that mean? Do you think this is the *Washington Post*? Until someone from the appropriate police department says for the record that they are investigating a murder, it's a suicide, do you understand? We put out newspapers here, not mystery novels."

"All the story said is that police *think* foul play *may* have been involved, and that's absolutely true."

"Apparent suicide, three grafs, inside. Philo will take care of it." I looked over at Philo, who looked away from me, his phone on his ear. Fuck me, I thought. "Frankly, Gus," Kerasopoulous continued, "I have zero time— zero, is that clear?—for your vendettas. Please plan on being in my office tomorrow morning."

"Wait, there's—"

"Nine o'clock. Sharp."

He ended the call. I hung up my phone. Philo was still on his. I'd hoped to read my leftover mail before heading to Enright's for a beer before the River Rats game, but I just grabbed my coat and went for the back door. As I swung it open, Philo called out, "Late for a drain commission meeting?"

"Fuck you, Philo," I said as I slammed the door shut behind me.

The crust of snow covering the beach splintered beneath my boots as I trudged toward the shore of the lake. The serrated ice dug into my shins. I stopped at the frozen edge of the lake and finally buttoned my coat. I took a deep breath, felt the cold air singe my lungs.

I liked the lake in winter. Of course I loved the lake when the summer sun lit the water and the afternoon music was boat motors and ice cubes being dropped into glasses and Ernie Harwell telling us a young fellow from Rawsonville would take that foul ball home as a souvenir. But the winter beach took me into a cocoon of wind and wet and cold that kept out the tinny claptrap surrounding the town's preoccupations of the moment.

I'd barged out of the *Pilot*, snatched the accordion folder from the truck and scrambled down South Street, furious with Kerasopoulos and Philo, but furious mostly with myself. I had assumed that Haskell burned me, when in fact it was Kerasopoulos. My assumption hadn't been unreasonable. But of course Kerasopoulos knew about the coach announcement, and probably all about my meeting with Haskell, how Haskell and I hadn't really become best buddies. So Kerasopoulos did what he did.

But I had assumed nevertheless, which was unforgivably lazy and stupid—a mistake, I told myself, that I never would have made back at the *Times*. Here I was unmarried, no kids, thirty-five, living at Mom's house, dating a married woman. No wonder I was already getting soft.

I walked toward the old marina Soupy had sold out of his family. Two streetlamps hovered at either edge of the eight concrete docks invisible beneath the snow. Just inside the first lamp's pool of light, a brass bell fringed with corrosion and ice sat silent on a stanchion. I sat down with the bell at my back and looked around to see that I was alone. I slipped the Pine County Sheriff's Department police report, S-950863, out of the accordion folder.

An ambulance was called to the Hill-Top Motel at approximately 2:14 a.m. on that muggy Saturday, August 26, 1995. The date sounded familiar, though I didn't immediately recognize why.

Dingus' neat block lettering made it easy to read. I admired his meticulous reporting.

The Hill-Top offered seventeen small rooms, $23.95 a night, in a peeling one-story building atop a low rise along U.S. 131. It was a favorite of truckers making runs between Chicago and the Soo Locks in the Upper Peninsula, and of lovers from Mancelona and Kalkaska conducting illicit affairs.

The owner, a man named Clarence Kruger, was a bald sixty-two-year-old with shrubs of white hair sprouting around his ears. He was at the office desk when a silver Jaguar, top down, roared up the gravel drive shortly before midnight. The couple in the Jaguar weren't the kind of people Kruger preferred to have stay in his motel, or at least that's what he would later tell Dingus.

The woman got out of the car and wobbled up to Kruger on high heels. She wore a silken white summer dress splashed with polka dots the size and color of strawberries. The man in the Jaguar shouted at her across the lot.

"Cash," he said. "No neighbor." He seemed to have an accent.

Kruger noticed the neck of a bottle of gin protruding from the woman's purse. "A room with nobody in the rooms next to it, please," she told him.

Number 7 was such a room, but Kruger had just repainted it. He considered telling the woman he had no vacancy at all, but it had been a slow summer, what with the drizzly weekends, so he took her three five-dollar bills and nine ones and handed over the key to number 14. "There's someone in thirteen but nobody in fifteen," he said. "Best I can do." The woman combed her hair with one hand while waiting for her nickel change.

The phone at his desk woke Kruger an hour later. His copy of *Boxing Illustrated* slipped off his chest and fell to the floor. He snatched up the phone. "Hill-Top," he said. "How can I help you?"

"Room thirteen here," came the man's voice on the other end of the line. He was whispering. "There's some scary noises coming out of the room next to me. Sounds like somebody's choking or something."

Kruger sat up in his chair and peered across the lot. Of course the rooms were all dark. He told the man in 13 he'd look into it.

He dialed number 14. Kruger counted the rings. Ten. He hung up and redialed. Eight more rings. The woman answered. She sounded upset. "It's . . . oh my God . . . please," she said.

"What's the matter, ma'am?" Kruger said, but she just kept sputtering incoherently and then hung up.

Kruger plucked his master key off the hook beneath his desk. He walked out to number 14 and leaned an ear against the door. The woman inside seemed to be weeping. "Wake up," she kept saying. "Wake up, please, wake up."

Kruger decided against knocking. He walked back to his office and called an ambulance, knowing it would also bring the sheriff or a deputy. He locked the door to his office, turned off the lights, and waited in the darkness, watching through the slatted blinds over his window. He put one hand to his heart. It was pounding. As he would tell Dingus, he'd had plenty of trouble in the Super 8s he had owned in Flint. How far north did a man have to travel to get away from it?

The phone rang again. Kruger let it ring three times before picking up. "Yeah?"

"Jesus, guy," the man in 13 said. "It sounds like they're tearing the room apart next door. I just heard a hell of a crash."

"Help is on the way, sir," Kruger said. "Please be sure your door is locked and the dead bolt is in place."

He heard the first siren just as the door on number 14 burst open and a man, naked and barefoot, staggered out into the light and fell. Kruger stood up from his chair.

The man crawled haltingly around on the pavement outside 14, grabbing at his throat, his skin glowing yellow in the wash of the bare bulb next to the door. The woman emerged, still in her summer dress, a shoulder strap fallen onto her arm. She dropped to her knees and placed a hand on the back of the man's neck. She leaned down to his ear and said something. He shook his head no, pushed her away. She leaned in again. He pushed her away harder. She stood and backed into the doorway and pulled the shoulder strap back over her arm.

The door on number 13 opened. A man came out. Kruger considered going out himself, almost put his hand to the doorknob, but the siren was growing louder.

He thought better of it.

The man from 13 was barefoot in jeans and a wrinkled white V-neck undershirt. His left forearm bore a faded, shapeless tattoo.

The naked man slowly stood. Kruger saw that he had a penis like a section of garden hose, much darker than the rest of his ashen body. Kruger grabbed the crank on his window and opened it enough to hear. The sirens, more than one now, swelled in his ears.

"Jesus H. Christ, man, you all right?" the tattooed man was saying. The naked man seized his penis in his right hand and yanked something rubbery and black away. He tossed it at the woman, who caught it and threw it into the room. "What in hell is going on here?" the tattooed man said.

The naked man stepped forward and said something Kruger couldn't make out. The woman clapped a hand over her mouth, laughing. The tattooed man took a step backward toward his room. The naked man offered him a hand. As he did, the light illuminated a scar on the right side of his neck the shape of a jagged crescent moon.

"Get the hell away," the tattooed man said.

It happened so fast that Kruger would have trouble explaining it to the police. The naked man stepped forward and took the tattooed man by his shoulders and hammered the butt of his head into the other man's face. The tattooed man staggered backward, grasping at his nose and cursing as blood spurted between his fingers. The naked man watched for a few seconds. Kruger thought he looked amused. Then the naked man turned and ran to the Jaguar, snickering as he hopped gingerly across the gravel. The woman gave chase but he leapt over the door into the driver's seat and stomped on the gas. She threw up her arms to shield her face against the flying pebbles.

The woman was uncooperative with Deputy Sheriff Dingus Aho, refusing, at first, even to acknowledge that she was Grace Maureen McBride. She denied knowing anything about the peculiar equipment the police found inside number 14, insisting it had been there when they checked in.

An eyebolt had been screwed into a stud inside the wall just above the bed, about three inches below the ceiling. Hanging from the bolt the police found shreds of sheet that appeared to have been torn from the bed in the room. The bed had been stripped to a bare mattress on which police found bits of drywall plaster and a tangle of frayed yellow twine. The materials were marked as evidence and sent to the state crime lab in Grayling for further analysis. Dingus's report noted that the black rubbery item the naked man had removed from his penis appeared to be a vacuum cleaner attachment.

The ambulance took the tattooed man to a hospital in Traverse City. No charges were filed against Gracie, despite Kruger's protests that he was entitled to recompense for the shredded sheet and the damage to the wall in number 14. A warrant was issued for the arrest of the naked man, but if he was apprehended, that was not reflected in Dingus's written report.

Gracie at first told police that she did not know the naked man's name, but she apparently slipped and referred to him as "YAR-ek", or at least that's how Dingus wrote it in his report. I had never heard such a name before. Gracie then insisted that she really did not know this man well, that his last name was too long to pronounce or to spell, that he came from somewhere downstate but she could not remember exactly where.

Dingus's report said he released Gracie into the custody of Beatrice

Carpenter. When I read this, I looked away from the pages and stared down the beach to my left, in the direction of my mother's house. I imagined Dingus walking Gracie up to the back door, his hand lightly on her elbow, the kitchen lights coming on, my mother in her fuzzy blue robe hugging Gracie and thanking Dingus, who would have kept his lights off so as not to alert the neighbors.

My mother had never said a word to me about this.

Then I remembered why the date—August 26, 1995—had resonated. Darlene and Jason had married on that Saturday. I had heard about the wedding from Soupy but of course had not been invited and remained in Detroit that weekend, working.

My mother later asked me if I had heard that Darlene had wed. By then it was Labor Day weekend and we were sitting on the bench swing that overlooked the lake. I took a long sip on my can of beer and told her, yes, I had heard. Mom then told me the wedding had been nice, but nothing special, which was her way of letting me know that she was sorry—not for herself but for me—that I had not been at the altar with Darlene.

Darlene never said anything about the incident at the Hill-Top Motel. She may not have known about it. In August of 1995, she hadn't yet moved to the sheriff's department; she worked then for the Bellaire Police.

I scanned Dingus's report again quickly, turning it over and back, letting the wind ruffle the corners of the pages. As I was slipping it back into the accordion folder, I noticed a piece of notebook paper crumpled inside.

I pulled it out. Someone had written on it in neat block letters:

J Vend
26669 Harman Street
Melvindale Michigan 48122

twelve

The old rink shuddered with cheers as I walked in.

Through the glass doors between the lobby and the arena, I saw Taylor Haskell glide away from his net with the puck cradled against his chest in his catching glove, his stick held high to ward off opponents who might think of giving him a little after-the-whistle bump. Three young River Rats in their blue-and-gold uniforms coalesced around him, whacking his leg pads with their sticks as Taylor flipped the puck to a referee. Whistles trilled and Taylor returned to his net. The stands exploded again with applause.

The scoreboard said River Rats 1, Maroons 0.

I'd had to park in the First Presbyterian lot a quarter mile from the arena because cops were waving vehicles away from the jammed rink lot. Pickups and SUVs lined the road shoulders for two hundred yards in either direction. A handmade sign taped to the arena's double-door entrance announced TONIGHT'S GAME SOLD OUT! Luckily, as a Rats alumnus I needed no ticket, regardless of my allowing that title-blowing goal in '81.

I squeezed into the crowd lining the glass to the left of Taylor Haskell. Though I didn't play goalie anymore, when I watched a game I still liked to be near the furious action around the net. Be they pros or teens or squirts in jerseys that hung to their shin guards, I liked to see the expressions on their faces, hear the shit-talking between opponents, watch the goaltender try to keep a clear line of vision to the puck through all of the crisscrossing bodies.

From up in the bleachers, hockey looks like a game of savage grace and swift beauty, which it is, but only up close can you see how hunger and poise and guile and anger can make a player who lacks wheels and hands the best player on the ice at any given moment, sometimes the moment that decides a game. Only up close can you see the difference between someone who knows how to play ice hockey and someone who is a genuine hockey player.

As the skaters glided into the face-off circle to his left, awaiting the next drop of the puck, Taylor skated slowly back and forth between his posts, settling himself after his last save. HASKELL read the white-and-gold nameplate across the back of his shoulders, over the numeral 19. Goaltenders usually wore number 1 or 30 or 31 or 35, but I had heard that Taylor wore 19 because it was the number of his favorite Red Wing, Steve Yzerman, and of his most hated Red Wing opponent, the wily sniper Joe Sakic of the Colorado Avalanche. I had never heard of a kid wearing the number of a player he didn't like; I guessed Taylor had a mind of his own.

The teams lined up at the face-off dot to Taylor's left. He got into his squat, square to the dot, his catching glove open at his left shoulder, his stick pressing flat against the ice. I wondered if he had always been a goaltender. Many a player becomes a goalie by default: as a six- or seven-year-old, he's the weakest skater on the frozen lake or the flooded backyard, so he gets stuck standing at one end of the rink, stopping pucks and jumping up and down on his blades to keep warm when the action's at the other end. But many goalies develop into strong and agile skaters who can stay with the fleetest defensemen and forwards on their teams, even while wearing all that extra armor. And some can shoot as hard as any of them, too, for their arms and wrists have grown sinewy wielding that big stick with those potholder gloves.

But, at least on the ice, they remain alone, always.

I'd thought I quit tending goal because I was tired of waiting around for things to happen. Which is what goalies do, a lot of the time. But now, as the referee dropped the puck and I followed it between one center's skates to a winger's stick blade and off the high glass and outside the blue line where the River Rat center gave chase against a Marquette defenseman, I thought maybe I had stopped because I no longer wanted to feel alone.

In the dressing room, in the hockey shop, in the tavern, the goalie is one of the boys. On the ice he is stranded, lost inside his bloated pads, hiding his face behind a mask. When he gives up a goal his teammates figure he should have stopped, he is alone, circling his crease, dousing himself from his water bottle, wishing he had another chance at the shot he was sure he had with the toe of his skate until it hit someone's knee and deflected just inside the post.

He knows that on the bench the other guys are muttering about the pylon or sieve or funnel between the pipes. He knows that even if he had a chance to explain—the puck took a funny hop, the defenseman left a guy uncovered—he would not be understood. Because nobody sees the game as a goalie does: as a low, flat, horizontal puzzle of bodies and blind spots and caroms and bounces that is constantly being assembled and disassembled on his left, his right, behind him, his left again, in front of him, beneath him, down low, up high. All of which he feels responsible for trying to control. Even if he isn't, really. Even if it's ultimately impossible to control, or even make sense of.

Not terribly unlike my day job. Or my life.

Marquette's number 6 collected the puck and slapped it across the rink to his defensive partner, number 4. Beyond the boards behind him I noticed Darlene and Deputy Skip Catledge standing in uniform at the entrance to the Zamboni shed. No yellow police tape was in sight. The Zamboni driver was dead but the game would go on.

Number 4 shoveled the puck right back to 6. High above 6's helmeted head at the top of the bleachers perched the private box Laird Haskell had built. A banner proclaiming "The Rat Pack is BACK" hung the length of the box. I couldn't see inside the box from where I was, but usually Laird Haskell stood at one end with a mixed drink in hand, chattering with whatever guests he might have without ever taking his eyes off his son. Whenever the puck was around Taylor's net, Laird Haskell would stop his conversation and shout clipped commands at the boy: *Stop it! Kick it! Grab it! Freeze it!* And just before face-offs, always: *Focus!* I never heard him say "Taylor"; instead Laird Haskell called his son "19", or "number 19". I couldn't tell if Taylor heard his father. He never looked up at the box or made any other sign of acknowledgment, unless you counted the way he sometimes bowed his head when his father snapped, *Nineteen! Focus!* Maybe Taylor was focusing. Or maybe not.

Next to Haskell's box, the bleachers were filled top to bottom, blue line to blue line with high school kids wearing gold sweatshirts embossed in blue with the slogan THE PUCK STOPS HERE. The Rats had started selling the shirts after the Haskells arrived the autumn before and Taylor, the brand-new goalie from downstate, started the season by shutting out the first five opponents he faced. He snapped his catching glove like a bull-whip, and he got down and up and from one post to the other faster than goalies who were years older. Some of the kids passing me to go to the concession stand and the pay phones had had their sweatshirts autographed by the fourteen-year-old guarding the Rats goal tonight.

I had met Taylor Haskell once, a few weeks before.

I had gone into the rink pro shop to buy a stick. I was looking at the rack with left-hand curves when I noticed a kid in River Rats sweats picking through the right-curve sticks on the opposite side of the rack. TAYLOR said the gold stitching over his left breast. He selected an Easton and held it in both hands like a right wing would. He leaned down on the shaft until it bent a little, testing its stiffness.

"Fresh lumber?" I said. "Aren't you in the wrong rack?"

He looked up and his cheeks flushed as if I had caught him doing something wrong. He glanced quickly over his shoulder at the door to the shop.

"Um," he said. "Just waiting for my mom."

"You want those, don't you?" I pointed at a rack of paddle-bladed goalie sticks across the room. "That little thing you got isn't going to stop a slapper."

"I'm just looking."

I walked around and offered my hand. We shook. He was a little taller than I'd thought. His damp brown hair—he'd just showered after practice—glistened over blue eyes flecked with green. He had a pinkish sprinkle of acne along his forehead. Except for the eyes, he looked like his father.

"Gus Carpenter," I said. "I used to have a jacket like that."

He looked down at his jacket, as if he'd forgotten he had it on. "You were on the Rats?"

"A long time ago. Played goalie, too. Not anymore, though."

"Huh. How come?"

"How come what?"

"How come you stopped playing goal?"

It was not an idle question asked by a bored adolescent. Number 19 of the Hungry River Rats really wanted to know why I had chosen to leave goaltending behind. I wondered if Taylor Haskell knew that I had been the goat of the '81 title game. Maybe he hadn't been in Starvation long enough for that indoctrination.

"I don't know," I said. "Guess I had enough of people shooting pucks at my head. Time to have some fun for once, you know?"

I was joking, but Taylor didn't take it that way.

"Yeah," he said. "What's it like?"

"Playing out of the net?"

"Yeah."

I really hadn't given it much thought. I knew I didn't feel nearly as much pressure playing wing. That was probably the best part. Even in a men's league where games started at 11:45 p.m. and guys showed up stoned or drunk, I got butterflies before going out to tend goal. Wingers can screw up two or three times a shift and nobody cares. A goalie screws up twice in a game and their buddies start yelling at them to start fucking trying already.

"It's fun," I said. "I mean, I'm nothing great on wing and, from what I've seen, I wasn't nearly the goalie you are."

"Taylor, what are you doing?"

The woman was standing in the lobby just outside the shop in a white ankle-length parka trimmed with fur. She gave me a once-over without meeting my eyes. Taylor turned around and said, "Can I get a stick?"

"Taylor," she said. "We don't have all day."

"Come on, Mom."

The woman gave me a look that said this was none of my business.

"We'll talk to your father again tonight."

Taylor's shoulders drooped. "Oh, right."

"We'll see." She waved him out. "Let's go."

Now Marquette's number 6 faked around a Rats wing and veered left toward the center of the ice. Jeremy Bontrager, Elvis's nephew, stepped up to cut him off but 6 wound his stick back behind his left ear and, one stride outside the blue line, slapped a long, chest-high, flip-flopping shot at Taylor Haskell.

Following the fluttering puck while watching Taylor out of the corner of my eye, I knew immediately that he'd come out of his crease half a second too late. The crowd didn't know it, but I could feel them holding their breath anyway, because Taylor Haskell, for all of his shutouts and spectacular stops, had gradually gotten a reputation for giving up soft goals.

It's one thing for a goalie to stop back-to-back shots then watch a third one go in as he's sprawled on the ice. It's one thing for a goalie to be beaten by a sniper firing a bullet of a shot through a tangle of bodies. It's one thing for a goalie to succumb to a skater bearing down unmolested who knows exactly what he's going to do with the puck. But it's another thing entirely for a goalie to let in a goal he should not let in: A middling wrister that sneaks between his legs or wobbles high when he guessed down. Or, worst of all, a long dying quail of a shot that the shooter himself never imagined would score, that the shooter was just flipping toward the net in hopes of a rebound or a face-off.

Soft goals are death to a hockey team. Almost nothing—a stupid penalty, a missed empty net—is more demoralizing. A team can totally dominate a game, outskating their opponents, beating them to every loose puck, blasting shot after shot at the opposing net, but if their own goalie then lets in a shot that everyone in the rink knows a blind man could have stopped, the game can change as suddenly and unforgivingly as if the teams had traded jerseys. A goaltender never wants to give up any kind of goal. But when I played in the net, there were nights when I would rather have faced the other squad's best skater on a breakaway than a tumbling puck sliding toward me from a hundred feet away.

Nobody in Starvation Lake was saying it out loud, because the softies surrendered so far by Taylor Haskell had come late in games, with the Rats enjoying comfortable leads. But there were whispers nonetheless. About the high one against Muskegon that he seemed to lose in the lights. The weak backhander that dribbled between his skates against Panorama Engineering. The one from behind his net that bounced in off of his butt against Compuware. The titters and the whispers became nervous little jokes that Taylor was so impenetrable that he had to actually *let* other teams score once in a while.

The night Compuware scored off of his rear end, Channel Eight was waiting in the arena lobby when Taylor emerged from the dressing room. Usually his parents whisked him out a side door to their idling SUV, but tonight Laird and Felicia had gotten intercepted by Elvis Bontrager, and they weren't about to cut off the chairman of the town council. By the time they reached Taylor, he was standing in a ring of teammates and their moms and dads, bathed in camera light and speaking haltingly into a microphone held by Tawny Jane Reese. I happened to be there, standing behind a gaggle of girls getting up on their toes for a glimpse of number 19.

Tawny Jane asked him about the game—the Rats had won, 4–1—and he grinned and said it was a lot easier to be a goalie when the puck was in the other end most of the time. Good answer, I thought. She asked what he thought of the new rink going up and he said he hoped it would be ready for next season. Oops, wrong answer, I was thinking when I felt someone push past me: Laird Haskell. Felicia had him by a sleeve but he pulled away and pushed through the throng. Tawny Jane was asking the boy what had happened on that butt-bounce goal.

Taylor didn't seem to mind. "I guess I wasn't paying attention," he said. He shrugged. "I was kind of bored."

"Miss Reese," Haskell said. "Please."

Tawny Jane looked up. Taylor turned around, eyes wide with apprehension, looking like he had in the pro shop when I'd seen him shopping for regular sticks. I turned and saw Felicia standing with her hands clapped over her mouth, looking mortified.

"Please turn that off," Laird Haskell said as he emerged into the camera light. "Miss Reese, I really wish you would have asked me about interviewing my son."

Tawny Jane looked over her shoulder at her cameraman. The light stayed on. "Mr. Haskell," she said, shoving the mike in his face. "Taylor tells us he hopes the new rink is ready for next season." She smiled her widest fake smile. "Does he know something the rest of us don't?"

Haskell shook his head no as he took Taylor by the shoulders and moved the boy behind him. "He's fourteen years old, Miss Reese." Beads of sweat had broken out on Haskell's forehead, but he pasted on his own phony smile. "I worry about the rink, he worries about keeping pucks out of the net."

"Yeah," one of the mothers said. "Stick to hockey, lady." Others chimed in. Tawny Jane glanced around, saw me. I was grinning, as much in sympathy as amusement. She lowered her mike. The light went off.

"Could we talk later, Mr. Haskell?" she said.

"Of course," he said. "Call my attorney."

I watched Felicia grab the boy, wrap an arm around his shoulders, and hurry him away, Laird Haskell trailing behind. "Bored?" Haskell snapped. "What do you mean, bored?" Over her shoulder his wife shot him a look of searing disdain as she ushered the boy through the lobby doors.

Whoa, I thought. Bet they'll be having a chat tonight.

Now, as the fluttering shot from Marquette's number 6 reached Taylor Haskell, I could see that he was in trouble. Because his initial reaction had been late, he had overcompensated, trying to catch up. He was off balance, his stick had come up from the ice, and his body wasn't square to the puck. He should have snagged it easily with his catching glove, but instead it smacked him just under his mask on the left side and bounced up and over his shoulder while he flailed with his glove. The crowd groaned. The puck bounced in the crease and rolled toward the goal line and a 1–1 score. Taylor toppled over backward, twisting his body around, stretching his glove out for the puck.

He grabbed it just before it crossed the goal line. Players crashed into one another above him. Whistles blew. The stands exploded with a cheer of relief. I felt a sharp poke in the back of a shoulder and turned around.

"Got a minute?" Jason Esper said.

He threw the inside bolt on dressing room 3. I sat in the spot where I always sat for both the Rats and Soupy's Chowder Heads, on a bench along the cinder-block wall. The tang of disinfectant stung the air. Johnny Ford must have just swabbed the shower mats.

Jason grabbed a folding chair. He spun it around in front of me so that he sat facing me with his elbows propped on the chair back.

"Not a bad little 'tender," he said.

"The Haskell kid? Yeah."

"But something ain't right."

"Gives up a softie now and then."

"Got lucky on that last one. But it's more than that. He doesn't want to be out there." Jason smirked at me. "Kind of like you, eh, Carp?"

"He's fourteen, Meat. I'm thirty-five."

"Fuck," Jason said, and he guffawed. "He's the fucking future of Starvation Lake. And you're the past. God fucking help us all."

"What do you want, Jason?"

"What do I want?"

I waited.

"What the fuck do you care what I want?" he said.

I didn't want to have this discussion. "How the hell did you end up here anyway?"

Jason shrugged. "Ah, you know, this guy knew that guy. Hockey's a pretty small world. You know."

He hitched the chair forward a foot. I caught a whiff of whatever goop shined in his tight blond curls.

"Let me ask you something," he said. "How the hell did Wilford fuck up his marriage? Wasn't he married to that Brenda babe?"

"Brenda Mack."

Why did Jason Esper care about Brad Wilford's failed marriage?

"The calendar thing finally do him in?"

At the start of each season, Wilf dutifully noted all of his scheduled hockey games on a calendar hanging in his kitchen. He would add a fictitious game or two and, when those nights came, tell Brenda he didn't really feel like playing, he'd rather just spend the time with her. This, he bragged to us, was the surest way to get laid without having to get his wife plastered.

Of course, this being Starvation Lake, Brenda found out.

"Among other things," I said.

Jason studied his right hand, turning it around as if he were examining it for the first time. The stringy scars crisscrossing his knuckles made the hand look like he'd stuck it in a lawnmower. "You know," he said, "I wasn't just a goon. I wasn't even a goon. I could skate. I had size. I had hands."

"You played for the Pipefitters."

"Yeah. But I got better after that. I had a real shot, did you know that?"

"At the pros?"

"The Flyers. Twenty-one years old. Bus gets me to Philly the afternoon of the game and I figure no way they're putting me on the ice tonight—shit, they're playing the Habs—so I'm getting something to eat. I go in a bar, get a couple beers and a cheesesteak, maybe another couple beers. Love those cheesesteaks with mushrooms. I walk over to the rink just to check out the locker room and I'll be goddamned if my name isn't on the lineup card. Dude, I'm penciled in on a line with fucking Zezel and Kerr."

"Really."

"I'm like, oh fuck, what do I do? I go out into the concourse because I don't want anyone to see me in the locker room and I find a men's room and lock myself in a stall and jam two fingers down my throat. Got a little out but the goddamn cheese just wouldn't come up."

"Did you play?"

"Yeah. Three shifts. Tripped a guy after he got by me because I was gassed. Stupid fucking penalty. Of course the Habs score on the power play. Coach moves me to the fourth line. I get one more shift. And that was it. One of the guys said I looked like Casper the Ghost."

"And you never played in the bigs again."

Jason didn't like the way I said that.

"Always figured I would," he said. "But that was it. One chance and I blew it. Bounced around in the minors. Started to fight, thinking I might get the call-up as a goon. Got my ass kicked a bunch but finally learned how to go and got a pretty good reputation as a hammer." He looked at his hand again.

"Did you like fighting?"

"I don't know. You like typing?"

"Depends what I'm typing."

"Exactly," he said. "Which brings us to what I'm about to tell you."

In one quick motion he had my left wrist in his hand, squeezing the bones between his thumb and forefinger. It hurt. I tried to pull away but my arm stayed where it was. Jason leveled his eyes on mine.

"I'm done fucking up my life," he said. "And you are done fucking my wife."

A shiver rippled down the backs of my arms. Not because I was afraid; Jason Esper, coach-to-be of the River Rats, wasn't about to kick my ass in a dressing room in the middle of a game with half the town in the arena. But the certainty with which he said what he said made me wonder: Had he told Darlene the same when they spoke in the parking lot behind the sheriff's department? Had she told him to go to hell? Or had she said something that made him think he could succeed in scaring me away? Or winning her back?

"She's only your wife," I said, "on a piece of paper."

Jason let go of my wrist. He stood. He picked up his chair in one hand and set it back against the wall near the shower. Then he came back and stood over me. "Maybe I should've got a prenup like the one old Laird stuck his old lady with, eh? Now that's one happy fucking household. If she wants out—and believe you me, she wants out—she gets her panties back dirty, that's about it."

"Serves her right for negotiating with a scumbag lawyer."

Jason leaned back and considered me.

"You know," he said, "I had the hots for Darl way back when we were in high school. But I wasn't one of the hotshots on the River Rats."

He stepped forward and angled his face in close to mine.

"Now I'm the coach, motherfucker."

"Good for you. Beat the Pipefitters, will you?"

"Uh-huh. And that piece of paper? It says we're married. If she wanted to get divorced, she could've gotten divorced. I wasn't stopping her. Now I am."

"Sorry, Jason, but—"

"Listen," he said. "Listen fucking good. Whatever you did with her up to this minute, count yourself lucky, because I ain't holding it against you. But from now on, she's my wife, and I'm going to make amends, and you goddamn better well respect that." He showed me his cleverest smile. "Man, I'm the new coach of the new River Rats. For the sake of the team, for the sake of the *town*, I can't have my wife running around with some shithead reporter who doesn't even want a new rink built around here."

"The rink has nothing to do with your fucked-up marriage."

"It does now. You heard me. I ain't fucking this up anymore. If I hear—"

It sounded like a firecracker. A huge firecracker, out in the arena. There was one booming pop, then nothing, then the screams, the women loudest and shrillest, *Oh my baby my baby* . . . "What the fuck?" Jason and I said in unison. He threw the bolt on the door and we scrambled out.

My nostrils filled with the smell of gasoline cut with something bitter that I did not recognize. I saw a cloud of black smoke turning to gray obscuring the bay where the Zamboni was stored. On both benches, coaches were yelling, "Down, get down!" and pushing their players to the floor. Parents were rushing out of the bleachers and around the boards to get at their boys. Some of the kids in the sweatshirts followed them into the lobby while others hung in the stands, hugging one another, staring across at the Zam shed.

Oh Jesus, Darlene was down there, I thought. I couldn't see her for the smoke and the chaos of people running back and forth, so I pushed past Jason and ran down the aisle behind the benches, clambering over the young skaters cowering on the floor. Jason followed me. "Darlene," I heard him yell and then I yelled myself, "Darlene, where are you?" I glanced up at the scoreboard. The game clock read 1:14 left in the first period; above the scoreboard, a real clock showed the time was 8:01. I slammed into Poppy Popovich, the outgoing Rats coach. "What the hell's going on around here?" he said as Jason grabbed me by the back of my coat, tossed me aside, and hurried past.

"Halt." Deputy Skip Catledge stopped Jason and me with both hands held high. We were about thirty feet from the Zam shed. Smoke billowed out both sides of the Zamboni's flat snout. I saw Darlene on one knee near the back wall of the rink, her hat off, holding her head in one hand. A man I recognized as Doc Joe knelt down beside her.

"One more step and you're going to jail," Catledge told Jason and me.

"Is she all right?" I said, the stink burning my sinuses.

Darlene heard me, lifted her head.

"A little shaken up. She should be OK."

"What happened? Did the Zam explode?"

Jason took another step forward, then another, until he was almost touching Catledge. "That's my wife."

Catledge placed a hand on Jason's coach jacket. "Stand back, sir."

"I'm the new coach. That's my goddamn wife. Let me through."

Catledge looked around at Darlene. He looked at me. "Quickly," he said, letting Jason pass. Jason gave me a glance over his shoulder as he trotted to Darlene. I started to follow him but Catledge stopped me.

"No."

"Come on, Skip." What was I supposed to say? I'm sleeping with her?

"Sorry."

"Darlene," I shouted, but now her face was obscured behind Jason's wide back as he moved toward her. "Darlene!"

Now she half stood. Her cheeks were streaked black with soot or motor oil. Jason put his arms around her. I didn't see her arms wrap around him but neither did she push him away. Then she caught my eye. She shook her head no, glanced up at Jason, turned around, and disappeared into the smoke.

My mother answered on the fourth ring. I pictured her sitting in her chair in the living room. I hoped she wasn't still grieving to Robert Goulet.

I was sitting in my idling truck in the road in front of the rink. Police tape ringed the parking lot, filled now with flashing police cruisers, fire trucks, and ambulances. Locals huddled in small groups up and down the road, trying to comprehend the possibility that someone had set off a bomb in their quiet little town with its sole traffic light at Main and Estelle, its willow-lined streets, its cozy family diner, the clear blue lake where they had learned to swim and fish and drive a speedboat. I'd jotted everything I could recall in a notebook, even though we wouldn't have another *Pilot* for five days. I didn't even know if I'd still have a job then.

My mother listened while I told her what had happened: the Zamboni had exploded. It wasn't yet clear what had caused it. No one had been seriously hurt, including Darlene, who'd been closest to the blast. Even the Zam itself hadn't sustained serious damage.

"Gracie's killers did this," Mom said.

"Well, they were a little late then."

"Maybe this was the real plan."

I supposed it was possible that a bomb—if it was a bomb and not just something that had gone wrong inside the Zamboni—could have been set days before and that whoever set it wouldn't have been foolish enough to risk going back to unset it after Gracie was found dead. Luckily, no one was near enough the explosion to get seriously hurt. It just scared the hell out of everyone.

"Maybe," I said. "Tell me, Mom, do you have any idea what exactly Gracie did all those years she was downstate? How did she make a living? Did she actually live in Detroit or one of the 'burbs?"

"I know she waitressed."

I pictured the Gracie I had glimpsed at the Red Wings game. She didn't look like a waitress.

"Anything else?"

"Let me think." I couldn't tell if Mom was struggling with her failing memory or just deciding whether to tell me something. I wished she would just go to the damn doctor. My impatience got the best of me.

"Did she ever say anything to you about an abortion?" I said.

"Why . . . an abortion? No. I don't—I think I would remember that."

"Would she even have told you?"

"Yes. Yes, I think she would have."

I wasn't so sure of that. I put my truck in gear. I had to steer around Tawny Jane Reese and her cameraman doing a stand-up in the middle of the road. I resisted the urge to honk my horn as I slid past her. As Kerasopoulos had told me, we were all a team now under the valiant Media North banner.

"All right," I told Mom. "I'm heading down there."

"Yes," she said, talking on without hearing me, talking faster as she went, "I definitely think she would have told me that. When we had coffee Saturday, she was talking, a little wistfully I thought, about having children and—"

"Wait," I said. "Saturday two days ago?"

"Yes, Gussy, we had coffee at Audrey's, late in the morning. Gracie was just out of bed. Is that all right with you?"

"Fine, but you told me this morning the last time you saw her was in the drugstore last week."

"Did I?" She hesitated. Had she let on something she didn't mean to let on? Had she just forgotten what she was supposed to fib about? "Well, what difference does it make? I saw her again Saturday. We had coffee and a nice little chat and it was the last time I got to see her." I heard a catch in her voice. "I'm getting a little tired of being interrogated. I didn't kill Gracie."

"I thought you wanted me to get to the bottom of this."

"I think you need to get out of town."

The cop lights flickered in my rearview mirror. I decided I had to make a quick stop at the paper.

"I just said I'm going to Detroit."

"Good. Go safely. I'm going to bed now. I love you."

I found the letter on my desk at the *Pilot*. It actually wasn't postmarked Detroit, as Mrs. B had said, but Dearborn, a suburb abutting Detroit on the west that also happened to border on Melvindale.

I sliced it open with a penknife. Inside I found a single piece of unlined white paper, folded once. I opened it in the pool of light thrown by my desk lamp. Someone had scrawled six words across the page in red ink:

Build it and they will die

What the hell is this, a movie? I thought. I considered whether I could have helped avert the explosion at the rink if I had opened the envelope earlier and told someone about it, maybe even Dingus. I decided not.

I folded the note and the envelope into my wallet.

I called Darlene. She didn't pick up. "I love you," I told her voice mail. She wasn't going to like my story in that morning's paper, making Gracie into three paragraphs of apparent suicide. I'd have to explain later.

I called Kerasopoulos's office number. I told his voice mail I had an emergency family matter that I had to attend to downstate. In a way, it was true. He'd either believe it or not. Either way, my days at the *Pilot* were probably numbered.

I took the penknife and descended the stairs to the *Pilot* basement, ducking cobwebs dotted with the carcasses of flies. A naked overhead bulb cast a dim light across the floor, revealing a puddle of water covering a rusted drain cover.

In the shadows along the walls stood racks built of two-by-sixes holding black binders of *Pilots* dating back nearly three decades. I found what I was looking for in the binder marked March 15–31, 1980. On page A3 of the March 18 issue, I found an eight-inch story beneath a two-column headline that read, "Anonymous Donor Bequeaths Scholarship on Local Girl." A black-and-white school picture of Gracie was wedged into the story. With the penknife I cut the story out of the binder and put that in my wallet, too.

Back upstairs, I sat at my computer and did a quick search for clips under the byline of a certain *Detroit Free Press* reporter. I selected half a dozen, printed them, scanned each one, and jotted a few notes about them on a piece of paper I also folded and stuffed into my wallet.

Then I dozed for a few hours in an armchair that our fired photographer had used for afternoon naps. I woke at 4:47, put my coat on, and went out the back door, shivering against the cold.

Audrey seemed surprisingly unsurprised to see me at her back door an hour before she would open the diner.

She pushed the door open and told me good morning and asked me if I wanted something to go. Yes, I told her, a fried-egg sandwich with bacon and cheddar on toasted pumpernickel. And a large coffee, black.

Audrey bustled about her griddle in a white apron over a peach-colored smock. A song played on a transistor radio propped on a shelf against a bag of brown sugar, Peggy Lee singing "Is That All There Is?" Audrey would turn it down to a murmur when her first customers arrived.

I had always loved the diner. When I was a boy, Mom would bring me there on Saturdays, when Audrey made her special concoction, the egg pie, an envelope of Italian bread bubbling with eggs, cheese, sausage, onion, mushrooms, and whatever else you fancied. We'd sit at the counter so Mom and Audrey could gossip while I tore into my pie, shredding the top crust, letting the steam warm my cheeks, savoring the only thing in the world that mattered at that particular moment in my young life.

Gracie didn't like Audrey's, though; she said it smelled like old people. When Gracie stayed with us, we didn't go to Audrey's on Saturdays; instead, Mom made Gracie's favorite, chocolate-chip-banana pancakes. I ate them only after picking out the banana.

"How is your mother doing?" Audrey said.

"As well as can be expected."

"Are there funeral arrangements yet?"

"Not that I know of. I think the cops have to finish first."

Audrey shook her head without looking back at me. "Looks like they have a lot more work to do after last night, huh?"

I let her bring the two eggs to a sizzle before I asked whether my mother had been in with Gracie on Saturday. She told me yes, they had come in late, in between the breakfast and lunch rushes.

"Did you happen to catch any of their conversation?"

With Audrey, the answer to that question was almost always yes. The real question was how much she would tell me. She liked me, though. She'd known me all my life. That helped.

"Not much, actually," she said. She flipped the grilled slices of Canadian bacon and cheddar onto the eggs, covered it all with the toasted pumpernickel. "Molly wasn't here and I was busy getting things ready for the lunch crowd."

"They had coffee?"

"Gracie had coffee. Your mother had tea. Why do you ask?"

"Come on, Mrs. DeYonghe. You know."

She wrapped my sandwich in wax paper, poured my coffee into a foam cup, handed them to me. "Where are you going?"

You know the answer to that, too, I thought. "Downstate."

"And you're coming back."

"Yeah. Why wouldn't I?"

"I don't know, Gussy. Years ago, you ran when your hockey went bad. Then you ran back here when things went bad downstate. I don't want you running again. Your mother needs you."

"I understand."

"You can't just keep running. Eventually you have to make your choice and stand your ground."

"Uh, OK," I said. I'd taken a stand at the *Pilot* the night before and wound up standing on my dick. "Any particular reason for the five a.m. lecture?"

Audrey plucked a dishrag off the counter and wiped her hands. "I was a little surprised to see Gracie in here. I don't think she'd been in since she came back to town. Your mother didn't look very happy with her. And she didn't stay long, left without Bea."

"Huh. OK. Thanks. For the food too. Here." She waved off my offer of a five-dollar bill. I tossed it on the counter. "I better get going."

I was ten steps out the door when I heard her call after me: "Gussy."

I turned. Audrey stood with her rump propping the door open, arms folded against the chill. "They were arguing," she said.

"Arguing about what?"

"I'm not sure. They kept their voices down. But it had something to do with an envelope."

Down from the walkway behind me the Hungry River lay frozen in the morning dark. Sometimes you could hear the burble of the water flowing beneath the ice. "Who brought the envelope?"

"I don't know. But it was pretty clear that Bea didn't want it. Then she almost left without it. I had to chase her down the sidewalk."

"Yeah?"

"A manila envelope." She held her right thumb and forefinger about two inches apart. "About yay thick."

Goddammit, Mother, I thought as I pulled my truck out of Starvation and aimed it toward Interstate 75 south.

thirteen

She was smoking a cigarette in a booth at the back of the Petros Coney Island on Michigan Avenue in east Dearborn. The tall Greek behind the counter nodded at me as I made my way to the table. His given name, I recalled, was Phaethon, though he went by Fred. Perhaps he remembered me, too. I savored the aromas of onions and chili and eggs fried in butter. I had fond memories of Petros.

Michele Higgins and I used to have long breakfasts there when I was writing about the auto industry for the *Detroit Times* and she was covering cops and, later, federal courts for the *Detroit Free Press*. We both lived near downtown at the time, but when we first started seeing each other, we didn't want to take the chance that someone from either of our papers would see us together, sitting on the same side of the booth, and think we might be sharing secrets between competitors. It was silly to think so; there were plenty of dalliances, affairs, and even marriages across the two dailies. Maybe, like those reporters who prefer to quote anonymous sources, we just thought it sexier to carry on a clandestine relationship.

"Hey there," I said. I slid into the booth opposite Mich. My butt scratched across a piece of duct tape that had been used to patch a tear in the red vinyl. I set the accordion folder Dingus had given me on the table next to the napkin dispenser. Mich glanced at it as she crushed out her cigarette. She pulled her blond locks off her forehead, only to have them fall right back. Her hair never stayed where she put it.

"Hey," she said.

It must have been too much for her to smile, especially this early in the morning. Her blue eyes were bloodshot and the smell of cigarettes hung on her black leather jacket.

"You look good."

"Ah," she said, dismissing my compliment, probably knowing it was halfhearted. She did look good for a forty-year-old, though she'd looked better. "What brings you to the real world?"

Fred appeared at our table. "The usual?" he said.

He really did remember, and not just me. I wondered if Mich still came to Petros. I looked at Fred. His thin salt-and-pepper mustache was neatly trimmed, as ever.

"Not for me," I said. "Just coffee, black, and some rye toast."

"It's good to see you again, Mr. Carpenter."

"You too, Fred. But it's Gus, OK?"

He smiled. We'd been over this a few years before. "OK, Mr. Carpenter," he said. "And Miss Michele?"

"Grapefruit juice." She hated the stuff but insisted that it helped cure her hangovers. "And two eggs, soft-boiled."

"Three and a half minutes?"

"Yeah. Thanks."

Fred went back behind the counter.

"Nice piece on the judge with the three families." The story had been among the ones I'd found in my search back at the *Pilot*. "What the hell was the guy thinking?"

Mich lit another cigarette without taking her eyes off me. "I don't need you blowing smoke up my ass. You don't read the *Times* or the *Freep*. Let's just get to it, all right?"

"Sorry."

"And the next time you use the sorry word, I'm out of here."

I wished I could've just paid and left. But I needed Mich. She was the best crime reporter in Detroit—sourced up her pretty butt, like lightning on a keyboard, and when it came to competitors, ruthlessly efficient.

In her own newsroom she'd dismiss her rivals' stories as "wheezes" or "snoozers" or "history." But when she ran into one of them at the cop shop or a crime scene, she was all smiles and flattery, softening them up, getting them off their games. "I worshipped your story on the twelve-year-old drug runner," she'd say. Or, "Man, you blazed a trail I'll have a hell of a time following." Veterans weren't so easily snowed, especially after she'd scooped them a few dozen times. Youngsters were another matter.

Once, she was sequestered in a room at the federal courthouse with a young *Times* reporter. They were supposed to have equal access to a box of documents on a money-laudering case involving a car dealer.

"Oh, I know your byline," Michele Higgins told the *Times* rookie."I hear you're on the fast track."

He actually blushed."I don't know about that, but thanks," he said.

The *Times* reporter, who obviously didn't know Mich, left to use the men's room. Mich plucked out some of the juiciest documents and hid them in her purse. Only after the *Times* reporter finished going through the paper and left to write his story did Mich return the documents to the box. The next morning, Mich's front-page story blew away the eight-inch piece inside the *Times*.

And the blushing one—me—got his ass chewed by his bosses.

Some time later, I encountered Mich again by the jukebox at the Anchor Bar. It was late and I was about to play Patsy Cline's"Crazy" when she reached over me to punch in B86 for"You Shook Me All Night Long" by AC/DC.

"Hey there, rookie," she said."You really like Patsy Cline?"

I turned, recognized her, may have blushed again.

"I do," I said."Why'd you do that to me?"

"What?" she said."You don't like AC/DC?"

"No. The auto dealer story."

"Oh." She reached past me again and punched in A18 for "Crazy." Her perfume washed over me as she turned her face close to mine.

"You know, they had paper clips in there," she said. She smiled."Maybe you should've put one on your cock."

From that night on we were together, sort of, except when we weren't. There was occasional talk of marriage—most of it on the newsroom grapevine that ran past the Anchor between our papers—but we both knew that getting married would require divorces from our jobs. I couldn't recall ever telling her that I loved her, at least not when I was sober. She could have made the same claim, with the exception of the morning after her Chihuahua McGraw was killed on the street outside her apartment in Indian Village and she was a puddle.

The fact was, I was no match for the police radio on her nightstand, and Mich couldn't compete with the half-in-the-bag union guys and cranky auto chiefs who called me late at night to brag and whine and squeal and leak. Our *thing*, as Mich called it, was hardly the stuff of Hallmark cards. But it rarely lacked for excitement. Each of us had keys to the other's apartment. We never knew when one of us might come home after midnight to find the other waiting naked and hungry.

I liked it but most of the time I did not crave it, and neither did Mich. Or so I thought. After my job blew up and I moved back to Starvation, I put our thing behind me along with everything else from Detroit. I stopped returning Mich's calls, partly because I was embarrassed, partly because I didn't believe she'd ever care enough to venture as far from her precious cop shops and courtrooms as Starvation Lake.

Then one night I opened the door to the apartment I'd had over the *Pilot* until Media North kicked me out. There she was in my recliner, a glass of Crown Royal on the rocks in one hand, a bedsheet bunched at her breasts in the other. "Oh, fuck," said Darlene, who'd come home with me after dinner at a bistro in Bellaire. Oh, fuck, indeed. Darlene turned around and walked out. It took me two weeks to untangle that mess.

Michele Higgins and I had not talked since, until that morning when I had woken her with a call from my truck as it descended the freeway bridge at Zilwaukee, a couple of hours from Detroit. She'd told me to leave her alone, but I had talked fast and told her it was about my second cousin, my mother's favorite girl in the world, and there was no else who could help me. I figured I had her when she said, "Why don't you call one of the dumb shits at the *Times?*"

Now I told her in more detail about what had happened to Gracie. About the shoe tree, the absence of a car or a ladder, Gracie's long hiatus downstate, the calendar hanging over her bed, the explosion in the Zam shed. I didn't bother to tell her about the brush or the baby shoe or the key.

While I was speaking, Fred brought our breakfasts and left the bill, which I took. Mich had one spoonful of her soft-boiled eggs and pushed the porcelain cup aside. Her gaze went to the accordion folder again. I grabbed it, pulled out the police report, and shoved the stapled pages across the table.

"Take a look."

I waited while she read. Near the end she nodded her head and smiled. She pushed the pages back to me, picked up her cigarette, took a long drag.

"What do you think?" I said.

She blew the smoke over her right shoulder. "Is that all?"

I pulled out my wallet and showed her the piece of paper with the name Vend on it. "Bingo," she said, sliding the paper back. "Remind me: what was that country song you liked? 'For the Old Times'?"

"'For the Good Times.' My dad liked it."

"You liked it too. You used to play it at the Anchor."

"Only when I was drunk. What's that got to do with anything?"

"'And make believe you love me one more time,'" she sang, way off key. "Brother. Buck Owens?"

"Ray Price."

"So." She put out her cigarette. "Your friend was mixed up with some dangerous people."

"My cousin. Second cousin."

"Whatever. You ever heard of this Vend dude?"

"Should I have?"

"I knew you weren't reading the Detroit papers."

I almost said I was sorry.

"Owns a bunch of strip clubs, here and over in Windsor. Bottomless across the river. Brings in chicks from all over the place: Michigan, Ohio, Quebec, even Poland."

"Is he from there?"

"Canada. The clubs all cater to different clienteles—Livonia autoworkers, Trenton steel guys, right up to the doctors and lawyers in the Pointes and Bloomfield. You can stick a buck in a garter to slobber all over a fat chick from Garden City or you can have a private room where you can jack off on a nineteen-year-old's face while she pulls on a dog chain around your neck. A real marketing genius. Or at least that's what I read in the blow job your old paper gave him on the business page last year."

Strip-club owners did make for good reading.

"And he's a bad guy?"

"No, Gus, he's a saint, like all guys who run strip clubs—all guys who run businesses, for that matter." She shook out another cigarette. "Boy, once a business writer, always a business writer."

"Give me a break, will you?"

She lit the cigarette and blew the first puff across the table. "I gave you a break. I'm here."

"Please tell me more."

"The guy's constantly under investigation by the cops and the feds. Drugs, prostitution, guns, tax evasion. Even kid porn a ways back, though I think he got away from that. They'll never catch the guy. He's too smart, too generous with his money, too much the, you know, the whole bootstrap entrepreneur shtick. He's good, I got to hand it to him. I mean, have you ever met a bad Canadian? Off the ice, I mean."

I could think of only one and he was in prison.

She gestured toward the accordion file. "And he lives in Melvindale, for God's sake. Brags about it. Blue-collar churchgoers, tree-lined streets, brick ranches. Just the place for a criminal mastermind, eh? He just built a new gym for some Catholic school there."

He's making more progress than Haskell, I thought.

"Al Capone lived in a neighborhood like that," I said. I took a sip of my coffee. It was as bland as I remembered. "YA-rek, right? And Vend?"

"Shortened. Used to be Vendrowska or Vendrowski. He has some goofy nickname, Knobs or Knobbo or something. He has a huge head. Saw him once."

Knobbo, I thought. It rang a bell.

"But you haven't nailed him yet in the paper?"

"Got a file this thick"—she held her hands a foot apart—"but the guy's slippery as an eel."

"Is he from Windsor?"

"Sarnia."

"I went up there once on a hockey trip. For twenty-five bucks, the chicks would blow you under the table."

"I don't need to hear that, thank you. He actually owns a piece of some team up there. He plays, or played. A goalie. Like you."

Another bell went off.

"I'm not playing goal anymore," I said.

"Really? Quite the changed man, huh?"

"Got bored with it."

"Uh-huh. But you're still fucking that cop?"

In reply, I sighed. She leaned back and looked at me like a skeptical judge might peer down at a defense attorney. "You really happy up there?"

"Sure."

"I could still get you into the *Freep*, you know. They think you got screwed by those pussies at the *Times* who wouldn't go to bat for you."

My bosses at the *Times* had indeed run scared when the auto company discovered I'd raided its voice mail system. I also shouldn't have done what I had done, even if every story I had written was true.

"Thanks," I said. "Could we just talk about Vend? Is that his address?"

"Why? You don't plan to go there."

"Why not? I just want to ask him a few questions."

"At his house? Gus. This isn't the business beat. Vend isn't some pasty-faced guy in his sixties who thinks hitting a squash ball makes him a bad-ass. People who piss this guy off pay for it."

"Got it."

"You said there was a bombing up north?"

"Yeah. Nobody got hurt, though."

"Nobody was supposed to get hurt. It was a warning. What's-her-name must have known something she wasn't supposed to know."

Build it and they will die, the note said. Whoever had sent it clearly intended it for public distribution. But why would Vend or anyone else outside of Starvation care about a new hockey rink? And who would send something so crude and obvious?

"Gracie," I said. "But he already—she's already dead."

Mich stopped to think. "Well," she said, "maybe somebody else there knows something they shouldn't."

"Yeah, well, it ain't me."

We sat in silence for a bit, Mich smoking, her eyes wandering around the diner, me spreading grape jelly on my toast.

"Hey," she said. "I hear your old ambulance chaser buddy is up there now."

"Who? Oh, Haskell." I put the knife down and noticed Mich looking directly at me. She had been with me when I'd had my unfortunate encounter with Haskell in Detroit. "Yeah. His son's a hockey hotshot. Haskell's trying to build a rink. I don't think he has the money."

She leaned slightly forward. "How could he not? The guy's made a pile."

"I don't know. But he's not paying his contractors. Work's come to a stop. And now he's trying to shake the town down for a hundred grand."

"Huh. Have you written about it?"

"A few stories. Ticked everybody off."

"Of course. How's old Laird?"

"Same. Like you said about Vend. Slippery as an eel."

"Yep." She gathered up her purse and shimmied out of the booth. She seemed to be in a hurry. "Gotta meet a guy."

I started to stand but Mich raised a hand that said don't bother.

"Thanks," I said. "Let's stay in better touch."

"Tell Ray Price."

I finished my toast while checking my two phone messages. One was from Philo, who told me Kerasopoulos was not happy that I'd skipped out of our meeting, but I should call anyway for some other information. Darlene's message was merely, "'Apparent suicide'? What happened, Gus?"

I left two dollars on the table and walked to the cash register. One side of the register was covered with school photos of smiling little girls in plaid jumpers, white bows in their hair, front teeth missing.

"Those your grandkids?" I said

"Yes, sir," Fred said. He craned his head around to admire the pictures as if he'd never seen them before. He smiled. "Four of them, sir. I am very proud."

He popped the register drawer open, slipped my bills in, handed me my change. "It is very good to see you again."

"You too, Fred."

I was stepping through the door when he called after me.

"Sir," he said. "Excuse me for—I couldn't help but hear."

"Yes?"

"Please, sir. Be very careful."

I pointed my truck down Michigan Avenue toward Melvindale. I thought of the scar on the neck of the man at the motel. I thought of the blood coursing from the other man's nose. I wondered what the hell I was doing.

T
he one time Gracie and I had seen each other in Detroit, I was in my third year at the *Detroit Times*. We had set several dates previously for drinks or dinner, and each time Gracie had canceled or failed to show. My mother kept pushing me to invite her out, telling me my second cousin was struggling with life just like me.

"Just like me?" I said. "Mother, I'm working sixty-five hours a week. I'm paying rent. I bought a car. They're thinking of sending me to Japan for some stories. I'm doing just fine. I got some school loans to pay off but—oh, right, Gracie doesn't have those because she got a freebie."

"All the more reason, honey. She needs a big brother."

"I'm not her brother. She ought to talk to whoever dragged her down here in the first place."

Still, I promised to try again.

This time I was late. My computer had crashed—ten minutes before deadline, of course—and I had to redo an entire story about Chrysler threatening to shut an assembly plant in Wisconsin. The Red Devil, a beer-and-pizza joint on the west side, was almost empty on a Monday night. But there was Gracie filing her nails at one of the Formica-topped tables near the bar. Melting ice cubes and a cherry impaled on a plastic spear sat at the bottom of a glass. I could just barely hear "Sweet Child O' Mine" playing on the jukebox.

"Sorry I'm late," I said. "Computers."

"I wouldn't know," she said, without looking up. "Don't have one."

"Did you order?"

She dropped the nail file in her purse. Her perfume wafted across the table, cutting through the garlic and oregano on the air. She looked at me. Her eyes seemed to have trouble focusing. They were on me, then looking behind me, then on me again, then on the table, rolling around like marbles in a bowl. I wondered if the empty glass was only her first drink.

"No," she said. "I was waiting for you."

I signaled for the waiter.

"This place," she said. "It's so . . . so you, Gus."

"What does that mean?"

"Oh, you know. Low lights, but not romantic. Peeling vinyl seats. The whole fake unpretentious shtick." She looked at me and giggled.

"You must frequent much classier places."

"Maybe I do," she said. "It's charming. And it would be even more charming if . . ." She whipped her head around toward the bar. "Hey," she shouted, "is my drink ready yet? I'm not used to being ignored."

"He's coming," I said.

"He better fucking hurry." She picked up her glass, shook the ice around. "Sorry. Don't want to cause any trouble. How's Bea?"

"Fine. I haven't talked to her in a week, the job's been so busy."

"The job, the job, the job," Gracie said. "You need to get your priorities straight, boy. Call Bea."

"When's the last time you called her?"

"I'm calling her tomorrow."

I grinned. "Do you even have a job, Gracie? Or priorities?"

She gave me a dreamy smile. "I have my priorities. I just don't happen to have them all in order." Then she laughed, a little too loud.

A spindly young man in a white button-down shirt, shiny black slacks, a skinny black tie, and an apron smeared with spaghetti sauce shambled over to our table. The plastic name tag pinned to his shirt said he was Randy. He set a full glass in front of Gracie. Her usual gin and Squirt.

"Can I get you something to drink?" he said to me.

I ordered a Blue Ribbon. Gracie glanced up at Randy, then took the menu out from between the parmesan and pepper flake shakers. I watched her eyes as she pretended to look at it. One lid drooped. She dropped the menu on the table and looked up at the waiter. Her eyes seemed to brighten.

"So," she said. "You're Randy."

"Yes, ma'am," he said.

"Ha," Gracie said. "I'm not 'ma'am.' I could be your little sister."

Randy smiled nervously. "What would you like?"

"Gracie," I said, wishing the computer had crashed a second time.

"Don't have a fucking—" She stopped and closed her eyes momentarily. "Don't have a fucking cow, all right?"

"Calm down."

"Hold your horses," she said. "Randy's not in any hurry, are you, Randy?" She gave him a smile I had seen her use on a hundred unsuspecting boys.

"I'm fine," he said.

Now Gracie swiveled around in her seat to face the young waiter. "I'll say," she said. "Tell me—tell the truth now—will you tell me the truth?"

"Uh, sure," he said.

Gracie must have seen me start to interrupt, because she raised a hand to stop me. Then she used the same hand to pick up her drink, lift it unsteadily to her lips, and drink it down in one determined gulp. She dropped the glass on the table and it tipped over, spilling the ice cubes and cherry across the red-and-white checked tablecloth.

"Gracie!" I said.

"OK," she said, ignoring me. "Tell me—are you a randy man? Huh?"

"Gracie, come on. Just tell him what you want."

"I'm about to."

She stood and stepped into the boy, almost knocking him over. He tried to back away but she grabbed him by his tie and pulled him into her. "Ma'am," Randy said, looking helplessly over his shoulder toward the bar. No one was there. I leapt out of my chair too late. She pulled harder on Randy's tie and got up on her toes to plant a kiss on his mouth, getting mostly chin. Then her arms and legs went limp and she collapsed in a heap at Randy's feet.

"Oh, my God," he said, jumping back. "I didn't do it. It wasn't me."

I crouched on the floor and turned Gracie over, cradling her head in one arm. Blood trickled from the corner of her mouth. She had bitten her tongue. "Gracie, Gracie," I said. "What the hell happened to you?"

As she'd fallen, she had bumped her purse off the table and some of its contents had spilled across the red carpet. I looked to see a change purse, a tube of K-Y Jelly, three tubes of lipstick. And my old blue hairbrush—*the* brush. I put it all back in her purse, brush first.

It took me fifteen minutes and a twenty-dollar bill to keep Randy and the chef, a sweating stump of a woman named Rhonda, from calling the police. Gracie looked drunk to them, but I suspected she'd taken something that didn't mix well with booze. I wouldn't have minded her going to jail—it might have done her some good—but I would have had to answer to my mother for the rest of my life.

From a story I had done on car crashes, I happened to know an emergency doctor at, of all places, Grace Hospital. I wrapped Gracie in a Maple Leafs jersey I had in my trunk, laid her on my backseat, and took her to the hospital. The doctors pumped her stomach. Out came Dilaudid, Quaaludes, cocaine, some alcohol. My doctor acquaintance explained that this was a dangerous mix, especially for someone who had been driving. He asked if Gracie might be willing to seek counseling. I told him I doubted it.

I slept on and off on a chair in the ER waiting room. The doctor nudged me awake around six the next morning and told me Gracie would be OK. I left thirty bucks at the reception desk for a cab. I had to get to work.

For the next two weeks, I called Gracie almost every day, trying to get her to see me, foolishly, vainly thinking that I could talk her into getting some help. She didn't return my messages, unless you count the registered letter a lawyer sent on her behalf to the publisher of the *Detroit Times*.

The one-page letter said I had made "persistent and inappropriate advances" on one Grace McBride. It said that if I did not cease and desist immediately, "further action" would be taken, including a court order barring me from any future contact with my second cousin.

The publisher gave the letter to my boss at the time, a guy named Virgil Ropolletti. Rope sat me down in his glassed-in office in the newsroom, put his unlaced Hush Puppies up on his desk, and lit a Camel. He'd won a Pulitzer as a young man for stories on a state lawmaker who had created a secret stash of taxpayer cash he doled out to buddies. He was on his fourth wife—all from circulation or ad sales—and was now obsessed with finding the body of Jimmy Hoffa.

"Well, sweetie," he said, "what do I do with this?"

I told him what had happened at the Red Devil. Rope knew the place, knew the owner, the barmaids, everybody. He could check it out if he wanted. But he wouldn't bother. He knew me, too.

"This chick hot?" he said.

"Jesus, Rope. She's my cousin."

"Sorry."

"Frankly, I don't know how the hell she can afford a lawyer."

"Hot-shit firm, too," he said. He dropped his half-smoked cigarette in a Coke can. "Sounds like my second wife. Families are all fucking crazy, if you ask me."

I thought of Mom, decided there was no need to tell her any of this.

"Yep."

"So what are you going to do?"

"What she wants me to do. Nothing."

"The old man," he said, pointing up at the fifth floor where the publisher's office was, "he's a little worked up over this. He's worried it's going to show up in the *Free Press*."

"Nope," I said, knowing I'd be calling Michele Higgins as soon as I left Rope. "Won't happen."

"OK. But why don't you make yourself scarce, take a couple days off?"

I didn't see Gracie again until she moved back to Starvation Lake— except, if it really was her, at that Red Wings playoff game, sauntering down to the rinkside seats with the dapper man in the turtleneck.

fifteen

Dirty white splotches of rock salt pocked the gray boulevards of Melvindale. I waited at a red light at the intersection of Greenfield and Schaefer. Not a single car passed in front of me. I supposed many locals would have been working the day shift at the Ford plant just across the Rouge River in Dearborn.

The light changed. I steered my truck slowly along the wide streets, six and eight lanes across. Streets that were almost empty of cars and trucks. Melvindale apparently had expected more, believing the auto industry would keep it growing forever. I'd root for it anyway. I liked the towns downriver from Detroit—Romulus, Trenton, Allen Park, Lincoln Park, Ecorse, Wyandotte, Melvindale. I'd played a lot of late-night hockey at the rinks there while employed at the *Times*, drunk more than a few early morning beers at the redbrick bars, scarfed and invariably regretted scarfing sliders from the White Castle at Dix and Oakwood.

I'd played there as a kid too, tending goal for the River Rats. I loved the Yack Arena in Wyandotte, with its polished oak beams arching gracefully over the ice surface; we'd beaten Mic-Mac there to win a Christmas tournament when I was sixteen. In Ecorse, we were down by a goal late in a game against a local team when a dad standing in the mezzanine over our bench dumped a Coke on us and earned his team a two-minute penalty; Soupy scored the tying goal on a low slap shot from the left face-off dot and, in overtime, slipped a backhander between the befuddled goalie's legs for one of our sweetest wins ever.

Then there was the rink in Trenton, home of the Pipefitters, a cramped, frozen box with a corrugated tin roof and bleachers along one side of the ice that swayed under the weight of more than a thousand people, almost every one in 'Fitters black and gold. One game, we had a 4–1 lead after two periods and came out in the third determined to grab our first win ever against what most people believed, year after year, was the best team in Michigan. When the Pipefitters tied it up with three goals in four minutes and thirty-six seconds, I looked out through my goalie mask and swore that the roof was trembling with the crowd's ferocious din. With fourteen seconds to go, Zilchy had a chance to break a 5–5 tie. His hurried wrist shot beat the 'Fitter goalie over his left shoulder but hit the crossbar and sailed harmlessly over the glass.

After the game, Zilch sat on the floor against the dressing room wall, his head in his hands. Nobody noticed him sobbing at first, but then he began to weep, louder every second, and then to scream, shaking, hysterical, tears streaming down his cheeks, tearing his helmet off and slamming it against the floor until it split in two. "Fuck, Zilch," Soupy said. He jumped up and crossed the room, one skate on and one off, and slapped Zilchy once, hard, across the face. Just like we'd seen on TV. And just like that, Zilchy stopped.

We never did beat the Pipefitters.

I turned onto Allen Road. I wasn't going anywhere in particular, not yet. I had no idea where Gracie had lived. But Mich had given me rough directions to Vend's address. Now I was working up the courage to go there. As a reporter, I had never grown comfortable with confronting people face-to-face, no matter how many times I did it. I did not envy the cop reporters who routinely had to show up on people's doorsteps to ask what they felt about their teenage daughter being found raped and knifed to death in a viaduct along the Lodge Freeway. I wasn't sure I wanted to present myself on the porch of a man who took joy in breaking another man's nose with his head, who I was beginning to believe had a hand in the death of Gracie McBride.

I passed a radiator shop, a two-story condominium complex trimmed with shake shingles, a Moose lodge, three gas stations, an awning shop, a motel with Christmas lights strung around its windows. There was an Italian bakery, a bar, a bank branch, two liquor stores, a pharmacy, a McDonald's, a Chinese restaurant called Ming Sun, a Slavic one called Putka's. I slowed my truck as I passed Wally's Wonder Print, trying to see in through the windows.

Bare maples and oaks and ragged piles of mud-crusted snow lined both sides of Harman Street. The sidewalks were clean. Neat bungalows nestled behind the matted brown lawns, patchy with snow. Basketball hoops with their nets removed stood outside one- and two-car garages. I passed the house twice, once going south, once north. I circled around Hanna Street to Elizabeth and back up Harman again. I parked across the street and two doors down from Vend's house, beneath an enormous oak that could have doubled as the tree in which Gracie was found.

I shut off the ignition and made sure my doors were locked.

The one-story ranch was the last place I would have looked for a strip-club magnate. It was dressed in clean white aluminum siding. The white awnings over the front windows and porch were trimmed in royal blue. The lawn surrounded a rock garden set off by a neat curving border of beige bricks. In the middle of the garden stood a statue of the Blessed Mother.

What was I going to do? Just walk up and say, "Is Knobbo here?" I wasn't even sure that Vend lived there anymore. The address I'd found in Dingus's file was almost four years old, after all.

I picked up my cell phone. There were messages from Darlene and Philo. I dialed Darlene, ready to be yelled at.

"'Apparent suicide'?" she said. "Three paragraphs? You know we have a bomb squad here from Traverse? Does it sound like we're treating this like a suicide?"

"It's not what I wrote," I said. "The fucking fat ass in—"

"Why do you let them push you around?"

That wasn't as simple a question as she might have imagined.

"I don't, Darlene. But it's not my paper."

"Whatever. The *Pilot's* so irrelevant anyway."

"Thanks."

"I just hope it doesn't make people who might have information think it's OK to keep quiet."

"Look, I'm sorry. At least Dingus seems to be letting you in on things."

"Where are you?"

"Beautiful Melvindale, Michigan."

"Good. Gracie lived there. Or at least that's where I mailed my letters . . . Hang on. I'm drying my hair. Finally got a shower."

Her hair had been wet the first time I had really noticed Darlene. I was thirteen. I crossed her yard next door to mine to catch the school bus that stopped in front of her house. I leaned against the mailbox facing Darlene's house, my books under one arm. Next door my mutts, Fats and Blinky, started barking as the bus approached.

Darlene's screen door opened halfway and then banged shut and then opened again. She stepped out onto her porch in her white parka, a stack of books cradled against her chest, her damp, dark hair shining in the sun. I heard the bus rumble to a stop behind me but I kept watching Darlene. She didn't even look at the bus. She bent forward at the waist and with her free arm shook out her hair as it fell over her face. Then she tossed it all back and shook her head some more and ran her hand through her hair again and again, smoothing it back and over her hood.

The bus driver beeped her horn. A year before, a month before, a day before that morning, I would have yelled, "Come on, Darlene, move!" But today I just stood there watching her take care of herself. Of course she was being selfish and vain and disrespectful. And that thrilled me. She wasn't afraid to believe that she knew what mattered at that moment, and that it wasn't the bus or the school bell or anything else but that she looked her very best before she started her day. As I watched her cross her lawn and climb the bus steps without a word or a glance for the bus driver or for me, I knew that I wanted to matter to her.

"It's crazy here," she said now.

"The coroner say anything yet?"

"No. Dingus is trying to hold him off. We think the bomb was set off remotely. You can do it with a phone call to a beeper or a cell phone."

"Can you trace it?"

"Pretty hard without the beeper or the cell. We're working on it. Actually, I'm working on it."

"Has anyone taken credit for it?"

"Credit?"

"You know what I mean."

"No one has stepped forward. No one has contacted us. We can only conclude it was someone who had it in for Gracie."

"Could it be somebody trying to send a message about the new rink?"

"What would the message be?"

Build it and they will die, I thought. But I said, "I don't know. Why would somebody kill Gracie and then bother with a bomb that apparently wasn't intended to hurt anyone?"

"How do you know it wasn't intended to hurt anyone?"

Because Michele Higgins had told me.

"I don't," I said.

"We think the bomb was planted on the underside of that stool Gracie used on the Zamboni. So it could have hurt her, or somebody else driving it. I don't know. Maybe there was a screwup. Maybe there's more than one person involved. Maybe there's more to this than just Gracie."

"Any prints?"

"Just Gracie's and a couple from that kid who works the concession stand, but that's no surprise."

"I suppose Tawny Jane's been all over this."

"She was waiting for me when I left the department an hour ago."

"What'd you tell her?"

"I told her I liked how she colored out the gray in her hair. How about you? What are you doing?"

"Driving around mostly." I didn't mention Mich. Instead I told Darlene about Vend and that police report from 1995. She went quiet for a minute.

"I see," she said. "So that's what happened the night before the wedding."

"I don't suppose Gracie ever told you."

"No."

"Did she make the wedding?"

"No."

"Of course you forgave her."

"Not at first. At first I said I'd had enough. I mean, I didn't even see her, barely talked to her, for years. Then she wrote me this long letter about her life, about how she knew she'd gotten mixed up with the wrong people and now she was finally getting herself together. This was after she got back, last year sometime. I just reread it last night."

"I'll bet she didn't name any names."

"No. Except one, which is why I called, partly. Maybe you can find this woman. Looks like she might have been trying to help Gracie."

"Gracie never said anything about her before?"

"Not that I can recall. Her name's Trixie."

"Trixie what?"

"I don't have a last name."

"Great. I'll just look in the phone book under Trixie."

"I thought you were a reporter." She waited for a reply that I wasn't about to give her. "She works at some kind of center for abused women. She apparently went by Trixie the Tramp, or at least that's what Gracie called her."

Darlene's landline phone began to ring in the background.

"Trixie the Tramp," I said. "I'll figure it out."

"I know you will."

"By the way, your hubby and I had a little talk last night."

The landline phone rang for the fourth time.

"Jesus—hold on."

The ringing stopped as Darlene picked up. I pressed my cell phone to my ear to hear. "Roger," Darlene said. "OK. I'll be there in ten."

She hung up the landline and came back to me. "I have to go."

"We have to talk about Jason."

"Not now," she said. My heart sank a little. "That was Dingus."

"OK. Go."

My cell phone battery was almost out, and I'd forgotten the charger. But I wanted to call Philo. He'd sounded oddly urgent on the brief message he'd left for me to call him. Maybe he's cleaning out my desk, I thought.

"Were you aware," I said when he picked up, "that there really was a drain commission meeting today? Eleven a.m. at the county building."

"I know. I went."

I almost dropped my phone.

"Really? How was it?"

"Boring, mostly. A collection of old fat white guys dithering. How do these people order in restaurants?"

"That's the drain commission."

"And what the heck is a 'wet-bottom pond'? Are there ponds with dry bottoms?"

"Welcome to the big time, Philo."

A blue Suburban that looked newly washed pulled slowly past me and parked two driveways ahead, directly across from Vend's house. I watched for the driver's door to open. It didn't. The tinted rear window kept me from seeing inside.

"Where are you?" Philo said.

"Downstate, like I said."

"The boss is not happy. Is it really family you're down there for?"

"It is."

"That woman who hung herself—she was family, wasn't she?"

"She didn't hang herself. But, yes, she's family."

Philo went silent for a moment. I kept one eye on the house's big front window, watching for the blue-on-white curtains to move.

"I doubt the boss knows that," Philo finally said. "But I'm supposed to tell you, if you're not in his office at eight o'clock tomorrow morning, you are no longer employed by Media North or the *Pine County Pilot.*"

"Thank you. Is that all?"

"No." Philo lowered his voice. "Do you really think somebody killed her?"

I hesitated. Was Philo spying for his Uncle Jim? Or was he genuinely curious? Had I somehow gotten through to him the day before?

"I don't have to think anything, Philo. Just following the bread crumbs. Tell me about the drain commission. You got a story?"

"I don't know. Of course, I don't have a paper for four days. But they had a pretty lengthy discussion about sewer service at the new rink. Apparently the developer—"

"Haskell."

"Yes, Laird Haskell. Apparently he has asked to modify his proposal for financing the system out there."

"That wasn't on the agenda, was it?" I always checked the drain commission agenda. A lot of a little town's money could literally go down the toilet in fifteen tedious minutes on a Tuesday morning.

"No. They just showed up like they owned the place. Made me late for a meeting at headquarters."

I could tell that worried him. "That's too bad. Haskell was there?"

"Well, not at the meeting itself. I saw him later. Let me just tell you—"

"Let me see," I said. I wanted Philo to see this as clearly as possible. "Just two months ago, Haskell was going to pay for the whole thing. Read my lips and all. I'm betting he proposed an *improvement.*"

"His lawyer, Mr. Gilbert, did the talking. He called it an *enhancement,* actually."

"For which the town and the county would pay."

"That's approximately right. I thought this one commissioner—I forget his name—might spit up his dentures. Then that Elvis guy was trying to say everything's all right, nobody ever expected Haskell to pay for everything, the rink is the future of the town, yadda yadda."

I let that sit there a second, savoring the thought that Philo might be coming around to the possibility that Haskell, for whatever reason, didn't have the money to build the new rink. Which meant, of course, that he wouldn't need all those *Pilot* ads he was promising to buy.

"So did the commission actually do anything?"

"Tabled it till next month. But, listen, I wanted to ask you—you got a couple of pretty thick envelopes in the mail this morning."

The Suburban doors remained closed. I peered into the rearview mirror on the driver's side. A pair of aviator shades on a wide face looked back. I averted my eyes, first to the house, then to the other side of the street. I turned the key to start my truck. It coughed twice, clicked, and died.

"Shit," I said.

"What?" Philo said. "I didn't open them."

"No, no, it's my damn truck, needs a starter. What about the mail?"

The driver's side door on the Suburban swung open.

"You got two big envelopes from Lansing."

I looked at the house. I wasn't going in there now. Maybe later. Maybe never. I tried the ignition again. Philo was saying something but I wasn't listening. The truck finally wheezed to life and I pulled it out onto the street. I tried to keep my eyes straight ahead but as I passed the Suburban I glanced to my right and saw a man approximately half the tonnage of the vehicle itself turned sideways in the driver's seat. He had a face like a moon, complete with craters that looked like someone had taken a ball-peen hammer to him.

In my rearview I saw him step out of the Suburban and stand in the street, watching me leave.

"Gus," Philo said, "what the hell's going on?"

"Nothing. City drivers. What were you saying?"

The large man was still standing in the street, shades off and arms folded across his chest, when I turned right on Martel. I took that to Allen Road, swung another right, and hoped I'd lost him.

"I'm guessing these envelopes have to do with those freedom-of-information requests you made a while back on Mr. Haskell," Philo said.

"Probably, yeah."

"Would you mind if I took a look?"

My heart was pounding. What a wuss I was. Why didn't I just get out and talk to the guy? Maybe he knew something. I couldn't think about it now. Philo suddenly wanted to pry his way into the Haskell story.

"Why do you want to look at that stuff?"

"Fair question. I don't blame you. I haven't been, shall we say—well, let me put it this way. When I was leaving the drain commission meeting this morning, that Elvis fellow took me by the elbow and steered me into the men's room, where he proceeded to, as he put it, 'advise' me of his confidence that the *Pilot* wouldn't write a word that would jeopardize the future of the community. He also mentioned he's having dinner with my uncle tonight."

"Elvis is a pillar of the community, you know."

"And while he's talking to me, Haskell walks in and takes a leak."

"Just like hockey. It's all about two-on-ones."

"Yes, well, frankly, it ticked me off a little. Plus I missed that meeting at headquarters."

So maybe it wasn't me that had gotten to Philo, but Elvis. And Haskell. And that meeting he missed.

I crossed Oakwood going south, watching my rearview for the Suburban while keeping an eye out for Wally's Wonder Print. "Are you planning to cover the town council meeting tomorrow?"

"I'm considering. Somebody told me it was routine and I probably didn't need to bother."

"Somebody, huh?"

"Yeah. Somebody."

I considered telling Philo about the note I'd received in the mail, decided his new interest in real stories had come up a little too abruptly for that. But I thought maybe he could help me.

"Can you do me a quick favor?"

"I'll try."

"Go online, do a clip search. Just the Detroit papers. Look for someone named Trixie the Tramp. See if you can figure out who she is, where she is."

"Trixie the Tramp. Is this family too?"

"You could say that. And go ahead and look at what's in the envelopes. You probably won't find much. But you never know. If you see something interesting, give me a call."

"Will do. And Gus?"

"Yeah."

"Don't forget. Eight a.m. tomorrow. Sorry."

"Uh-huh. Gotta go."

I swung my truck into Wally's, over the paved lot, and into the back. I parked between a Dumpster and a utility pole where I thought the truck would be hidden from the road.

I stepped outside. The wind snapped my coat collar against my cheek. I pulled the zipper all the way up and stuffed my hands in my coat pockets. *Knobbo*, I thought as I walked around to the front door. If anyone could refresh my memory, Wally could.

The three glass walls that enclosed Ron Wallman's office faced out on a room filled with laser printers, computer terminals, paper cutters, and tall steel racks stacked with boxes and rolls of paper. Signs hanging from the ceiling cheerfully exhorted the workers bustling between printing jobs to bustle a little harder: "Attitude is a little thing that makes a big difference" and "Don't judge those who try and fail, judge only those who fail to try."

Dozens of photographs, plaques, pennants, and certificates crowded the plaster wall behind Wally's wooden desk. Most of the pictures hung in cheap black frames at haphazard angles: Wally posing on a rink with his hockey pals; Wally on the tee with his hockey pals; Wally hoisting a frosted mug of beer in a bowling alley with his hockey pals. A row of plaques pronounced him Melvindale Chamber of Commerce Businessperson of the Year from 1992 to 1996. At the center of it all were professionally framed photos of his wife, Sheryl, and their kids, Joe and Roy.

"What happened to the jersey?" I said.

I was sitting in a cushioned folding chair across from his desk, nursing a Labatt Blue and still feeling the hurt Wally had put on my ribs when he had hugged me in the reception area. The last time I'd been in his office, drinking Scotch after a late-night hockey game a few years before I'd left Detroit, the centerpiece of the wall had been a framed display of his old gold-on-black jersey with the name PIPEFITTERS running diagonally down from the shoulder. Wally had been the star defenseman on the team that had beaten us in the 1981 state final, a six-foot-six, 225-pound bruiser with agile feet and pretty fair hands for a big man.

"Ah, you know, time to grow up," he said. He was sitting on the front edge of his desk, which I could barely see for his bulk. He grinned and winked. "Got it hanging behind my bar at home. The wife never goes down there."

I smiled. "Looks like you're doing OK, Wall."

"Can't complain. Wife's good, boys good, life's good." He thrust his right hand forward again. It swallowed mine. "Always good to see you, buddy. What brings you to town? You bring your gear? I got a nine forty skate now every Tuesday at the Yack. I can tell one of the 'tenders to stay home tonight."

"Nah, gotta get back. Got a game. And I'm not playing goal anymore."

"I thought I heard that. What the hell?"

"Like you said, gotta grow up some time."

I'd gotten to know Wally playing late-night hockey against him during my years at the *Times*. He sponsored a thirty-and-over team in Melvindale called Wally's Wonders. On the ice we'd scrap and bitch and try to beat the hell out of one another. Then we'd have a beer in the parking lot before closing Nasty Melvin's. We got to be friends over bad Buffalo wings and worse nine-ball.

Wally had only teased me once or twice about the state title game. I'd only teased him about a thousand times about his ballooning up to three hundred pounds. I noticed he'd grown another chin since I'd last seen him.

"Hell," he said, "maybe I'll bring the boys up there for a couple of games some weekend." He'd been talking about coming up for years. Thinking of my liver, I hadn't encouraged it. "Hell, the hockey, I don't even care. Seeing all the boys, having a few pops, that's the thing, right, man?"

"Absolutely."

"How's old Soup?"

"Still skating."

"Still dangling? That fucker could play, boy. He went by me once like I was a turnstile. I think he grabbed a token." It was an old hockey line, but Wally laughed like he'd just thought of it. He lifted the Blue to his mouth and drank half the bottle in one long pull.

"Yeah. He bought the bar on Main Street."

"You've got to be kidding. Now there's trouble. You know, I've done some work for his ex. She's got a nice little business in Lincoln Park."

"Didn't know she'd moved there," I said. "Small world. Speaking of which, I've been working on this little feature story and came across a guy I think might've played for you or played in your league a while back."

Wally was leaning over his fridge again. "Ready?" he said.

"I'm good."

"Pussy."

"No news there, pal."

"Which guy?"

"I don't remember his name, but his nickname was something like, I don't know, Knobs or Knobby or Knobbo?"

"Oh, fuck. That guy." Wally twisted the cap off the fresh Blue and snapped it at the plastic wastebasket behind me, missing. "Fucking Knobbo, man."

"Jarek Vend."

"I've seen him in the paper. He's mixed up in all sorts of shit now. Ever been to one of his strip joints?"

"No. Didn't know the guy."

"I dropped like seven hundred in one of them once. That was some high-end foo foo, boy. Thank God I'm married. It's cheaper."

"He played goalie for the Wonders?"

"Yeah." Wally shut his eyes, thinking. "Ninety-one. You in the league then?"

"No. I was still playing in St. Clair Shores."

"East side homos. Anyway, we made the finals and lost to Paxton Van Lines, best of three. We win five to one the first night, Blummer gets a hat trick. Next game we shit the bed, blow a two-goal lead, lose four to three in OT. Paxton comes out in the rubber with this ringer, played at ND, guy named Schneider—his brother played for the gold medal team in eighty—and just fucking swamps us, four-zip."

He had a memory like that. I was sure he could have told me the starting lineups on each team and where each guy played his kid hockey.

"And Knobbo was in the net? Why do they call him Knobbo?"

Wally cracked a big smile. "If you don't know, I ain't telling you."

"Fuck you then."

"Hey, maybe the knob on his goalie stick, eh? Anyway, he could play, too. And he was like, I don't know, forty. Played for the Junior Wings way back when Gordie Howe's kids were still playing." Wally stood and waved his arms around like a goalie stopping shots, beer slopping out of his bottle and onto his carpet. "Total flopper. But, man, what a weirdo. Always with the blow in the dressing room."

"Cocaine?"

"Yeah. One line before the first period, two before the second, three before the third. A little superstitious, are we? Some nights he'd be the life of the damn party; other nights, not a word. You definitely didn't want to fuck with him, though. I know all you goalies are crazy, but this guy took the cake."

"Really."

"Oh, man." His face burst into a smile. "You heard about Antonoff."

"No."

Wally told me. Antonoff played for a team called the Gray Hawks sponsored by a mortgage company in Southgate. Everybody mistook him for a Russian because of his name and because he talked funny, but he was just some East Coast guy in for a year to consult with Chrysler on some manufacturing stuff. It took him only a few games to establish himself as a major asshole on the ice, always chopping guys, kicking legs out, running goalies. Always after the whistle.

One night, late in a game, the Wonders were blowing out the Gray Hawks when Vend—Knobbo—made a save and smothered the puck with his stick-hand glove. Antonoff came flying in after the refs had blown the play dead, sprayed Knobbo's head with ice, then slapped the side of Knobbo's mask with his stick blade. Knobbo jumped up, said something to Antonoff in a language other than English. Antonoff told him, *Go back to your worthless fucking country.*

As Antonoff skated away, laughing, Knobbo pulled his mask back on his head and said something else and looked up into the stands where he had two buddies with three young women dolled up in furs and silk scarves, smoking, drinking something that probably wasn't 7Up from giant 7Up cups. Knobbo gave them a furious nod and waggled his big flat goalie stick in the direction of Antonoff. Both guys nodded back. The chicks giggled.

"Late that night, man," Wally said, "they fucked him up."

"Antonoff?"

"Yeah. He was always the last guy out of Nasty's. Those jag-offs were waiting."

"Knobbo?"

"No. The guys from the stands, talking in Polish or Ukrainian or whatever the hell it was. They beat the shit out of him, messed up his face so bad he had to have reconstructive surgery. Left him in a Dumpster back of Nasty's. Supposedly Knobbo showed up at the very end and got up on the Dumpster and pissed all over him."

"Wow. I think I'll take that other beer now."

Wally went around to the fridge again, plucked out two Blues. "What's your article about?"

"I don't really know yet," I said. "Knobbo apparently has some business interests up our way."

"Better be careful what you write, eh?"

"Yeah. He only played that one year?"

"He got hurt, man. Old Meat cut him."

"Meat?" I said.

Wally's door swung open and a woman ducked her head in. "Hey, boss," she said. Wally swiveled his big body around.

"What's up, Claudia?"

"Got to get Annie up to Fraser."

"Fraser? That shithole? What's the matter with you? Rinks around here aren't good enough for your little girl?"

"The sacrifices we make for hockey." She grinned and pointed at Wally's Labatt bottle. "Getting an early start, are we?"

Wally spread his arms wide in supplication and nodded toward me. "I have a guest. Meet Gus, an old hockey bud down from up north."

"Hey there, Gus."

"Nice to meet you, Claudia," I said, but all I could think was, Meat? Jason Esper knew Jarek Vend? Could it be that there was no coincidence in Jason returning to Starvation not long after Gracie had?

"Don't forget to punch that clock on your way out," Wally said.

She chuckled. "Right on, boss."

The door closed. Wally said, "Mark my words—her kid's going to be the first babe to stick in the NHL. Great kid."

"You talking about the same Meat I know?"

"Meat? Oh, yeah, Jason . . . Jason . . . Esper—yeah—he played with me on the 'Fitters. He was just a beanpole back then."

"Yeah. He's living in Starvation. What's he got to do with Knobbo?"

"You don't know?"

The Wonders were playing Big Bill's from Inkster, Wally said. During a scrum at the net, a Bill's center named McSween slashed Knobbo across the forearm. Knobbo went down just as Jason came zooming in with his stick up around his elbows, aimed at McSween's forehead. McSween ducked. Jason went flying. As he catapulted over the pile, one of his skate blades sliced through the right side of Knobbo's neck.

"I swear, man, I almost lost my lunch," Wally said. "The blood shot up this high"—he held a palm flat at his shoulder—"and Knobbo was rolling around and screaming like he was going to die."

"But he didn't."

"Nope. Meat, man, Meat saved his life. He cut him and then he saved his life. He got down and jammed his hands down on Knobbo's neck until the ambulance came. It was lucky we were close to the hospital." Maybe I imagined it, but I thought Wally went a little pale. "I can still see Meat in the dressing room, blood all over him, shaking like a leaf."

"And that was it for Knobbo?"

"Yep. For Meat, too. Next time I saw him—the last time I saw him— was at one of Knobbo's clubs, working the door."

"No shit, bouncing? When?"

"Last fall?" Wally looked sheepish. "I mean, I don't go to those places usually, but Poke had a bachelor party. Meat didn't look all that glad to see us. We didn't stay long."

"Good old Meat."

"Yep." Wally sneaked a look at the clock on his desk. I stood up, set my second bottle on Wally's desk.

"I better get going."

Wally pointed at my half-full bottle. "Alcohol abuse, man."

"What can I say? I'm a wimp."

Wally deserved his good life. I wondered what he would have said or done if I had told him about my life, how I was just trying to hang on to my job and my girlfriend. He stretched out a hand. "Good to see you, bud."

Jason Esper had cut Jarek Vend. Then he had saved his life. Then he was working for him. Then he came up north and married Darlene. But something was missing. His life went to shit and drink and video golf.

He left Starvation, went back downstate. Back to Vend. They were brothers bound by spilled blood. Now Jason was back in Starvation again, supposedly cleaned up. I was betting he and Knobbo were bound by something other than just blood. Probably not something pretty.

Philo had left me a message. I scribbled the Prospect Street address for Trixie the Tramp—a.k.a. Patricia Armbruster—on the side of a foam coffee cup. Not bad, Philo, I thought. Not bad.

Then I dialed Darlene. I just wanted to hear her voice. My phone died in the middle of the first ring.

"There's no need for you to see anything here," she told me.

"But isn't this—"

"What happens here is none of your business." She gave me a prim smile. "My car's out back."

Trixie Armbruster did not look like a tramp, or at least the sort of tramp her nickname brought to mind. Taller than me, she carried her boxy frame in a baggy cotton dress. The dress was printed with tiny flowers that had all faded to the same shade of pale lavender. On our way out to the muddy lot behind her building, she wrapped herself in a worn brown bomber jacket. The zipper didn't work so she clipped the jacket together beneath her bosom with a safety pin. Her gone-white hair stuck out over the jacket collar in a stiff, wavy perm. She walked with purpose, two steps ahead of me, limping with each step, favoring her left leg.

All I knew of Trixie's past was what I had heard on Philo's short phone message: She was once a prostitute and heroin addict. She had broken free somehow and started the center for abused women, mostly abused prostitutes. She called it Trixie's Place for Tired Women and Girls. The name helped get her some publicity, a few grants, some pity donations from a rich liberal or two, a little extra police protection from the city. When I heard it on Philo's message, all I could think was, Gracie, what did you get yourself into?

Trixie had sounded oddly expectant when I'd called her from a pay phone outside a party store to ask if I could drop by. I suppose that someone who did what she did was always ready for anything. I had explained how Gracie had been found dead in the shoe tree, how she was extended family, how I had come at the behest of my mother, Gracie's favorite aunt, to see if I could gain a clearer understanding of how she had lived her life, why it had ended.

"I don't know," she had said. "I don't see what good it would do."

"Maybe Gracie told you—"

"Yes, I'm aware that you're a newspaper reporter. If her aunt sent you, I suppose I can show you a couple of things."

The center was in a dreary brick building that looked like it might once have been a corner store or a bar, tucked into a neighborhood not far from the Ford factory across the river. The only thing identifying the center was a semicircular plaque hanging on the front door and carved with the words "Trixie's Place." Beneath the plaque hung a plain wooden cross painted along its borders in gold.

I had pushed the doorbell and immediately a buzzer had sounded and a woman's voice had come over an intercom: "Step inside, please. I'll be out in five." I'd waited in a space barely bigger than a closet, gazing down at a floor of muddy tile. There wasn't a sound until I'd heard footsteps descending stairs inside and then the jingle of keys. The inner door had opened and I had presumptuously begun to step inside when Trixie blocked my way, closed that door behind her, and pointed me to her car.

"Thank you for meeting me," I said.

Trixie was steering her Honda Civic through another neighborhood of snug bungalows. I tried to watch the street signs to see if we had wound up back at Vend's house. Trixie was taking rights and lefts and rights again, seemingly doubling back. I thought we'd gone down the same block twice but couldn't be sure because the houses looked alike. I thought maybe she was trying to make it so confusing that I couldn't find my way back.

"Please understand," she said without taking her eyes off the road. "I am not happy that you are here. I am not happy that this day has arrived. I never am. But in all honesty, I can't say that I'm surprised."

"Tired Women and Girls?" I said.

"Tired of being abused?"

"So why not just abused?"

"Too many others with names like that."

"I'm sorry for your loss," I said.

She continued to drive without speaking. A gentle smile made its way onto her face. Then it was gone. She turned to me.

"I don't mean to be glum," she said. "It's hard." She reached across and touched my forearm. "I'm sorry for your loss, too. Although, again, in all honesty, I can't say that I think you appreciate it."

"Thanks, I think."

She withdrew her hand. "It's all right. Grace was not easy to know. For anyone. It didn't matter how much you loved her, or how hard you tried."

"Then you obviously knew her well."

Trixie tilted her head to one side, smoothing the crinkled skin along her jaw. A slender necklace of gold lay on her pale white neck. I decided she had been a beautiful woman once. "Sometimes, yes," she said, "I thought I did. But that's just vanity, isn't it? Most of us don't even know our own selves."

She turned a corner and eased off the gas as the Civic approached a cul de sac. She parked at the curb in front of a house that looked like so many there, only a shade of paint or a set of shutters different than Vend's. The aluminum siding was a dingier white and there was no rock garden or statute of the Blessed Mother. An orange-and-brown paper turkey dangled in the front window. It reminded me that Gracie had declined Mom's invitation to Thanksgiving dinner because she had been going for a visit downstate.

A piece of white paper was tacked to the front door.

"This is where Gracie lived?" I said.

Trixie looked past me at the house. "I know she could have used the money," she said. "Now I'm glad she didn't sell it, so you can see."

"She owned the place? Gracie had a mortgage?" I pointed at the house. "What's the paper on the door? That a foreclosure notice?"

"Details like that don't really matter now."

"Yes, they do. Unless you think Gracie really killed herself. I don't."

Trixie's gray eyes moved to mine. "Why are you here again?"

"To find out what really happened to Gracie."

"Do you think that's possible? Without hearing it from Gracie's own lips?"

"I guess I must, or I wouldn't be here."

The car was still idling.

"You know," Trixie said. "We didn't call her Gracie. We called her Grace."

"We?"

"Her sisters back at the house. Me."

"Gracie always called herself Gracie. She said Grace sounded old."

Trixie looked out the windshield. "The will of God," she recited, "will never take you where the grace of God won't protect you." She turned the car off. "Let's go."

Trixie had a key. As she swung the front door open, she blocked my view of the piece of paper. Then she closed the door.

"OK," I said. I reached into my back pocket for my notebook.

"Be kind," she said. "This is not a crime scene."

"I don't have such a good memory."

"You reporters are so full of it." She tapped two fingers on her chest. "Imprint what you see and hear on your heart. The story will be much clearer."

"I'll do my best," I said. For now, I left my notebook in my pocket. "Are we on the record?"

"You can write whatever you like. But for the sake of the women in my care, I don't want to see my name in your paper. I'm already having enough trouble with my landlord."

"What's the problem?"

"None of your business. This way."

The inside of the house was clean and sparsely furnished but obviously lived in. In the living room, another afghan like the one Mom had made me—identical to the one I'd seen in the Zamboni shed—lay in a bunch at one end of a sofa. An unlit lamp stood on an end table. An armchair faced the sofa across a coffee table. A television perched atop a mostly empty bookshelf. On the mantel over a fake fireplace stood a framed black-and-white photograph: Gracie and Darlene stood with their arms around each other at the end of a dock, smiling and squinting against the sun, ripples of lake water glinting behind them.

"I don't understand," I said.

"What?"

"Why would Gracie leave all this stuff here if she was moving back to Starvation?"

"Good question."

"I mean, did she have to leave suddenly or something? Was she in trouble?"

"Well," Trixie said, "if she wasn't in trouble before, she obviously found it. I don't know. Maybe she just didn't know if she wanted to move up there permanently. Grace didn't tell me everything. Let's go in here."

The kitchen smelled faintly of Murphy's Oil Soap. My mother used up a big bottle of Murphy's every few months and said its lingering aroma was her favorite in the world next to that of a cinnamon cake baking.

There was a breakfast table with two chairs covered in flowery green vinyl, white cabinets, Formica counters the color of bananas. The table held an empty schnapps bottle sprouting a bouquet of dried hydrangeas. Lacy cotton curtains dressed a window over the sink that looked out on a tiny backyard, a concrete side drive, and a one-car garage. In the dish drainer rested a chipped black coffee cup embossed with a Detroit Red Wings logo.

It was the cup more than anything that made me silently marvel: Gracie had had her own house. I pictured her standing in that kitchen, sipping coffee from that cup, looking out the little window to see whether the morning promised sun or rain or snow. Was it really hers? That wouldn't be too hard to find out. I made a mental note to check before I went back up north.

I opened a cabinet next to the sink. There were half a dozen each of plates, bowls, coffee cups, and milk glasses. I looked in the next cabinet, saw a platter, two serving bowls, an empty shelf. I crossed to the other side of the sink and opened another cabinet. Inside I glimpsed a collection of flower vases before Trixie's hand appeared and pushed the cabinet shut.

"Hey," she said. "Are you looking for something?"

"Booze."

"You won't find it here."

I looked over at the schnapps vase on the table. Peach schnapps, I noticed.

"Ancient," Trixie said. "Come on."

A hallway off the kitchen led to a pair of facing bedrooms. The door on the left stood halfway open. The door on the right was closed. Trixie stopped just short of where I could see into the rooms and placed her big body in front of me.

"How did you know to find me?" she said.

"Someone told me."

"Who?"

She seemed determined to know. The implication seemed to be that if I didn't tell her, I wouldn't see the rooms. I had no idea what I might find in there, but I definitely wanted to see.

"Darlene Esper," I said. "A friend of Gracie's. Do you know her?"

"I know of her. She's the wo—the girl—in the picture in the living room."

"Yes."

"And you've been in love with her your whole life."

Her certainty startled me.

"Isn't that right?" she said.

"Pretty much." I nodded toward the rooms. "Which was Gracie's?"

"Wait," she said, stepping forward and placing a hand against my chest. "Do you know what Grace did when she came to Detroit? Have you ever really given it any thought—a girl of, what, eighteen or nineteen, leaving her tiny little town up north to come to the big city?"

"Forgive me, but what's the big deal? Lots of kids leave up north every year to go to college downstate. I did. And they do fine. And they don't have rich benefactors paying their tuition for them like Gracie."

"So your answer is no, you have not given it much thought."

"What is that supposed to mean?"

"Grace's *benefactor*? You mean the man—it could only be a man, or more than one—who promised her an education? She got one, all right."

She told me about it.

Gracie had enrolled in the freshman program at Wayne State University in the fall of 1980. She had hoped to declare her major as English. One semester of tuition and room and board had indeed been paid for in full. But no money had been provided for her required texts. At the campus bookstore Gracie learned that the bill for those would come to nearly $350. She had saved barely half that from her summer job at Dairy Queen. Her appeals to her mother for the rest met first with promises, then with lectures about saving money, then with unreturned phone calls. Grace started classes without books.

Finally she contacted her anonymous benefactor. The only requirement the donor had was that Gracie write a short letter at the midpoint and the end of each semester reporting on her academic progress. There was a post office box to which she was supposed to mail the letters. Now she wrote

explaining her book dilemma. In the letter she apologized for her ignorance and promised to repay any book money provided.

Soon Gracie heard from a man. He didn't say whether he was her actual donor, but he had a job for her waiting tables. Late one afternoon she
showed up for her first six-hour shift. Although it served food and drinks,
B.J.'s Office wasn't a restaurant. B.J.'s was a strip club on Michigan Avenue
in Dearborn, about a fifteen-minute drive from Gracie's dormitory. When
she drove up to the place, she thought maybe she'd gotten the address
wrong.

"I'm aware that Grace was no angel in her youth," Trixie said. "But even
she was, shall we say, taken aback."

"But she took the job," I said.

Trixie shrugged. "This wasn't some smoky pit frequented by guys missing teeth and stuffing dollar bills in G-strings. This was a gentleman's club.
A jacket was required. You had to pay twenty-five dollars just to get in the
door. The girls were from everywhere but here."

"Canada? Poland maybe?"

"How did you know?"

"Just a guess."

"Hm. Well, on a good night, Grace could make two or three hundred
dollars in tips. So she really only had to work one or two nights a week,
which left her more time to study."

"And I'm sure she used it for that," I said.

"I didn't know her then, of course, so I can't say for sure. But she told me
she tried, and I'll take her word." ·

"Did she dance at the club?"

"No. She waited tables." Trixie folded her arms and gazed down at the
floor. "But she might have been better off dancing."

The middle-aged men who sat with their $7.50 Heinekens at the little
round tables in the shadows of B.J.'s Office hadn't made their fortunes by
pursuing things that were easily available. The dancers, of course, were easily available; the waitresses were not, or at least not as obviously so. To bed
a slinky young woman who peeled off her clothes before men as routinely
as she poured herself a morning coffee was one thing. To seduce a waitress—especially that pretty college student named Gracie—now that was
something else.

Midway through her second semester at Wayne State, Gracie stopped going to classes. She moved out of her dorm and into an apartment in the Bricktown neighborhood near downtown Detroit. She continued to work at B.J.'s one or two afternoons a week. Her nights were given to other employment that paid her much more. There was a man, a very rich man, many years her elder, who paid her rent and bought her things. After a while there were other men, other apartments, more money and things.

"So she was a hooker," I said.

"Of a sort," Trixie said. "Unfortunately, it wasn't strictly about having sex for money. Grace became very good at satisfying a particularly difficult-to-satisfy customer. And, unfortunately for her, she came to enjoy it. At least for a time, she enjoyed it at least as much as the customers."

"Jesus. What kind of customer?"

"Please be respectful of the Lord's name."

"Sorry."

"Tell me, Gus. Are you familiar with sexual bondage? Autoerotic sex asphyxiation?"

From the Lord's name to autoerotic sex. This woman was tough. I studied her face for any sign of weariness. There was none. She looked to be in her sixties. I wondered if she merely looked older than she was because of the past life she had led.

"I've heard of it. Can't say I'm familiar."

"You'll see."

"So," I said, "this whole anonymous donor thing was bull."

I pulled out my wallet and showed Trixie the clipping I'd cut from the *Pilot* of March 18, 1980. She scanned the article quickly, smiled wanly at the picture. "Look at her," she said. "Just a child. Can I keep this?"

"It's yours," I said. "Whoever paid her tuition was really a"—I searched for the word—"a recruiter."

"Essentially. Small-town girls from troubled homes, out of sorts in the big city. We had two others at the center. Grace brought them to me."

"Goddamn b—excuse me."

"That's all right. All these guys were bastards."

She pushed open the door to the room on the left and let me step in before her. The room was lit by the flat afternoon light coming in through the window facing the street. The first thing I noticed was the poster on the wall at the head of the single bed. Red Wings star Sergei Fedorov was spraying ice and snow at the camera in a sideways hockey stop. He wore a bright red jersey, number 91, and a wide smile on his boyish face. Beneath the poster a red bedspread was emblazoned with the Red Wings' white winged-wheel logo. Three foot-high stacks of Red Wings game programs sat on a trunk at the foot of the bed.

A small desk and a chair stood next to the bed. Atop the desk was a red plastic cup filled with pencils and pens, a photograph in a standing frame, and a single piece of construction paper.

I stepped over and picked up the photo frame. Eddie McBride—Gracie's late father, cousin and drinking buddy of my own father—reclined across the backseat of a boat, shirtless, in a yellow bathing suit that set off his deep tan. On his lap sat a baby girl with reddish curls and a cloth diaper. She was smiling.

There was no picture of Gracie's mother, Shirley McBride.

I set the photo down and took up the sheet of paper. It held a pencil drawing of a hockey player with his arms and stick raised over his head in celebration of a goal. It was crude enough to have been rendered by a child, but I supposed it could just as easily have been Gracie's work.

"Whose room is—was this?" I said.

"Grace," Trixie said. "Grace slept here."

"When she wasn't at the center?"

"Here mostly, at least the last couple of years. Until she went back up north."

I went to the closet on the opposite wall and slid the doors open. The hangers were filled with simple cotton dresses and jumpers and frilly tops. The floor was covered with pairs of shoes piled on one another. There were pumps and flats and mules and slingbacks, sneakers and moccasins, clogs and knee-high boots and flip-flops and slippers. I shoved the door closed and turned back to Trixie.

"Except for that, looks like a boy's room," I said.

"Grace loved hockey. Loved the Detroit team, that player especially."

Fedorov, one of the Wings' Russians, was a gifted skater who could play as well as anyone in the world at either end of the ice—when he wanted to. Some nights he played as if he didn't much care. I wondered if his occasional ambivalence appealed to Gracie, whether she saw whatever struggle she was going through mirrored in her hockey hero.

"I had no idea," I said.

"Why would you?"

Out of the corner of my eye I saw something moving on the street outside. I turned and saw the back end of a blue sport-utility vehicle sliding slowly past the house.

"What?" Trixie said.

"Nothing."

I moved to the foot of the bed and started riffling through the first stack of programs on the trunk. I was looking for one from that Detroit-versus-Chicago playoff series when I thought I had seen Gracie. But Trixie grasped my shoulder and pulled me toward the door.

"Come on, I don't have all afternoon."

She left the door to Gracie's room open, stepped across the hall, and produced a pair of keys that unlocked the two locks on the door to the other room. She pushed the door half open and stood across the threshold. "Gracie called this her dark room," she said.

"Not for photography, though."

"No."

I peered into the room, couldn't see a thing. I looked at Trixie. "Can I ask you something?"

"Go ahead."

"Did Gracie have a son?"

Trixie held my gaze for what seemed like a full minute. Then she looked away. "No," she said. "Grace . . ." She looked back at me. "Her employer said she couldn't be pregnant. But Grace let . . . let the baby go. It was her choice."

"What employer?"

Trixie looked at me again. "You'll see."

"I will? What about that drawing in the other room?"

"Part of her rehabilitation was volunteering at a local grade school. The kids in Melvindale love the Red Wings, too."

So Darlene was right about the abortion. I thought of the baby shoe Gracie had hidden in the Zam shed. Something approaching sadness swelled then receded in the pit of my stomach.

"When did she have it?"

"What?" Trixie said.

"The abortion."

She pursed her lips. "I don't think Grace would want me talking about it."

"Grace is dead."

"Not yet. Not to me, at least. And not to you, either, or you wouldn't be here now, would you?"

"Do you talk in riddles with the women at the center?"

"Do you want to see what's in this room or not? If you prefer, we can leave right now and you can go chase down whoever was outside the bedroom window."

Trixie didn't miss a trick. "All right," I said.

She stepped aside and let me pass.

seventeen

The room was tiny, more like a sewing room than a bedroom, with the musty smell of a place no one had been in for a long while. And it was indeed dark, the shades drawn on the window opposite the door. Trixie flicked a wall switch. A bare bulb in the center of the ceiling threw a dim oval of yellow light that left the corners of the room in shadow.

Next to the window hung a glassed-in frame containing a medal pinned on white satin. The Purple Heart.

"Is that her father's?" I said.

"Why else would she have it there?" Trixie said.

"Don't tell me—she got it off the Internet."

"How did you know?"

For $33.50, I thought. "Things get around in Starvation Lake."

Cardboard boxes sat along the baseboards on two walls. Above them, to my left, hung four pages that had been clipped out of newspapers and thumbtacked to the wall. I stepped past Trixie to see them up close.

"Holy shit," I said.

The first was the front page of the *Detroit Times*, Sunday, March 3, 1996. A thirty-six-point headline ran across the top: "*Teen's Fiery Death Shines Harsh Spotlight on Superior Pickup Truck*." The story beneath it ran under the byline of A. J. Carpenter. Augustus James Carpenter. Me.

"What does she have this up here for?"

"Maybe you had a fan," Trixie said.

I shook my head as I read the first few paragraphs of the story, remembering. "Gracie never gave a damn about what I did. She used to call me a fag if I got an A in school."

"I don't know what she used to do. Keep going."

The next page, yellower than the first, was also from the front of the

Times, Friday, January 31, 1992. Under my byline again, barely above the fold: "*Local Attorney Nabs Another Big Verdict; GM Vows Appeal.*" The amount of the verdict, which someone had underlined in red ink, was $28.3 million. The copy wrapped around a small black-and-white photo, circled in red ink, of the local attorney, a handsome smiling man named Laird Haskell.

That's quite a coincidence, I thought.

I turned and glanced at Trixie. She was leaning against the doorjamb, watching me. "What?" she said. "Something wrong?"

I ignored her and turned to the third page, which was not from the *Times* but the *Free Press*, page B4, Friday, September 1, 1995. "Strip-Club Owner Acquitted of Role in Explosion" read the headline over the story by Michele Higgins:

> The prosecution of a prominent area strip-club owner blew up in Wayne County Circuit Court yesterday when a judge dismissed charges that Jarek A. Vend paid to have a bomb planted in the kitchen of a rival gentlemen's club in Romulus.
>
> Vend, 46 years old, owner of more than a dozen strip clubs in Metro Detroit, had insisted he had nothing to do with a minor explosion that occurred at the Landing Strip one afternoon in May. But he told reporters he was amused that someone appeared to have played a prank on a competitor. No one was injured in the blast, which police said appeared to be designed to frighten rather than inflict real harm.

There was no photo.

"Jesus," I said.

"Please," Trixie said.

I spun around to face her.

"This is the guy who gave Gracie a job when she needed book money?"

"Who?"

"Vend."

She shook her head. "No," she said. "He was probably the guy's boss. Vend doesn't talk to the help, unless he's sleeping with them."

"I was at his house earlier."

"Over there?" She jerked a thumb over her shoulder. "That's his mother's. His late mother's. It's in his name. The press eats that crap up about him being a local guy. He has a high-rise in Windsor overlooking the river. Just in case the cops here ever decide to really go after him, which they never will. Talk about a goddamn bastard."

And I thought Starvation was a small town. She probably knew who was in that Suburban cruising past the house too.

"What about this lawyer?" I said, pointing at the page with the Haskell story. "Why was Gracie so interested in him?"

"What's his name?"

"Haskell. You haven't looked at these?"

"Grace's hobby, not mine." She nodded past me. "What's the last one?"

The front page of the *Times* was dated Thursday, July 24, 1997. I knew what was there. After forcing me to resign, the *Times* had agreed to publish a retraction of my stories about Superior Motors' deadly pickup trucks. Four hundred and fifty-two words ran in a one-column slot at the bottom of the page, next to the index. Gracie had carefully clipped it and tacked it up as part of her "hobby." I didn't have to read it. But I stared at it anyway, cursing Gracie, picturing her in the Zam shed telling me I played hockey like a pussy, wishing she were alive so I could tell her to go to hell. Even things she hadn't intended for me to see wound up stinging.

"She's a fan, all right," I said. "What's in these boxes?"

The four boxes were closed but not taped. I bent over, flipped one open, reached in, and pulled out a tangle of black leather.

"What the—," I said, holding it up in front of me. A collar equipped with a drawstring was attached to thick straps that ran down to an adjustable belt that presumably wrapped around someone's waist. More straps fitted with buckles and Velcro jutted from the belt. I dropped it on the floor and pulled more leather from the box. A hooded mask with a zipper running down the back. A girdle with thin silver chains dangling from the crotch.

I put it all back and looked inside the next box. It looked like it had come from a hardware store. Or the Zamboni shed. There were chains and pulleys and clamps. Eyebolts, screwdrivers, needle-nose pliers, a hammer, a can of WD-40, a jar of Vaseline, two packages of Saran wrap. I sifted through the jumble and found three pairs of handcuffs at the bottom of the box, two of blue plastic, one of nickel. The next box was stuffed with plastic tubes, leather belts, and rubber hoses of various lengths. I picked up one of the hoses and noticed small, curly hairs stuck to the open end.

My stomach turned over once, then again.

I thought of Vend, the naked man, bursting out of the motel room up north with something black and rubbery attached to himself. I turned to Trixie and took a deep breath.

"I think I've seen enough," I said.

"What about the other box?" she said.

"I've seen enough."

"Are you afraid?"

I thought, What is this, hockey? Why doesn't she just come right out and call me a pussy? "All right," I said.

I opened the fourth box. Inside was a small safe, gray with a black handle. "Do you mind?" I asked Trixie. She nodded. I lifted the safe out of the cardboard box, set it on the floor. I tried the handle. Locked.

"Well," I said. "I don't suppose you have the key."

"No. Sorry."

"Oh, jeez, hang on."

I got down on the floor and dug out my key chain. I found the little rust-colored key that had been tied into the ribbon on the baby shoe in Gracie's hiding place. I held the key up for Trixie. "Maybe this'll work," I said.

"Where did you get that?"

"Gracie left it to me in her will."

The key slid into the lock and turned. I lifted the cover. Inside were half a dozen black plastic boxes. Along the spine of each box was a piece of white tape marked with what appeared to be initials and a date:

DTJ 7/26/92
LKH 3/19/90
MXR 2/8/93
JAV 12/31/91

"Videos?" I said. I picked up one of the boxes and opened the plastic shell casing. A videotape fell out into my hands. The tape, too, was fixed with a label marked with initials and a date matching the ones on the box.

I waggled the tape at Trixie. "Gracie got a video player?"

"Not that I know of."

"Then what are the videos for?"

"I don't know."

"You got a tape player back at the center?"

"You're not going in the center."

"Can I take these then? I'll return them."

"Nothing leaves the house."

"Why?"

"Nothing leaves the house."

"Trixie, I can't do my job—"

"I thought you'd seen enough," she said. "We've pawed through enough of Grace's things. We're not taking them away. This is her home."

I held the tape up next to my head. "Please?"

"Sorry."

"Will you at least think about it?"

"Put it back, please."

I set the tape back in the safe, closed the safe, lifted it into the cardboard box. I'd try her again later. I could always come back downstate if she relented. When she relented. I got up off the floor.

"Tell me," I said. "If you knew, why didn't you just come out and tell me Gracie was mixed up with this Vend character?"

"Because," she said, as if the answer was obvious, "you're a reporter. I've dealt with plenty of reporters. You're skeptical. You have to find things out for yourself or you don't want to believe them. That's the way you are. Besides, Gus, face it—you'd never believe what Grace told you anyway. She could have given you chapter and verse about Vend or Laird Haskell and it would've gone in one ear and out the other."

"Ah, so it's my fault," I said, though I knew she was probably right. "What do you expect? She was drunk or high every time I saw her."

Trixie stepped forward and pointed a finger in my face. "Of all people," she said, nearly shouting, "*you* should know that appearances—oh, never mind." She turned away, shaking her head. "Never mind."

"What happened to the others?" I said. "The women Gracie brought you. Are they OK now?"

She let out a sigh, collecting herself. Trixie the Tramp obviously didn't like losing her cool. "I have to be going now."

"Come on," I said. "I'm listening."

"One of them is managing. I try not to let her out of my sight. The other . . ." Trixie's voice trailed off. I waited. She closed her eyes. "They found her a few weeks ago in Sarnia, near the beach, hanging from a swing set."

"Oh, man. No."

"Suicide." She opened her eyes. "At least that's what the cops said."

We rode back to the center in silence. I thought of what Trixie had just told me. A "suicide" in Sarnia followed by a "suicide" in Starvation Lake formed a gruesome pattern. I had to get to a phone.

She parked the Civic in a dirt lot next to the center. I opened my door. The inside light came on. Trixie didn't move. She still had her hands on the steering wheel.

"Thank you for coming," she said.

"You're welcome."

"I know it probably upset you, even though . . ." She swallowed. "You should know, Gus, that Grace was trying to turn her life around."

She shut off the car. We sat in the dark alongside the center, cars swishing past us on the road. "She would've been happy that you came," Trixie said. "Even if it won't do any good."

"You don't believe she killed herself."

She let her hands drop into her lap. "Sometimes I do. It's easier because, let's be honest, what difference does it make? These are clever men. They didn't get to where they are by leaving fingerprints all over their mistakes."

She turned in her seat to face me.

"I know what I said before, but . . . I didn't realize until I started to show you, but I wanted you to see. Grace would have wanted you to see. Now go home and bury her and forget all of this. You don't have to ruin your life trying to prove something you can't."

Either she was trying to be nice or she was daring me.

"Would it ruin my life if I got a look at a couple of those videos?"

Trixie opened her door. "I'll let you know."

"One last thing?" I said.

"One last thing."

"Did she regret it?"

"Regret what?"

I chose my words carefully. "Her baby."

"Very much."

I watched her walk back into the center with her determined limp, her dress swaying beneath the bomber jacket. Trixie the Tramp was a good woman. She was not a good liar. She'd said she hadn't really looked at those newspaper pages; it was Gracie's hobby, not hers. But she knew enough to call Haskell by his first name. I could only wonder if that was her only slip.

The pay phone at Nasty Melvin's was right where I remembered it, beneath the Bud Light sign—used to be a Miller Lite sign—hanging on the wall in the back of the bar alongside the chalkboard menu. The price of a cheeseburger had gone up since I'd drunk there with Wally and other hockey pals a few years before, from $3.25—with fries and a dill pickle—to $3.75.

With my cell phone dead, I had no choice but to use a pay phone, but I didn't mind visiting Nasty's. I'd had a lot of fun there and managed to keep myself out of the occasional fights that broke out between the middle-aged bikers who tried to keep to their Bud longnecks and the overserved yuppies who insisted on playing pool for money, then tried to sneak out before paying their debts. Not once in my years of drinking at Nasty's did I see a hockey player get into a fight. Fights were a part of the game on the ice, but skaters carry no illusions about hockey being some metaphor for life. Life was quite a bit harder than hockey, as was getting up for work with a busted face.

I ordered a bottle of Blue Ribbon and five dollars' worth of quarters.

I figured I would make my calls, grab a cheeseburger or two to go, and head back up north. If all went well, I'd be back in time to make the playoff game against the Minnows before I went looking for Darlene.

I set my Blue Ribbon on a table and stepped over to the phone, the soles of my boots peeling off the linoleum floor. I had to get someone at the Wayne County Clerk's Office before it closed at five o'clock. Then I'd see if I could dig up a cop in Sarnia.

The phone at the clerk's office rang six times. Then came a recording. I hit a few buttons, hoping the options hadn't changed. A man came on the line. I asked for Nova Patterson.

"She's left," the man said.

"No," I said. "Look in the back. She always stays late."

"I am not allowed to leave the front desk, sir."

I didn't bother asking the guy for what I wanted. He'd tell me I needed to come in, and I didn't have time.

"Listen, do me a huge favor. Just tell her—yell it out if you have to—that Gus Carpenter is on the line. She'll want to talk to me."

"Sir, this is a place of business, I can't be—"

"Look, look, you're right," I said, changing strategy. "I'll just come in. Let's see . . . I got twenty minutes. I'll be there in five. I have a pretty big request and I hope it doesn't keep you there late."

"Sir, you might want to consider—"

"Or you can just put Nova on the line and forget it."

He thought about it. "Hang on." He put me on hold.

A minute passed. The phone clicked. A big sweet voice came over the line, louder than it needed to be. "Where the hell you been, sugar?"

"Nova," I said. "How's Michael? Is he playing for the Lions yet?"

She had helped me a thousand times when I was working in Detroit. You needed a friend like Nova Marie Patterson in the Wayne County Clerk's Office, where a reporter seeking public records was treated with all the respect of a rat scrounging in a trash can. I brought her chicken paprikash from Al's Lounge. I told her she was way too nice to be working at the clerk's office. We talked about her boy, Michael, who wanted to play in the NFL. He was tiny for his age, his head too small for the smallest helmet. Nova blamed the drinking she'd done as a teenager, when Michael was born. She drank sloe gin, "but not slow, if you know what I mean," she'd told me. She was clean now.

"Oh, my Lord, I hope not," she said. "He plays for the Lions, he's going to get killed." She laughed. "So where've you been, stranger? Thank you for the tickets, but I want to see your handsome face."

I smiled and leaned over and grabbed my beer. I had a hockey buddy who knew a guy who knew a guy who worked for the Lions, and every season I sent Nova two tickets.

"Long story," I said. "Basically, I had to get back up north and take care of my mom."

"You're such a good son. Are you going to come see me?"

"I wish I could. That's why I called. I need a favor."

"Well," Nova said, "I am obliged to tell you that the stated policy of the Wayne County Clerk's Office is to respond within forty-eight hours to written requests submitted in a timely fashion."

"That's what you tell all the boys."

She laughed. "What do you need?"

I read her the addresses for Gracie and Vend. She put me on hold.

I sipped my beer and looked around the bar, tapping my foot to the jukebox, Bob Seger's "Heavy Music." Cigarette smoke twisted through the stilled blades of the ceiling fans. TVs flickered silently across the back of the bar between the potato chip racks, the glowing booze bottles, and the fifteen-dollar Nasty Melvin's T-shirts. A pool table stood near the front door where my hockey pals and I once had sat, as many as twenty of us from both teams, after hockey games. Every night I promised myself I'd have two beers and get out of there, and every night I'd be begging our favorite barmaid, Double D, for one last pitcher ten minutes after she'd bellowed out last call.

It wasn't home, but it felt like it for now.

Nova came back on the line.

"Where you at?"

"Where do you think?"

"Never mind, I don't want to know. All right, I got your stuff."

I took out my notebook and pen. "Go ahead."

She told me the house on Harman with the Blessed Mother statue in front was owned by Jarogniew Andrzej Vend. It had been purchased in 1986 for $48,500. The taxes were current.

"And the other one's in foreclosure, isn't it?"

"How'd you know?"

"I'm a reporter, Nova."

"Oh, yeah."

It didn't make sense, though. The house I had visited didn't look like one Gracie was planning to give up. It looked like she herself might have visited it recently. She'd come back to Starvation five or six months before. If she had planned to return for good, why wouldn't she have sold the house? Why would she have let the payments slip?

"And who's the owner?" I said.

"Hang on."

I heard papers rustling, then the muffled sound of Nova's voice calling out to someone in her office, "Goodnight, Robert. Have a good one." Then she said to me, "Man, this place . . . no matter how many times I get it all shipshape, somebody comes behind me and messes it all up."

Shit, I thought. "What's the matter?"

"It's all right, I got it here, just one second . . ."

Before she could say another word, a fleshy hand wearing a gold ring and matching watch grabbed me by the wrist and pulled my arm away from my ear.

"What the fuck?" I said.

I turned to see the man with the moon-cratered face who had stepped out of the blue Suburban on Harman Street. With his other hand, he snatched the phone out of my hand and set it back in its cradle. I tried in vain to remove myself from his grip. He smiled, revealing a lower jaw of teeth as yellow as a hamster's. "You will come with me," he said. He turned me toward the door.

"Hey!" I yelled in the direction of the bar. "Help!"

A second man, almost as big as Crater Face, had stepped between me and the bar and was saying something to the barmaid in a language I did not understand. I heard her laugh as Crater Face shoved me stumbling out into the parking lot, where the first thing I saw was a light flick on inside a large vehicle parked in the dark alley behind Nasty Melvin's—the Suburban.

I remembered I still had my beer and tried to swing it at Crater Face but he snapped my arm back behind me so hard I thought it might tear loose from its socket. "Motherfucker!" I screamed, and I felt the beer being removed from my hand and looked up to see the second man hold it up in front of my face, taunting me, before he threw back his head and swallowed it in one gulp.

"Ha ha ha," he said.

Crater Face reprimanded him in that foreign language and pointed at the Suburban.

They forced a pillowcase over my head and pinned me between them in the backseat. A third man drove. Inside the pillowcase, the smell of sweat, someone else's sweat, made me gag. We might have driven for two minutes or ten minutes or half an hour. The second man started to say something and I felt Crater Face reach across me and heard the thump of his fist against the second man's chest. The rest of the ride was silent.

The vehicle came to a stop. We had parked. I heard the doors opening. Someone yanked me out.

A hand rough with calluses shoved me forward by the back of my neck, holding the rancid pillowcase tight to my head. There was a short flight of stairs then a walk down a dark corridor. Then we were on an elevator. I counted eight dings before the doors opened again.

They shuffled me down another corridor. We stopped and I heard the men whispering and then an unfamiliar woman's voice, blurting from an intercom. There was a clicking noise and the sound of a large glass door whooshing open. We entered. We turned left and then right and then they stopped me and sat me down in a chair. I felt leather soft on my palms, smelled cigar smoke.

The pillowcase came off.

A man sat against the front of a desk, his legs crossed, facing me. He leaned slightly forward, his shaved head pale as a winter moon. Smoke wafted from a cigar in an ashtray to his right.

His black T-shirt clung tight to his flat belly and muscled chest. The shirt was emblazoned with the silhouette of a woman wearing a fireman's helmet and swinging on a pole; a logo encircling her read, THE PUMP ROOM. SOUTHGATE. REDFORD. MOUNT CLEMENS.

The man tilted his head to the left, sizing me up. I saw the crescent scar on the side of his neck. I recognized the man who had ushered Gracie— yes, it was Gracie, I was certain now—to her seat at that Wings playoff game. And perhaps the man who had killed her, as well as the young woman in Sarnia.

Prickles of heat skittered down the back of my neck.

Michele Higgins had been right.

The man smiled and scratched his chin.

"You know," he said, "you look like her."

eighteen

"H ow is Mr. Ron Wallman?" Jarek Vend said.

"Fine," I said.

Vend had introduced himself with a handshake, offered me a cigar that I declined, and, without asking, set a glass of Scotch with ice on a small table next to my armchair. Crater Face and his two partners had hovered behind me until Vend told them, "Leave us. I will call when you are needed."

I wished he had said "if" rather than "when."

The low lighting made it hard to see, but the office was as big as any I'd ever been in, and I had done interviews in the offices of the chief executives of every auto company in Detroit and two in Europe. Except for the twin sculptures of naked women—one marbled white, one polished bronze—standing on opposite ends of Vend's desk, the office could have been that of anyone running a company that made designer jeans or tractor axles or cell phone accessories.

"I am sure he is doing fine," Vend said. He paced as he spoke, slowly circling his desk, using his cigar to gesture. I noticed that when he moved to his right, he unconsciously dropped his left shoulder slightly, like a goalie might, if he was left-handed. "Fine is not good enough for me."

As he passed the window that spanned most of one wall, I tried to peer through it to get an idea of where we were, but the vertical blinds were closed tight. He circled behind his desk and stopped at the bronze sculpture, gazing at me through eyes half hidden by his heavy lids.

"Excuse me—wouldn't you like to write down what I say? Isn't that why you traveled all the way down here? To hear what I have to say?"

"I don't really know, to be honest."

"Ah, well, an honest journalist." He picked his own glass up and took a sip. He smacked his lips. "So refreshing. Please. Take notes. As you can see"—he laid one hand atop the sculpture—"I have nothing to hide."

I pulled out my pen and notebook.

"Now, concerning Mr. Wallman," he said. He spoke with a trace of a Polish accent. But his "ows" came out sounding more like "oohs," like the Canadian he was. "Let me tell you a story. I attended a chamber of commerce luncheon, oh, a year ago, maybe two. I assume Mr. Wallman has many customers, or prospective customers, in that gathering. I see him walking through, a beer in one hand, always with the beer, shaking hands and clapping this one and that one on the back. They are all his long-lost friends."

"That's Wally."

"And I see him even shaking hands and clapping on the back men and women who are also in the business of printing things—excuse me, why do you stop writing in your notebook?"

I was waiting for him to say something I cared about. "Just listening."

"I am not going to harm you, Mr. Carpenter."

Maybe you aren't, I thought, but maybe Crater Face and those other guys are. "I appreciate that."

"Good. So, Wally. As you say, he is a very good guy. He will never be a great businessman, though, because a great businessman cannot be friends with competitors. He cannot be friends with those who are trying to take bread and jam from the mouths of his children. He cannot slap them on the back and offer them a bottle of beer."

I started to ask a question, but Vend held up a hand to stop me.

"Please. Do not patronize me with, 'Keep your friends close and your enemies closer.'" He stuck the cigar in his teeth and talked over it. "I am well versed in the verities of the American businessman. They are lies." As he said "lies," his lips pulled back, baring his teeth.

He removed the cigar from his mouth, walked to my chair, and lifted one black loafer up on the arm. The mix of his cologne with the smoke smelled like black licorice.

"The true goal of capitalism is monopoly," he said. "That is all—total control of whatever market it is you choose to enter, so that you can do with it what you wish: raise prices, hire people, give to charity, fuck beautiful women. It is not about competition. Nobody wants competition. Only in textbooks do we want competition, not here"—he pointed the cigar at the floor—"in the fierce and arbitrary world of the real. Competition is angst and worry and hoping that your competitor is not so dumb that he takes you down with him." He stepped back and spread his arms wide. Ropes of muscle spiraled along his forearms. "I know," he said. "A paradox."

"Not really. Stupid can be dangerous."

"That is correct. And *wealthy* plus stupid, that is the worst of all."

He reached back and pushed something on the surface of his desk. Five television screens that were sunk into the wall above and behind him burst into brilliant life. They were all tuned to the same station. The sound was off. On each screen, the same pretty young woman talked as a glowing skein of numbers scuttled across the screen beneath her. Then her five faces disappeared and the screens filled with graphs showing how the stock price of a company identified as GX had performed that day. I had never heard of GX. Its bumpy price line stretched from the lower left corner of the screen to the upper right.

The woman's five faces then reappeared, all of them smiling.

Vend stood facing the screens. "I digress, Mr. Carpenter. But wouldn't you love to fuck her?" He looked over his shoulder at me, grinning like we were teammates scoping out the talent in the bleachers.

"She's all right," I said. "But no, actually."

"Oh, please. You would not like to fuck her? Right there on her desk while the little numbers go past?" He laughed and laid a hand across his heart. "Is it because you have someone back home that you love with all of your heart? Is that it?"

"What is your point, Mr. Vend?"

"You are a man of unusual discipline, Mr. Carpenter. But, as I said, I digress."

He turned back to the TVs. "The committed capitalist, Mr. Carpenter, is bound to do everything in his power to eliminate or, at the very least, incapacitate every one of his competitors. Otherwise, like your friend Mr. Wallman, he is doomed. Otherwise, he will, in time, become no better than the rest of them. Look at the auto companies, how they squandered their advantage, how they frittered it away on businesses they knew nothing about. They ignored their competitors, but their competitors did not ignore them. And so we have Detroit."

"There is no middle ground?"

Vend smiled wistfully. "Ah, yes, the middle ground," he said. "How you Americans love to talk about the middle ground, that place where we all can agree. But really, Mr. Carpenter, if you think about it, there rarely is one that makes anybody happy. It's really the place where we all disagree."

He reminded me of CEOs I had interviewed. While you were listening and taking notes, they sounded colorful and provocative. You imagined you were getting good stuff for your story. But later, when you looked through your notes, you realized that they really hadn't said anything you could use, that it was all bromides and platitudes and generalizations. You had nothing that stuck.

"Why are you telling me this?" I said.

"I have read your fine articles from the paper in Detroit. I like that paper. I'm not so fond of the other. So I thought you might understand. I am hoping that you would understand. Do you?"

"Have you eliminated or incapacitated all of your competitors?"

He studied me with a face at once curious and amused. "I am constantly at work," he said. "How is your drink? It's a Campbeltown malt, Springbank, fifteen years old. Not easy to get."

"You said I looked like her. You refer to Gracie McBride, yes?"

I was sure by now that Jarek Vend had recruited Gracie all those years ago. Small-town girl, troubled family, long past virginity at the age of seventeen. She had worked for him, certainly slept with him, indulged with him in the kink that filled the cardboard boxes in her dark room. She must have known things about him, things he would not have wanted others to know. But things bad enough to compel him to kill her?

Vend ignored my question. "I have also enjoyed the stories you've been writing at your new paper."

"Excuse me?"

He hit another button on his desk. All five TV screens filled with images of hockey players weaving to and fro. Vend reached into a fax machine on the credenza beneath the TVs, plucked out a page, and held it up for me to see. It was a copy of one of my stories about the new rink.

"You seem to be the only one who sees the reality of your situation." He tilted his head to one side. "Why do you look so surprised?"

"Why would a strip-club owner in Detroit care about a hockey rink in Starvation Lake?"

"You love hockey, don't you?"

"I play."

"So did I." He turned his head and put a finger to the scar on his neck. "Played very hard."

"There are plenty of rinks around here. What does Jarek Vend care about ours?"

"Excellent pronunciation, Mr. Carpenter, thanks no doubt to your new friend, Miss Patricia Armbruster."

An image of the woman hanging from the swing set in Sarnia appeared in my head. I focused on the tip of my pen moving across my notebook.

"I come from a small town in Ontario, LaSalle, where I grew up playing in a barn. You know—with the dressing rooms that made you duck your head, and no Zamboni, just a Jeep with a large brush attached to the front. So I can well appreciate how much a splendid new arena would mean to your town."

"Understood."

"But please tell me: why should I pay for your splendid new arena?"

"You? What are you talking about?"

He drained his glass and set it down hard on the desk. His smile had vanished. Ice cubes crunched in his teeth.

"You have written extensively about it," he said. "There was the money, and then there was not. You used your skill to figure that much out, Mr. Carpenter. I commend you. But you have yet to determine where the money came from in the first place or where it went when it suddenly disappeared. Isn't that right?"

He squeezed a lighter out of his jeans pocket and slowly relit his cigar, the flicker of flame flashing in his eyes. Then he turned his back and with two fingers pushed a button on his desktop. Four of the TV screens went dark. The middle screen remained on. "Observe."

A man wearing nothing but a pair of white socks dangled from a rope attached at his back to a canvas harness wrapped around his torso like a girdle. The harness trussed him up at the elbows and ankles so that he looked like a chicken ready to go into an oven. His head was hidden in a black plastic garbage bag cinched at his neck. He spun slowly in the air, twisting his head back and forth in the bag.

A woman in a black leather halter and matching thong pranced around. She tugged lightly at the ropes, a pair of pliers clutched in one hand, her skin pallid as a perch belly. She had her back to the camera, but she was too tall to be Gracie. Still I thought of Gracie again, working at the bench in the Zamboni shed, the tools natural in her hands, a finger smear of grease on her cheek. The woman on the screen squatted down and propped herself beneath the man in the harness. I turned away.

"What the fuck?" I said.

"Yes, indeed, Mr. Carpenter, that is the appropriate response, the response a great journalist is always seeking from his readers, no?"

"You can turn it off now."

"Now you have a headline. You can tell the fine, upstanding citizens of Starvation Lake that this"—he waved his hand toward the screen with a flourish—"is one very important source of funding for their excellent new rink, the rink that will catapult them once again to hockey greatness."

"Bullshit."

"There, Mr. Carpenter, is that better?"

I looked back at the screen. Hockey players again were gliding where the hooded man had been writhing.

"You see, we provide a full array of services for our clientele," Vend said. "The clubs are merely a point of entry—a lucrative point of entry, to be sure, but just a starting place, not unlike the Chevrolet that a young man buys before he graduates to a Pontiac and then a Buick and an Oldsmobile and, finally, a Cadillac. You have now seen the Cadillac. Or perhaps these days Lexus is the more appropriate analogy."

He reached back and pushed the button on his desk again, keeping his hand there this time. The hockey players disappeared and all five screens lit up again. They were filled with close-up shots of five different men.

"No way," I said.

"Of course," Vend continued, "not everyone can afford every dish on the smorgasbord. Certain services begged for a rarefied sort of client, a man of certain tastes and bearing and means, who would pay a handsome premium for our services and, naturally, for absolute discretion."

"Jesus," I said, pointing at the first screen. "Judge Rapp? And that's Davis McInerney." McInerney was an executive vice president at Superior Motors. From my days at the Detroit Times, I recognized the others, too: a real estate developer, a state senator, a retired outfielder.

Now I had an idea what was on those videotapes in Gracie's house. I tried to remember the initials I'd seen on the sides of the tapes. She must have figured out a way to smuggle out her own copies. She probably had more tapes hidden away somewhere else, somewhere safer. In my mind I scanned the rafters in the Zamboni shed, looking for hiding places. Vend must have known. Maybe Gracie had threatened to use the tapes against him, or his customers.

"It's quite an illustrious gallery," Vend said. He hit the button again. Five more men appeared: two attorneys, a city councilman, two men I didn't recognize, one of them wearing a police uniform. Vend hit the button again and there were five more. He kept hitting it until the faces were flashing too fast for me to tell who they were.

"And these guys were all into the kinky stuff?"

Vend took a puff on his cigar. "Not necessarily. As I said, we offered—offer—a multiplicity of services. That is one. The presence of the young woman enhances the aesthetic of the experience while at the same time offering some peace of mind in the knowledge that she is there to prevent any unfortunate accidents."

"But Gracie wasn't just a minder, was she, Mr. Vend?"

"Our associates perform a wide array of services for a wide array of customers."

The TVs went black.

"Unfortunately," Vend continued, "I personally did not have access to a certain, shall we say, *strata* of clientele, at least not back then. I had the product; I needed a partner who could provide the proper customer."

"And you found one. One who clearly was in that strata."

"Indeed." I knew what he was going to say next. "Mr. Haskell was the best money could buy."

It was surprisingly easy to believe. While part of me didn't want to think a man of Laird Haskell's public stature would risk his career and family on such an enterprise, the part that knew Haskell, the part that had encountered many a rich and powerful man who had succumbed to the illusion that he could become invisible, accepted it as easily as if Vend had told me that Haskell favored suits and ties in the courtroom. I could see him first as a customer, then as a recruiter of talent, then as Vend's pipeline to the wealthy and powerful.

"And now," I said, "your partner is stealing from you to build his rink."

"There appears to have been some diversions. But not just from me, Mr. Carpenter. I assume he is stealing—that is, diverting monies—from others as well. I just happened to be—what do ambulance chasers like Mr. Haskell call it?—a deep pocket."

"That's funny," I said. "He's going to the town council tomorrow for a little loan of a hundred grand."

"So I have heard," Vend said. "Mr. Haskell is a most resourceful man, and we have benefited. He has been an enormously creative and productive member of our team. But he has let personal distractions cloud his focus. Obviously, for the sake of our employees and other various interests, I cannot indulge these distractions with my hard-earned assets."

"By distractions, do you mean . . . his son?"

Vend blew out a thin ribbon of smoke that disappeared in the shadows above him. "We were all going to play in the NHL at one time in our lives, weren't we?"

I thought of Taylor Haskell on the ice, slapping the goalposts with his stick. Then of the smoke floating out from the Zam shed the night before. Then of Gracie, and of the *Free Press* story she had tacked up on the wall of her dark room.

"Oh, no," I said.

"What is it, Mr. Carpenter?"

"He brought Gracie into this?"

Haskell had moved to Starvation full-time only in the past year. But he'd had a summer cottage on the north side of the lake for as long as I could remember. In Starvation Lake, it wouldn't have taken much to have known about Gracie, the small-town girl from the troubled family, and about her father, blasted from the sky over the jungles of Vietnam.

"I will leave you to your own conclusions," Vend said. "As for Mr. Haskell, I now consider him my competitor."

"And so," I said, "'Build it and they will die.'"

Vend cocked his head ever so slightly. I thought he might smile but he did not. The skin tightened around his cheekbones. He came off the desk, dropped his cigar on the carpet, and crushed it beneath the sole of his loafer.

"For the record," he said, "we support Mr. Haskell's efforts to extort—excuse me, extract—additional monies from your elected leaders."

"I'll bet."

"Indeed, we believe Mr. Haskell ought to seek even more support from your town's benevolent elder statesmen. Will you be in attendance?"

"The chances are better if I get out of here."

Now he smiled. "Of course."

I wondered if he knew that I knew about him and Gracie at the Hill-Top Motel. He certainly couldn't have known that I'd seen him with her at that Wings playoff game. "Tell me, Mr. Vend," I said. "Could this thing with Haskell be about more than just money?"

He looked past me, snapped his fingers, and called out something I didn't understand. I heard footsteps approaching, the door behind me swinging open. Vend looked at me.

"What is it you journalists like to say when you've been backed into a corner by your own recklessness? 'Don't shoot the messenger'?" He stepped up and pushed his face to within an inch of mine. Other, lighter, shorter scars became apparent along his neck. "Here is a message," he whispered. "Your Gracie gave up on life because the people who supposedly loved her gave up on her. When you are all weeping around her grave, you should remember that there is no tragedy in the inevitable."

He stepped back. Hands grabbed my shoulders from behind and jerked me out of the chair. Vend reached out and snatched my notebook away.

"Hey," I said. I tried to wrench free but the men held me fast. "Come on."

"Worry not," Vend said. "I will return it momentarily."

He dropped the notebook on the floor next to the flattened cigar butt. He unzipped his pants and removed himself. I understood then how he had gotten his nickname. It had nothing to do with the knob of tape on his goalie stick.

He zipped up and gestured toward the soaked notebook.

"There you go, Mr. Carpenter. I very much look forward to your next article, if you can get it in your little paper. I would hate for you to have come all the way down here for nothing."

I left the notebook lying on the floor.

The flickering lights looked like fireflies through the tinted windows of the Suburban. As the vehicle rolled to a stop, the window to my right edged down, and the smell of burning gasoline leached in. Crater Face, sitting to my right, grabbed my arm and yanked me forward.

"Look," he said.

The lights, I could see now, flashed from police cars and fire trucks and an ambulance. Flames and smoke were spewing from the roof of a house.

Gracie's house. We were parked one street over, close enough to see but not be seen. Every few seconds the lights illuminated neighbors standing around in parkas. I thought of the Red Wings cup waiting in the drainer.

And those videotapes I would never be seeing.

"Motherfuckers," I said.

Crater Face turned and grasped me by the neck and squeezed, turning me sideways, his fingernails biting into my skin. The man behind me pinned my elbows back. I felt my neck muscles collapsing as I struggled to remain conscious. The window went back up. The vehicle started to move. The men let me go. They spoke in their language, laughing.

They were still laughing when they threw me onto the gravel of the parking lot at Nasty Melvin's.

My hamstrings didn't stop quivering until I veered onto Interstate 275 heading north. I pulled off at Eight Mile Road to fill up. The smell of gasoline made me nauseous. Ten minutes up 275, I was still smelling the gas. I pulled onto the shoulder and flicked on my emergency lights.

I found the four empty five-gallon cans under the cover of my flatbed. I glanced around, looking for police flashers. There were none yet. I waited until there was a break in traffic and took the cans and flung them into the high weeds poking through the snow across the road shoulder.

I stayed on back roads, keeping my eyes peeled for state police cruisers, all the way back to Starvation.

nineteen

T he cop lights flashed on in my rearview mirror just as I parked behind the Starvation Lake Arena. "Fuck me," I said.

I had stopped earlier and called Darlene from a pay phone outside a Grayling tavern called Spike's Keg 'O Nails. She hadn't answered, so I'd told her voice mail I'd see her after the game. She wasn't much of a hockey fan.

I'd also tried the Sarnia police. The night dispatcher told me only the chief was authorized to speak to the media, and he was out of town until the next night. I left my name and number.

Now in my side-view mirror I saw Sheriff Dingus Aho approaching, alone. It wasn't like Dingus to be out on patrol; he had to have been looking for me. I shut off the truck, opened the door, and stepped out. A fluorescent lamp on the back of the rink threw diffuse light across the snow-packed asphalt. Dingus walked into it, arms folded across his chest.

"Can this wait?" I said. "I've got to be on the ice in ten minutes."

"Can't go in this way," Dingus said. "The Zamboni area is still off-limits."

"Oh. OK, I'll walk around front. Sorry."

"What are you parking back here for anyway?"

"Got in the habit when I was playing goalie. Had to do with some superstition I've long forgotten."

I grabbed my bag and sticks out of the back of my truck. "You hauling gasoline?" Dingus said.

"Soupy ran out the other day and I spilled some giving him a hand."

"Uh-huh." He stepped between me and the rink. "So how was your trip to Detroit? Find out anything?"

I had debated while driving back exactly what I could or would tell Dingus and Darlene. I didn't have a paper for four days and I had serious doubts about what, if anything, the publisher would allow the *Pilot* to print. Journalists weren't supposed to be snitches for cops. But Dingus had pointed me to Vend. And Darlene, well, hell, Darlene was my girlfriend. One of them could probably get to the Sarnia police. I decided I wanted Darlene to hear about that first.

"Not much that I can say anything about," I told Dingus. "I've got to make some calls in the morning."

His frown bunched his handlebar up beneath his nose.

"I wouldn't be holding out on me, son. Your little story about Soupy is believable, but bullpuckey. My sheriff friends in Wayne County gave me a call. You were seen going into a house this morning that later went up in flames."

Trixie, I thought. Would she have been implicated too?

"I am not an arsonist, Dingus."

He sniffed at the air. "If you say so."

"Gracie was murdered, all right," I said. "But you knew that."

"By whom?"

I had been sure that Vend was responsible for Gracie's death. Until I had heard about Haskell. It could have been Vend, or Haskell, or both. Gracie's videotapes—and whatever other evidence she had hidden away—could have put them out of business and in jail. I thought of the girl in Sarnia. What had she known and how had she threatened these men?

What did I really know? That Gracie had become ensnared, probably by Haskell, in a prostitution ring that included among its specialties asphyxiation for wealthy gentlemen. That Gracie had apparently tried to escape that life and make a saner one of her own while struggling against the knowledge that she had given up a child. That both Haskell and Vend could have had motives for killing her, depending on what she knew and what she was willing to reveal. That Vend and Haskell were embroiled in a conflict over large amounts of money and—I only guessed—Gracie's affections.

But if Gracie was truly out of their business, as Trixie seemed to have been saying, why would Haskell and Vend have cared about her anymore? She must have wanted something. Money? Her house? A job at the new rink? Her dignity? Could they have somehow given that back to her?

"Not sure," I said.

"Well, Doc Joe appears to disagree."

"Doc Slow reported already?"

"Surprise, surprise, the county commission sent a letter yesterday to the good doctor asking for input on his budget."

"And so he produced his report in record time. What'd he say about Gracie?"

"The proximate cause of death was strangulation, the result of a broken neck," Dingus said. "Strongly suggesting suicide. Of course ol' Doc didn't come down too hard on any one side, trying to keep all parties happy. But he cited no specific evidence of homicide, no real signs of struggle, no marks other than the striations on her neck."

"Come on. She walked out there in a snowstorm, shinnied up a tree, and hung herself?"

"I'm sure you'll be shocked to hear that the good doctor did not address those issues directly."

"Can I get a copy of his report?"

"I doubt it. I myself have yet to see it. The county attorney said it would be made available in due time."

"After Haskell gets his way with the town council."

"Maybe so."

"So we can get that fabulous new rink."

"That is paramount."

"Son of a bitch."

"I was thinking the same."

We stood without speaking for a minute. I heard slap shots echoing off the dasher boards inside the old rink.

"You know," I said, "Gracie had an abortion."

Dingus knit his hands behind his back. "Go on."

"Not sure when. Probably in the last few years."

"Aha. That's why she killed herself."

"It's a story."

"Yes. Well. I'll be candid, Gus, I suspect you know quite a bit more than you're letting on. And I can appreciate that you've probably had a tough day, traveling back and forth and all. So I'll let it go for the moment."

"Thanks."

"I'm in more of a sharing mood than you, so I'll let you know: while you were gone, Channel Eight's reporter stopped by my office. She seemed very interested."

"Playing hardball, huh, Dingus?"

"Aw, that's nothing. Go play your game. Then sleep on it. If I don't hear from you by tomorrow, say, five or so, I'll be calling Sheriff Brice."

"Who?"

"Wayne County sheriff Sam Brice. He might be interested in running some tests on your truck, see if you've been hauling large amounts of gasoline."

"Come on."

As Dingus turned for his cruiser, he called over his shoulder, "Go out there and smoke 'em tonight."

"What the fuck, Trap?"

It was Soupy. He was dressed and ready to go, his skates tied, his two sticks freshly taped, his red Chowder Head jersey pulled on, his old taped-together helmet resting next to him where he sat on the bench against the wall, the last man remaining in dressing room 3.

One of Soupy's countless superstitions prevented him from going out onto the ice until I had sat down next to him. I'd thought he might let that one die when I stopped playing goaltender, but he did not.

"Sorry," I said. I sat and unzipped my bag.

"Where the fuck were you?"

"Had to make a quick trip downstate."

"Uh-huh. You heard the news?"

I was pulling gear out of the bag—shin guards, elbow pads, cup, gloves, helmet, pants. All of it stunk of mildew and sweat.

"You mean the coroner?"

"Yeah."

"Yeah. Heard. Sorry, man."

"Sorry for what? It wasn't my fault."

"I know. I mean—"

"You think she offed herself because of me?"

"No, I do not think that."

Soupy plopped his helmet on his head and braced his elbows on his knees. I stripped off my shirt and pants and started pulling on my long cottons, still damp from Sunday night. Soupy remained silent, staring at the floor. I heard a whistle shrilling on the ice. The door to the dressing room swung open and a grizzled guy wearing the black-and-white stripes of a referee ducked his head in.

"Tonight, fellas," he said.

Soupy didn't even look up.

"You can start without me," I said. I elbowed Soupy. "Go on."

"You got a funnel?" the ref said. He meant a goalie.

Soupy turned to him. "Yeah. Be right out."

The ref glanced over at me for some reason. "You sure?"

"I'm sure. Don't you dare drop that puck yet, Jack."

The door shut. Soupy looked down at the floor again.

"What's wrong, Soup?" I said.

He sighed. "Ah, fuck, man."

"What?"

"We've got to talk. But not now. Later maybe." He reached down and grabbed my right arm. "Over there, man." I looked across the room and saw a set of goalie equipment stacked on the bench facing me. I had seen it on my way in but paid it no mind. I realized that Soupy wanted me to put it on.

"No," I said. "Are you crazy? I'm not playing goal."

"I left you like sixty fucking messages."

"My cell phone was dead. Where's E.B.?"

Ernie Block had been our goaltender since I had retired. Soupy loved it that his name was Block. Like most goalies, E.B. had some games where he could stop anyone short of Gretzky on a breakaway and others where he couldn't keep a beach ball from going between his legs. On the bad nights, he did a lot of yelling at his teammates, which was fine because it gave us fodder to make fun of him with at the bar afterward.

"E.B.'s in jail."

"What?"

"Yeah. He was playing a pickup game in Gaylord and—brace yourself now—he got to screaming at one of his D. The guy turned around and popped him pretty good. E.B. goes down but then he comes up with his stick and shoves it halfway up the guy's ass. Turns out the guy is a cop."

"Shit."

"Yeah. So E.B.'s spending the night. I went up and got his gear."

I imagined E.B. using his sole phone call to let Soupy know he wouldn't be playing tonight. He was probably sick about it. Not only was it hard to win without a goalie, the fun of the game was ruined for both teams.

But I didn't really care.

"Well, I'm not playing goal, man. I haven't played in a year. I don't have my goalie skates. I'd get killed out there."

"Don't pussy out on us now, Trap. We can beat these assholes. I don't give a shit if they've got Meat."

"Oh, great. Meat's out there. And what's his specialty aside from beating guys senseless? Steamrolling goalies."

"What are you talking about?"

"Nothing. Forget it. I'm not playing."

Soupy stood, his sticks gripped in his right glove. He popped in a mouthguard and snapped his chin strap.

"Fuck it, then, Trap. Don't even bother getting suited up."

"Fuck you. I'm playing. Wing."

"We don't need you on the wing. We got plenty of benders who can cough up the puck." He pushed the door open. "We need you in between the pipes. Don't bother coming over to the bar later either. We don't serve pussies in Enright's."

Later, I thought. He had me. And he knew it.

"Wait," I said.

Soupy let the door close. I looked over at the goalie stuff. I looked at Soupy. "What is it you need to talk to me about?"

"Nothing, man."

"Don't fuck with me."

He grinned, the bastard. "Any more than I already am?"

"Goddammit. You will talk to me."

"Later. Yeah."

I got up and went over to E.B.'s goalie stuff. I picked up one of the leg pads. A hairy wad of cotton padding was spilling out through a tear along the stitched-on Cooper patch.

"Jesus," I said. "Did he get these for his sixth birthday?"

"It ain't about that, Trap," Soupy said. "It's about you." He started out the door, then stopped and turned back to me. "And hey—better keep your head up, pal. Meat looks extra pissed-off tonight."

I dressed in the silent room surrounded by emptied hockey bags and blue jeans hung on hooks. I stood and snatched up my goalie stick—E.B.'s goalie stick—and clumped out to the rink. Nothing felt right.

E.B.'s pants were too baggy. His cup was too tight. His shoulder and arm pads smelled like spoiled gravy. Worst of all, his goalie skates, with the protective hard-shell plastic along the sides, were at least two sizes too small. I couldn't get into them. So I had to use my own regular skates, which had none of that extra padding. One hard shot off an instep and I'd be in the hospital.

The rink opened before me, two circles of guys skating counterclockwise at either end of the ice, flipping pucks from stick to stick, snapping them into the mesh at the backs of the nets. I pulled the mask down over my face. It was too tight; I jiggled it until my cheeks weren't pinching my eyelids. I skated across the ice to the front of my net and began to slide sideways back and forth between the goalposts to scuff up the ice in my crease and pile snow at each post to bog down passes coming from the corners. Soupy and Wilf and Zilchy and Danny Lefebvre and my other teammates whacked me on my leg pads with their sticks as they glided past. *Good game, Trap. Fuck 'em, Gus.* I felt the old butterflies flutter.

I slapped the blade of my stick off one goalpost, swung it back off the other, did it again and again, counting to eleven, the ritual complete. The two referees skated to center ice. I took a quick look around the rink. Down at the other end, there was Jason Esper, a tree trunk on skates, his long crossover strides propelling him around the back of his net and up the boards. Past him through the glass I saw the crisscrossed police tape that obscured the Zamboni shed. In the bleachers, a dozen people in parkas and lap blankets sat in clumps of twos and threes, cradling foam cups of coffee.

My eyes fell on a woman sitting alone at the top of the stands behind the other team's bench. She was talking into a cell phone, her head tucked into the collar of her navy pea jacket. It was the first time in more than a day that I had seen Darlene out of her deputy's uniform. And the first time I had seen her at one of my hockey games in I couldn't remember how long. I wanted her to look my way, but she kept talking into her phone.

One of the refs blew a short blast on his whistle. The Chowder Heads of Enright's Pub and the Mighty Minnows of Jordan Bait and Tackle broke their huddles at their respective benches. I banged my gloves together in front of me and got into my ready squat, my shoulders square, my stick hard against the ice, my catching glove out to my left and open. *What the hell is Darlene doing here?* I thought. *Why is she sitting way down there?*

All but one of the other skaters hunched over their sticks in face-off position. Jason Esper remained upright. He was still glaring at me when the ref dropped the puck.

Clem Linke of the Minnows won the face-off. He chipped the puck back to his twin brother Jake, who deked around Wilf and flipped the puck end over end into our zone, halfway between my left post and the corner. My heart thumped as I slid out of my crease and caught the puck on my stick blade. Soupy was coming fast with Jason on his heels.

"Leave it," Soupy yelled.

I yanked my blade back, leaving the puck for Soupy, and started to pedal sideways and backward into my crease. But my skates were too sharp; wingers use sharper blades than goalies, who are constantly moving side to side. My right blade jammed. I lunged forward to keep myself from toppling over backward but overcompensated and fell forward.

"Fuck!" Soupy yelled as he tripped over my left leg and went flying, the puck dribbling away. Jason stopped hard. Shards of ice sprayed the left side of my face. I saw Jason's stick blade collect the puck and flip it to his backhand. I got up on one leg and flailed with my catching glove. Way too late. The puck bounced through my crease and onto the stick of Jake Linke, who smacked it into the back of the net. The refs' whistles shrieked. "Fuck yeah," Jason yelled. He spun to skate backward as he whipped past Soupy sprawled behind the net. "Easiest hundred I'll ever make," he shouted.

"Fuck off, Meat," Soupy yelled back.

I got to my feet. "You bet him?" I said.

"Fuck him," Soupy said. He got to one knee and looked through the eyeholes of my mask. "I bet on you, Trap. Get your fucking game together."

"What?" I said. "I didn't want to play fucking net."

"Do your job," Soupy said, skating away.

Five minutes later, Frank D'Alessio slapped a sloppy pass out of the air, crossed into our zone, and let fly at me with a wobbly slap shot, shoulder high, not unlike the one Taylor Haskell had struggled with the night before. I saw it all the way but the wobbles fooled me a little. I mishandled it with my catching glove and fumbled it back out in front of the net.

Slinky Jake Linke slid his stick between Soupy's backpedaling legs and whacked the bouncing puck to my left, where Jason was waiting. Stevie Reneau had his stick hooked on the cuff of one of Jason's gloves but Jason brushed it off and with one hand snapped a shot over my shoulder as I flopped to stop it. The puck whanged off the left post and trickled into my crease. "Shit," Jason yelled. "Post." I dove to my left to smother the puck but it squirted back out to Jason, who fired again, catching me so hard on the wide part of my stick that I dropped the thing.

Now I was lying on my back in the crease with no idea where the puck was. I felt my stick beneath my left leg pad and reached under to grab it but it was upside down so I had it by the fat blade instead of the knob, almost useless. Then Stevie fell backward across my legs, pinning me to the ice. I craned my neck to the left and saw the puck lying loose about six feet away, Soupy diving for it, and Jake Linke's stick about to flip it over me and into the net. I couldn't move my lower body, so I just shoved the thin upper shaft of my stick into the air and hoped for the best. The puck hit the two-inch-wide shaft just above the Sher-Wood label and dropped onto my chest. I covered it with both gloves as the referees blew the play dead.

"You lucky fuck." It was Jason. Out of the corner of my left eye I saw him bearing down on me with his stick leveled across his chest. I twisted my body around and tucked my head. Jason came to a hard stop an inch from my head and jabbed the side of my mask with his stick. Soupy came crashing over me into Jason, spitting, "Get the fuck out of here," while Wilf slammed into Jason from behind. I looked up to see Jason grab Wilf by the front of his jersey and toss him aside like a rag doll. Other players came flying and tumbling into the scrum, piling up on top of me, cursing, grunting, threatening to beat the living shit out of one another, forgetting for the moment that in fact most of them would be laughing and drinking together later at Enright's.

The refs pulled us apart. I stood up and flipped the puck to one of them. Jason stood behind one of the refs, regarding me.

"You got shit in your ears?" he said.

"Did you like that save, Meat?"

"You didn't fucking hear me yesterday, did you?" He looked down at my feet. "Ah," he said. "Nice skates. Might want to test those out."

"Do what you've got to do."

* * *

He didn't get his chance until the second period.

By then we were down 3–1. I'd let in another softie—a Clem Linke wrist shot that fooled me under my stick-hand glove—and the Minnows got another on a nifty tic-tac-toe passing play that I didn't have a prayer of stopping. We were having trouble getting much offense going. If we stayed within two, though, we had a decent shot at coming back. I had to keep us in the game.

Now Jason caught a pass just inside our blue line, driving toward me. My defenseman on that side took the middle, giving Jason a long angle from the wing to my left. I pushed out a foot from my crease and crouched lower, forgetting my vulnerable feet, expecting a puck at my neck. Jason had room to shoot from outside the face-off circle but took another loping stride down the boards, hoping to turn me, the rusty goalie, sideways.

He wound up high. The puck exploded off his stick blade barely an inch off the ice. Before I could turn my pad the puck smacked the inside of my right skate just behind the toe. I felt something crack inside my foot as my knee buckled and I collapsed to the ice, screaming, "Goddammit" for the pain while searching for the puck. I felt it bounce once against my left hamstring and I squeezed my legs together, hoping to trap it there before it dribbled into the net. Jason's knee caught me hard in the side of the head as he crashed the crease. I toppled over.

The refs whistled the play dead. My foot was on fire with pain. "Asshole," I was yelling, "You fucking asshole."

Jason was not through. He grabbed my shoulder and rolled me over and shoved the palm of his glove into my mask, snapping my head back. One of the refs tried to get between us but Jason shoved him aside with his other arm. He had about forty pounds on the ref and sixty on me.

"You got shit in your ears?" Jason said.

"What the fuck do you want?"

The ref was pulling Jason by the back of his jersey collar but Jason didn't budge. "I'm giving you two for roughing, Meat," the ref said. "Don't push it."

Jason grabbed the bottom of my mask and pulled my face in close to his. I smelled the tobacco dip on his breath. My gut churned with nausea. My foot felt like it might burst the seams of my skate.

"It's over, pal," Jason said. "Got it? She's here for me. Don't be fucking calling her anymore. You hear me? Don't be fucking calling her."

"It ain't over with Vend, though, is it, Meat?"

A look of surprise spread over his face. He loosened his grip on my mask.

"You're his bitch up here, aren't you, Meat?"

"You don't know what you're fucking talking about."

"Or are you Haskell's bitch? Better get it straight who you're working for, Meat, or you'll wind up like Gracie."

He shook his head. "You're dead," he said. The refs pulled him toward the penalty box as he stared at me over his shoulder. Before he stepped into the box, he pointed his scarred right hand at me. "You're a little fucking pussy, Carpie," he yelled. "And you're fucked."

Soupy and Zilch helped me to my feet. I couldn't put much weight on my right skate. "You going to be all right?" Soupy said.

"He broke my goddamn foot," I said.

"OK," Soupy said. "Maybe I can get them to play the rest later."

"No," I said. "No, I'm going to play."

"You can barely stand up."

"Just give me a couple of minutes, I'll be all right."

I moved away from him, skated little circles back and forth, most of my weight on my left skate.

"Fuck it, Trap," Soupy said.

"No."

I put my stick-hand glove under my left arm and grabbed Soupy by his jersey. "Listen," I said. I looked him in the eyes. Then I turned and looked behind my net. "Just get that bastard within reach."

The ref dropped the puck on the face-off dot to my left. I leaned hard on my left skate, gritted my teeth against the pain. Soupy gobbled up the puck and skated it out of our zone. I watched him weave between the Minnows, moving away from me. My gaze moved to the bleachers. Darlene was gone.

Jason was as trapped by Vend and Haskell as Gracie had been. He probably thought he was clever, working both against the middle. Haskell must have thought he had a spy in Vend's camp. Vend must have thought he had one in Haskell's. I figured Jason was the one faxing Vend those copies of my stories, keeping him apprised of the town council's doings. The two of them were, after all, bound by blood, and then money, and probably drugs and blackmail and who knew what else.

Maybe I should have felt for the guy. Right.

Jason came back on the ice with just under a minute to go in the period. Goalies are supposed to keep their eyes on the puck. But I watched Jason, waiting, knowing he didn't think I had it in me.

One of the Minnows shoveled the puck into the corner to my left. Jason charged down the boards to get it. Soupy swooped in ahead of him, scooped up the puck, and veered behind my net. That's where he left the puck.

Jason saw it sitting there and put his head down, churning at full speed.

The heel of my stick blade caught him full on the Adam's apple. He flew up and back so hard that one of his skates almost knocked my stick out of my hand. I heard his helmet crack against the ice and watched as Jason threw off his gloves and clutched at his throat, choking. One of the refs rushed over and knelt over him. "Holy God," he said, "somebody call nine one one." I rested my arms on the crossbar and watched Jason kick his skates this way and that.

The ref turned to me. He was just a kid, maybe seventeen, played for the River Rats and made a few bucks refereeing games for old guys like me. He looked scared. "You better go take a shower, Gus," he said.

"Fucking-ay," I said. As I started to skate off the ice, I called out to Jason, "Winners win, motherfucker. Players play."

I left E.B.'s gear in a pile in the dressing room and swung out of the rink parking lot as an ambulance shrieked in.

twenty

All the shoes were gone.

Stars glimmered on a black sky between the snowy branches of the shoe tree. I looked way up where Gracie's pink sneaker had hung with Ricky's football cleat. My eyes moved down and across the boughs where other sneakers and boots and sandals and galoshes should have been dangling.

They weren't there anymore.

Darlene looked up into the tree. She was standing at the trunk in snow to her knees. She held one hand on the tree, as if she was reassuring it.

She had left a note under a windshield wiper on my truck: *Midnight at the shoe tree.* She was in her brown-and-mustard uniform again, her hair tucked up into her earflap cap. Reflections of stars sparkled in her onyx eyes.

"What happened to the shoes?" I said.

"Evidence," she said. "We took them all down this morning."

"Huh. Did you see my skates?"

"What skates?"

"The skates you made me hang up there with your softball spikes."

"Oh, those." A sad smile flitted over her mouth. "I don't know."

I walked up to within a few feet of where she stood.

"You're limping," she said.

"No shit. Since when are you interested in hockey?"

She ignored my question. "D'Alessio told Jason to press charges."

"Right. The last thing Jason wants is cops messing around with him. Do you know the kind of crazy shit he's involved with downstate?"

Darlene folded her arms, looked down at her boots.

"Darlene?"

"I can't talk about it now."

"Can't talk about what?"

"Jason. Downstate. Anything."

"Why did you ask me out here?"

"I wanted to see you."

"I'm right here. Why didn't we just meet at the apartment?"

"Not smart at the moment. I have to work anyway."

"Not smart? Why? What the hell is going on?"

"A police investigation is going on."

"I didn't set fire to any house downstate, Darlene."

"I know." She reached up and briefly took my collar in her gloved hand. "You have to trust me. Things have gotten complicated."

"I'll say. Would you like to hear about my trip?"

"I've got a few minutes; go ahead."

"Are you going to spill to Dingus?"

Darlene didn't say anything.

"I want you to know because you loved Gracie," I said.

"I can't promise anything."

I explained how Kerasopoulos had killed my original story about Gracie and made it a brief about an apparent suicide. I told her about Gracie's house, about the darker of the two bedrooms, about Trixie, about Vend, about Haskell, about the woman on the swing set in Sarnia. Again I didn't mention Michele Higgins. Darlene said, "My God," once or twice. The expression on her face shifted from surprise to anger, from anger to sadness. The surprise wasn't quite shock, though; it was as if she had heard bits and pieces of the story already.

"Did you ever see her house?" I said.

"No. Until—" She stopped herself. "I mean, I didn't know she had one."

"I'm not sure it's actually hers. You never saw it when you visited?"

"No. But I hadn't been down there for years." She steepled her gloves beneath her nose, thinking. "I hadn't been down there to see Gracie since she was still in school."

"Or pretending to be in school."

"I guess. Every time I made plans, she came up with some excuse to cancel. Now I guess I know why."

There was another reason Darlene didn't go downstate: I was there.

"She never said a word about Vend or Haskell?"

"Not by name." She sighed. "No, Gracie didn't mention anything about . . ." Her voice trailed off. "Although I do remember her mentioning that Trixie woman once or twice. Said she was the only real friend she had down there."

"I'm sorry."

"Why?"

"I don't know. I bet that kind of hurt."

Darlene shrugged. "She didn't even make my wedding. A bridesmaid. I should have cut the bitch off then."

"But you didn't."

"No. I mean, I tried, I tried to just forget her a bunch of times, but then I'd go to the mailbox and there'd be a letter, and I'd be right back on the hook again. And when she came back here, we took the time to catch up. Or at least I thought we did."

"How perfect that you kept those letters in a shoe box, eh? Have you had a chance to look through those?"

"Most of them. Even with twenty-twenty hindsight, they don't tell you much. There's all this girly chatter about how she's dating this guy or that guy, and he screwed her over or she blew him off, and she hates her job and her boss is a butthole but it pays well so she's going to hang in there."

"Vend."

"I'm so stupid."

"Darlene." I stepped forward and reached for her shoulder, but she put a hand up to stop me.

"No. I am so stupid. Every now and then, she'd make a joke about how she was going to die young, it was her destiny. I just figured it was the usual Gracie drama. But it was all there. She was destined to die young and it just . . ." She looked up into the tree, struggling not to cry. "It just sucks."

"Do you think it was Haskell or Vend?"

Darlene went on as if she hadn't heard me. "Then she came back, and we'd go to Riccardo's and she'd talk about how she was trying to get a real plan in her life, she just had to get out from under some things."

"The abortion."

"Well, that's what I thought. Or maybe that's what she wanted me to think. Obviously there were other things going on. God. I thought, I really thought she was sounding better, even last week."

We both turned our heads toward the sound of sirens coming from the direction of town. I saw the lights of a police cruiser blinking behind the tree line a mile from where we stood, heading north along the eastern shore of the lake. It was followed by a different set of flashing lights, perhaps a fire truck or an ambulance.

Static crackled over the microphone clipped on Darlene's shoulder. She turned away. "Oh, God," I heard her say. "Another?" She said something else I couldn't make out, then "Ten-four" before she turned back to me.

"I have to go."

"Where?"

She just looked at me.

"OK. Why do you say Gracie was better?"

"I don't know. Just her attitude. She ordered double pepperoni on her pizza. She was talking about how she was having fun with Soupy, how she thought she might be able to save up enough to at least rent a little cabin on the lake and get out of that disgusting Zamboni room."

"Haskell or Vend?"

"Doc Joe says she killed herself," she said. She fished her keys out of her coat pocket. "I have to go."

"Doc Joe's covering his ass."

"It's in his job description."

She started to walk past me to her cruiser parked on the road.

"Wait," I said. "Will I see you later? Or tomorrow?"

She stopped and put a gloved hand flat on my chest. "I'm glad you're safe," she said. "But I don't know. Maybe not till this is over."

"Then I hope it's over soon. You're holding back."

"It's my job."

"I don't mean your job."

She turned away quickly and started for the car. I trudged behind her. She stopped and turned back to me again. "Why is it, Gussy, that the people you love the most hurt you the hardest? Huh? Why is that?"

"Darlene. What's the matter?"

She trudged up the bank and onto the road.

"Do not follow me," she said without turning around, "or you will go to jail."

"Darlene."

I stood in the road and watched the rear lights on her cruiser recede in the dark. I felt helpless. She veered up the same shore road that the other vehicles had taken a few moments earlier. I couldn't think of anywhere else they would be going at that hour in that direction but the home of Laird Haskell.

Soupy jumped when I hissed at him from the kitchen behind the bar at Enright's. I had slipped in through his alley door.

"Jesus, Trap," he said. "What the fuck?"

"Any of the boys out there?"

"Nah. We're cleared out. Just me, cleaning up. The game got over early, as you know."

"Yeah. Sorry."

"No you're not."

"No I'm not. So you didn't play it out?"

"Without a 'tender? Shit. We played out that period, blew off the rest. Clem Linke was all pissed off that he had two goals and wanted to go for a hat trick. But the Chowder Heads said, See you at the bar, and we left. Six to one final."

Soupy stood in a white apron spattered with hot wing sauce, scrubbing out a bar sink with a Brillo pad. In his other hand he held a spatula. He had turned the bar lights up, illuminating the pall of cigarette smoke floating just below the ceiling. Silence fell as "Ring of Fire" ended on the jukebox.

"Jason didn't come in, did he?" I said.

"Last I heard, he was at the hospital. You got him good, man."

"Good."

"You want a beer, help yourself. And help me too."

I opened a wooden fridge door beneath the back bar and yanked out two Blue Ribbon longnecks. I flicked the caps off and handed Soupy one. He put down the Brillo pad and we both took a long pull.

"Yes, sir," Soupy said. "First one of the day always tastes best."

It wasn't quite one o'clock, so I guessed Soupy was trying to make me laugh. I didn't. I just said, "I came to settle up."

"OK. Three fifty."

Again, I didn't laugh. "You know what I mean."

The spatula clanged into the sink. Soupy untied his apron and threw it on the bar. He took two small glasses and a bottle of peach schnapps off the back bar and motioned toward the kitchen. "In there," he said.

I sat down on some boxes of paper napkins. A Hungry River Rats calendar hung on the wall behind my head. The February picture showed Taylor Haskell in full legs-splayed flop, snagging a puck out of the air with his catching glove.

Soupy propped himself against his griddle. He undid his ponytail and his blond hair fell around his face. He pulled it back onto his head and nodded toward the calendar and said, "What do you think of the messiah?"

I glanced at the calendar. "Ha. Yeah. Watched him last night. Good glove, good on his feet. Gotta keep his head in the game."

"Don't we all."

We sat and sipped our beers for a minute. "Yeah," Soupy said. "Grace used to say, 'That kid doesn't even want to be here.'"

"Gracie said that?"

"She'd surprise you, man. Surprised me. She knew some hockey. I don't know a lot of chicks who understand the two-line pass."

"Loved the Wings, eh?"

"Yeah. Fedorov was her man."

Soupy unscrewed the cap of the schnapps bottle, set the glasses down, and filled each halfway. He handed me one, clinked it with the other.

"To Grace," he said.

"Gracie."

We gulped them down.

"Jesus, Soup," I said, grimacing. "Peach schnapps?"

He capped the bottle and set it aside. "Yeah," he said. "I'd prefer Jack Black. But Grace hated this shit."

"You mean she loved it."

"No. Despised it. That's why she drank it."

"You're not making any sense. And what's with the 'Grace' instead of 'Gracie'?"

Soupy grabbed his beer and took a sip. He cradled the bottle against his chest and looked up at the ceiling.

"She liked 'Grace' better," he said. "I wish I'd called her that before.

Maybe" . . . He waved his bottle around in front of his face. "Ah, nah, fuck it, man. She liked 'Grace' better. Enough said."

"What about the schnapps? Why'd she drink it if she hated it? Whenever I saw her, she was parked behind a gin and Squirt."

"No," Soupy said. "Hang on."

He set his beer down and went back out to the bar. He came back holding a half-filled bottle of Gordon's gin. The label was marked with a big black "G." He shoved it toward me. "Try it."

"No thanks. I know what gin tastes like."

"Trust me, Trap. Just take a sip."

I took it, uncapped it, and raised it to my lips, expecting the smell of alcohol. There wasn't any. I took a sip, swished it around, took another.

"This is not gin," I said.

"Remember the time we fucked with Stevie on his birthday?"

Soupy and a few of the other boys had brought big blond Stevie Reneau down to Detroit to celebrate his thirtieth birthday. We'd spent most of a Friday night at the Post Bar, ordering round after round of tequila shots. Except only Stevie was drinking tequila. The rest of us were drinking shots of tap water, thanks to the ten spot Soupy threw the bartender when Stevie wasn't looking. We let him in on it after the tenth or eleventh shot. He took a wild swing at Soupy and fell on his face while the rest of us howled with laughter. We had to carry him to Lafayette Coney Island for 3:00 a.m. dogs.

"So it's water," I said. "I don't get it."

Soupy took the "G" bottle back and swigged from it. "Gracie wasn't really drinking, except for a shot of peach schnapps every now and then."

"Let me get this straight. She wasn't drinking. But she drank schnapps."

"Whenever she had the urge to drink, she took a shot of the peach shit."

"Which she hated."

"Hey, I didn't say this was the straightest-thinking chick I've ever hung out with. Although she was Einstein compared to my ex. But look, Grace knew what people thought of her. She basically wanted nothing to do with them. Best way to do that, she figured, was let them think what they wanted."

"That she was a fucked-up drunk."

"Yeah."

"So they'd leave her alone. Talk about esteem issues."

"I'm telling you, man, she was working on it."

"That and a bottomless glass of Squirt and water."

I took a long pull on my beer. Gracie had faked me out. I recalled the last time I'd seen her, in the Zamboni shed. She'd seemed shit-faced to me. I recalled how Trixie had gotten in my face when I'd said Gracie was always high or drunk. *Of all people, you should know that appearances . . .* she had said, without finishing the thought.

"You really did like her, didn't you, Soup? It wasn't just the fucking."

He pulled his hair back on his head again, held it. "Yeah." He chuckled. "She kept saying she wanted to hang one of her shoes and one of my skates in the tree."

I smiled. "Of course."

"She was messed up, but she was all right. Good heart."

Kind of like Soupy. Except he wasn't dead.

"So that's it?" I said. "That's what you had to tell me?"

"Don't get pissy with me, Trap."

"I'm not pissy. It's late."

He set his beer down and came across the room. "Move," he said. I stood up from the napkin boxes. Soupy took the River Rats calendar off the wall. He flipped inside it to the month of November.

The top half of the page showed a photograph of the Rats mobbing Taylor Haskell after a win. The bottom half was obscured by a piece of loose-leaf paper folded and taped across the days and dates. Soupy peeled it away and handed it to me. It was a photocopy of what appeared to be a letter.

I read the four short lines twice before I looked up.

"Where did you get this?" I said.

"Grace."

"When?"

"Technically, last week."

"Around the time she found out the new rink wasn't going to hire her."

"Yeah, about then."

"What do you mean 'technically'?"

"She gave it to me then. She told me to keep it in case something happened to her. Then something happened."

"Did she give the original to Haskell?"

"She never said. I don't know what she did with it. If anything."

"She obviously intended to give it to him."

"Looks that way. But I don't know." He waggled his empty beer bottle. "Another?"

"No thanks. Jesus, Soup. If this is real . . ."

"Looks pretty real to me. Though who knows if Grace would've followed through. She kept saying she was done with all that."

I thought of the boxes in her dark room.

"Why didn't you give this to the cops?" I said.

"Almost did," he said. "Dingus put the heat on me, man, the whole interrogation room with the lightbulb thing. Said he'd do everything he could to bust me for underage drinkers. But I honestly didn't know shit. They just got me because I called."

"What do you mean you called?"

"I called, man. I called her in. Grace. I found her."

I imagined Soupy's pickup truck rolling up to the snowbank on the road shoulder by the shoe tree. Sheets of snow blowing across his windshield, his wipers beating vainly against the blinding white. He might not have seen Gracie right away. Maybe he backed the truck onto the road sideways so that his headlights shined over the bank past the dangling silhouette.

"You closed early," I said.

"Fucking-ay, huh? I must have been out of my goddamn mind."

"But how did you know she was out there?"

"I didn't. But I was worried. It was after ten, and she still wasn't here. She was always here by ten. Then I got a call."

"A call from who?"

"No idea. They didn't say and I didn't recognize the voice."

"A man or a woman?"

"Whoever it was wanted me to think it was a man. The connection wasn't so hot either, and I couldn't hear shit because of the bar. But I'm pretty sure it was a woman."

A woman? My chest tightened. What woman could have known that Gracie was hanging in the tree? Darlene? Trixie?

"And she said what?"

"'She's waiting for you at the shoe tree.'"

"Good God. So you closed the bar? Nice move, man."

"I know. I freaked. But I guess I'm not so paranoid, huh? I mean, she'd given me that letter and all I could think was—"

"Did you open it then?"

"No. It was at my house. I read it later."

"So you went out there and called it in but what? You just bolted?"

"She was dead, man. There was nothing I could do. Maybe I'm fucking stupid, OK, but what would you have done? I'm her boyfriend. I closed the bar early. I'm the only one out there. Here, Dingus, slap the cuffs on. I freaked."

And you're Soupy Campbell, I thought. Still a boy.

"But the cops traced your call."

"Fuck, man." Soupy shook his head. "You know how sometimes you think you shut your phone off but you didn't?"

"Nice. So Dingus brings you in. What'd you tell him?"

"What I saw."

"Gracie hanging in the shoe tree."

"Yeah."

"So, again, why didn't you give the letter to the cops?"

"I want a beer."

He walked out of the kitchen. I looked around. His makeshift desk, a folding table with a checkerboard etched into the top, was pushed into a corner beneath a bulletin board covered with pink-and-yellow invoices. I counted three stamped OVERDUE. It made me sad. Soupy had given up his family's marina along a soft stretch of beach for a tunnel of darkness and smoke and hourly replays of "Freebird."

He returned with a fresh Blue Ribbon. "She didn't want me to," he said.

"She didn't want you to give it to the cops? Then why would—"

"She told me to make sure you saw it."

"Me? No."

"Yeah. You. She said you'd take care of it."

Of course she wouldn't have gone to me directly. She thought I couldn't stand her. I thought she couldn't stand me. And yet there she was downstate with my stories hung on her walls, and here she was up north, trusting me from the grave to find her murderer. I tried to stop the pang of grief I felt by reading the letter again.

"So what was all the horseshit you were giving me yesterday when I was in here?" I said. "Why didn't you give me this then?"

"For one thing, I didn't have it with me. For another, I wasn't about to spill my guts in front of those losers who sit at my bar all day drinking three two-buck beers. My brain wasn't exactly working right, Trap. I mean, the last thing I need right now is to have my name splashed all over your paper. I'm barely holding on here."

I finished my beer and stood the empty on Soupy's folding table. "Sorry, Soup," I said.

"You, too, man."

We shook hands. I waved the letter at him. "You don't mind if I take this now, do you?"

"You going to put it in the paper?"

I wasn't sure how to answer. At that moment, I had no idea how I would confirm that the letter was authentic. The person who'd signed it was dead.

"How about I just take it for now and if I want to write anything, I'll tell you?"

"Cool. But you get it, right?"

I slipped the paper into my jacket. "Get what?"

"It wasn't my fault, man. Either way, it wasn't my fault."

"Understood. Get some sleep, Soup."

I pushed the back door open. The wind had kicked up.

"Hey," Soupy said. "Good to have you back between the pipes."

"It was a one-night stand, pal."

"Nah. Once you got the kinks worked out, you looked pretty good."

"Go to hell."

I sat in my pickup rereading the letter beneath the flood lamp outside my mother's little yellow house.

It was dated Wednesday, February 3, a few days before Gracie died. It looked like she had used a marking pen, perhaps blue or purple, given the gray shade of the letters on the photocopied page.

L—

Here is YOUR letter.
You have taken everything from me.

And left me with nothing.
Except what I KNOW.
—G

Motive, I thought. It obviously goes to motive. I thought of those video-tapes again. And I thought, Why wouldn't Haskell at least have tried to appease her? He'd made a career of negotiating, of finding that middle ground that made Vend sneer. Why not give Gracie whatever she wanted—some money, a lousy little job driving the Zamboni at the new rink?

Unless, of course, Gracie could not be appeased. Unless she really did want her dignity back, and neither Haskell nor Vend—who might well have received the same sort of note from Gracie—could give it to her.

I stepped out of my truck. I watched the boughs of the evergreens along Mom's bluff swaying gently in the night wind, heard the pulley cable on Mom's flag clanging off the metal pole.

I folded the letter and slipped it into the inner pocket of my jacket. What would I do with it? What could I do, without knowing whether Gracie had actually presented Haskell with her notion of blackmail?

I thought of Haskell and his wife and his son sleeping in their mansion beyond Mom's evergreens, across the frozen lake, two of them more than likely knowing not a thing about Gracie and Haskell and the things they had done downstate. Unless Haskell had really killed her, or had her killed, what claim did Gracie really have on him and his family? Yes, Haskell was a goddamn bastard, as Trixie had said. So was Vend, who seemed a lot more capable of doing what had to be done. But Gracie was a big girl. She'd known what she was doing.

I supposed I could just go to Dingus, or Darlene, give one of them the letter. And watch Tawny Jane Reese tell the world about it on Channel Eight.

Oh fuck, I thought.

I had to be in Traverse City—I looked at my watch—in about five hours. As Philo said, eight o'clock sharp or I would no longer be employed by Media North or the *Pine County Pilot*, as if it mattered anymore.

twenty-one

Voices in the kitchen woke me at 6:34.

I found Mom and Darlene's mother sitting at the dining room table. Mom was in her flannel pajamas, Mrs. B in a faded violet housecoat. Her galoshes stood dripping on the carpet by the sliding glass doors that led to the yard. I smelled the coffee they were drinking out of matching mugs labeled B for Bea and R for Rudy, my father. My mother had the R mug cupped in her hands.

"Good morning, Gussy," she said.

Blinking against the hanging lamp, I peered past the table into the living room. A dozen or so bouquets of flowers adorned the floor beneath the picture window facing the lake. Through the window I saw scattered lights winking on the bluffs on the north side of the lake. I remembered my father taking me on my first snowmobile ride on a yellow-and-black Ski-Doo he had borrowed from a friend. Dusk was just falling. We shot down the slope in front of the house, across the snow-covered beach, and out onto the hard white lake. I almost fell off the back as I tried to turn and wave to Mom watching from shore.

"Morning," I said. "You guys are up early."

Mrs. B regarded me through her Tweety Bird glasses. "Dear, I've been up since two. Can't sleep for all the excitement around here."

"What did you do, Gus?" my mother said.

"What do you mean?"

"The police called here last night. And you're limping."

"Took a puck off the foot. What police?"

"The D'Alessio boy. He said he needed to talk to you."

"Ah. Just hockey stuff."

More likely, it was Dingus turning up the pressure on me to talk. If he only knew what I had in my jacket pocket.

"Why are you up so early?" Mom said.

"Got a meeting."

"Where were you yesterday? You didn't return my calls."

"I was out of town. Did you call my cell phone?"

Lately Mom had been calling my office when she meant to call my cell, and vice versa. Mrs. B reached across the table and took one of my mother's hands in hers. "Bea," she said.

"Of course, yes," Mom said. "How did it go?"

"Fine." I assumed Mom had told Mrs. B where I'd gone. I decided to change the subject. "Who sent these?"

A glass vase holding a bouquet of white lilies and carnations stood on the snack bar in the kitchen. I picked up the card lying in front of it.

Deeply sorry for your loss.
With sincere regards,
Felicia Haskell

"Huh," I said. "That's nice. I didn't know you knew her. Or that she knew Gracie was . . . you know."

"Who are you talking about?"

"Felicia Haskell."

Mom thought for a second. "Oh," she said. "I don't think I know her."

"It's all just part of the campaign," Mrs. B said.

"Campaign?" For a second her suggestion eluded me. "Oh. You mean for the rink? Come on. They know me better than that."

An idea popped into my head. I fingered the letter in my pocket.

"They came late yesterday," Mom said. "I was just running out to ceramics and didn't have time to move them."

"If it was me, I'd feed them to the deer," Mrs. B said.

"I might just do that."

"We don't need that rink, and we don't need a new coach either. Poppy does just fine with those boys."

I set the card back down. "I better get in the shower."

"We're going to Audrey's, dear. Would you like to join us?"

That gave me another idea.

"No thanks. I'm already running late. See you at the office later, Mrs. B."

The bathroom sat between the two bedrooms and had doors on either end. I went in one door, locked it, and turned on both the shower and the sink. I listened. Mom and Mrs. B were still talking. I opened the door at the other end and slipped into Mom's room.

I found the manila envelope Audrey had told me about in the middle drawer of my mother's desk. It was torn open at one end. As quietly as I could, keeping one ear on the conversation in the dining room, I slipped two sheaves of pages out of the envelope.

The first was bound within a cover of light blue cardboard. "Haverford Variable Life Insurance Company" read the logo on the front. I scanned the first page quickly. On January 7, Grace Maureen McBride had signed up for a term life policy for the sum of $250,000. I flipped through the pages, wondering who was the beneficiary. On page six I found a notation that the beneficiary "will be as shown in the application unless you change them."

I switched to the other sheaf of pages, Gracie's application for the policy. I found what I was looking for at the bottom of the fourth page. Fifty percent of the death benefit, it said, would go to Patricia Armbruster of Melvindale, Michigan, the woman I knew as Trixie.

The other 50 percent would go to Beatrice Carpenter of Starvation Lake, Michigan.

"Oh, holy shit," I whispered.

"Gus?"

My mother's voice came from behind the opposite door of the bathroom. I stuffed the papers back into the envelope. She knocked on the door.

"Gussy. Why is the sink running?"

I slid her drawer closed, tiptoed back into the bathroom, and eased the door on my side shut. I turned off the running water.

"Just shaving," I said.

"Are you all right in there?"

"I'm getting in the shower."

"Gussy. Are you going to be all right? At your meeting?"

Mrs. B must have known where I was going.

"Everything's going to be fine, Mom."

I stood there staring at the door, waiting for my mother to go back to the dining room. I could tell she was waiting herself, probably thinking, *What does my son know?* while I wondered the same about her.

* * *

My cell phone rang as my truck descended the big hill overlooking Skegemog Lake along M-72 west. If I didn't hit traffic along the Traverse bays, I'd be on time for my appointment with Jim Kerasopoulos.

"Hello?" I said.

"Where are you?"

There was something unpleasant in the tone of Darlene's voice.

"Got a meeting with the fat ass in Traverse. Did you talk to the cops in Sarnia?"

"Really?"

"Yeah. Why?"

"I don't know. Sometimes you're as slippery as an eel."

"Huh?"

I heard a newspaper rustle in the background.

"You haven't heard the news?"

"What news?"

"Looks like you got scooped again."

I had watched a few minutes of Channel Eight's 7:00 a.m. report at Mom's house and seen nothing about Starvation Lake.

"Scooped how?"

"The Detroit Free Press. You know. Front page, too. Here, let me read you the headline: 'Feds Investigating Car Makers' Nemesis.'"

Car makers' nemesis, I thought. Ralph Nader? Why would I care about the feds and Ralph Nader? Then it came to me.

"Haskell?" I said.

"Correct," she said. "Would you like to hear the first paragraph?"

In my mind I saw Michele Higgins sitting across the table at Petros, cigarette jutting from her hand, her face lined with disdain.

"Go ahead."

"'A federal grand jury is considering evidence that renowned plaintiffs' attorney Laird Haskell avoided paying taxes in excess of two million dollars, sources familiar with the matter say.'"

"Jesus," I said.

"It gets better." She continued reading. "'Haskell, who left Metro Detroit last year and moved to the northern Michigan town of Starvation Lake, has had his assets frozen by the federal government and is said to be struggling to avoid personal bankruptcy, sources said.'"

She stopped. In a way, the story was a complement to what I'd written about Haskell's inability to finish the new rink. But I doubted that was why Darlene was reading it to me.

"That's quite a story," I said, bracing myself.

"Here's the best part." She read:

A. J. Carpenter, executive editor of the local paper, the *Pine County Pilot*, said Haskell has stopped paying contractors he hired to build a new hockey rink in the town. "Work's come to a stop," Carpenter said in an interview Tuesday at a diner in Metro Detroit. "He's trying to shake the town down for a hundred grand."

Carpenter, a former *Detroit Times* reporter who resigned in the wake of an ethics scandal two years ago, described Haskell as "slippery as an eel."

"I'll bet you can guess the byline on the story."

"It was strictly—"

"But not strict enough that you would mention it to me last night? Or the other day? I know you had all that other business to attend to and of course you had to get back in time for your precious hockey game but maybe you had a few minutes to squeeze in a quickie, huh?"

"Darlene, we had coffee."

The line went silent. My tires whined on the plowed asphalt. Darlene spoke so softly then that I could barely hear what she said.

"You lied."

"I—no. Darlene, I didn't lie, I just didn't—"

"You lied. And I don't know who to believe anymore. I don't know who to believe."

She hung up.

I pulled my truck into a gas station at the corner of M-72 and U.S. 31 and parked. My foot hurt when I stepped on the brake, and I remembered Jason hovering over me, telling me to stay away from Darlene.

I stared at my cell phone lying in my lap.

I remembered how Mich suddenly had been in a hurry to leave Petros. The Mich who had a good story going, who'd probed me about Haskell to see what I knew, who must have gotten nervous that I would get to it before her. And just for the hell of it, shoved her knife in and twisted.

I thought of Darlene hunched over the paper, reading. She must have read it at the sheriff's department. She didn't get the *Free Press* at home. Somebody must have given it to her, pointed out the story, the quotes, made her blush with embarrassment.

"Damn, Darlene," I said to no one. "I'm sorry."

I tossed the phone aside and pulled my truck onto U.S. 31.

Downtown Traverse City was what Starvation Lake longed to be. Before noon fell, shoppers would be scuttling along the brick-trimmed sidewalks of Front Street beneath old-fashioned gaslights hung during summer with baskets of flowers. The cheerful shop windows would beckon with antiques and books and bathymetric maps of Lake Michigan and jewelry and fudge and pastel sweatshirts embroidered "Up North." There were banks and bars and art galleries, a movie theater that actually showed movies, and restaurants boasting of sushi and wild boar tacos and fresh walleye with a nut crust *du jour*.

Still, I didn't feel jealous in the least as I peered down on the street from a fourth-floor conference room at Media North headquarters. I would have taken Audrey's egg pie over nut crust *du jour* any day. Envy was for people like the town council members who deluded themselves into thinking that an influx of rich downstaters like Haskell—Haskell, the man with the feds chasing him—would return Starvation to whatever glory it imagined it once enjoyed.

A door opened behind me. I turned. Kerasopoulos swept into the room. "Betty," he said to his secretary. "No calls."

He closed the door and motioned at the conference table. "Please."

"Good morning, Jim."

"I'm afraid it's not. Sit."

I took a seat facing him across the table. He had a thin sheaf of papers rolled up in one meaty hand. He set them facedown on the table between us and sat. The strands of his navy tie with the pinpoint pink dots splayed in opposite directions across his belly, like a bib. He pressed his palms together and set his hands on the table so that his fingers pointed at me.

"Gus," he said. "It's been a year of firsts for this admittedly young company. First time gross margins exceeded forty percent. First time selling an all-in-one mobile-phone, long-distance, cable-TV, and Internet package.

First time recognized by the Michigan Association of Ad Agencies as a prime partner."

He tapped the tips of his fingers on the table with each sentence, his eyebrows knitted into a single salt-and-pepper hedge across his forehead.

"OK," I said.

"Now, thanks to your reckless and irresponsible reporting, we are confronted with our very first libel lawsuit."

He slapped the papers with his right hand but left them facedown. "But let's take things one at a time. First, your specious and highly speculative article about the unfortunate young woman who hung herself. Thank God we caught that before the first press run. Did you think you could sneak it past me, Gus?" He pointed at the wall at one end of the room where a trio of diplomas hung in wood frames. "Did you forget that, as an attorney who takes his profession very seriously, I've spent more than thirty-five years paying attention to every single little detail?"

Fat ass, I thought. "She didn't kill herself. Wait. The cops are going to prove she was murdered."

"Oh, they are, are they? Well, I guess they better let the Pine County medical examiner know, because he says she committed suicide."

I dearly wanted to tell him that his pal Haskell might well be implicated. But I didn't need him squealing about what I knew.

"All Doc Joe said was that strangu—"

"Shut up!" Kerasopoulos lifted his wide body halfway out of his seat and stabbed a finger in my direction. "Just shut your damn mouth. This is not an argument. This is not a negotiation. This is me, the president and chief executive officer of Media North Corporation, telling you what's what. Understood?"

"Understood."

"We would look like fools today if we had needlessly stirred the town up with your cockamamie triangulations of half truths and rumors with a few irrelevant facts thrown in. I will not have it." He was bellowing now, his baritone booming into my face. "Do you hear me? I will not have it. And I will not have my neph—Philo learning that this is the way to publish a community newspaper."

He sat back down, took a deep breath. His starched shirt collar dug into his mashed potato neck. "A word of advice, though I sincerely have no expectation of you taking it: you really should keep your family matters within your family."

"Excuse me?"

"You wouldn't happen to have something to gain from a finding that your cousin was actually murdered, would you?"

"No," I said, without thinking. Then I remembered the life insurance policy. My mother would benefit, but of course I was living with my mother, so—but how the hell would Kerasopoulos have known about the policy?

"Enough on that subject. Were it our only problem."

He grabbed the papers, flipped them over, and shoved them across the table at me. The word COMPLAINT blared from the top of the cover page. *Haskell v. Media North Corp. et al.* included as defendants the *Pine County Pilot*, a number of contractors I had quoted in my stories, and me. I looked first for a docket number, which would have indicated that the lawsuit had actually been filed. There wasn't one. I quickly skimmed the next twelve pages.

The lawsuit asserted that my stories had maliciously defamed Laird Haskell and, in doing so, deprived him of the ability to complete a project— the new rink, of course—in which he had invested considerable amounts of his own time and money. He was seeking damages in excess of $10 million. Just seeing that number, I thought, must have puckered Kerasopoulos's wide butt.

I actually smiled. "He hasn't actually filed it yet, has he?"

"Does this amuse you somehow?" Kerasopoulos leaned into the table, his face reddening. "A libel verdict against this company could render—"

"This is bullshit." I slid the papers back. "He's just trying to scare us into paying him a pile of money he desperately needs."

"Let me assure you—"

"He hasn't filed yet, right?"

"No, he has not. But I assure you that Mr. Haskell is dead serious."

"Uh-huh. Have you seen today's *Detroit Free Press*? Or don't you read papers that don't cuddle up to advertisers?"

He gave me one of those long, hard, penetrating looks that men who imagine themselves to be powerful give to men who don't burden themselves with such illusions. It told me that the answer to both of my questions was no.

Kerasopoulos didn't reply, though. He sat up straight and smoothed his tie across his torso.

"Well, Gus," he said, "I'm afraid we can no longer tolerate your particular brand of journalism. Perhaps you found it easier to practice in Detroit. Although, as we both know, things didn't work out so well for you there either."

OK, I thought. My time at the *Pilot* was up. What did I need it for anyway? How could you tell anybody anything when the next paper was always three or four days away? And it wasn't like the weekly paycheck of $412.50 was going to make me rich, even in Starvation Lake.

"Let's see," I said. "The feds are coming down on Haskell but we should be afraid of him. Gross margins are through the roof but you're whacking the *Pilot* budget. Shit, Jim, you should be grateful for a big bad libel suit. It gives you the perfect excuse to shut the *Pilot* down."

"We're done here." He picked up the papers and stood.

"You can make a big show out of firing me, wait a few weeks, then tell the good people of Starvation Lake, Sorry, this libel suit is too much for your little rag and its subpar profit margins, we've got to shut it down. Then you throw a few hundred grand at Haskell to make him go away—if he's not in jail by then—and your year-end bonus will be secure. Great plan."

"I would fire you this minute if the lawyers would let me."

"Go ahead. Stand on principle, Jim. Or is now not really the time?"

The door behind him opened. A slender young man in a security guard's uniform stepped into the doorway and stood with his hands folded at his belt. He had a badge but no gun. He also seemed to be trying to grow a mustache, without much success.

"This gentleman will show you out," Kerasopoulos said. "You are hereby suspended from your job indefinitely, pending further consideration by the Media North board of directors. In the meantime, you are barred from the *Pilot* newsroom and any of its facilities. We will arrange for you to collect your personal items in due time. In the meantime, please do not attempt to contact any of the newspaper's employees, including Mr. Beech. If you choose noncompliance, rest assured we will promptly take appropriate legal or other actions."

"Other actions?" I said. "I thought you were just a lawyer."

He glared at me one last time and left the room.

The fuzzy-lipped rent-a-cop placed a hand on my elbow and led me silently to the elevator, down to the first floor, and across the lobby to the glass double-door entrance. Outside, a thin gray sleet had begun to fall. As I started out the door, I turned to the guard. "I hate fucking Traverse City," I said.

"Have a good day," he said.

My windshield wipers made slurping slaps as I steered my pickup past the fudge shops along the bay east of Traverse. I turned on the radio, thinking naïvely that I might catch a bulletin on Haskell's IRS troubles. A country song came on. Despite myself, I laughed. I had nearly lost my job and my girlfriend. "Good thing I don't have a dog," I said aloud.

What was I going to do now? A newspaper reporter wasn't much without a newspaper. Even if I did get to the bottom of Gracie's death, who was I going to tell? Not Michele Higgins, that was for sure. There was my mother, of course, and Mrs. B. They would listen and tell their bingo and bowling and ceramics partners only those things they wished to believe. And those women and men in turn would translate only those things they wished to believe, until it all became a fiction.

But there was Dingus, of course, who could do the right thing. And there was Darlene. Maybe. Besides, a man had pissed all over my notebook. I had to know why.

My phone rang. I snatched it off the console, hoping Darlene was calling to say she had lost her temper.

"Did you hear about Laird Haskell?" Philo said.

I didn't answer right away.

"Gus?"

"Yeah. On the libel suit? Or the IRS?"

"Pardon me?"

"Never mind. You go first."

"All right. I hear he's going to do some sort of mea culpa at today's town council meeting."

"Who told you that?"

"Let me put it this way. At first I was told not to bother with the council meeting and instead cover a girl's volleyball match at the high school."

"I remember."

"Then I got a call about fifteen minutes ago saying go to the council meeting."

Of course, I thought. Kerasopoulos had made his secretary run out and get him a *Free Press*. Then he called Haskell or Haskell's attorney.

"So Uncle Jimbo's running coverage now, huh?"

"I didn't say that, but . . . Gus?"

"Did you see the *Free Press* this morning?"

"I have it here on my desk. But listen—"

"I'm afraid I can't help you any more, Philo. Your dear, fat-assed uncle just told me I'm no longer welcome at the *Pilot*. I'm reckless and irresponsible. If I were you, I think I might just go to the high school. Tough to be reckless and irresponsible covering volleyball."

"Gus, would you please just shut the hell up and listen?"

It was the second time I had been told to shut up that morning. By members of the same family no less.

"Sure," I said.

"I went through those documents you FOIA'd."

He pronounced it *FOH-ahd*. "FOY-uhd," I corrected him.

"OK. You told me to call if I found something interesting."

"Right. But I'm not supposed to be talking to you."

"I need to talk to you about these documents."

"Go ahead."

"I can't now. I have to go take a photo of a new pizzeria."

At the *Pilot*, we routinely published photos of new businesses, the owner smiling in front of a burger stand or a real estate office. They were essentially free ads, handed out in the expectation that the business would reciprocate by buying an ad or two. Some did, most didn't.

"What new pizzeria?" I said.

"Roselli's, up the hill across the river."

"Roselli's? You mean Riccardo's?"

"Well. Yes."

"That's not new. They're just changing their name again."

"Exactly."

"Jeez."

"It pays the bills."

I slowed my truck as I neared the intersection with U.S. 131 in

Kalkaska. Waiting at the light, I considered detouring north to the Twin Lakes Party Store for one of their tasty egg sandwiches. What was I bothering with Philo for anyway?

"Listen, Philo. How do I know you're not just spying for your uncle?"

He waited before he answered. "Look. I think I might know something that you probably don't. You want to know what it is or not?"

"Fair enough." I pushed the pickup straight through the light. "Tell you what. I'll meet you there—Riccardo's, Roselli's, whatever—around noon. Don't worry, it'll be empty. Bring the documents."

"Done."

"And, Philo? Could you look up a phone number for me?"

Felicia Haskell jingled a wine charm on the stem of her half-full glass and gave me an innocent smile. "I am not a drinker, Mr. Carpenter."

"Gus. Didn't think you were."

We stood on either side of the butcher-block island in her kitchen with the wall of windows overlooking the frozen crescent of the lake. Beyond Felicia Haskell was a room bigger than a two-car garage. Half of one wall was consumed by a fireplace at the bottom of a tower of cut granite. Muddy boot prints marred the carpet in front of the hearth. There was a hint of smoke in the air.

Across the room, a grand piano stood before the wall of glass. Outside, the sleet had given way to snowflakes the size of silver dollars. Mom's house was invisible in the gauze of white.

"I just—" Felicia Haskell shrugged. "I have to have something that reminds me of civilization."

"Understood."

"Once in a while. I'm sorry. I know you love it here."

"Some of it, yes." I drank from my glass of orange juice.

I had waited until I was driving along the lake's north bluff, seconds from the Haskell house, and called her from my truck, figuring her son, Taylor, would be at school and hoping her husband would be with his attorney, drawing up their strategy for dealing with the feds, plotting whatever form of extortion they planned to present to the town council. I'd told Felicia Haskell that I had been moved by the bouquet she'd sent my mother. Could I drop by for just a minute?

Of course, she'd said. Maybe she felt sorry for me.

"Please forgive the smell," she said. "We had a little chimney fire last night. I've been telling Laird to get a sweep out here but he's been so busy with the rink and everything."

I remembered the flashers moving behind the tree line the night before. "Everybody OK?" I said.

"Yes, everyone's fine. It just—you know, scares the heck out of you."

"Police come?"

"They did. Didn't get much sleep. They were here till almost three."

"The cops, too?"

"Whoever. I was with Taylor in his room. We'll be fine. Just can't use the fireplace for a while." She gave the wine in her glass a swirl. "Now, haven't I seen you at the rink? Aren't you a hockey player?"

"Yeah. Not much of one. But it keeps me sane."

"Nice for you. I have to say it makes me insane. Driving here, driving there, practice, workouts, chalk talks, games. It never seems to end."

"I remember."

"I'll bet." She couldn't have weighed 110 pounds, her fake boobs accounting for everything over 100. She wore a red sweater with the tails dangling over black tights that ended in a pair of fur-lined boots. Her silver hair was pulled back in a black leather catch, bringing the angles of her cheekbones and slender nose into sharp relief. Again, I thought she looked older than she was. She still had the bandage on her left wrist.

"Thanks for letting me drop by, Mrs. Haskell—"

"Felicia."

"Felicia. I was just thinking that no one has asked your—"

"Excuse me, I'm sorry." She produced a cell phone from under the island. "Hi, Tay," she said, without turning away. She listened. "No. No. Yes, I understand, honey, but you have balance training after . . . No, maybe this weekend . . . Taylor . . . No . . . No, you need to get your rest."

I heard the boy's voice grow louder, though not loud enough for me to make out what he was saying. "Yes, I understand, honey," she said. "You can talk to your father, but that's the way it is until the season's over."

She set the phone down and blew out a long sigh. "Gus," she said, "did you ever think you would play in the NHL?"

The question caught me off guard. I chuckled. "No."

"Why do you laugh?"

"Well, I just . . . my mom. I mean, she was fine with me playing and all, came to most of the games, though she said she thought the game was dumb and she couldn't bear to watch me. I play—I played goalie. Like your son."

"I see."

"After games, my mom would make cocoa for me—she makes great cocoa from scratch, with the unsweetened stuff—and we'd sit in the kitchen and replay the game a little. And she'd always say, 'How come all the other parents have Gordie Howes and I don't?'"

Felicia furrowed her brows.

"Sorry," I said. "He was a big star for the Red Wings back then."

"Oh. That seems a little mean."

"She didn't mean it that way. It was our little joke about the parents and how they all thought their kid was going to the pros, but me and Mom, we had our heads on straight."

"That's funny. You did."

She set her glass down and walked over to the wall next to the fireplace. I sneaked a look at her cell phone. The area code was 248: suburban Detroit, where she and Haskell had come from. She fiddled with some knobs on a console built into the wall. Piano music filled the room.

"Do you know this?" Felicia said.

"Can't say I do. It's pretty."

"Horowitz. Playing Chopin. Vladimir Horowitz."

"Ah."

She turned the music down and came back to the island. "I wish I could interest my son in *that* Russian."

It took me a few seconds, but I got it. "Ah, he must like those Russkies on the Wings, eh? Larionov. Fedorov. Kozlov. Fetisov."

"His father certainly likes them."

"What about Osgood?"

"Who?"

"The Wings' goalie." Osgood let in a softie every now and then. "Does Taylor like him?"

"Gosh. I have no idea."

"Does he like playing goalie, Felicia?"

She looked momentarily baffled. "Who?"

"Taylor."

"Oh. Of course." She looked into her glass, carried it to the sink, poured the wine out. "It keeps him busy."

"Yes, but does he *like* playing goalie?"

"I don't know what else he would do here except get in trouble."

She didn't sound too convincing. I decided to change the subject.

"You've certainly had your hands full, with the new rink and the fire and . . . did you by chance see the *Free Press* today?"

"Unfortunately, yes." She was awfully cool for a woman with fire trucks and cops and the IRS on her doorstep. "That's why I'm glad you called."

"Really?"

"The man I read about in the papers, Gus, is not the man I know."

"No?"

I probably shouldn't have challenged her. I couldn't help but think of what Jason had told me about the happy Haskell household. She backed away from the island now, sizing me up.

"No," she said. "I realize Laird's not an easy man to get to know. I realize a successful attorney is going to make some enemies. But he's not just a collection of jury verdicts and bank accounts."

"It is hard to get to know someone who won't talk to you."

"Don't take it personally."

"If you say so."

"I know, I know. For all of his many talents, my husband hasn't handled things so well of late. I mean, why not just tell your story? Tell the truth, you have nothing to hide. Why let the critics and the naysayers get all the ink?"

"I'm all ears."

"I know what you think. You know Laird Haskell the plaintiff's attorney, the guy who makes the tear-jerker speech to the jury, who gets up at the press conference and works up the crowd. But you know what? When he's not on stage, he's actually quite shy. He doesn't talk about the good things he quietly does for people less fortunate than him. I'm reading in your paper about how he doesn't have the money to build the rink and I'm looking at our checkbook and seeing thousands of dollars going to charities. Especially for women."

Especially for women. She wanted me to know that. Why? I was feeling good about my hunch about Felicia Haskell. When I had seen the bouquet at Mom's, I'd had a gut feeling that she felt somehow guilty, maybe because she knew Gracie had been turned down for that job at the new rink. Or maybe not. But Felicia Haskell had reached out, and when people reach out, they want to be heard. So I was there to give her a chance. But women? Laird Haskell had a soft spot for *women*? It would have been funny if it wasn't so sad. Especially if that prenuptial agreement was as much of a straitjacket as Jason had said.

"Why women?" I said.

"His mother. She married a jerk. Heavy drinker. Liked to smack her around in front of Laird and his sister."

"Did she ever get away from the guy?"

"Yes. When she died. Anyway, I wish I could read about that Laird in the paper once in a while. Something positive. I guess you people have to emphasize the negative to sell newspapers."

She couldn't possibly have been talking about the *Pilot.* "Could be that people like to read those stories. I will do my best. But Mrs. Haskell—"

"Felicia."

"Felicia. I suppose the *Free Press* story is, as you say, negative. But would you know if it's at all true that your husband's assets have been frozen and he might be looking at bankruptcy?"

She pursed her lips, then said, "I know Laird's been under a lot of pressure. I try not to pile any more on by asking him a lot of questions. As I said, someone who does what he does tends to make a few enemies."

"I'm sure that's true."

"That's not for you to quote."

"I understand." I reached into my jacket pocket and pulled out the photocopy of Gracie's letter to Haskell. I'd stopped at a shop in Traverse City and made a second copy, which was back in my truck. "Got something here I wanted to show you. Might be bull. Might upset you."

"I'm a big girl."

I handed it to her. She unfolded it. Her eyes scanned it once, twice. Then they slid up to me. "What is this?"

"I can't be absolutely sure. But it looks like a note my second cousin might have sent to your husband."

Felicia didn't move. She read the letter again. "Why?" she said. "Because it says 'L'? That could be Larry or Lenny or Louie or a million other people."

Or it could have been Laurie or Linda or Lucinda. But Felicia Haskell chose not to even consider a woman's name.

"We're thinking it's your husband," I said.

The paper was trembling in her hand.

"Who's we, Gus? Where did you get this?"

"I got it."

"What are you trying to say, that my husband was . . ." Her voice caught. "That my husband was sleeping with her? That little white-trash slut? Who slept at the rink and drove the damn Zamboni?"

"No," I said. "I just thought maybe you could—"

"How dare you show me this. How dare you walk into my home with your ugly insinuations." She tore the paper in two. I watched. She tore it again. And again. She flung the pieces in my face. "Get out," she said.

"So it wasn't your husband?"

"Get out of my house. I'm calling the police."

I looked around as I walked to my truck, hoping no one had heard her outburst. Not a chance. I hopped in and backed between the snowy walls of pines and out onto North Shore Road. I figured I had the confirmation I'd come for.

ey there, did you try to call me?"

"Call you? You hung up on me and I'm supposed to call you?"

I had called Nova Patterson from the parking lot behind the pizzeria that only the day before had been called Riccardo's. A red, white, and green banner that said "ROSELLI'S—UNDER NEW MANAGEMENT" now covered the Riccardo's sign stuck in the ground. A corner had come loose and was snapping in the noon breeze.

"I'm sorry. Got myself in a little trouble. I'm OK now."

"I was worried," she said. "But you didn't give me your number. And I'm not allowed to make long-distance calls anyway."

"That's OK. Got anything for me?"

"Hang on."

From my pickup I could see down the hill and over the river to Main Street. A snowplow rumbled down the south side of the street, steering around Mrs. B's Mercury in front of the *Pilot*. Had she been ordered to call the cops if I walked in the door? Soupy leaned out of Enright's and flung a bag of trash at his Dumpster.

A teenaged boy wearing a River Rats jacket came out of the dentist's office, stuffed his hands in his pockets, and hunched his shoulders against the cold. It was Dougie Baker, the Rats' backup goalie. Decent with his gloves, still figuring out how to use his feet. Taylor Haskell's teammate would not be playing in the NHL or anything remotely close. He went to the dentist, not balance training.

My gaze drifted toward the lake. A blue Suburban with tinted windows emerged from behind the marina and turned onto Main.

"Uh-oh," I said.

"Something wrong?" Nova was back.

"No," I said, keeping my eyes on the Suburban as it moved slowly down

Main then turned up Estelle Street into the neighborhoods behind. "What do you have?"

"All right," Nova said. "Where were we? I told you the one house, the one on Harman owned by that one guy."

"Mr. Vend," I said. I reached into a jacket pocket for a pen and notebook and felt something else there: the brush. I kept forgetting I had it. "And the taxes were paid by?"

"Something—I'll spell it out: KNB LLC."

"KNB?" I said, writing it on the notebook cover. "'K' as in kitten?"

"'N' Nancy, 'B' boy, yeah."

Short for Knob. Or Knobbo.

"Brother."

"What's wrong?"

"Nothing. What about the other house—the one in foreclosure?"

"Got that right here. The old owner was a company called . . . not sure how to say this . . . fee-liss . . . ?"

"Felicity?"

"Tuss."

"Felicitous," I said.

"Felicitous Holdings."

"Yeah. Right."

"You've heard of them?"

"I think so."

"Good, because I did a little extra checking for you."

Nova told me that over the past few months, Felicitous—it had to be Laird Haskell—had sold thirteen properties in Melvindale, Dearborn, and River Rouge. KNB had bought each of them for a dollar. Except the one where Gracie had lived.

I added it up in my head: Whenever his money problems had started, Haskell must have tried to avail himself of some of the cash in that lush niche business he and Vend ran, the one Gracie had been so good at. Now he was trying to get square with Jarek Vend. I had my doubts that cheap bungalows in downriver Detroit were going to do it.

No wonder that blue Suburban was trolling Starvation Lake.

"Wait a minute," I said. "The house in foreclosure? I was in—I mean, the person living there still has the house. Doesn't the bank padlock it or something?"

"Not always," Nova said. "This one's going up for a sheriff's sale. But the owner gets to try to pay back the money. You know, to redeem themselves."

Redemption and Haskell didn't quite go together. But apparently he had held Gracie's house back from Vend. I wondered why. For some reason, he must have hoped Gracie would go back downstate.

"One more thing, Nova Marie?"

"Please?"

"Please."

Out of the mess of old newspapers and fast-food rubbish on the passenger seat floor, I dredged up a foam coffee cup.

"Does your list have an address on Prospect?"

"It does indeed." She read it to me. It matched the one for Trixie's women's center I'd scribbled on the coffee cup.

Trixie might never have known it, but her landlord had once been Laird Haskell. Now, whether she knew it or not, her landlord was Jerek Vend. Of course she was having trouble. Had Haskell discounted her rent because he felt such pity for unfortunate women? Had Vend raised it beyond her means?

It made sense in the twisted, incestuous way that the last few days made sense.

Philo came walking up the hill. He waved and went inside the pizzeria.

"Thank you, Nova," I said. "I owe you one."

"I low about two —like two tickets to a Lions game?"

I saw Soupy come back out of Enrights, let the door close, and just stand there in the cold, head bowed, arms wrapped around himself.

"You there?"

"Yes, yes," I told Nova. "I'm on it."

Soupy went back inside. I thought of the calendar hanging in his kitchen. I looked down the street for Dougie Baker; he was gone. I remembered the piano music spilling over me in the Haskell kitchen. Something about it bothered me.

"And don't be hanging up on me no more."

"Shall I spread these out in grease or marinara?" Philo said.

We were sitting in the corner booth at the pizzeria. The only other person in the place was the owner, Belly, who was in the kitchen. Philo held a file folder against his blue-and-black argyle sweater and surveyed the table with a look of utter disgust. Belly hadn't yet changed the old *Pilot* covering the table.

"Who cares? They're just photocopies, right?"

"I would prefer not to wallow around in some stranger's lunch." Philo came halfway out of his seat. "Waiter?" he shouted. "Can you bus this table?"

"Hold your fucking horses," Belly yelled from somewhere behind the counter. "I'm a one-man show here."

"Well, excuse me," Philo said, sitting back down.

"Here," I said, peeling one edge of the newspaper away and folding it in half to expose the bare plastic tabletop. "Let's see what you know that I couldn't possibly figure out for myself."

Philo laid the folder flat on the table and flipped it open to reveal a two-inch-high stack of photocopied documents. Most of them had come from the Michigan Department of Treasury, although I'd sent my freedom-of-information requests to every agency I thought Haskell might have had to file with. Sticky tabs in red, orange, green, and yellow jutted from the edges of the pile.

"I'm impressed," I said. "Are you sure you want to do this?"

"Do what?"

"Show me all this stuff, given that I'm persona non grata at the *Pilot?*"

Philo gave me a hard look through his horn-rims. Then he said, "Do you plan to go to the town council meeting today?"

"Why do you care?"

"I might need your advice when I write my story."

Philo was serious. "I'm flattered," I said, "even if you won't be publishing for three days. Anyway, if Haskell's going to apologize, I want to be there. Who knows? Maybe he'll apologize to me."

"Good." Philo placed one hand flat on the stack of pages. "They didn't give us everything you asked for."

"They never do."

"And this stuff doesn't tell you very much."

"Nope."

"A lot of it's just routine. Some is blacked out. But there are a couple of things that might be helpful. You were obviously trying to figure out where

Laird Haskell was getting his money, or where things might have gone awry for him." He fingered the pages back to the green tab he had marked "dt." He slipped out a few stapled pages and handed them to me. "This could be informative."

I scanned the cover page quickly. It was a state registration for a business called ExpertWitness Trading LLC. I found the description on line 6A: "Trading of securities and related assets."

"No way," I said. "He was trading stocks? Himself?"

"Looks like it. You can't tell for sure."

"Good way to piss away a fortune in a hurry."

I flipped through the other pages. Haskell was not required to report how much he'd made or lost on the business. The last page listed the principal owners of ExpertWitness Trading as Laird Haskell and Felicia Quarles Haskell. I wondered if she knew she was co-owner of a one-man day-trading firm. I thought of Vend showing me the TV screens in his office, the comely young women furrowing their brows over the latest market news, the stock charts pointing infinitely up. Vend knew just how Haskell had been seduced.

"Yes," Philo said. "And from reading your stories about him, he strikes me as a man who would believe he could master anything."

"You read my stories? My *Times* stories?"

"Just a few. Found them online."

"Yeah, well, if you can kick the auto industry's ass, why not Wall Street?"

"Exactly."

"Plus, it's a fun way to fill up a lonely winter day up north."

"Though I don't really understand why he'd bother filing the paperwork."

"Easier to write off the losses on your income tax," I said. "Or to have a legal cover for laundering money."

"Why would Haskell need to launder money?"

"Did you read this morning's *Free Press*?"

"Yes. Of course."

I handed the pages back. Philo fitted them back in the original stack. I had never seen him so focused on something other than a budget.

"What else you got?"

"The rest of the stuff really just indicates how many different businesses Haskell was trying to run in addition to whatever legal work he might have had. Real estate, a little retail, the new rink, a bunch of residential down-state. But there was one thing, in particular—"

"Nothing about kinky sex?"

Philo stopped arranging the pages and looked at me. "Kinky—oh, the waiter."

Belly stood at the table glowering at Philo. "I am the proprietor, sir," he said.

I grinned. "Hey, Bell. Meet Philo Beech of the *Pilot*."

Neither of them offered a hand. Belly grunted. "What the hell kind of name is that? Philo? Sounds like something you use to wash a pot."

"I was named for my great-grandfather."

"BFD," Belly said. He looked at me. "You guys going to order today?"

We ordered Italian subs to go, mine with peppers, Philo's without. "Here, let me grab this," Belly said, tearing the newspaper away from the table and balling it up in his hands. "I'll bring you another."

"Did you say kinky sex?" Philo whispered.

"Just a joke. Let's see some more."

"Well." He took a deep breath. "There's this one thing."

"The thing I couldn't have figured out."

He ignored me and pulled out another stack of pages. "This particular collection of documents seems to show that Mr. Haskell, along with some other individuals, owns a great deal more property than we thought, right next to the property where the new hockey rink is being built."

"Really?" It immediately made me think that Vend might like to get his hands on that too. Which may have been why he seemed so interested in the town council meeting.

"Yes. Much of it is owned by a company called—"

"Felicitous Holdings," I said.

"How did you know?"

"Lucky guess. Does it say what they plan to use the land for?"

"No, just 'future development.' But you can imagine, if the rink is a suc-cess, that land could become valuable."

"Big if, but yes."

"If it doesn't, they have problems."

He had no idea. "Correct," I said.

"What most interested me, though, was this." He turned the first few pages back to one listing the company's board of directors. There were nine directors, including Haskell and his wife; Haskell's local attorney, Parmelee Gilbert; and other names I didn't recognize. Philo placed a forefinger on one.

"Here," he said.

The name he pointed to was Linda Biegeleisen. Her address was given as Suttons Bay, Michigan, a village on the Leelanau Peninsula jutting north from Traverse City. Jim Kerasopoulos, I knew, lived in Suttons Bay.

"Who's she?" I said.

"She's listed by her maiden name. I suppose that's legal, if that's the name you have on your driver's license."

"So what?"

Philo took another breath. He seemed, to my surprise, angry. "A few years after my great-grandfather came to this country, his wife made him shorten the family name. Some of his nine children adopted the altered form. But some chose to revert to the old one, out of respect for their ancestors. My father did not. His sister did."

"Get to the point, Philo."

He tapped the name twice. "This is my aunt."

"Your aunt as in—holy shit. No."

"Yes."

I almost jumped out of the booth. "You've got to be fucking kidding me. Kerasopoulos has a piece of Haskell's business?"

"His wife certainly does."

"Same thing, man. Same thing. So your uncle has a direct interest in that rink. Direct. Man, I'm dumb. Here I thought he was just shilling for ads. Jesus. How the hell did he think he could get away with this?"

Philo took off his horn-rims and rubbed his eyes with the heels of his hands. He put his glasses back on and stared at the table. "Believe me," he said. "My uncle thinks he's smarter than everyone. I'm sorry."

"Sorry for what?"

He looked up at me. "For being a little bitch."

I wasn't sure what to say. I thought of saying I always knew his uncle was a fat ass, but that wouldn't have helped.

"Never mind," I said. "Your uncle could be in a lot of trouble." I was thinking now of Vend. "What are you going to do?"

"I'm going to cover the story."

"Right. Kerasopoulos will want to banner that baby across the front: 'Publisher of This Newspaper Linked to Slime-Ball'—oops."

Belly showed up with our sandwiches in one hand and a wrinkled piece of newspaper in the other. "Two subs, one peppers, to go. That'll be six dollars and thirty-five cents."

"Thanks, Bell." I set a five and three ones on the table, took the sandwiches, and stood up.

"Hey," Belly said. "Remember that broad you were asking me about?"

"Who? When?"

"The broad was with your cousin in here." I had totally forgotten about that. Belly shoved the piece of newspaper at me. "Didn't know her name, but I never forget a face."

The date at the top of the clipping was November 8, 1998. The headline on the story said, COUPLE RENEWS WEDDING VOWS. There was a black-and-white picture of the couple: Laird and Felicia Haskell.

"Her?" I said, pointing at Felicia. I didn't remember the story; it was probably written by one of our blue-haired freelancers. Philo leaned in to see. "She was here with"—I hesitated—"with Gracie?"

"Yep. Didn't look like she wanted to be here. No wonder because your cousin, she got pretty worked up there for a while."

"About what?"

"Fuck do I know. Girl stuff. This broad"—he pointed at the paper again—"she wore sunglasses the whole time, like she's a movie star or something."

"You're absolutely certain?"

Belly dropped his arms to his sides. "Are you deaf?"

Outside, Philo followed me to my truck.

"Aren't you walking?" I said.

"Wait," he said. "Kinky sex. That wasn't a joke."

"Not really."

"Gus," he said. "As I said, I'm sorry I wasn't much help to you before. But frankly, I'm not in much better shape than you."

"No."

"And if I'm going to do what I have to do—what we have to do—I'm going to need to know what you know."

I looked down Estelle Street. The blue Suburban sat on the opposite end of the Estelle Street Bridge, peering up the slope and across the Hungry River at Philo and me. I could feel the stare of that cratered face.

I turned to Philo. "So," I said, "is now the time to stand on principle?"

Philo didn't flinch. "I think so."

I opened my truck door. "Hop in. We got a little time before the council meets. I think it's going to be interesting."

Town hall sat on Elm Street just up from Main, in sight of the preserved remains of the dam the Civil Conservation Corps built in the 1930s to create the lake they christened Starvation.

A fire in the 1970s destroyed the grand four-story edifice of brick and granite that had once towered over the spot. Before the fire, the council had been deadlocked over the budget, and *Pilot* headlines screamed of lawsuits and countersuits and citizens demanding recalls. Amid the uproar, the council neglected to appropriate enough money to pay the insurance premiums on the building. Today, town hall was a low-slung rectangle of beige brick that could have passed for a post office. Two willows flanking the walkway to the glass double-door entrance were all that remained from the old days.

Now a long line of locals, most of them retirees, waited beneath the willows for seats at this afternoon's town council meeting. The snow had stopped but the wind had not and many of the women had wrapped their faces in scarves. I watched from the open window of my truck on the street, keeping an eye out for the blue Suburban. I had dropped Philo at the *Pilot* after telling him some but not all of what I knew about Gracie's doings downstate. I was taking a chance that he wouldn't squeal to Dingus or his uncle. I didn't think he would. Betrayal can change a person.

I stood near the street watching the queue waiting to get into town hall. I'd been checking my voice mail all day for something from Darlene. Now I checked again, and again there was nothing. With so many people, I thought, maybe she'd be working the council meeting.

The milling crowd at the head of the line parted and I saw Gracie's mother, Shirley McBride, with her back to the double doors, her blond head wrapped in a white wool headband, a cigarette in one hand and a sign in the other. She had duct-taped a poster board to a metal clothes hanger bent into a crude handle. On the poster she had written in black felt-tip pen, UNFORGIVEN: MY DAUGTER OR HASKEL'S HOCKEY? Sheriff's Deputy Frank D'Alessio stood a few steps away, his eyes fixed on the ground, looking like he wanted to scream, or at least haul Shirley off to jail.

"We've got lots of police for a town hall meeting," she was yelling. "But not enough to find out who killed my daughter."

"Not enough to shut you up either, Shirley," shouted someone from the waiting line. "Get her out of here, Frank."

D'Alessio turned his head to Shirley and said something I couldn't hear. She continued her yelling.

I looked down the street and saw the Channel Eight van rolling up from Main. Walking along the sidewalk next to it was my mother. She didn't go to many town council meetings, so the rumors about a Haskell apology must have reached her. Mom took her place at the end of the line, craning her neck to see what was going on at the entrance. Then she slung her purse over a shoulder and started to jostle her way around and past the waiting throng, meeting their annoyed stares with smiling hellos and good afternoons until she came face-to-face with Shirley McBride.

What are you doing, Mom? I thought. I jumped out of my truck and started walking, then trotting, toward the hall. Mom tried to take Shirley by the hand, but Shirley shook her off and thrust the sign into Mom's face, saying something I couldn't hear amid the voices rising around them. Now Mom disappeared in the mob. I heard Shirley telling her, *Go to hell, I'm not your charity case,* and Mom saying, *Shirley, please listen to reason, for once just listen.*

I made my way through the line just as D'Alessio stepped between my mother and Shirley. Shirley was yelling louder and Mom didn't like it but she wasn't backing off. I grabbed her by a shoulder. "Mom," I said. "What are you doing?" She shrugged me off without a glance and put her hands up to Gracie's mother in supplication. "We can work this out, Shirley," she said. "We can work this out like adults."

"OK, ma'am, that's enough now," D'Alessio said. But Shirley lunged toward Mom, almost knocking D'Alessio over. He grabbed her by her down-filled vest and forced her back against the wall. Her sign fell to the sidewalk. "Take her to jail where she belongs," some old guy shouted. D'Alessio struggled with Shirley, who was just as short as Gracie but twice as wide. "Settle down, Mrs. McBride, or I will take you in."

She turned and shouted in his face. "Why don't you go do your job and find my daughter's killer instead of picking on me? Oh, I'm sorry—we need every penny we can find for a goddamn hockey rink."

"Please calm down, Shirley," my mother said.

"Mom," I said, pulling at her again. She took a step back, still without acknowledging me, as the others closed in around us, shouting things about the rink and Haskell and Gracie and Shirley. D'Alessio had one hand on the cuffs dangling from his police belt and the other palm up in front of Shirley's face, warning her back. Her headband had come off and her hair flew around her pickled beet face as she screamed and pointed at my mother. "She wants my money. She got my Gracie, now she wants my goddamn money."

"No, Shirley," Mom said. "Please."

Once more Shirley tried to force her way past D'Alessio. The cuffs came out. She kept yelling as he dragged her away. "You can't have it. You bitch. You got what you wanted. You got what you wanted. Now you don't get a penny. Not a fucking penny. Do you hear me? Not a goddamn penny."

Mrs. B stepped between me and my mother and embraced her. "Bea, are you all right? Never mind her, sweetheart."

Mom pressed her face into Mrs. B's parka. "My God," she said.

I stepped around Mrs. B and took my mother by an elbow. "Mom?" Behind me I heard the town hall doors being opened. The line began to move past us. I saw Philo beneath one of the trees, snapping photographs. "Come on. It's all right. Let's go over here."

She yanked her elbow away. The look on her face was defiant.

"Mom, what is going on?"

"I came for the meeting, Son. Come on, Phyllis."

She and Mrs. B locked arms and pushed past me. I watched the rest of the people pass, heard them mutter, "Some people should just avoid each other" and "Like a couple of damn cats."

I entered last. Just before I turned to go in, the Suburban pulled up to the curb across Elm and parked. The driver must not have seen the fire hydrant half buried in snow.

Laird Haskell turned his back on the seven members of the Starvation Lake town council and faced the rest of the room.

"This," he said.

Next to his head he held up a copy of that morning's *Free Press*. He pointed to Mich's story. He turned slowly to his left then to his right so that everyone in the room could see.

He read the headline aloud to the people filling all the seats to his left, standing along the wall beneath photographs of former council members, most of them dead. "'Feds Investigating Car Makers' Nemesis,'" Haskell said. He swiveled toward his right, where I was standing, but he avoided my eyes just as I was avoiding those of Jim Kerasopoulos, sitting at the opposite end of the front row, eight seats down from Haskell. On the wall beyond Kerasopoulos stood Jason Esper, his neck wrapped in gauze. Philo sat in the back row on my side of the room, scribbling in his notebook.

"'Feds Investigating,'" Haskell repeated. He let the paper fall to his side. He was wearing his denim shirt and a tan corduroy jacket with cocoa-brown patches on the elbows. Denim and corduroy went over fine in Starvation Lake, but usually not with starch and elbow patches. At the moment, it didn't matter. Laird Haskell was going to bring a new hockey rink to Starvation Lake, a new attitude, new championship banners to hang in the rafters. We just had to help him a little more than he'd told us before.

The council had dispensed quickly with the early items on its agenda, referring one concerning potholes back to the roads commission and approving the Girl Scouts' request to set up cookie tables at hockey games. All that remained was the executive session that folks had been hearing would get the new rink back on track to open for the start of the next season.

Before the council went behind closed doors, though, Haskell wanted to say a few words.

"Forget the rest of the headline," he said. "All I could see this morning, as I was sitting down to breakfast with my wife, Felicia, and our beautiful son, Taylor, was 'Feds Investigating.'" He bowed his head. I took note of Taylor Haskell, in his blue-and-gold River Rats jacket, and Felicia, her hands enfolding her son's, sitting in the front row next to Haskell's attorney, Parmelee Gilbert. Haskell looked at his wife and son.

"I'm so sorry that I've brought this on our family," he said. Felicia nodded. Taylor just sat there, probably not knowing what to do. I felt uncomfortable watching him. Haskell turned back to the room.

"And I'm sorry—deeply sorry—that I have brought this opprobrium on you, the good people of Starvation Lake. You've been so good to me and my family." He set the *Free Press* down on his chair and brought his hands together gently in front of his chest. I'd seen the moves before, in front of a jury. "But you won't see Laird Haskell issuing any blanket denials. Those might go over well down in the big city. But not here. You deserve better. You deserve an explanation. No more hiding. I want to come clean with all of you."

Two or three people clapped. Then a few more, until the council chair, Elvis Bontrager, lightly rapped his gavel.

Then Haskell explained. It took a while. In fact he had gotten over his head financially on "certain unrelated projects" downstate. He'd had to follow through on some charity commitments he'd made when things were better. He hadn't expected some of the rink construction permits to take so long to obtain, not that he was blaming anybody here.

He'd shifted money around among his businesses to make sure the new rink was taken care of before anything else. In doing so, he may have neglected to cross some T's and dot some I's, tax-wise. The IRS had noticed. Now he was "cooperating fully" with the IRS to ensure that he paid his fair share of taxes. It was an "unrelated matter" that would have "zero effect" on his ability to complete the rink "so long as I have the support of your elected officials today."

It was as simple as that. No mention of his forays into day-trading or his other businesses downstate. Not that I expected any.

"I had hoped, and I was truly confident, that I could handle this quietly, without burdening my family or anyone else," he said. "This morning, of course, part of it found its way into the public eye. But I want you to know—and I wouldn't blame you if you didn't believe this—but even before that article appeared, I was thinking about what I needed to do. Because there's something else, too, that has weighed on my mind, something more flesh and blood, more life and death, than taxes and permits and construction projects."

A low murmur slid through the room. Haskell pursed his lips and shook his head, as if to reprimand himself. "A young woman," he said. "A young woman with a long life to live, and who-knows-what good things to bring to this world, chose to end her life last week." I heard my mother gasp. Then a few others.

"It is terrible," Haskell said. "A terrible thing indeed that happened to Miss McBride. I have to tell you, good townspeople, that I hold myself at least partly responsible."

The room grew so quiet then that I could hear the wind rustling the willows outside. I looked Philo's way. He was writing as fast as he could. Over his shoulder now I noticed my enormous friend with the bad complexion standing along the back wall, a hard-shell briefcase under an arm. He was smiling. I looked at Haskell. His cheeks had flushed red. He'd seen Crater Face too.

"People hear a lot of things in a town like Starvation Lake," Haskell continued. "I know some of you have heard that I sent Miss McBride a rejection letter regarding her application for employment at the new rink. Small detail: I personally did not send a letter, nor would I have. But I nevertheless accept full responsibility."

No you don't, I thought.

"And I ask, in all humility, for your forgiveness and the forgiveness of Miss McBride's family and friends." I looked at my mother. She closed her eyes. "It was, in fact, a tragic mistake," Haskell said. "Her application was mishandled. She shouldn't have gotten any letter, acceptance or rejection, until thirty days before the rink was to open. But with the uncertainties over financing, and some degree of uncertainty as to the local commitment to the rink"—now he glanced my way—"somebody took it upon himself or herself to send her a rejection. And for that, I am profoundly, profoundly sorry."

He paused again. "Some of you will, of course, be rightfully skeptical of my version of things, and of my motivations. I don't blame you. But you should keep this in mind." He moved to where Taylor Haskell sat. "My son—my only child—was in the rink the other night when that explosion went off. I cannot tell you how terribly that frightened my wife and me." He stopped, swallowed hard. "We're confident the police are doing everything they can to determine what happened." He chanced a look at Crater Face. "But all I can think is that somebody out there is trying to scare us. Somebody out there doesn't want Starvation Lake to move forward with its plans and dreams. I will tell you now, that they might have momentarily, and understandably, given us pause. But they will not stop us. They will not stop us."

Applause broke out again. Haskell sat and took his wife's hand. Crater Face, who did not applaud, set the briefcase on the floor behind his legs. He folded his arms. He wasn't smiling anymore.

Chairman Bontrager banged his gavel once. "Well put, sir," he said. "I know exactly how you feel. My nephew was on the ice that night when that whatever it was happened. And I'll be damned if it's going to scare me from doing what's right for this great town."

"Hear, hear," someone called from the back.

"Mr. Haskell," Elvis continued, "I'd like to thank you on behalf of the entire council and my fellow townspeople for that heartfelt apology and explanation, sir."

Haskell nodded.

"And now, in the interest of time and of moving forward from things we can't do a darn thing about, I would entertain a motion to take this meeting into executive session. Of course, the council will vote in full view of the taxpayers of Starvation Lake, but some matters, as we all know, are best discussed in private."

Now the council had the cover to give Haskell his $100,000. What was he going to do with it, though? Did he have to choose between the feds and Vend? Who scared him more? Some pear-shaped guy in a suit in downtown Detroit? Or the hulk at the back of the room who would be pleased to mangle his limbs?

"Do I have a motion?"

"So moved," said Councilman Ted Huesing.

I spied a flash of brown and mustard through the windows in the twin doors to the meeting room. Then Dingus's handlebar appeared briefly in one, Darlene's face in the other. Others cops were milling around out there too, wearing the blue of the Michigan State Police.

"Do I have a second?" Elvis said.

"Second," Floyd Kepsel said.

"Excuse me, Mr. Chairman."

It was councilman Clayton Perlmutter, who had tipped me off to the loan the council was preparing to give Haskell. He glared at Elvis. "Mr.

Chairman, are you suggesting that this council might be doing something under wraps because if we did it in full public view, the public might not like what it sees?"

Elvis stared straight ahead. "We have a second. All in favor?"

"Point of order, Mr. Chairman," Perlmutter said. "Wasn't the request we're supposed to discuss amended just a few hours ago? Are we not therefore required to postpone the executive session until our next meeting?"

So Haskell had asked for even more than $100,000, as Vend had suggested. Or demanded.

"Oh, get over it, Clayton," Kepsel said. "This isn't the CIA. We're just trying to build a skating rink for our kids, for Pete's sake."

"Sometimes it feels like the CIA, Floyd."

"The only spy in this room is you, Clayton, and you know it. And you're not going to get with the program until you get your little cut of the action, and you know that, too."

"Enough," Elvis said. "Mr. Haskell has been nothing but forthright and honest in his dealings with this council." He turned and stared at Perlmutter. "Which is more than I can say for you, sir."

"A man can have both a public and private life, Mr. Chairman."

Elvis ignored him. "We have a motion and a second to move to executive session to consider a matter regarding the new hockey arena. All in favor?"

"Aye," came six voices.

"Opposed?"

"Abstain," Perlmutter said.

"The council will now adjourn briefly. Folks, you may wait or—I'm sorry. Sheriff? Is there a problem?"

Dingus now stood at the back of the room near Crater Face. Darlene moved into the room behind him. She had her handcuffs out.

"Afraid so," Dingus said. "Mr. Haskell?"

Haskell stood and faced Dingus. "Yes?"

"Laird Kenneth Haskell, you have the right to remain silent."

"What?" Felicia shrieked, jumping up from her chair.

"No," Haskell said. "Sheriff, there's been a misunderstanding. This is strictly a federal matter. Please, my attorney."

Parmelee Gilbert stepped between Dingus and Haskell. "Sheriff, is this really necessary? My client isn't going anywhere."

Elvis was slamming his gavel again. "Sheriff! Sheriff, please forbear!" Most of the audience was now standing to see better. D'Alessio and Deputy Skip Catledge strode into the room and flanked Dingus. Four state police officers took up positions at the entrance. Across the room, Jason was sidestepping his way to the emergency exit behind the council bench. I looked the other way for Crater Face, saw his wide back exiting the room.

His briefcase remained.

"Step away, counsel," Dingus said to Gilbert, "or you'll be joining your client." Gilbert moved aside. Dingus addressed Haskell. "This has nothing to do with your financial matters, sir, but with something more flesh and blood."

Haskell's face went as white as the frozen lake. For a second I thought he might collapse. Felicia Haskell jumped up and put her arms around him from behind, screaming, "No, no, no!"

Their son stood, alone and looking around.

"Dad," he said.

Darlene moved behind Haskell with the cuffs. A TV camera lit the circle of cops and citizens pressing around Haskell. Tawny Jane Reese pushed a microphone in Haskell's face as Catledge peeled Felicia away from him.

"Mr. Haskell," Tawny Jane said. "How are you feeling?"

Darlene cuffed him. Harder than she needed to, I thought.

"You have the wrong man," Haskell said. "He's getting away."

Dingus used his big body to ease Tawny Jane aside, and she angled the mike over the back of his shoulder.

"Anything you say," he told Haskell, "can and will be used against you—"

"No, Sheriff, listen to me, you have the wrong man. My God, he was standing right there." He tried to point with his shoulder. Darlene started to push him through the crowd.

I slipped down the side wall and around to the back as Darlene shoved Haskell through the door. I tried to catch her eye, to no avail. I squeezed out and trotted down the corridor to the main entrance. Across the street, the man with the cratered face was frantically circling the Suburban, illegally parked and blocked in by the Channel Eight van.

I ran back to the meeting room. The cops were bringing Haskell out. Darlene pushed him past me, trailed by Catledge and Dingus. I grabbed Dingus by the elbow. "Sheriff, look," I said. He yanked himself away.

"What are you doing?"

"You want another Zamboni bomb?"

He stopped and followed me back into the room. I pointed at the brief-case still sitting on the floor against the wall.

"The guy who left that behind just bolted out of here in a big hurry."

Dingus stared at the briefcase for a hard second. "Oh, Jesus," he said. He yelled into the corridor, "Frank!" and D'Alessio hurried over. "Stay here," Dingus told him. "I've got to call the damn bomb squad again."

twenty-three

We had waited for almost an hour in the shift room at the Pine County Sheriff's Department when Dingus swept in followed by Darlene, D'Alessio, and Skip Catledge. The deputies lined up in front of pop and candy vending machines on the back wall, their hands folded behind their backs. Dingus stepped to a lectern set up between two long white folding tables. A TV camera light shined on his face.

"We are on the record," he said. "But, Ms. Reese?" He motioned to Tawny Jane, who stood with her cameraman behind the two rows of folding chairs where the rest of us sat. "No cameras, please."

"But Sheriff, we need some live—"

"I'm sure you have plenty of pictures from your little episode on the street this afternoon. Be thankful we didn't give you a ticket."

The Channel Eight van had blocked in the illegally parked Suburban. License plates were checked. The briefcase was whisked away. Now Crater Face waited in a cell somewhere in the building where we sat.

The camera light went dark.

"Thank you," Dingus said. He faced eight reporters, including Philo, Tawny Jane, me, the Associated Press guy from Grand Rapids, and others from as far away as Petoskey. Reporters from the Detroit papers were probably on their way. Maybe even Michele Higgins.

I sat at one end of the back row of chairs. In one jacket pocket I carried the *Build it and they will die* note; in another was Gracie's blackmail note to "L."

"First," Dingus said, "a little housekeeping. We will try to be as helpful as we can with information about the pending case. But we will not try this case in the media. We understand that you all have your jobs to do. We hope you'll understand that we have our jobs to do."

"Sheriff Aho?"

It was Jim Kerasopoulos, sitting ten chairs away from me in the back row, near Tawny Jane. I'd ignored the dirty look he had given me when I came in with a notebook in hand.

"Sir, I will take questions when I've—"

"I apologize, Sheriff." Kerasopoulos stood. "But there's something you probably should know before you continue. One of the journalists here—I believe you know him, Mr. Carpenter—has been suspended by our publication, the *Pine County Pilot*. I don't believe he legitimately belongs."

The deputies and all the reporters turned their heads toward me, except Darlene, who stared straight ahead, and Dingus, who said to Kerasopoulos, "Excuse me, sir, but who are you?"

Kerasopoulos looked surprised. He cleared his throat. "Forgive me. I am James Kerasopoulos, president and chief executive officer of Media North Corporation, parent company of the *Pilot*."

"What exactly is your interest in this matter?"

Keraspoulos clapped an earnest hand to his chest. "I believe we share an interest, Sheriff, in making sure we make a clear and factual record of what you're doing while not in any way hindering you in your endeavors."

"And what does Mr. Carpenter have to do with that?"

"Quite frankly, Sheriff, I think he should be removed."

Everyone looked at me again. I shrugged. I was a lot more useful to the sheriff than fat ass. Dingus turned to Kerasopoulos. "I'll take that under advisement," he said. "Meanwhile, do you have anything identifying you as a journalist?"

"Identification? My driver's—"

"A press pass perhaps?"

"No, sir, I do not have a press pass."

Kerasopoulos was growing annoyed. I was enjoying it.

"Then I'll have to ask you to leave, sir."

"I beg your pardon? Sheriff, please. This is really not—"

"This briefing is for journalists, sir, not the general public. I believe your paper is adequately represented. Deputy?"

Darlene ushered Kerasopoulos out. Again I hoped she'd look my way. She did not.

"Let's proceed then," Dingus said. He put his right hand on the butt of his holstered gun, the other at the top of the lectern. "As some of you may know by now, we arrested Laird Kenneth Haskell and charged him with murder in the first degree related to the Monday, February eighth death of Grace Maureen McBride."

Haskell was being held in the Pine County Jail. He would be arraigned the next morning in front of Judge Horace Gallagher.

Other "persons of interest," Dingus said, were being held for questioning: Jason Thomas Esper, of Starvation Lake, and Kazmierz Lubomir Geremek of River Rouge. Police also were seeking for questioning a man identified as Jarogniew "Jarek" Vend, of Windsor, Ontario.

"That's all I have for now," Dingus said. "I will take a question or two."

A few hands went up. Not mine. I figured Dingus would talk to me afterward.

"Yes?" Dingus pointed at Philo.

"Sheriff, can you give us an idea what evidence you have against Mr. Haskell?"

Dingus smoothed his mustache over with a hand. "I'm sorry, sir, we don't normally discuss evidence until we're in court."

"But Sheriff," Philo said, "Mr. Haskell, as you know, is a very well respected man in these parts and known well beyond Michigan, let alone Starvation Lake. His case is likely to get an enormous amount of attention."

Nice, Philo, I thought. I watched him squint skeptically at Dingus through his horn-rims, tried to imagine him at a White House press conference. Not quite there, I thought.

"Agreed," Dingus said. "What's your point?"

"Well, it seems like all you have is a body that was hanging in a tree. Is that it? I mean, when you arrested him, Mr. Haskell seemed to think it was about his problems with the IRS, not with some obscure killing up here."

Normally Dingus would have repeated what he'd said about trying the case in the media. But Philo's question, more of a well-aimed poke than a question, apparently got to him. He turned to Catledge and whispered something. Catledge left the room. Dingus held up a finger. "One moment."

It was Dingus's moment. He had spent the last three days working his way around town councilmen and county commissioners and a coroner who had tried to discourage him from chasing the truth. Now he would show them all.

Catledge returned holding two clear plastic bags that he handed to Dingus. Dingus held them behind the lectern so we couldn't see them just yet.

"During a routine response call to a chimney fire shortly before midnight last night, the Pine County Fire Department discovered evidence that appeared to be pertinent to an ongoing crime investigation.

"Pursuant to that, the Pine County Sheriff's Department secured a warrant which was executed on the premises at 72215 North Shore Road, a home belonging to the suspect, Mr. Haskell. We removed a number of items from the premises and have marked them as evidence."

No wonder Felicia hadn't gotten much sleep.

Dingus held one bag up in front of him. A white tag on one corner of the bag was marked "2." Inside we could clearly see a work boot, right footed, ankle high, brown, with a hard black sole. "This is the boot that the decedent, Ms. McBride, was wearing on the night of her death. When she was found, she was not wearing anything on her left foot."

He moved the bag back and forth and turned it around so everyone could see. He set it down on the table to his left, then lifted the other bag up. The white tag on this one was marked "3." It, too, contained a shoe. The shoe looked similar, but the surface visible to us was blackened, as if it had been in a fire.

"We believe this shoe belonged to Ms. McBride as well," Dingus said. He laid the bag on the lectern. "During our legal search of the Haskell residence last night, we found it lodged in a fireplace." He looked at Philo. "That's all I can share for now, son, but I hope that answers your question."

Philo didn't say anything. Dingus looked around the room, ignored the other outstretched hands. "Or anyone else's question, for that matter. That's all I'll be saying for now."

"Were there witnesses?" the AP reporter asked.

"No comment. That's all for now."

"Sheriff, could you just tell us—"

"I'm sorry, Ms. Reese, we've got to get back to work, thank you for coming, I'm sure we'll be talking again soon. Good afternoon, everyone." Dingus turned and addressed me: "Stay right where you are."

I stayed put. Philo stopped on his way out. He kept his voice down. "Meet me at my place after you get out of here."

"Why?"

He winked. "We have a deadline to meet."

* * *

"So," Dingus said, "I cannot wait to hear how you ticked off your boss."

The room was empty, the fluorescent lights humming. Dingus sat facing me on one of the tables.

"Same way you tick off yours, Dingus."

"Yes, indeed. It's Starvation Lake, eh? Everybody's talking, and everybody's holding out on you."

"Something like that."

"So what are you holding out on me?"

"Nothing you don't already know," I said. "You're going after Vend, so Deputy Esper obviously talked to you."

"You may reach your own conclusions."

"Got anything else besides the shoe? A witness? A helper? I mean, how the hell did Gracie hang herself in a snowstorm without a ladder or a—"

Dingus held up a hand to stop me. "Off the record?"

"Ha. You heard the guy. I don't have a paper anyway. Sure, off the record."

"Got a ladder."

"From Haskell's house?"

"Could be."

"You got lucky with that chimney fire."

"True," he said. "And it really wasn't much of a fire."

"You got forensics backing any of this up?"

"We will. Takes time. This is a small town."

"No shit. What about the briefcase? No bomb?"

"No bomb. But some pretty explosive photographs in there, if you know what I mean."

I knew. "Vend could've been involved too, don't you think?"

"Possible," Dingus said. "Seems more likely he set Haskell up. If he wanted Gracie dead, looks like he may have sent a boy to do a man's job."

"You heard about the woman in Sarnia, right?"

"What woman?"

I had called the Sarnia cop shop on my way to the press conference and the chief still hadn't returned. But I had assumed that Darlene had told Dingus by now and they were checking it out.

Now I told him.

"Will certainly look into that," he said.

"So," I said, "you think you have a motive?"

Dingus shifted on the table, looked away, scratched a forearm. He made a little show of looking at his watch. "She obviously knew some things," he said. "But that could look a little squishy to some juries. How about you?"

I thought of the burned-up videotapes down in Melvindale.

"Working on it."

"It's getting late, Gus. The state police would be glad to give you a ride downstate. The Melvindale police have some questions about a fire."

I could have handed over Gracie's blackmail note. But it was the best thing I had that was mine alone. I had no paper, but I hadn't lost the jealous need to hang on to the scoop.

"What about the Zamboni explosion?" I said. "How's that fit in?"

"Not sure it does. Maybe a prank, in the end. We don't have to prove Mr. Haskell had anything to do with it anyway."

I reached into a pocket, pulled out a piece of paper, and handed it to Dingus. "This came in the mail the day the bomb went off."

Dingus looked at it. "'Build it and they will die,'" he read. "Clever. I doubt Mr. Haskell would have sent it."

"Me, too. But maybe Vend? It came from downstate."

"That seems a little too obvious." He smiled and slipped it into a pocket beneath his badge. "I'll hang on to it."

"Consider it my get-out-of-jail-free card."

"For now."

Philo's A-frame cottage nestled in a copse of evergreens on the north bank of the Hungry River. I knew the house. In the summer there would be a dock and a pontoon boat and a deck lined with Adirondack chairs painted a green that matched the water. Now everything was draped in white.

"Nice place," I said.

I was kicking snow off my boots on the throw rug inside his front door. I smelled Windex on the air.

"Yeah," Philo said. "I rent it from Uncle Jimbo and Aunt Linda. Overpriced, though."

"Uncle Jimbo?"

"Yeah. I might need another place to stay tomorrow night."

"What do you mean?"

"This way."

He led me down a hallway into a small bedroom he had made into an office. Two framed diplomas, one from the University of Pennsylvania, the other from Columbia University, hung over a desk pushed up against a wall. On the desk sat a computer, a stapler, a Scotch tape dispenser, and a Washington Redskins coffee cup holding pens, pencils, and a pair of scissors. A swivel chair sat before the computer, and Philo had brought a straight-backed chair from the kitchen. I watched the photograph on the computer screen change from the Washington Monument to the Capitol dome.

"Take your coat off," Philo said. "Did you bring your notes?"

I slapped my back pocket. "Yeah. Why?"

"Observe."

He leaned over and clicked his mouse. The screen went blank. Slowly, the frame of a web page unfolded. Most of it was empty. But the top of the page bore a title resembling a newspaper's:

News of the North

"You've got to be kidding me," I said. "Jimbo let us—I mean you—have a website?"

"Not exactly."

I turned and leaned in toward the Penn diploma on the wall.

"Computer science, Philo?"

"I know a little."

"You built us a website? And it's not the *Pilot*? Or Media North?"

"What did I tell you?" he said. "The Internet to the rescue. It's a little crude, but at least we don't have to sit on our hands till Saturday. I'm tired of watching that Channel Eight chick get all the stories."

"Wow. So—what? We just write? And then what?"

He laid out the plan: We'd write a main story that included the particulars of the day—Haskell's arrest, the arraignment, the arrests of Jason and the others, the town council drama—as well as the exclusive stuff we had from my trip downstate. We'd write a sidebar about Kerasopoulos's entanglements with Haskell, based on the state documents we had.

Philo would post the stories online the next morning, then send an e-mail announcing the new website to all the people who had signed up for

Media North's Internet service. By nine o'clock, everyone in Pine County would know what we knew.

"Oh, man," I said. I was getting excited. I was a reporter again. I pulled out the blackmail note and gave it to Philo. "Look at this shit."

He scanned it quickly. "Awesome."

"Yeah. Yeah, man. We're going to stick this right up Tawny Jane's sweet ass." At that moment, I almost high-fived Philo Beech. Instead I said, "Hey. Are you sure you want to nail your uncle, Philo? We don't have to."

"Don't you think he deserves to be nailed?"

"That's a complicated question for me. But for you, well . . . there might not be a lot more budget meetings in your future."

Philo considered this for only a second. "I actually do have a trust fund," he said. Of course he did. He turned the swivel chair toward me. "You drive."

After the stories were written, Philo left the room and came back with two bottles of Amstel Light and a bag of Better Made potato chips.

"Amstel?" I said. "You're going to have to change your brand if you want to work for a real newspaper."

"If you say so." He sat in the straight-backed chair next to me. "I've never done a real story before. This is a real story."

"Yeah, man. Good work."

We clinked bottles. We leaned back and drank. I couldn't help but think of my best nights at the *Times*, when I had a great story all wrapped up and headed to the printing plant, a story that was going to cause all kinds of headaches the next morning for the *Free Press* reporter who had missed it. That first beer never tasted so good. Even an Amstel.

Philo said, "Can I ask you something?"

"Shoot."

"Did you ever ride on one of those Zambonis?"

"Nope. The guy who drove the Zam most of my years here wouldn't let us near it. Or her. He called it Ethel."

"My father took me to a Baltimore Skipjacks game when I was little. I won some contest and got to ride on the Zamboni between periods."

"Did you like it?"

"At first, sure, it was cool. It's really a totally different perspective from down on the ice, seeing all those people in the seats. The lights are really bright down there too, and you can see how the ice isn't nearly as smooth as it looks from the stands."

"Things never are what they seem, are they?"

"Well, no, and especially so in this case." Philo took a sip of his beer. "We were making our last little trip around the rink and I was looking up in the seats, waving to my father. We were supposed to turn but the Zamboni just kept going straight for the, what do you call them?"

"The boards?"

"The boards. I looked at the driver and he was slumped over, unconscious. I started screaming and yelling and all these men ran out on the ice but they were too late. We just slammed right through the boards and into the bleachers."

"Were you OK? What happened to the driver?"

"It turned out he'd had a stroke. I had a couple of bumps and bruises, but mostly I was scared. I haven't been to a hockey game since."

I shook my head. "Crazy. I guess Zam driving is a young man's game."

"Yeah." He set his bottle on the desk. "Talk about crazy. How about that Haskell woman? Did you see her outside?"

"Nah. I was dealing with Dingus and that briefcase."

"She was hysterical. She kept trying to get in the police car with her husband. It took two cops to restrain her. Her poor son just stood there like he was in shock."

"He probably was."

"Which reminds me," Philo said. "Was she the woman that fat guy at the pizzeria pointed out in the paper?"

"Supposedly."

"What was that about?"

"Supposedly she was in the place with Gracie last week. I don't know. Belly's full of shit half the time." I stood up, finished my beer, set the bottle down on Philo's desk. What Belly had said didn't make sense, at least not within the story line Philo and I had decided upon. I didn't want to think about it. "We'll have plenty more to write tomorrow. Maybe the cops will have grabbed Vend by then."

"You think maybe Dingus really does have the wrong guy?"

"I don't know." I pulled on my coat. "There was a city editor at my old paper who liked to say, 'They wouldn't have arrested him if he wasn't guilty.'"

Philo had a good laugh at that.

* * *

Starvation Lake was quiet as I drove to Mom's, almost as if nothing of note had happened that day, as if no one had been arrested and accused of murder. I planned to go home and make myself a big fat fried bologna sandwich with lots of ketchup and onions, drink a Blue Ribbon or two, and get a good night's sleep, get ready for my Internet debut.

I had to stop at the red light at the Estelle Street Bridge. I peered up the hill to the pizzeria. As usual, the place looked empty. I saw Belly's head, wearing a white paper hat, moving around beyond the lighted windows. The stoplight turned green, but I sat there a bit longer, staring.

Belly had to be yanking my chain, I told myself. Or he was just plain mistaken. I hit the gas.

twenty-four

The diced onions had just begun to sizzle. I was peeling the ring bologna when Mom emerged from her bedroom in pajamas and robe. One lamp was lit in the living room, the lake invisible in the dark beyond the windows. Mom sat down in her easy chair, wrapped herself in my River Rats afghan.

"I hope I didn't wake you," I said.

"I was reading. I thought I might watch the news."

The news wouldn't be on for another hour.

"Can I make you a sandwich?"

Mom turned her head, gave me a look. "Do I look like your father?" My dad had loved fried bologna sandwiches, taught me how to make them. Mom never cared for them. "Phyllis made us a nice salad."

"Good."

She turned back to the living room. The TV remote sat untouched on the table next to her. I took out a cutting board and began to slice the bologna lengthwise into the pan. The long curls of meat crackled in the bubbling butter.

"It was quite a day in Starvation Lake," Mom said.

I had decided I wasn't going to tell Mom about my job situation until the website appeared the next day. I had some questions, but Mom wasn't going anywhere, and I was hungry. I uncapped the ketchup and squirted it around the pan. The sugary tang filled my nostrils.

"I'll say," I said. "What was going on with you and Shirley? I thought she was going to punch you."

Mom made a show of folding her arms. "Are you just going to talk to the back of my head?"

I looked at the bologna and onions snapping in the pan, looked back at Mom. I turned the heat off and went over to sit on a footstool facing her.

"OK," I said.

She shook her head, threw the afghan back off her shoulders. "What did you ask me?" she said.

"About Shirley. The hockey fight you guys had at town hall."

"Hockey fight?"

"Shirley McBride, Mom."

She wasn't remembering. But she was trying. She closed her eyes and pressed her fingertips together in her lap.

"Shirley and I—oh, God. That was like a hundred years ago. The only person who gives a damn about it is Shirley."

"Gives a damn about what?"

She opened her eyes. "Eddie."

"Gracie's dad?"

"Yes. Eddie. Your father's cousin. The one who died in the war."

"OK."

"He used to come up here on weekends when he was in high school. I didn't really know your father yet. I actually met Eddie first. Down at the public access. He pretended to help my father put our boat in." She smiled. "He was standing on the stern and Daddy gunned the boat and Eddie went flying."

"Ah," I said. "You and Eddie had a little summer fling?"

"Well . . ."

"I'm not sure how much of this I want to know."

"Not a fling," Mom said. "I wasn't that kind of girl."

"Good."

She sat there thinking. She looked at me. "Shirley," she said. "That was her on the sidewalk today."

"That was her, yes."

"She was wearing braids. All sorts of braids." We were back in the distant past again. "After Eddie, she wouldn't braid my hair anymore."

"No?"

"No. She never forgave me for Eddie. Even after, especially after Eddie died, and she started in with the boyfriends."

I thought of the trailer where I would knock on the only door and sing out, "Graaaayseee!" Most days Gracie would come right out and close the door quickly behind her. Once in a while she'd ask me in because she hadn't finished her Frosted Flakes and tea. I thought her kitchen smelled like a doctor's office. Shirley might come to the table and sit silently smoking in her slip. Once there was a hickey the shape of a snail on the skin over her collarbone.

"All those men, every single one of them a piece of shit."

"Right."

"I'm sorry, son. Forgive my language. Shirley was drawn to that like a deer fly, but those men . . ." She brushed at her eyes. "What was I supposed to do? Turn Gracie away? Send her back to that revolting little trailer in the woods?"

"You did the right thing, Mom. Gracie loved you."

"She loved you, too, Gussy."

"I don't think so."

"Why won't you believe me?"

"Mom," I said. "When you saw Gracie at Audrey's the other day, she gave you an envelope."

"I didn't see Gracie at Audrey's the other day."

"Yes, you did, you told me you did."

"No."

"Yes."

Now she was telling the lie she'd forgotten to tell two nights before.

"All right. So what?"

"She brought you an envelope."

"I don't remember."

"Yes, you do. It was a life insurance policy."

"No—"

I stood. "Should I get it out of your bedroom?"

She gave me a look of reproach that she couldn't sustain. "Sit down," she said. I sat. "I brought the envelope to Audrey's. Gracie had sent it to me, she said for safekeeping. Of course I had to take a peek. And when I saw that . . ." She shook her head no. "I'm glad I peeked. I don't want that money."

The money Shirley had been talking about at town hall.

"So you tried to give it back?"

"I told her I didn't want that money, I didn't want her to die."

I leaned in closer. Gracie would have given Mom the policy around the time she gave Soupy her letter to Haskell, "in case something happened."

Around the time Gracie supposedly was with Felicia Haskell at the pizzeria. I looked over at the bouquets people had sent. Felicia's weren't there anymore.

"Mother," I said, "she was just giving you her life insurance policy. Did you have some reason to think she was going to die? Did she tell you she was in some kind of danger?"

"No."

"Or you don't remember?"

"I remember. She was fine."

"Did she say anything about—wait." I was thinking about the rejection letter, which made me think of the Zamboni shed, which made me remember what I had found there. "Hang on."

I stood and dug in my jacket hung on the back of a kitchen chair, then sat back down with my mother. "Look what I found."

I handed her the blue hairbrush.

"Oh." She took it in her left hand. "Where did you get this?"

"In the Zamboni shed. Gracie had it in a secret place."

Mom turned it over in her hands. As she did, her lips began to tremble. Her eyes welled.

"Mother?"

She clutched the brush in both hands and brought it to her chest. She bowed her head. She began to sob.

I reached across the chair and took her by an arm. "Mom. What's wrong?"

"She didn't have to—" Mom had to stop for a moment. "I told her you could have helped."

"What are you talking about?"

She thrust the brush at me. "Why couldn't you two get along? Why couldn't you both just—" She was struggling to talk. "I told her. I told her . . . I told her you could help her."

"Help her what?"

"She wouldn't listen. 'He'll never help me. He hates my guts.' That's what she said. But you, you . . ." She pulled the brush back into her, crying harder. "Shirley can have the money. I never wanted any money." She was sobbing so hard now that she could barely catch her breath. "I could have . . . I could have . . ."

"What? You could have what?"

She held up a hand to stop me. She set the brush in her lap and reached one hand out. I took it.

"Mom, what is it?"

"Those people. All those people from down there. I wish they'd just stay. Just leave us alone. We don't need their big houses and fancy boats."

"Mom?"

She tightened her grip on my hand.

"You know, I would give my life for you. You know that, don't you?"

"Yes. I know that."

My mother hitched forward in her chair, gathered up my other hand. "Any mother," she said, "a good mother, would lay down her life for her son."

I waited.

"Gracie didn't have an abortion," Mom said. She saw the quizzical look in my eyes. "There was no abortion."

"So there was no baby?"

"Yes. There was."

I looked down at our entwined hands. "I know who."

"No, you don't."

"You don't know, Mom. There's a really bad guy downst—"

"No, Gus. Think."

In my mind I walked into Gracie's good bedroom again, the one with the light coming in, the poster on the wall, the child's drawing of the hockey player. Then I heard the piano music again. I looked up at my mother.

"Are you—" I let her hands go. "No. My God."

"I wish she would have asked you for help." She picked up the brush again. "It's my fault that you two never got along."

"You knew? You knew all along? All this time? Fourteen years?"

"I'm sorry, son."

I ate the bologna sandwich cold, without tasting it, as I drove to the rink. I parked in front and grabbed my skates out of my hockey bag. Until then, I had forgotten about the pain in my foot. I limped into the arena.

A peewee team from Starvation Lake was playing one from Alpena. I didn't bother to check the scoreboard. Johnny Ford watched from his perch behind the concession counter. He held his gaze even after I plopped my skates on the counter. He was wearing the same River Rats sweatshirt he had worn the night he had caught me snooping in the Zam shed, with the same mustard stain on the "N," the yellow now turning brown.

"Hey, Johnny," I said. "Can you do these?"

He still didn't look my way. "Look at that," he said. He pointed the stump below his left elbow in the direction of the ice. I turned to see. "Three guys coming into the zone, all on the same side of the ice. What's the advantage in that? Might as well be two guys. Shit, one."

I had figured that Johnny Ford watched a lot of hockey, but until then I had no idea that he cared.

"Yep," I said. "All about two-on-ones, man."

"Really ain't that complicated." Now he looked at me; then, dolefully, at my skates. "It's kind of late, isn't it?"

"I don't need them tonight," I said.

"When's your next game?"

"Pickup skate, tomorrow night."

"I'll leave them under the counter. Four bucks."

I gave him a twenty. He turned his back and moved to the cash register. He punched something with his stump and the drawer flew open. I heard the bill-holders snap inside the drawer as he plucked out a ten, a five, and a single with his other hand.

"Hey, Johnny."

"Yeah."

"You ever find that phone?"

He shoved the drawer shut with his butt. He laid the change next to my skates. "Nah," he said. "She probably lost it."

I took the ten and the five.

"You get a new one yet?" I said.

He dug in his sweatshirt pouch, produced a cell phone. "This."

"They let you keep your number?"

"Yeah."

"That's cool."

"Yeah."

"Why the hell did you loan it to her anyway?"

"She let me drive."

"The Zam?"

"Yeah."

"How was it?"

"All right. A little harder with the—" He waggled his stump.

"I'll bet. But you're doing a fine job now, man. Ice was good last night."

"Thanks."

"I heard a funny story about a Zamboni driver tonight. He was—"

"No, no, no, man." Johnny waved his hand at me. "Bad luck."

"OK, OK." I laughed. "But look, I was just thinking, you know, the cops are all over Gracie's stuff since, you know. They might find the old phone. You can trade it in for, I don't know, maybe some cash."

He shrugged. "I don't want to mess with cops."

"I don't blame you." I looked at the skates. "Ready tomorrow?"

"Yeah."

I started to leave, then stopped and turned back to Johnny Ford. "Shit, you know, John, I'm talking to the cops about ten times a day. Give me your number and if it turns up, I'll give you a call."

"You don't have to."

"No trouble."

He had to get low to the counter, his hair hanging down over his face, so he could hold a napkin down with his stump while he scratched out the number.

The napkin was crumpled in my left hand as I knocked on the door of Darlene's apartment with my right.

She answered in an old white-and-green Michigan State football jersey that hung to her knees, number 23. She opened the door without a word, turned and walked into her little kitchen. I followed. She flicked on a light and took a glass out of the dish drainer and filled it with water from the tap.

I unzipped my jacket. "We have to talk," I said.

Darlene pulled her dark hair back with one hand and drank the glass down. She set the glass in the sink. She turned to me.

"Did you sleep with her?" she said.

"No."

"Did you want to?"

"No."

"Why didn't you tell me?"

I had no good answer for that. "Like you said, things got complicated. I was doing my job."

We didn't say anything for a minute. Darlene gazed vacantly at the wall behind me, thinking. "I was doing my job, too."

"When?"

"When you saw me at the rink. We had Jason under surveillance. Dingus had talked to someone in Detroit about him. I was the tail because he wouldn't suspect me."

"You?" I felt at once stupid and relieved. "Jeez. I'm sorry."

"Don't be." She lowered her eyes now. "We followed you, too."

"When? When I went downstate? No."

"Yes. D'Alessio."

"Frankie? He let those shitheads basically kidnap me?"

"You were doing your job, Gus. Isn't that what you wanted? You got to Vend, right? You figured it all out?"

"Isn't that what *you* wanted?"

"Why are you here? Haven't you had enough pain yet? This isn't hockey. You can't just swing your stick at somebody's head and make everything right."

I set the napkin on the counter, the number facedown.

"Whatever happened to Sarnia?" I said.

"You're such a boy."

"What about the chick on the swing set, Darlene? The Sarnia cops wouldn't talk because I'm a reporter. But they'd talk to you."

She wasn't going to tell me. Or she didn't know. Or she hadn't called. "You know I can't talk about an ongoing investigation," she said.

"Of course. Not now. So you can't tell me whether you ever tracked down that phone call, can you?"

"What phone call?"

"The one that set off the Zamboni bomb."

That stopped her, as I had expected. "Why?"

"What do you mean why? Did you track it down or not?" She started to shake her head. "Stop fucking with me, Darlene."

"Why are you fucking with me?" It was almost a shout. Tears were filling her eyes; I couldn't tell whether from anger or sadness. "What difference does it make? Gracie's gone. Nothing's going to bring her back."

Goddamn, I thought. She knows, too. She knows. Maybe not what my mother knew, but something nobody else did.

I flipped the napkin over and pushed it along the counter. "That's the number of the cell phone that ignited the bomb," I said. "Gracie got the phone from Johnny Ford, the one-handed kid at the rink."

Darlene wouldn't look at it.

"Am I getting a little closer to what really was getting complicated?"

She pulled the State jersey up to swab her cheeks. "Haskell's in jail," she said. "Jason's in jail. The state police are going to have Vend soon. Isn't that enough? Do you really want to bring in—" She stopped herself. She was going to say too much. "It's time for you to go."

"Bring in who? My mother? Your mom? Trixie?"

"Go."

She stepped forward and shoved the heel of one hand hard into my chest. I fell back a step. But I wasn't leaving yet.

"The phone that called this phone to make it ring and set off that little bomb   the area code was two four eight," I said. "Wasn't it? Only one person could have set that off and been sure it wouldn't hurt a certain someone. Only one person knew exactly where her boy was when she dialed that number."

Darlene grabbed the napkin and balled it up in her hand and drove both of her fists into my chest, driving me backward into the door.

"Get out."

"You knew."

"Get the fuck out."

I opened the door, felt cold wash over the back of my neck. "You knew," I said. "I mean, you didn't know what Gracie was going to do, but once she did it, you knew. And you kept it to yourself."

"Everything is," she said, "as it should be."

I stood at the bottom of Darlene's stairway for a while, shivering in the dark, wondering if she would reconsider. The outside light over her door went out. I walked away, feeling the ache in my bruised foot again.

"Sarnia Police," said the woman's voice. "Officer Poulin."

Her voice on the phone, husky and matter-of-fact, reminded me of Darlene's. I was at my desk in the *Pilot* newsroom. I told Officer Poulin I was a sheriff's deputy in Pine County, Michigan, and I needed to confirm the details of a recent suicide—or perhaps it had been reclassified as a homicide—in Sarnia. I described a young woman hanging from a swing set.

I was not terribly surprised to hear Officer Poulin chuckle. "A swing set, eh?" she said. "That's a good one. I have a feeling I'd remember that. Are you sure it happened recently?"

"That's what our source says. A few weeks ago."

"Who's your source?"

"You know, some goofball trying to trade info."

"Well, that explains things, eh? But you're calling awfully late—or early, depending."

"Picked him up on a DUI. He has a warrant out in Detroit."

"Right-o. He sure doesn't want to go back there."

"No, ma'am. So, you have no record of a suicide or a homicide occurring there in the last few weeks, or even months?"

"Wait just a minute. I'll double-check."

She set the phone down. Someone, probably Mrs. B, had cleared my desktop. All the pens and pencils in my Detroit Tigers beer mug were gone.

Officer Poulin came back on the phone.

"Deputy—I'm sorry, what did you say your name was?"

I hesitated, then said, "Esper."

"Esper? Hmm. We had a young man played for the minor league team here named Esper. Pretty good with his fists."

"Really?"

"Yeah. Some years back. Anyway, I checked and we have zero reports of suicides or homicides in the past six months, certainly none involving a swing set. Or monkey bars, for that matter."

"Sorry for the bother."

"No bother at all. You have a nice day."

I hung up the phone.

Trixie had lied about the girl on the swing set. And about the abortion. I should have picked up on it when she'd fibbed about knowing who Haskell was. She had been having trouble with her landlord, whom I now knew to be one Jarek Vend. Gracie's life insurance money would be good for her worthy mission. And, as Darlene had said, there was nothing anyone could do to bring Gracie back. The bad guys would get what they deserved.

I had a decision to make.

I could go home and get some sleep and let Philo post our stories online as we had planned. But now I knew that we had it all wrong, or a lot wrong. I didn't have to think hard or long about why Gracie did what she did. There was vengeance and there was love and there was the belief, however misguided it may have been, that she was out of options.

I picked up the phone and dialed. It rang fourteen or fifteen times before I hung up and redialed. After a dozen more rings, Soupy picked up. He coughed and I heard him drop the phone—"Fuck," he said—then he came on.

"What the hell, Trap?"

"How'd you know it was me?"

"Who else would it be? What do you want?"

"Listen," I said. "Some shit's going to come down tomorrow. I just want you to know, you were right. It wasn't your fault."

"Huh? What are you talking about?"

"Gracie. Like you said."

"Oh, Jesus, man." He fumbled around with the phone again. I heard something that sounded like a bottle banging off the floor. "What are you going to do?"

"I have to go. Just wanted you to know, buddy, you're a good guy. We'll talk tomorrow night."

I took my Tigers mug when I left the *Pilot*.

It was still dark when Philo answered his front door. I had managed two and a half hours of fitful dozing on Mom's sofa. Philo stood in the doorway in boxer shorts and a U.S. Navy T-shirt, rubbing sleep from his eyes.

"Why are you here?" he said.

"Remember what I said about imagining your corrections?"

"What?"

"We've got to rewrite our stories."

"You're kidding."

He made a pot of coffee and some peanut butter toast. We wrote and rewrote. We questioned every little thing we had written the night before. Around eight o'clock, Philo's cell phone started ringing every ten minutes or so. He ignored it. "No desire to talk to my uncle," he said.

The second the clock struck nine, I called Nova at the Wayne County Clerk's Office. "Let's make it two Lions games," I said. I asked her to run down one more piece of information. She said she would call me back.

Philo ducked out at ten to cover the Haskell arraignment. Haskell stood mute and Judge Gallagher entered a plea of not guilty. For some reason, Kerasopoulos was in attendance. He motioned across the courtroom for Philo to come see him, but Philo pretended he didn't see, then slipped out a side door.

We were ready a little before noon. The sidebar, on Kerasopoulos's business relationships with Haskell, was essentially the same. Philo had e-mailed his uncle a list of questions. *This is silliness,* Kerasopoulos had replied. *Won't dignify with answer.* Our sidebar quoted him.

The main story had been redone from top to bottom. The headlines read:

Murder Charge May Be Flawed
New Evidence Suggests Suicide

"Let's not post it until I hear from my source in Detroit," I told Philo. Instead of asking about my source, he went to his fridge for two more Amstels.

"Quite a morning," he said as he handed me a beer.

"Yeah."

"Are you all right?"

"Fine. Just thinking of something Dingus told me a couple of days ago. Something about the newspaper being a snapshot of the dark human soul."

"Hmm. They didn't teach us that at Columbia."

Nova called a little after twelve thirty. "This took some digging," she said. "Had to call in a chit with folks at probate. I think you owe Michael a Lions sweatshirt, too."

"Done," I said. "What do you have?"

On December 6, 1984, Grace M. McBride had given birth to a son. The birth certificate did not name a father. The boy weighed seven pounds, six ounces. A note in the file indicated the boy was adopted shortly thereafter. Gracie named him Taylor Edward McBride.

twenty-five

H ow did you find me?"
          She held the apartment door open only the width of her
          face. Through the crack I saw that her hair had gone from silver
to ash, with strands of white that fluttered away from her head like feath-
ers. In one hand she held something shaped like a bowl, wrapped in brown
paper.

"A hockey buddy," I said.

"They're all the same, aren't they?"

"Pretty much. Could I come in, please? I won't stay long."

"You're not writing a story."

I held my empty hands up. "Didn't even bring a pen."

Felicia Haskell opened the door.

It was late April. The ice on Starvation Lake had broken up. I had
driven down to Detroit to find Laird Haskell's wife.

She had borrowed the two-bedroom apartment from a girlfriend after
leaving Starvation Lake. The living room was strewn with cardboard
packing boxes. Some were open at the top, others taped shut and shoved
against a wall beneath a panoramic photograph of Detroit's skyline. Felicia
set the wrapped dish inside a box.

"Taking off again?" I said.

"Not soon enough."

She moved to a counter alongside the kitchen. It was stacked with un-
wrapped dishes and glassware.

"Taking Taylor with you?"

She kept wrapping and packing as if she hadn't heard me.

Doc Joe had held on to the coroner's report for weeks, even after Dingus
and the Pine County prosecutor had sheepishly agreed to drop the mur-

der charge against Laird Haskell. What Doc finally released told us little we didn't already suspect. The cause of death was indeed strangulation, in combination with fractures along the upper cervical spine—a severely broken neck.

I scoured the report for any signs of a struggle, even of Gracie struggling with herself. Had she changed her mind at the last minute? Had she decided, in the final seconds of her life, that she ought to live for her son, however unavailable he was, rather than die for him?

I tried to interview Doc Joe. He ignored my calls and e-mails. One unseasonably warm evening, I found him at his house. He was sitting outside in the dying daylight, reading a history of World War I, in which, I had heard, his grandfather had fought.

Doc Joe wore a wool sweater vest zipped halfway up. I stood looking down on his bald spot. Inserting a scrap of paper as a bookmark, he closed his book, put his reading glasses in his vest pocket, and listened. When I had finished, he gazed out at the lake.

"You know," he said, "I've always liked the color of your mom's place. But the missus, she's never going to let me paint our place yellow. No, sir." He turned back to me. "Why do you want to know, son? She killed herself. I understand that someone may have helped. But still."

"She was family."

"I am very sorry for your loss." He pinched his glasses to his nose, opened his book. "There's nothing I can do for you."

The next morning, I dialed Wally's Wonder Print in Melvindale. Wally was out, but five minutes later he called me from his cell phone. I invited his hockey team up for a weekend of games and drinking with the Chowder Heads. "Oh, fucking-ay, man, we are so there," he said, and he must have nearly driven off the road because I heard car horns honking angrily in the background.

Then I told him why I'd really called. I needed to find someone. Someone in hockey circles. "Yeah, the goalie," Wally said. "I heard the kid ain't even skating anymore. Some kind of head case." I didn't bother telling him that it wasn't so. He called me back that night with an address in Farmington Hills. "Just keep my name out of it, bud," he said.

So there I was with Felicia Haskell.

She had initially been charged with aiding and abetting a suicide for whatever role she had played in Gracie's death. But, without witnesses, the Pine County cops knew they'd have trouble making it stick. Along with the state police and the feds, they were also more interested in putting her husband behind bars than in punishing Felicia. She helped them. Probably still was helping. Though he was no longer charged with murder, Laird Haskell now faced multiple counts related to prostitution, solicitation, and fraud. And the IRS was still all over him and his enfeebled bank accounts.

"My lawyer would kill me if she knew you were here," Felicia said. She looked around the room. "Where's the goddamn tape? Oh fuck it." She set the plate she was holding in one hand back on the counter. "Sit."

She plopped on a stool. I took one facing her.

"What do you—wait." She covered her face with her hands. I waited. "Why am I doing this?" she said, not to me, but to herself. She brought her hands down. She wiped her cheeks with a sleeve.

"We are totally, completely, unequivocally off the record," she said.

"That's fine."

"I am doing this for you. And your family. Not for your newspaper. Not for the people in that godforsaken town."

"Understood."

"You're still with the paper?"

"I'm back with the paper, yes."

Our online story on Kerasopoulos's ties to Laird Haskell had not gone over well with Media North's board of directors. While they concluded that Kerasopoulos had done nothing illegal, they nevertheless asked for his resignation. He threatened to sue, but the board quieted him with a severance package rumored to be in the neighborhood of $3 million.

At Philo's urging, I had returned to the *Pilot* as if I had never left.

"All right," Felicia Haskell said. "It's not that I'm worried about getting arrested again or anything. It's just—my son. He knows enough."

I could have said, *He isn't your son*, but that probably would have ended the conversation.

"How's Taylor?"

"Fine. He's with my mother until I get things sorted out here."

"Then you're leaving."

"Then we're leaving."

"Where?"

She spun halfway around on her stool, surveying the boxes. "Ask me something else," she said.

"I hear he's not playing anymore."

"Not that either."

"OK," I said. "I just wish . . . it might have been nice to talk to him once before you leave."

"I'm sorry," Felicia said. "I thought about your request. But in the end, I just . . . couldn't."

"He's family."

"No, actually he's not." Felicia let that sink in. "He knows who his birth mother is, or was. Now she's gone, and it's best for a fourteen-year-old boy to leave all of this behind."

"I understand." What choice did I have? "So tell me why. Why did she—why did you—do it?"

Felicia placed her hands in her lap. They were naked of the rings and bracelets I'd seen before.

"You didn't know your cousin very well, did you?" she said.

"I know her a little better now."

"Well, I doubt I know her—knew her—any better than you. It's really not that complicated, Grace and me. We had a lot in common. We both hated someone. And we both wanted the best for Taylor."

"How could the best be for Gracie to die?"

"You're not going to want to hear this. But she was never going to have Taylor. She was never going to see him. She was never going to get near him. Never. I made that clear. I made it clear to her and to my worthless husband. Taylor was mine. Legally mine. All mine."

"That was your prerogative."

She came halfway out of her chair, slapped a hand on the counter. "I brought him up knowing—*knowing*—that he was the bastard son of a whore and her . . . her bastard lover, my husband. But I was a good mother. A damned good mother. And I still am."

I wanted to tell her not to call Gracie a whore. But I didn't want her to throw me out yet.

She sat back down.

"I'm sorry," she said.

"Don't worry about it."

"I'm so sorry."

Part of me felt for her. I thought of the prenup that I figured left her with whatever was in the boxes in that room and not much else. Then I thought of the boxes in Gracie's house. They were a lot different than the ones Felicia was packing.

"Tell me: Were you ever . . ." I decided to alter my question in midsentence. "Did you know Trixie?"

"This is not about me."

There was no point in disagreeing.

"So whose plan was it, exactly?"

Felicia wrapped her arms around herself. "I could tell you it was Grace's, because it was. But it took two, obviously."

"How did you even—"

"I knew about Grace long before she knew I knew. Before even Laird knew. He thought he was so smart. God, he thought he was smart."

She brushed an angry tear from a cheek.

"We knew we couldn't have kids. So we adopted. It all happened so fast. Everybody I knew who adopted, it took forever. But of course Laird knew all the right people, you know, he called in some chits, this judge, that lawyer, a social service worker, and the next thing you know we have this beautiful boy."

"Fourteen years ago."

"And for six or seven years, it was fine. I didn't know where Taylor came from and I didn't care. He was such a good boy. And then, one day, Laird was out of town, and this package shows up."

"In the mail?"

"In the mailbox. No postage. Just a little box. Addressed to me."

"What was in it?"

"A shoe." She had trouble getting it out. "A baby shoe."

"For the right foot."

"How do you know that?"

"Go on."

Haskell pleaded ignorance, she said. He called the shoe a prank, blamed it on another lawyer he said was messing with him over a case. Felicia hired a private investigator. A young woman, the investigator discovered, had been trying to make contact with the son she had long ago given up for adoption. A young woman who knew Laird Haskell quite well.

As Felicia spoke, I imagined Gracie sitting high in the rafters at the rinks around Detroit, arriving late and leaving early, her face hidden by a hat or a scarf, surreptitiously watching her son play hockey. And I thought of her again at the Red Wings game with Vend. She stayed close to him, I decided, so she could keep tabs on Haskell, and on her son. It wasn't the smartest way to go, but by then, what else did Gracie have?

"Did you finally confront him?" I said.

"At first I just decided it didn't happen, it didn't matter. Fired the investigator. Threw the shoe away. But finally it was just too much. So I went to him."

"And he denied it."

"Oh, no. It was too late for that. No, he just came clean, the son of a bitch. God, that man. You'd have thought I was sitting in a jury box." She reached out and grabbed my sleeve. I could feel the anger in her grip. "It was just like that day in town hall, all that confessional bullshit."

"I can imagine."

She let go of me. "You know, that was the hardest part of this whole charade. Sitting in that room with all those idiots, playing the good wife, screaming and crying like he fucking mattered to me."

"I'm thinking Gracie played the harder part."

She lowered her head to her chest, squeezing herself again.

"She followed us up here. She followed us. Our marriage had been shit for years. I'd hung on for Taylor. Then he moves us a million miles from civilization, away from our friends, and Taylor's friends, and then he has the gall to start in with the stock trading, sitting on his ass yelling at the computer all day. He thought he was so goddamned smart." Felicia shook her head, loosed a bitter laugh. "You know he was just bored. Like me and Taylor. Just plain bored up here."

"So you went to Gracie."

"Oh, no. Hell, no. She came to me. Woman to woman. I told her to go to hell, go back to Detroit, get out of our life. At first. Then the calls started coming. These men with strange accents. Coming to the house, where my son might answer the phone."

"And the money problems . . ."

"Unlike my husband, I wasn't counting on a pro hockey contract."

She looked tired. Tired of the conversation, tired of packing boxes, tired of trying to escape from her husband's grasp.

"You made Laird send that rejection letter to Gracie."

"Actually, I had one of his staff do it."

"And the explosion at the rink? What was that about?"

"That was Grace. She wanted Vend as badly as Laird. Bad idea, in retrospect."

I thought of the clipping in Gracie's dark room, of Vend acquitted of bombing a rival strip club, how the episode had amused him.

"The flowers were a bad move, too," I said. "In retrospect."

"Also Grace's idea. But I felt for your mother."

"Sure you did."

"Part of the plan. They had the intended effect."

"And you set the chimney fire so the cops would find the shoe? How do you a set a chimney fire?"

"You wait for your husband to go to bed and you build a really big out-of-control fire using lighter fluid and then you call the fire department and tell them you think you have a chimney fire."

"And of course they come, whether you have one or not."

"Silly women, huh? What do they know?"

"Right. What about the blackmail note? Why didn't you just get it to the cops somehow?"

"Grace figured it'd look better if you found it for them and gave it to your girlfriend."

"Jesus."

I thought of how Gracie had led us to this moment in this room filled with boxes. How she'd fooled me in the Zam shed and shown me the hiding place I later thought I was so clever to plumb. How she'd stocked her little fridge and left her Wings cap hanging and marked the calendar so that my piqued curiosity would lead me to where she wanted me to go. How she knew the pages hung on her walls would at once flatter and anger me to action. How her bogus blackmail note would neatly and easily satisfy my hunger for a motive.

And those videotapes at Gracie's house? They were probably blank. Of course Trixie wouldn't let me take one.

"That night at the pizzeria," I said.

It stumped her for a second. "Oh, that disgusting place. She made me go."

"Belly blew your cover."

"Belly?"

"Was Gracie having doubts?"

"Doubts about what?"

I was beginning to get angry.

"Doubts that she wanted to kill herself, Felicia. Doubts you talked her out of."

"No." Felicia held my eyes, made sure I saw that she was not lying. "She had no doubts. Once she saw that I would not bend on her seeing my son, she had no doubts. None at all."

I believed her. It sickened me, but I believed her.

"Gracie was fucked up," I said.

"Your words. But yes."

"So you made a deal. You could kill a lot of birds with that stone, eh?"

"I tried, Gus," she said. She wasn't answering my question. She wanted me to know something else. "Right at the end."

"Tried what?"

The women struggled across the road with the extension ladder Felicia had taken from the toolshed at her home. The snowstorm howled, the shoe tree a hulking phantom in the blizzard dark.

The wind kept grabbing one end of the ladder and whipping it away. Gracie held it fast to her shoulder, spitting orders as she bit down on a penlight in her teeth. Felicia kept glancing over her shoulder for headlights. Even here, she thought, the storm would keep most people inside. She had made sure her husband took an extra sleeping pill before telling him she was going downstairs to read. Beneath her parka she wore the cashmere robe and flannel pajamas she'd been wearing before she left him snoring.

They propped the ladder against the shoe tree.

It would look like a suicide so obvious that it could only be murder. Haskell would take the rap after Felicia planted one of Gracie's shoes in their fireplace. Haskell, in turn, would finger Vend. Both would go to prison for one crime or another. Felicia would disappear with Taylor. And Gracie's life insurance policy would take care of the only people who had ever taken care of her, my mother and Trixie.

The cool, clear logic of desperation.

Gracie climbed the ladder, tucking her head into her shoulders against the wind and pelting snow. Felicia followed two rungs below. They faced the road so Felicia could watch for cars.

Gracie had visited the tree at dawn to select a bough that appeared strong enough to hold her, high enough that she would not touch the ground. She had fashioned a noose from black nylon rope and foam sheathing, the same as the many she had made for her clients. She'd been wearing it around her neck beneath her coat when Felicia had picked her up on the service road in the woods behind the rink. Felicia had felt her stomach flip but decided not to say anything. This was how it would be and soon it would be done.

Near the top of the ladder, Gracie hugged the bough with her left arm, wound the rope around the bough, and knotted it in a loose-fitting loop that she slid out onto the branch as far as she could reach. The ladder wobbled and Felicia leaned right and grabbed at the tree trunk. In the branches above Gracie's head she saw the blurred white shapes of sneakers and boots and skates.

Gracie bent and slipped off her left shoe, an ankle-high work boot with a worn hard-rubber sole. She wasn't wearing a sock. She dangled the boot down by a lace and Felicia took it and stuffed it into one of the flap pockets of her parka. She looked up again and saw Gracie staring down at her.

Felicia closed her eyes. She counted slowly to five, six, seven . . . She hadn't known what to expect. Would she feel the weight of the body as the rope unraveled to tautness? Would she open her eyes to a woman struggling against her noose? She felt herself holding her breath, gripping the ladder so hard that her palms hurt. Would she be able to simply slide the ladder back into her SUV and drive home and slip back into the soft leather chair in her living room and pick up her book where she'd left off?

The ladder shook. Felicia felt the rattle, violent and abrupt, from her fingertips to the bottoms of her feet.

"And that was it?"

Felicia shook her head. She held her left arm up in front of me. "Remember, I was wearing a bandage when we last met."

"So?"

"I tried to grab her. I tried to reach her, pull her back. I tried. But I lost my balance and fell. By the time I got up, it was too late."

And once Gracie was dead, what choice did Felicia Haskell have but to follow through with their plot?

She let her arm fall to her lap. I stood.

"I'm sorry," she said. "I called her boyfriend. I didn't have to do that."

I didn't care anymore that she was sorry. I didn't care if she lived out of boxes for the rest of her life.

"All you had to do was tell her you'd share Taylor. But that wouldn't have solved your husband problem."

"I think it's time for you to go."

"What about Taylor? Is he ever going to get to play hockey again?"

"What difference does it make?"

"He's a good kid. He might like to play again."

"You people and your stupid hockey."

I went to the door. Felicia stayed put. I turned to say good-bye, but before I could, she said, "You still don't really know her, do you?"

"Maybe not," I said. "But I know she loved her son."

Late that afternoon, I knocked on Parmelee Gilbert's office door. He was getting ready to call it a day and walk home, but he invited me in.

I repeated for the fifth or sixth time my desire to speak with Gilbert's client, Laird Haskell. But before Gilbert could again inform me that he would not be trying Mr. Haskell's case in the media, I told him about my visit to Gracie's house, about the drawing of the hockey player, the photograph of Gracie with Darlene, the coffee cup in the dish drainer, the implements in the boxes in her dark room.

Only once as I told him did I glance at the picture of Carol Jo, the pigtailed cheerleader Parmelee Gilbert had lost to an unknown killer more than thirty years before. Gilbert listened to me. If the expression on his face changed from its usual flat calm, I didn't notice. He said he would get back to me.

The next morning, there was a message on my office voice mail: Haskell would see me at one thirty.

twenty-six

Three pickets walked a haphazard circle at the top of the driveway that wound down to Laird Haskell's house. I parked across the road. A silver mist blurred the edges of the fresh leaves in the trees. On the calendar, spring had come; in the air, it was weeks away.

"Councilman," I said as I walked past Floyd Kepsel. He was carrying a handmade sign that read, LET THE THIEF PAY FOR HIS THEIVERY. At least one thief was spelled right. "Any news today?"

"Hello, Gus," Kepsel said. The other pickets, Sally Pearson and Johnny Ford's mother, Harriet, stopped pacing. "Not a thing, of course," Kepsel went on. "Lawyers work by the hour, you know."

"Yeah," I said. "Lawyers tend to take their time."

"But this one didn't take his time raiding our budget, did he?" Mrs. Ford said, jabbing her picket sign in the direction of Haskell's house. The sign read, FEDS GO HOME—AND TAKE HASKELL WITH YOU. "He ought to be in jail."

"He ought to be hung in that tree," Sally said.

Laird Haskell was under house arrest while the various authorities sorted out who was going to prosecute him first. A local judge had decided it might not be safe for him in the Pine County Jail.

Most townspeople hadn't seemed to mind when Haskell was charged with murdering Gracie, so long as it didn't hurt the chances of the rink opening for the next season. Even when the seamier charges came down, some seemed willing to forgive so long as rink construction resumed.

Then came the lawsuits from contractors who hadn't been paid. And the subpoenas to town officials from the U.S. attorney. And the growing likelihood that the town, not Haskell or any of his businesses, would be liable for hundreds of thousands of dollars, maybe even millions, in unpaid bills. Not to mention the property taxes that Haskell wasn't paying now.

People had packed town hall at an emergency council meeting called to consider budget cuts necessitated by the financial mess Starvation now found itself in. When the clamor grew so loud and angry that it drowned out Elvis Bontrager's gavel, he stood up, announced he was resigning as council chairman, and walked out. Petitions for a recall election to remove the rest of the council were soon circulating on Main Street. Angry pickets sprung up around town hall, in front of Audrey's and the *Pilot*, and finally at Haskell's home.

Parmelee Gilbert won a restraining order to curb the pickets at the house, but Dingus and his deputies weren't too aggressive about enforcing it. Too short staffed because of budget cuts, Dingus said. Haskell had hired a pair of security guards. I saw them chatting where the driveway ended at Haskell's house.

"What are you here for anyway?" Floyd Kepsel said to me now. "Taking him some provisions?"

"If I'm not out in an hour, call Dingus, will you?"

"Haw," Kepsel said. "Tell Laird I said hello. He ain't been out of that house in two weeks, so far as I can tell."

"Will do."

Kepsel lowered his sign. "Tell me, Gus. Why in heck did the newspaper wait so long to tell us this guy was a damn liar? Why all the happy stories about what a marvel this rink was going to be?"

Floyd Kepsel was not joking. I wasn't sure how to answer him, though I knew it would be a waste of time to tell him he was full of shit.

"Ask Elvis," I said.

Laird Haskell stood facing the bay window in his office, hands clasped behind his back. The lake was a flat sheen of blue and purple in the mist. Haskell's starched denim shirt was untucked.

"Please sit," he said, without turning around. Parmelee Gilbert and I sat at the table where I'd been with Haskell and Jason Esper when I met Felicia. We waited. Haskell didn't move or speak for a full minute.

I hadn't come with a particular plan in mind. I really just wanted to see Haskell and let him see me. It wasn't quite like lining up to shake hands with the opposing team after a tough game. I didn't want or need to shake Haskell's hand, nor did I think he wanted to shake mine. But once I had seen Felicia, I wanted to make sure I saw her husband face-to-face once more to hear what, if anything, he had to say.

I had no such desire to see Vend.

Finally, Haskell said, "I guess I have you to thank, Gus. Is that right?"

"Thank me for what?"

I knew what he meant but wanted to hear him say it. He turned to face us, hands still behind his back. He looked as tired as Felicia had.

"For getting the murder charge removed."

"You're welcome."

"I'm confident, of course, that my very able attorney would have succeeded in doing the same, but it would have taken a great deal of time and money."

"You have plenty of one and not much of the other, huh?"

Haskell smiled.

"I see the River Rats didn't go very far in the postseason."

The Rats had won the regional title but lost in the state quarterfinals to—who else?—the Pipefitters, 3–2, in overtime. Dougie Baker played well in the net but surrendered a goal late in the third period that tied the game; some folks in town were griping that he should have stopped it, a wrist shot from the blue line, skimming just above the ice. But Soupy told me it had glanced off a Rats player's toe and changed direction. "Handcuffed him," Soupy said. "Tough break."

I had been hoping to bump into the kid at the rink so I could tell him he had done a good job.

"They did fine," I told Haskell. "Felicia says hello."

He was straining now to keep the smile on. "Really? Where is she?"

"I don't know."

"You said you saw her."

"I did. She's gone."

"How did you—" He looked impatiently at Gilbert. "Did we—never mind." He looked back at me. "She has Taylor with her?"

"So far as I know."

"That's *my* son," he said, stabbing an index finger into his chest. "It's not even her son. It's my son."

"What about Gracie?"

He slowly sat down, setting his palms flat on the table. "I must say, I am sincerely shocked and dismayed—increasingly so, at my advancing age—at the ingratitude of people."

"Who? Gracie? Are you kidding?"

"Of people who have absolutely no reason to be anything but grateful for what someone has given them. This town. My wife. Your family member. Every single one of them."

"My family member?"

"Wake up, Gus. I didn't hang her in the tree. That is an established fact. I didn't do it. You had all of your life to keep her out of that tree. Do you feel responsible? Maybe you do. But she did it. She put herself there. With the help of my lovely wife. She's the one who ought to be enduring this, not me."

"How about Vend?" I said. "Do you think he was ungrateful for everything you did for him, all that business you brought in?"

Haskell looked to Gilbert again. Without raising his gaze from his folded hands, the attorney recited, "My client cannot comment on pending legal matters."

Vend remained at large. Police supposedly were hunting him in Toronto, but they worried that he had fled overseas. Really they had no idea.

"Tell me, Laird," I said. "You feeling a little trapped? Are you more afraid of going to prison or not going?"

Gilbert started to repeat what he'd just said, but Haskell stopped him.

"You've seen Vend?"

Crater Face, Jason Esper, and other of Vend's cronies were in jail. But they were all flipping on Haskell and Vend so they wouldn't be behind bars forever. That couldn't have made Haskell feel too good. One of the rent-a-cops at his door was the fuzzy-lipped kid who'd told me to have a good day in Traverse. He was going to protect Haskell from Vend?

"Not recently," I said.

"What does that mean?"

I let the question sit there while Haskell's face got redder.

"'Recently' is one of those words newspapers find so useful when the only way to be accurate is to be vague," I said. "Like 'several.' Or 'expected.' Words designed to disguise we're not really sure what we're talking about, or we don't really want you to know we don't know. 'Recently' could be yesterday or two months ago. Who knows?"

Haskell threw up his hands. "So what are we doing here? Did you come here to torture me? Or to ask questions? If it's not—"

"I'm working on a follow-up story," I said. "A more detailed look at the relationship between you and Vend. Who was the real mastermind behind it all? Who called the shots? Who was whose bitch?"

"You'll never get that in your little rag."

"Sure I will. Suddenly, this place can't get enough stories that shit on Laird Haskell. Did you know the *Pilot*'s circulation is up thirteen percent in the last month? And funny, but nobody seems to give a damn about the guy downstate. He didn't screw them over on a hockey rink."

Haskell shifted in his chair and looked out at the lake, idly rapping the fingers of one hand on the table. I watched him calculate. He turned back to me, the red washed out of his face for the moment.

"I can help you with that story," he said. "I have documents. All sorts of documents. Boxes of them." He leaned into the table. "Copies of handwritten ledgers. Credit card slips. Photographs. Voice mails. E-mails, even. We could put away some of the biggest names in Michigan. And Vend—we could put that twisted pervert in prison for the rest of his life."

"You're one of the biggest names in Michigan, Mr. Haskell."

"Not even close. These are big. You can't imagine. Dangerous big."

I smiled. "I'll take whatever you want to give me. On the record."

"On the record?" Haskell said. "No. Be reasonable. I give you the papers, you quote from the papers. No need to say where you got it."

"Sorry." I stood to leave. "This is not a negotiation."

"Are you crazy? Are you fucking crazy? Some of these people—they would—fucking Jarek Vend is—you don't realize." He was halfway out of his chair, sputtering, spittle whitening the corners of his mouth.

Gilbert lifted his head to watch. He looked fascinated, as if he'd never seen this particular client before.

"If I see Vend, I'll be sure to tell him you said hello. Maybe he'll give me the documents. What do you think?"

"Wait." Haskell rushed around the table. He took me by an arm. I could smell the sweat on him. "Wait. Please, Gus, think about this."

"You already offered all that stuff to the cops. Right? But they're not playing, are they?" I pulled my arm away. "They're taking you down, Mr. Haskell. Or Vend will take you down. Either way's fine with me."

"What—what did I ever do to you? I didn't return your fucking phone calls, so you just hang me out to dry?"

I turned to Gilbert. "Thanks, Parm."

"Feel free to call if you have follow-up questions," he said.

"Follow-up questions?" Haskell said. "You don't even have a story."

"Well," I said, "you did say you have all these ledgers and credit card slips that could bring down the biggest names in Michigan. Including Vend. What did you call him? A twisted pervert? I mean, I'd love to have the documents, but the quotes I got are pretty good."

"We were off the record."

"I never agreed to that."

Haskell turned to Gilbert. The attorney looked at me, then at his client.

"It is customary," Gilbert said, "to make those sorts of agreements explicit at the beginning of an interview."

"Son of a bitch," Haskell said. He turned back to me. "Come on, Gus. For old times' sake. There must be some middle ground here."

I looked at him. His silver hair was mussed. The second-to-last button on his shirt was undone. His eyes were sunken with fear and weariness. I could have put him in front of a mirror and he never would have seen it. He would never see anything but smiling Laird Haskell, scourge of the auto industry, friend of the victim, doting husband, father of a future NHL goaltender.

"Yeah, sure, Laird," I said. "The middle ground is like this: You could have hung Gracie in that tree yourself. But you didn't. That's all."

I could still hear him shouting, *What in God's good heaven does that mean?* as I trudged up his driveway, ignored Kepsel and Sally and Mrs. Ford begging me to tell them what was going on, climbed into my pickup, and pulled away.

I never did write a story on that conversation.

Two days later, Parmelee Gilbert resigned as Laird Haskell's attorney. By the end of the week, he had closed his office, put his house up for sale, and left Starvation Lake for good.

twenty-seven

We took Mrs. B's rowboat about fifty yards out from Mom's beach. A Clorox bottle chained to an old sump pump on the lake bottom marked the spot. Our dive raft would float there once the water warmed up enough for me to paddle the thing out from shore.

My mother slowly stood between the bench seats in the bow of the boat.

"Careful, Bea," Mrs. B said.

"I'm all right."

Mom removed the lid from the tin containing Gracie's ashes. Mrs. B and I watched as Mom stood waiting for the boat to drift around until it was pointing downwind. Streaks of lavender and pink glimmered on the water, mirroring the early evening clouds.

Mom lifted the tin. "This was Gracie's favorite place," she said. "That I have not forgotten." She wanted to cry but she made herself smile. "May it give her peace for all eternity."

"Amen," Mrs. B said.

"Amen," I said.

Mom shook the tin. The spring breeze floated Gracie over the lake. She disappeared on the silver ripples.

"Stay here," Mom said. "I'll make tea."

I was pulling the boat up onto the damp sand. Mrs. B stood on a section of dock stacked on the beach, pulling her sweater close against the twilight chill. I dropped the bow rope and waited for Mom to go into the house.

"Darlene couldn't make it?" I said.

Mrs. B kept her gaze on the lake. "She had to work."

"Really?"

I didn't mention that I had seen Darlene's car outside Audrey's, but the look on my face must have given me away.

"She's going to need some time, Gussy. You'll have to trust her."

"Is the divorce going through?"

"Ask Jason. Now that he's in jail, he has even more reasons to procrastinate."

"I'm sorry," I said.

"No. No, I'm sorry."

"Cream? Sugar? Lemon?" my mother called out.

"Please be patient, son," Mrs. B said.

I looked up at my mother. The wail of a loon came from somewhere out on the lake. I remembered I had to get the swing out of the garage that weekend.

"Nothing for me, Mom," I said. "Got to get somewhere."

I hugged Mrs. B as I left. "Tell Darl I said hi."

"Of course."

The violet stripes were fading in the western sky by the time I ascended to the highest branch that would bear my weight.

It wasn't as high as Gracie had climbed all those years ago while her boyfriend gaped from below. But it would have to do.

From where I stood with my left arm hugging the trunk of the shoe tree, I could see all the way to Main Street. A light came on in Darlene's apartment window. I watched it for a few seconds, then looked away, past town to the lakeshore. I turned and saw the steel frame of the rink bathed in the yellow glow of safety lights. I looked up into the tree, and I thought of Gracie perched up there as a girl, asking the sheriff's deputy, "Didn't you ever do anything for love?"

I reached into my coat pocket. I tied the shoes together and looped them over a bough as high over my head as I could reach: A high-top sneaker dyed again to a brilliant pink, and a white baby shoe laced with blue satin ribbon.

ACKNOWLEDGMENTS

First, thank you to all of the people who read *Starvation Lake*. I hope you liked it, but even if you didn't, I'm grateful that you gave Gus a chance.

Thanks to my indefatigable agents, Erin Malone and Suzanne Gluck of William Morris Endeavor. I'm deeply grateful to my editor, Stacy Creamer; her assistant, Lauren Spiegel; and to all the enormously helpful folks at Touchstone: Marcia Burch, Renata Di Biase, Josh Karpf, Stacy Lasner, Cherlynne Li, Meredith Kernan, Jessica Roth, Alessandra Preziosi, David Falk, Ellen Silberman, and Trish Todd. Also to my meticulous copy editor, Amy Ryan; my T-shirt guy, Mike Manion; and my brilliant Web designers, Sunya Hintz, Todd Kneedy, and Justin Muggleton. For their advice, encouragement, patience, and party-organizing skills, thanks to Janet Adamy, John Anderson, Joe Barrett, Pete Bookless at the Hide-A-Way Bar, John Campbell, John Carreyrou, Helene Cooper, Kimi Crova, Sam Enriquez, John Galligan, Tony Gray, David Gruley, Michael Gruley, Terry Gruley, Michael Harvey, Bill Hayes, Julie Jargon, Dan Kelly, David Kocieniewski, Alan Murray, Bruce Orwall, Dan Radovich, Marcus Sakey, John Schroeder, Sean Sherman, Glenn Simpson, Doug Stanton, Andrew Stoutenburgh, Del Tinsley, Jeff Trachtenberg, Rich Turner, Ken Wells, and especially Jonathan Eig. Thanks always to Trish Grader and Shana Kelly, who gave Starvation Lake its start. And to my most important readers: my wife, Pamela; and children, Joel, Kaitlin, and Danielle. Last but not least, a deep and heartfelt bow to the Shamrocks, the Flames, the YANKS, the Hawks alums, and all the boys of Thursday hockey.

TOUCHSTONE READING GROUP GUIDE

The Hanging Tree

FOR DISCUSSION

1. The first line of the book is, "I have learned that you can be too grateful for love." Do you think this statement refers to the relationship between Gus and Darlene, or is the author highlighting a larger theme? Think about the various relationships in the novel in light of this sentence. Does it change your perspective on them, or on the book as a whole?

2. Gus has proven himself to be a reporter of persistence and talent. Is Gus wasting that talent by staying in Starvation Lake? Do you think he is hiding in Starvation Lake, still ashamed of what he did at the *Detroit Times*? Or are his reasons for living there—his mother, Darlene, his history with the town—genuine? Do you think he aspires to work for a big paper again?

3. Many people in Starvation Lake are annoyed by Gus's negative stories about the new hockey rink. Why does the new rink mean so much to the town? How do the prospective new rink and the existing old one function as symbols for Starvation Lake?

4. Gus and Gracie had a very troubled relationship, with tensions that seem to go beyond normal "sibling rivalry" (or, in their case, cousin rivalry). Do you think Gus's appraisal of Gracie's character is fair? How does his understanding change of who she was? Is it easier, or more appealing, to forgive someone who is dead?

5. Gus's mother withholds a lot of information about Gracie that could potentially help the investigation. If she weren't in a declining mental state, would she have let things slip at all? Or does she hide behind her forgetfulness as an excuse to withhold information at will? How would Gus's investigation have changed if she had kept her silence?

6. Is Gracie's slide into prostitution understandable? Do women truly have no other option at times or, as Trixie says, do they enjoy playing that role on a certain level? If prostitution were legalized and controlled, do you think stories like Gracie's would be less likely?

7. Gracie sacrifices her life for her child. Given Gracie's limited resources and options, do you agree this was the best way for her to help her son, or could it prove to be intensely damaging to him in the long run?

8. Gus tells Philo, "Just like hockey. It's all about two-on-ones." There are many "two-on-one" relationships throughout *The Hanging Tree*. Besides that of Gus-Darlene-Jason, can you think of any other love triangles? Or triangles that involve nonromantic relationships? Do you think these triangles were intentional on Gruley's part?

9. Felicia Haskell is, at first, a minor character, but she is central to Gracie's death and the unfolding of the plot. Is she a sympathetic character, forced to make difficult decisions, or a selfish manipulator?

A Conversation with Bryan Gruley

Tell us about the process of plotting a mystery novel. Do you have the story mapped out before you sit down to write, or do you discover it along with your characters?

So far, I'm not much of an advance plotter. I know where the story begins and I have a vague idea of how it ends. Then I start writing and, yes, I discover the story along with my characters. As I go, I jot notes to myself about story arcs I need to follow through on and loose ends I have to tie up, and these become a sort of rough, moving outline for what's to come in the next few scenes.

How is writing a sequel different from writing a debut novel? Does your writing process change at all?

Writing my first novel was hard because I had no idea how to go about writing a novel. Writing the sequel was hard because I had no idea how to go about writing a sequel.

I don't mean to be glib. In a sequel, you have to be mindful both of readers who have not read your previous book and readers who have. You have to give the former enough backstory to appreciate the setting and characters without giving so much that you either bore repeat readers or reveal so much of the first book that new readers won't go back and give it a try.

At least for me, another challenge on the sequel was quieting the echoes of reviewers, bloggers, readers, and others who had opined about my writing. Writing my debut, all I had to worry about were my own instincts and the suggestions of the few friends who read the manuscript. This time around, it was impossible at times not to recall the critics, professional or not, who'd complained about the hockey or the dialogue or the prologue or the way my hair was done in the author photo. It made for some second-guessing, but I tried to remind myself what my friend, the novelist John Galligan, told me: Write what's in your heart.

When you first conceived of this series, how did you decide which point of view to tell the story from? Did you ever consider using a character other than Gus to narrate, or telling the story from a third-person perspective?

In truth, I didn't conceive of a series; I just wrote one story, Starvation Lake, *and my friends at Touchstone told me it would be a series.*

I never gave serious thought to telling the story in anything but the first person. It just felt natural, and it really helped me to get to know at least one character, Augustus Carpenter. I sometimes feel envious reading stories told in third-person omniscient, because the narrator can honestly know things that the main character cannot know. I do not have that luxury with Gus, of course, but for now at least, I feel that it's his voice more than anything that connects with certain readers.

While you don't write from a female perspective, there are several strong female characters at the heart of *The Hanging Tree* (particularly Gracie, Felicia, Darlene, and Michele). Do any of the women in your life inform your female characters?

Absolutely. While none of these fictional characters are modeled on particular women in my life, I assume that virtually every girl or woman I've ever known has influenced the way in which I've drawn them—and the way Gus perceives them. The latter is most important because it tells us as much about Gus as it does about them.

Felicia and Laird Haskell put a lot of pressure on Taylor. Throughout the novel, Gus describes the dashed dreams of parents who believed that their sons were bound for the NHL. Do you think that this kind of pressure from parents is more intense in small towns like Starvation Lake?

I doubt it. Remember that the Haskells originally hail from the Detroit suburbs. The pressure there—and in Chicago, Toronto, Minneapolis, Montreal, Boston, and other hockey towns—can be intense. The best parents understand that the odds of their kid playing pro hockey are infinitesimal. They instead encourage a love of the game that the kid can embrace for the rest of his or her life.

Philo's belief in the potential of the Web to change journalism is pivotal to the story. You have experienced the changes affecting journalism firsthand. Do you think that the essential role of reporters has shifted in the information age, or is their basic purpose and process the same? Are you optimistic about the future for newspapers in America?

The reporter's missions is as ever: tell people things they didn't know five seconds ago, and tell them stories that make them think, laugh, debate, cry, act. Today, a young reporter is likely to be as adept with a video camera as she is with a pen and notebook, and he's likely to deliver information in shorter, faster blasts than before. But the essentials remain unchanged: What's new? What's interesting? How does it affect me and my world?

I'm not optimistic about the future for print newspapers, per se, because the business model is broken beyond repair. But the demand for news, compelling tales, and insightful analysis in an increasingly connected, increasingly complex world is greater than ever. The challenge is finding ways to deliver that material in ways that people will actually pay for it.

Tell us about your plans for Gus and Starvation Lake. Will the series continue? Any thoughts on how many books there might be?

At least one more, according to the folks at Touchstone. I can envision more beyond that, because I enjoy the characters so much. I'm dying to know what will happen to Soupy and Bea and Darlene and the River Rats. The only way to find out is to sit down and write it.

Enhance Your Book Club

1. Gruley shared in a Pulitzer Prize for the *Wall Street Journal*'s coverage of the September 11 attacks. You can read some of his articles online at his website, www.bryangruley.com. Pick a piece to read together and note the differences in his style as a journalist and as a fiction writer.

2. Hockey, and the position of goalie in particular, are important to the storyline of *The Hanging Tree*. Watch some of a hockey game on TV or online (or attend a local hockey game!) and try to imagine it from a goalie's point of view.

3. *The Hanging Tree* takes place in 1999, before Internet news had become popular. Philo, Gus's boss at the *Pilot*, expresses a belief that it's the wave of the future for reporters. Discuss among the group where and how you get your news, and how that has changed in the past ten years.

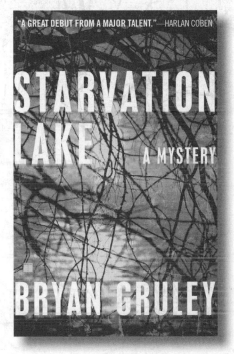

Mosby's Manual of Diagnostic and Laboratory Tests